PRAISE FOR JAY ERICKSON

Jay Erickson delivers a riveting fantasy tale filled with seafaring, intrigue, a diverse range of characters, compelling settings, and enjoyable dialogue laced with wit and humor! Sirens of Sowle will have readers unable to resist the siren's call of the next book in this series!

Stephen Zimmer, Award-winning author of the Rayden Valkyrie and Ragnar Stormbringer Tales.

Sirens of Sowle is a rollicking tale of the high seas that couples swashbuckling, heart-pounding action with an eclectic cast of compelling female characters. Jay Erickson's skillful plot construction and breakneck pacing have come together to spin a ripsnorter of a yarn that is sure to entrance any lover of pirate lore.

Dr. Scott Simerlein, author *Rudger Rump and the Mage of Ages*

Epic fantasy in treacherous waters - Jay Erickson takes his unique flair for action to the high seas and delivers a fun swashbuckling adventure. The characters each tell the tale in their own way and really get the reader rooting for them. If you like suspense on the waves with a little touch of romance in your fantasy adventures, you will love meeting all of the *Sirens of Sowle*.

Anastasia M. Trekles, author of the *Chronicles of M'gistryn Series*

Jay Erickson has done it once again! Loyalty, betrayal, deception, heroism, and coming into one's own destiny. Marissa de Cantor y Castile and her band of misfits are driven into breaking the law in order to save her homeland from a tyrant who just happens to be her ex-lover. Mr. Erickson's depth of character development and the relationships of the crew on the Bella Dahlia drew me in like an anchor. I could not put the book down! I couldn't put the book down! I eagerly await where Mr. Erickson takes the Bella Dahlia next!

JP Strohm, author of *Broken Order*

SIRENS OF SOWLE

JAY ERICKSON

Photography credit Marcus J. Ranum.

ISBN: 978-1-948374-89-7

Hydra Publications

Goshen, Kentucky 40026

www.hydrapublications.com

Citadel

Sowle
Sea

Loja de
Cantor

Castile

Cuddle
Cove

N

Stonewall
Pale

PART I
BELLA DAHLIA

PRELUDE

The Bella Dahlia

A titanic vessel cut across the glasslike waters, sluicing white ribbons into the reflective azure sea and leaving a wan froth in its wake. Rows of cannons glistened across its hull in the noon day sun, a sparkling reflection of the doom this terror had in store. The goliath of the sea barked annihilation from those cast iron cylinders, and the sound it brought – a heavy swell of thunder that pealed across the horizon – became a deathly dirge that rippled across still waters.

This was the *Bella Dahlia*, scourge of the Sea of Sowle.

The mariners stared out across the depths at their impending end. Aboard the merchant cog *Triall*, many men muttered in fear. Few tried to save face, but most couldn't hide the mounting dread that was looming inside them as this terror of Sowle bore down on their ship, its black banner whipping violently in a wind that only existed for that one haunting vessel.

The *Triall's* own sails were limper than a man heavily drunk on whiskey. Where the galleon was finding wind was beyond anyone. "Sorcery!" a deckhand on the cog cried. No one argued.

The *Bella Dahlia* was a beast of the sea; nothing like it existed within a thousand leagues. It plagued the waters about the port of Castile – indestructible and unstoppable.

Gossip burned through mariners like wildfire that the ship was crewed by women, but as the men looked to the midday sky and the windless calm they found themselves trapped in, they knew the truth – these weren't women, they were sirens.

The *Bella Dahlia* closed on the cog, massive and imposing. It pulled hard to port, eclipsing the *Triall* in its starboard shadow.

Her song pierced through the din of their combined trepidation. A lilting harmony, so beautiful, so ethereal, that many men found themselves crying at its majestic grace. They all knew the stories of the sirens. When the song ended it meant only one thing for them – death.

As the mariners of *Triall* stared up at the passing leviathan, they saw *her*. Standing tall, proud, and coldly beautiful on the quarterdeck of the *Bella Dahlia,* singing pure and true, was the true siren of the Sowle Sea – Captain Bloody Mari.

She looked down upon them and smiled as the cannons of the *Bella Dahlia* began their iron rain.

CHAPTER ONE

Marissa de Cantor y Castile

Nothing breaks the spirit more than the hopeless cries of children. Hanging her head, hands firmly pinned against her ears, Marissa tried to smother out the wails of misery.

She felt the press of the bodies against her, on all sides. Their heat sweltered against her own, mostly bared flesh. Their filth rubbed and chaffed against her filth. Long ago she had gone nose-blind to their stink, but she knew what they all smelled like – animals.

Like cattle corralled in a pen, awaiting slaughter.

In a way, that's exactly what they were awaiting, but it would not be a quick death. It would be a slow, agonizing one. A death of the will. A death of the soul. This was what awaited Marissa and those around her.

For they were slaves.

She felt a slight tug against the thin burlap loincloth tied around her waist. Quickly, her hands shot down to hold on to one of the only garments she had left. Marissa picked her head up to look crossly at her would-be thief.

It was a girl of perhaps ten winters in age, dressed in less than she. Wide brown eyes stared at Marissa in surprise. Clearly the thieving girl had thought by Marissa's state that she was catatonic, driven mad from months caged at sea.

Marissa shook her head at the young girl, and the girl hissed in return, pulling away from her, pushing through the throngs of oily, naked flesh to find an easier mark; An even younger child, perhaps.

Marissa thought for a moment that maybe she should stop the girl, even try and protect her, but a squeeze on her right arm quickly pulled such thoughts away. That squeeze was a familiar one. It was a way of saying *no*.

Marissa turned her head, a swath of knotted raven hair falling like a curtain over her own dark eyes. The woman next to her smiled very weakly, but encouragingly. "It will be okay," she mouthed to Marissa.

Marissa hung her head once more. Everything was far from okay, but the woman next to her gave her encouragement and strength. Her name was Isa, and she was Marissa's closest, most intimate of friends.

She felt Isa's hand slide down her arm and take Marissa's hand in her own, holding it for strength, as she did for so many countless nights now. Marissa held it tight, afraid to let go.

The wooden planks above her groaned and whined under strain. Marissa could hear the scurrying of feet above scraping against the water-logged wooden slats.

They were pulled hard to their right, some women and children screaming in surprise. A loud thud echoed across the keel, and there were screams above, orders in a language that Marissa still couldn't understand even after months at sea with them. Then, nothing. Absolute silence. No voices. No skittering on the deck. Only the ever-present whimpering of terrified women and the laments of the children.

With a crash of a trapdoor, both Marissa and Isa started amidst dozens of startled cries of surprise. Marissa looked up, trying to peer between all the heads around her to see what was happening. Though she had lost all sense of time, trapped in the cell for as long as she had been, it felt too soon for a meal.

Slowly, almost painfully, Marissa waited until she saw the first foot descend on the worn wooden step. Short claws clacked against the sea-rotten boarding, the tips sinking ever so slightly into salt-saturated oak. Across that clawed foot was a dark green line of scaly skin. As it secured its perch, another clawed foot entered in view. Soon Marissa recognized the once-vibrant orange pantaloons, followed by the swishing of a thick, heavy tail. As the creature fully entered her view, Marissa felt her lip curl in disgust – a scales.

Rather, that was the informal name for the race of reptiles who called themselves the Kii-Aur. Golden frills and a small ridge of horns decorated the creature's crown. Its ears were non-existent. Instead, Marissa could make out the disc-shaped membrane of a slightly darker hue than its scales, just beyond the jaw line on the sides of its head.

Its cold gaze drifted across the gaggle of women and children, and Marissa shivered as those alien eyes passed over her. A scales' eyes had no visible sclera. It was all deep green irises with speckles of gold around vertical slits for pupils. The caiman-like race bore a blunt snout with two nostrils that sat above its large, oversized mouth. Within that pronounced overbite, Marissa could see the sharp daggers of its yellow-tinged teeth as they extended over its lower lip.

Scales were thin, lithe creatures. But it was mostly a decep-tion. Their muscles were long and narrow, as strong as any well-labored man, only hidden beneath thick-scaled flesh. Marissa called it an "it" on reflex, though she knew the scales in front of her to be a male. She learned to identify them early on – their ridge of horns protruded higher than the females, while the females had far larger frills.

Only a baldric slung over his shoulder, he wore no armor over his orange clothing. Hanging from the baldric was a scabbard, complete with a sword that was unique, exclusive to the scales. The long-knotted scar across her back spasmed as her eyes fell on the hilt of walrus ivory. They called them *yataghan*, a form of scimitar that held a single-edged curved blade of forged steel. Unlike traditional scimitars though, a yataghan was longer, and the blade curved inward rather than sweeping back. She felt the bite of such a blade once.

Within seconds her slave masters also descended, three men, soiled almost as much as the slaves, all armed with crossbows pointed at the cage. They were a dark-skinned people, Islanders from the Scorchglass Archipelago. They spoke their bizarre language to the scales, who nodded, clearly in understanding. It responded in kind. Marissa understood what was happening just as one of the slavers reached the cell door.

This scales was a buyer.

Isa's hand tightened in hers, as she too understood. Marissa had hoped to make it to a major city. She had held the fleeting glimmer of a dream that perhaps someone in the Jasian Enclave would be there and recognize her. Now those hopes were dashed hard against a coral reef, as the scales raised a pointed claw directly at her and spoke in heavily-accented trade tongue, "Let me see that one."

THE SEA OF FLESH IN FRONT OF HER PARTED IN A SURGE LIKE she was plague-infested. Truth be told, maybe she was. The buyer singled her out before even looking over any other "merchandise."

Two slavers kept their crossbows trained on the women while the key master slung his weapon over his shoulder and fumbled with a large ring of keys. Marissa held her breath, as the first key failed to open the lock, and then a second. Isa's grip on her hand tightened as the slaver inserted a third. With a large groaning clink, the rusty lock yielded.

He pointed at Marissa and rambled his unknown dialect. She didn't move. She was frozen in fear. If this scales liked what it saw, it was going to buy her. Her eyes drifted to the creature and its mouthful of razor-sharp teeth. Judging by the dripping from its lips, she held no illusions of what it wanted her for.

Marissa shook her head no and tried to back up. The slaver began to chatter faster, pointing to his feet. Still she shook her head no. The dark-skinned man stepped away from the cage for only a second and was back in a flash, a long pole with a loop of wire hanging from the end in his hands.

"No!" Marissa screamed as he tried to reach at her with the wire noose. She let go of Isa's hand and grabbed at the pole, pushing it away, "No!"

Horror drove at her stomach as two more men descended the plank steps and rushed towards the cage. All around her, the women and children cowered like docile sheep.

The slavers charged in towards her. Marissa screamed all the louder as they grabbed at her arms. She fought and wrestled. She tried to bite them, but they pinned her hard against the two of them, sandwiched between their slick, odorous bodies. She twisted and writhed, but they were too strong, and she felt the wire braid drop over her head and tighten against her throat.

Tears flooded her vision, blurring everything. She gasped as the wire tightened and bit into her skin. Terror threatened to consume her. She was no longer yelling, but mewling incoherently, as they pulled her out of the cage like the livestock she was.

Through hazy eyes she searched for Isa, as the reality of what was happening hit her in the gut like a hammer. Isa was nowhere to be found.

Marissa stared at all of the faces she had shared a cell with for so long. They all refused to look at her. Refused to make eye contact. She was the dead walking, and they had already abandoned her.

Marissa slipped and struck the slimy boards, choking as they drug her the rest of the way out of the cell. She came to a stop directly in front of the soft clicking of claws against the wood.

Her dark eyes wide in horror, she looked upwards at the lizard leering over her. His yellow teeth glinted in the faint torch light. "*Yesss*," he said. "You will do splendidly."

"Let her go!" A husky voice growled from Marissa's right side. Air-deprived, she struggled to see who was defending her. It sounded nothing like Isa.

Her focus coalesced around the cell opposite of hers, full of the ones meant to fight in the gladiatorial coliseums. Her eyes fell upon the obsidian gaze of a green-skinned orc. "I said let her go. She's Enclave."

The scales above Marissa hissed and looked down at her in shock. His clawed foot lashed out and hooked her by the shoulder, violently slamming her onto her back. Marissa cried out in pain as the tips dipped into her flesh.

"She is Enclave!" the scales hissed in agreement as it stared at the worn and faded holy symbol of a circumpunct on the torn tabard that now served as her tunic.

"Yes," another voice agreed, one that Marissa knew too well. Marissa cried out as the scales pushed harder against her. She looked pleadingly at the voice, now at the entrance of the cell she came from – Isa. Three men surrounded her, their crossbows all aimed right at her chest. "Should you take her, surely her people will find out," she said simply.

The scales looked down at Marissa, and then back to Isa. "If no one has come for her yet, no one will," he decided aloud.

"Perhaps," Isa agreed. "Do you really want to risk it though?"

Hope glimmered for a moment as the scales' pressure on her shoulder faded slightly. Clearly, he was thinking, considering the implications of what he was about to do. Then she felt that pressure renewed. "It matters not from where she hails. I have other things in mind for this one."

Marissa felt herself begin to whimper as doom consumed her.

"Then take me."

The words came so simply that Marissa was certain she had not heard them right. The scales too seemed at a loss. "Take me," Isa told it again. She stepped forward, holding her hands in front of her, unafraid. "Let me go, in her place."

Marissa felt the scales' eyes on her as it studied her, thinking. She refused to look at it, and instead looked at her closest friend. Isa wouldn't make eye contact with her. "Isa no..." she began, but one of the men tightened the lanyard around her throat cutting her off.

"I choose this willingly," Isa told the confused scales, stepping out fully into the small area between cells. The men surrounded her with crossbows.

Marissa felt the pressure of the scales' foot on her shoulder break away. "Such courage," he said in admiration. "I shall enjoy devouring you."

The steel cord loosened from Marissa's neck and was gone. Instantly, she fell into a fit of coughing. She felt the pebbled texture of the scales' tail as it slid across her scarred back. "Isa!" she croaked.

Marissa looked up, her eyes blurred in pain, trying to find Isa.

She could make out her shape between the scales and the men, but little else. "Isa, no!" she tried again.

Marissa heard the groan of the wooden step as Isa began to ascend. "No!" Marissa keened, as a pain grabbed at her so deep it tore at her soul.

"Jasian, get a hold of yourself," the husky voice whispered. "Accept your friend's sacrifice with honor."

Marissa rolled over to glare at the owner of the voice. On the face of the green-skinned orc, she stared through strange tattoos that seemed to glow azure to her obsidian eyes. Those eyes stared back at her with no ire or malice, just acceptance. "She dies so you live – remember that."

The orc nodded in the direction of Isa. Marissa rolled her head to look back at her friend, before she disappeared from her life forever. Instead, she saw something else that surprised her – an opportunity.

The men and the scales were disappearing to the next level, all eyes on Isa. Only the key master remained behind, distracted by the scene. The pole and noose lay discarded to the side.

Fear clenched at her nerves. It fought to keep her pinned on the floor, submissive and frightened. But something else within battled against that fear – anger. Anger that her best friend was being taken away to be consumed like some lamb. Anger at the oppression that drove her down for months, culling her will to fight. Anger that she felt powerless, even during this moment of opportunity.

She latched onto that anger and let it fuel her. Slowly it helped her put her hands to the floor and push herself silently into a crouch. She refused to let the anger that she was never going to see Isa again defeat her fear. Instead, she would work around it. Curtail and control it. She still felt it keenly through her body, just like the throb of the wound on her shoulder, but she wouldn't answer to that fear, to the whisper that if she failed, she would die.

She could be killed, or eaten, or worse. But she pushed that voice down. If she did nothing, the result would still be the same.

Her hand reached out for the pole. The key master still didn't even acknowledge her.

"Jasian!" the orc whispered in surprise. "Jasian, what are you doing?"

Marissa's fingers wrapped around the damp wood. She held it tight as she slowly lifted herself from the floor. The key master was watching as the last swishing of the scales' tail disappeared above.

Marissa stood up fully, lifting the pole and dangling noose up behind the key master. She hovered there, for only a fraction of a second, fear of failure still coursing like fire through her veins. It told her she wouldn't be strong enough. She bit her lip, her resolve beginning to wane.

The key master began to turn.

"Now!" the orc screamed.

Without any more thinking, without any more hesitation, Marissa reacted. Like a scorpion stinging its prey, Marissa lashed out. The wire noose flailed wildly as it swung up and wide, falling over the key master's startled head.

Marissa yanked with all her might as the cord fell across his throat. The noose snapped tight. Eyes bulging, the key master turned as Marissa fought to control the pole. She pulled and twisted as the key master writhed, his swarthy skin taking on color as he struggled to find air.

Marissa stumbled, her bare feet sliding on the slick floor. She couldn't hold against him; he was stronger than she. He yanked back and her feet slipped against the slime. She fell hard on her backside, letting out a yelp of pain. Fully twisted around, the key master gripped the other end of the pole, his oxygen-starved eyes alight with murderous intent. He pulled her forward, and she slid helplessly across the deck. He was going to kill her.

Her eyes darted in panic, and she saw only a single chance. As he slid her forward, she angled herself back to the cell. Her bare feet wedged between the bars and she anchored herself to them. Her slide stopped.

The key master bucked at the sudden stop in alarm, a weak wheeze escaping his lips. Marissa pulled at the pole now, her strong legs controlling the momentum, not her arms.

The key master gasped, spittle flying from his mouth, and snot poured from his nose as he tried vainly to fight. He was too weak, though. Marissa wrenched the pole hard, and it drove him to his knees. She pulled again and he slid forward.

His eyeballs began to hemorrhage as the blood fought for a place to go. His grip was weakening, but he still had some strength left. He could still overpower her. And then, she felt herself pull free from the bars, propelled backwards.

Confused, she looked back in surprise. Bulging green forearms gripped the end of the pole – she had pulled the pole far enough back that the orc could reach it. Marissa got her footing back underneath her, and together, they conquered the man, pulling him to the ground. The orc leaned down hard against the pole, and with a violent cracking of cartilage, the man's neck collapsed. He fell into a fit of seizures, and then went still.

Marissa gasped as the adrenaline began to leave her. She stared down at the dead man at her feet, and then at the reddening of her palms. She did this. She killed him.

"Jasian," the orc said, right next to her ear. Marissa spun in alarm to look at the stranger. Now standing, the orc towered over her. The orc pointed to the ring of keys on the dead man's belt. "Free me."

Marissa took a step backward. Orcs were feral savages, creatures who lusted for blood and gorged themselves on the organs of their conquered. They were a race of monsters never to be trusted.

The orc held her hands out, imploring Marissa. "Please," she cried. "I will help you. We can save your friend."

Marissa looked back to the cells with the other human women and children. None of them even made eye contact with her. She would receive no help from them.

The orc pressed against the bars, imploringly. "Please. Time wanes before we are discovered, and your friend dies."

Marissa studied the dark eyes of the savage woman before her. She did not know this woman, this creature, but they shared a common bond. They were slaves heading to a bitter, slow, and painful end. But they would not die this day, she decided. Trusting her instincts, she reached down and pulled the keys from the dead man's belt. Holding them aloft, she stuck each one into the lock and twisted until she found one that turned freely.

With a click, the door released and swung open. The massive woman slid from the cell, casting Marissa in her eclipse.

Marissa was surprised to see that she was not very broad for an orc, but rather lean. Sinewy long muscles rippled over her arms, legs, and abdomen as if activated for the first time since she was caged. This woman was coiled strength, with not an ounce of fat to be seen.

The orc looked down upon Marissa, an unfathomable appreciation glittering in her eyes. Marissa took a step backward as the tall woman clapped her on the shoulder. "Thank you Jasian. Let us save your friend."

CHAPTER TWO

Marissa de Cantor y Castile

Marissa took point as she worked her way to the next level of the ship. Lanterns played with the shadows, creating false assailants in every corner. Her heart hammered as her vision slowly adjusted to reveal a distinct lack of slavers in the area. In fact, there was little of anything remaining, considering how long they were at sea.

The orc came up behind her and quickly ducked behind a large rack of barrels tied together with twine. Marissa's stomach ached when she realized what those barrels held – fresh water. She couldn't remember the last time she was allowed more than a swallow, and by the time the bucket made it to her, it was usually only some dregs and the backwash of those before her.

The orc seemed of the same mind, and before Marissa could even voice her concern, the large woman cracked the top of the cask and plunged her head within. Marissa watched in sick fascination as the orc took large drafts of water, drinking as if she were a horse at a trough. When she came up for air, she pointed to the barrel. "You must have strength for what is to come."

Marissa's insides roiled with need, and she needed no further invitation. Warm, liquid life filled her belly, raced through her veins, and invigorated her. Though she hardly drank the amount the orc had, Marissa had to agree on the necessity.

A wry smile came across the orc's face, punctuating her protruding canines vividly. "Now we kill." She nodded her head violently behind Marissa, and her hair swung like water laden whips, sending a filthy spray Marissa's way. "We avoid crew quarters and climb to the galley to arm ourselves with knives and whatever else we can find, yes?"

Marissa nodded dumbly. "Yes." She had absolutely no idea where to go on this ship.

Again, the orc smiled and then, quieter than Marissa would have expected, she made her way forward.

Marissa was amazed at how the orc seemed to know her way around the ship. She moved with precision and grace, guiding the Jasian worshiper to the safest points possible, avoiding the entire crew. Before she knew it, the orc was stopped in front of a hatch.

"Why are we stopping?" Marissa whispered.

"Galley," the orc replied.

"Right. Isn't this where we want to be?"

The orc put a finger to her lips and pressed her ear toward the hatch. Marissa waited impatiently. Isa was likely on the main deck by now, and she didn't think her friend had much time before the scales transferred her to his ship.

"There are people in there," the orc hissed. "Three, maybe four."

Marissa's guts knotted once more. They were hoping to arm themselves in there, not fight bare-handed.

The orc seemed to read this. "We must go this way. If we take any longer, we will lose your friend."

Marissa tensed, but she forced herself to strengthen her resolve. "I will not leave Isa."

"This will be ugly," the orc warned.

"I can handle it."

She nodded at Marissa and then reached for the handle. With a twist and a flex of hard muscle, the orc pulled the lever down. She then opened the portal swiftly, and Marissa charged in.

Two slavers turned to look her way, confused. It took them a second to realize that she was one of the slaves. In that breadth of time, the orc barreled into the room like a stampeding bull, colliding with one of the men and taking him to the floor.

The other reached for a sharp cleaver that was sticking out of a cutting board next to him. He raised the weapon, ready to rend the flesh from her body. Marissa looked around the galley for any accessible defense, saw a wooden soup ladle, and grabbed for it. The man's lip snarled in satisfaction, and he lunged for her.

Marissa raised her weapon when, without warning, a small black figure rose behind the slaver. Before either she or the man could react, the little shadow drew a line across the man's throat.

For the second time in less than a minute, confusion danced across his face. Then, to Marissa's revulsion, that line on his neck opened into a hot acrid spray of lifeblood. Marissa gasped as hot crimson spattered across her face and chest. Instantly the slaver dropped his cleaver and clutched at his throat. Blood pulsed between the gaps of his fingers with every beat of his heart.

Marissa scrambled for the cleaver, grasping it with hot, sticky fingers. She looked back at the slaver as he collapsed to his knees and swayed to his side, his vice-like grip releasing from the viscous wound. After several moments and an inordinate amount of blood, the spray subsided to become merely a trickle.

Behind his body stood a small gnome holding a regular dinner knife. The childlike creature smiled up at her mischievously. "Oi! Works better than a spoon!"

Marissa's mouth fell open, dumbfounded, until a sharp crack brought her back. Marissa looked over to the orc, who staggered to her feet. The orc's hands were skinned raw across the knuckles, and Marissa cringed at the sight of her opponent, the man's face turned into little more than mashed pulp.

The orc looked down at the armed gnome before them. "What's this?"

"What's what?" the gnome said indignantly. "Haven't ye ever seen a gnome afore, tusker?"

"She's got a mouth on her," Marissa said.

"Ah, brains of the group, I take it?" the gnome replied. "Look I'd love to chat all night until the Ayjub come back and kill us all, but I think we should move first, then escape, and then share our feelings, savvy?"

The small woman raised her arms up, and Marissa could see they were bound at the wrists. At further glance she realized the gnome had shackles around her ankles and another on her waist. "You're a prisoner too?"

The gnome sighed, "Aye, definitely the brains." She looked up at Marissa, "Yes, I'm a slave too, but unlike ye, a few of us actually have useful skills on this boat, besides bed warming, so they put us to work. I'm a sawbones. I mend wounds." She held up her wrists. "Mind cutting me free?"

Marissa looked to the orc next to her. She shrugged. "Strength in numbers," she said, as she reached for the shackles.

FIVE MINUTES LATER THE THREE WOMEN, ALL ARMED, FOUND themselves on the upper gun deck. Marissa knew that the odds of avoiding the slavers now were impossible.

All around, Marissa could see the long rows of demi-culverin guns, or cannons, as they were commonly called, on both sides.

She marveled at the amount of firepower this slave ship possessed. Above their heads, they could hear the active footfalls of the sailing crew.

The orc's jaw tightened, causing her lower teeth to bulge out even more. She cocked her head upwards to the deck, listening and sniffing. She looked to Marissa. "They are getting ready to set off."

Urgency covered Marissa like a blanket. "We must hurry!"

"Much as I love a scuffle, there's no way we canna fight all the Ayjub on this ship," the gnome pointed out.

"We have to try – I won't let Isa die," Marissa said flatly.

"Why canna we escape on a longship under cover o' darkness?" the gnome asked.

"I vowed to save her friend," the orc replied.

"'er friend?"

Marissa barely listened to the two women hoarsely whispering back and forth on the merits of bravery versus stupidity. Her mind was elsewhere. She was not in agreement with the gnome on merely escaping. She was there for Isa. And what about the others? If they fled, they'd be leaving other women and children to die.

Fear found a familiar nest in her chest, one that she gave into often. She wasn't a leader, or a strategist. That *was* Isa. Marissa was the timid one, the follower. She always had been. Why did these two look to her? She couldn't help them – hells, she couldn't help herself. In her moment of weakness, as she looked to the barrels of shot and black powder around her for a way to save her best friend, that familiar comfort of cowardice began to wash away as the spark of an idea came to mind. She looked out the gun port to the scales' sloop that was tethered to the ship they were on and that spark became a fire that momentarily blinded out the fear.

"I... I have an idea."

CHAPTER THREE

Marissa de Cantor y Castile

A maniacal grin split the gnome's face. "All hell is going to break loose when we do this. Ye know that right?"

"And it's going to hurt like you won't believe. The ships are too close," the orc added.

Marissa looked at the both of them. "We don't have time for pleasant options. You are sure this will get their attention?"

The gnome nodded excitedly. "Oh, it'll get their attention."

"Then do it," Marissa told the gnome.

Eyes alight with anticipation, the gnome looked out the portal to the sloop below. "Aimin' fer the mast!" Using the flint striker, she lit a fuse they had put into the touch hole. "Brains, steer clear of the rail," the gnome said, still smiling that childlike smile that dominated her entire cherubic face.

"What rail?" Marissa managed to ask just as the gnome covered her ears. With one finger the small figure pointed down.

Marissa looked down and saw a steel rail at her feet. She took a single step backward, just as her world exploded around her.

There was a single clap, followed by a roar that drowned out her own scream. The cannon rolled across the deck, violently slamming into the center of the ship just where her bare feet once occupied. Marissa had no time to ponder how close her feet had come to being sheared off when the blast pressure struck her.

The concussive force of the blast slammed into her like a battering ram. Unprepared, it threw her from her feet, hurling her into nearby barrels of powder. Her world spun, as pain wracked her body. It felt as if all her bones were struck by mallets at the same time.

Choking smoke quilted the room. Marissa gagged on it and reflexively waved her arms in front of her. Her ears rang and she groaned as she stood up. She shuffled to the portal. She looked through the smoke, out into the dusk, searching for the sloop. Through the dense haze, she could just make out the mast, or what was left of it.

At about seven feet up from the deck of the sloop, where the mast had once been, was a sundered hunk of wood. Lying in the waters, slowly gaining weight, was the remainder of the mast and its sails. The attached rigging to the mast was pulling hard at the sloop. The ship listed away, held on only by its mooring to the galleon.

A growl brought her back, and she looked to see the orcish woman sitting up. The brute wrapped her left hand tightly around her right forearm. Marissa bent to the terrifying woman. "Are you all right?" She was surprised that her voice sounded so distant.

The orc assessed her arm, "I've had worse. Did it hit the mast?"

With a nod Marissa added, "I don't think that sloop is going anywhere."

"And then neither are we," the orc answered. "It's time to stand and fight, Jasian. I hope your plan works."

Marissa nodded. "Me too."

Marissa stood facing the forward hatch where the majority of the slavers would come. Terror wracked her body as the heavy footfalls echoed around them like thunder.

It seemed like an eternity for the first grime-laden foot to appear in her vision as the lead man, assumedly the Master Gunner, came to see how and why his blessed cannon fired at their attached allied vessel. Following him, dozens of other filthy men raced down, intent on laying low any slave uprising before it grew out of control.

Marissa could feel the orc stiffen behind her. The green-skinned warrior was facing opposite her, towards the crew quarters that they previously avoided. "There are many," she muttered.

The blood drained from her face, as even more slavers followed the Master Gunner. How many were there on this ship? She fought to control the fear that liquefied her innards. Still, she knew her voice quavered as a single word escaped through gritted teeth. "Hold."

The Master Gunner came towards her, a rueful smile at his lips. Marissa grimaced at the sight of the voids and blackened stumps where most people had teeth. His dark skin held a waxy sheen of sweat that made the filth of his body almost glisten. Naturally curly hair was locking into dreads from lack of cleaning.

He was stocky, but not fat, and he easily doubled her in weight and arm length. Not to mention, he was armed with a curved cutlass, a real weapon of violence compared to her pitiful kitchen utensil.

The men gathered in front of her, and she held her cleaver up at the ready. They were twenty feet away. Marissa didn't look behind her. "How many?

"I don't know how to count," the deep voice came back. "They're lined up though."

"Hold," she breathed.

The Master Gunner began yelling at her in his native language. He pointed at her and then pointed to the deck.

Marissa knew he wanted her to drop the cleaver, even though she couldn't understand his words. She shook her head no. The Master Gunner laughed at her brazenness and turned to glance at all the other men. They laughed, too.

"Drop or die," he said in Trade Tongue, his accent thick and heavy.

Every fiber of her being wanted to do as he asked, but the orc's words held her in place. Marissa took a deep breath, fastening her resolve as she shouted, "Come and get me, big boy."

The Master Gunner smiled even more lewdly. She could feel his eyes drinking her in, an intent upon them that made her skin crawl. He stepped forward, raising his cutlass and closed to a mere ten feet away, his men drawing steel behind him.

Marissa let out the faintest whisper, "Hold."

The Master Gunner took another aggressive step forward and he froze. All the men behind him clamored and scrambled, trying not to stab one another with their drawn weapons. The slaver's nose wrinkled, and then took one deep sniff in the air.

That was when Marissa really did smile at the group of slavers. Her eyes lit with intensity. With raised eyebrows she mouthed a single word. "Boom."

Marissa stepped aside to reveal a demi-culverin facing towards them, and the gnome holding a smoldering slow match hovering just above the touch hole of the cannon. There was no wick for this one. With devilry in her eyes, the gnome drove the slow match home into the gun powder. The orc dove out of the way and for the second time in less than three minutes, a peal of thunder tore across the gun deck.

Bar-shot exploded from the barrel of the cannon. At such close proximity, not a single slaver could react in time. The result was a level of carnage so calamitous that it seemed like a theater play before her eyes.

At the head of the line, the Master Gunner simply disintegrated beneath the sheer force of the bar-shot, turning into a fine plume of red-misted gore. Following his entrancing demise, the swath of men behind him met no easier fate. The bar shot swung and like a guillotine sheared through the entire pack of armed men, erupting behind them as a spinning crimson-soaked lasso. It continued through the rest of the deck, shattering oak and pine before brilliantly exploding out of the stern of the ship into the deep blue beyond. A stream of flotsam could be seen glittering in the dying sun.

The pirates behind the cannon itself fared no better. For every action, there is an equal and opposite reaction. Unrestrained, the loose cannon erupted backward, becoming a recoil-driven projectile of its own. The twelve-hundred pound culverin, now a battering ram of doom, vaulted backward, destroying everything around it and crushing the line of men until it finally tumbled and lodged into the hatch that led to the crew quarters.

Marissa could only blink at the totality of butchery around her. Through the ringing in her ears, she heard the gnome cry out jubilantly, "Fire in the hole!"

"Little late for that," the orc said with a grin. When her eyes fell to Marissa, that smile disappeared.

Unease gripped at her belly. Was she hurt? Was the adrenaline so strong she didn't realize that the bar-shot hit her too? She looked down at her hands... they were covered in blood.

MARISSA STARED AT HER ARMS IN ALARM. IT WASN'T JUST HER hands – it was her arms, belly, breasts and thighs. She was soaked in blood.

"Oh Maker, where am I hit?"

The gnome whistled in surprise. "I'm fer thinkin' you were a might bit too close to the Master Gunner."

"Did the bar-shot get me? Am I dying?" Panic laced her words as she began patting her body, looking for the wounds.

The orc surveyed her, and then a tusky smile lit upon her face once more. "It's not yours, Jasian."

"Not... mine?" Marissa continued patting at her body, everything sticky as her hands slid across the cruor. Slowly, the realization began to enter her brain. The Master Gunner pretty much exploded. That dawning brought with it a new understanding as she began to taste the copper tang, rich upon her lips. Disgusted, she spit it out on the floor. "It's in my mouth! Oh, he's in my mouth!"

The gnome barked in laughter.

"It's so disgusting!"

The orc shook her head, "We must act fast. I'm sure they are already recovering. We must go to the deck now."

Accentuating her words, the orc strode forward and plucked up the Master Gunner's cutlass. His hand was still holding on to the grip, the only visible piece of the man left.

"Oh lord, I'm going to be sick," Marissa commented as she watched the orc peel the fingers away from its quite literal death grip on the weapon. She bent over, gagging on the deck.

"Be sick later," the wild gnome added, slapping Marissa on the hindquarters as she passed.

Marissa shot upright with a start, watching, bewildered as the gnome began to filch all the knives she could from the deceased slavers. "Grab a weapon – we've so much more death to deliver these pigs."

When the gnome drew an odd-looking cudgel, she smiled and said, "I think this is just yer speed, Brains." The small woman tossed it at Marissa.

Marissa barely caught the strange weapon. She guessed it was maybe sixteen or eighteen inches long. It was exceptionally sleek along a very smooth metal shaft that bore a hole at the bottom of it. She noted that it made a very poor handhold with her grimy hands.

The strange weapon transitioned from steel to wood which ended in a sharply-curved knob. Opposite the knob there was a small steel mechanism that was pulled back. There seemed to be a small chip, of what Marissa guessed was obsidian or flint, at the tip. Perhaps for piercing? It was the strangest club she'd ever seen.

The gnome was paying her no more mind, and so Marissa tucked the cudgel into the strap of fabric around her waist and grabbed for the nearest cutlass on the cruor-drenched floor.

Marissa was no stranger to battlefields, and the fields of dead men, but never was she the direct cause of such a thing. She fought to keep down the bile that rested thick in her throat. Wrapping her fingers around a dead man's sword, she took a deep breath and pulled the weapon free of the claret mire.

"Lady?"

Marissa spun; her cutlass raised. All she could see was the wreckage the cannon wrought. She squinted her eyes, trying to take in the dark recesses of the gun deck. Immediately the orc and gnome were at her side. Marissa could make out large golden eyes in the shadows. Very large eyes. She held up her cutlass. "Who are you?"

The creature scurried forward into the light. Marissa blinked in confusion. It was small, smaller than the gnome, looking more like a very young child. It was dressed in clothing just as ragged as Marissa's, so it did nothing to hide the fact that it had only three-clawed hands and feet, and a tail. On top of its head were dense rows of what appeared to be blonde plumes, but Marissa could tell at once what they really were – quills. She opened her mouth to speak, but it was the gnome who spoke first. "Blimey, that's a sprig-gan. Where did ye come from?"

"Orlop deck," the spriggan answered.

"Ye followed us?"

The blonde-quilled head bobbed a yes.

Those large golden orbs blinked up at Marissa, "We want to help you fight!" As if punctuating her words, she held up the club she liberated from one of the bodies. It took several seconds as the words processed in Marissa's head. "We?"

The spriggan turned her head, nodding back into the dark confines of the deck. More eyes became visible in the light as women stepped forward. At first, there were only a few, and then Marissa realized there were almost twenty of them.

"Yes!" the orc growled.

A smile took to Marissa's blood-stained lips. "Let's take this damned ship!" Marissa turned and followed after her green-skinned ally, an army behind her.

"WE ARE NOT TOO LATE!" THE ORC WHISPERED EXCITEDLY AS Marissa joined her behind rank barrels of what smelled like sour wine.

With a nod of her head, the large warrior directed Marissa to look to the stern. Marissa complied, pulling away the curtain of her dark, clumpy hair and looking in the direction the orc nodded.

She could see the scales, whose sloop they handicapped, screaming at the Ayjub Captain, his fringe a deep burnished bronze, in agitation. Clawed hands gesticulated wildly as he yelled. Armed slavers, all with crossbows and sharp instruments of war at their sides, were slowly flanking the creature as it became angrier about its current situation.

Isa stood at his side, and the caiman-like creature barely

noticed her. Marissa was about to bolt up and scream to her dearest friend, when a strong hand clamped her down. "No!" the orc hissed. "Look beyond your friend."

Marissa fought down the desire to ignore the orc and scream for Isa. She was so close now, only fifty feet away. All Marissa needed to do was charge in and fight less than a dozen men. She had the women now. It was not so impossible a feat...

"What are we waiting on?"

The orc nodded to the aftcastle, and Marissa saw what the orc had seen – two slavers acting as overwatch.

"I got this," the gnome said confidently. "Brains, ye and Tusker do yer thing as soon as I clear em,' ye savvy me?"

Marissa looked down to the little woman, "Okay..." Clearly, she didn't fully savvy.

The gnome winked. "You'll see." And then she was moving. In seconds, the gnome was gone from view. "Where...?"

Marissa watched in amazement as one of the Ayjub overwatch suddenly toppled backwards in alarm and disappeared out of sight, without so much as a sound. Seconds later, the other slaver, oblivious of what happened to his friend less than fifteen feet away, met a similar fate.

"Who is this chick?" Marissa asked in awe.

"I'm not sure we desire to know," the orc answered her honestly. "She has cleared the way for us, now it is up to us to do the rest."

"Right, ten men, and one scales. We can do this," Marissa said. As if hearing her cue, the spriggan lifted her head out from below deck. "Say the word, lady!"

A tusky grin took to the orc's lips, "I will see this through, Jasian. I owe you that much."

Marissa took a deep breath, the orc's confidence bolstering her own. "When this is over, I would like to know your name."

The brutish woman stared at her quizzically. "Your kind cares little for mine..."

Marissa shrugged. "Maybe, but I think friends should share names. Mine is Mari."

The orc worked her jaw several times, before the word left her mouth. "Friends?"

Marissa nodded. Inhaling deeply, she stood up and moved forward. Behind her, the orc dipped around the barrels and came around the other side of the mast, a walking shadow of her. Marissa focused her gaze on the slavers in front of her. She could do this. She would do this – for Isa.

The gap closed to about thirty feet when one of the Ayjub finally noticed her. For a moment, he could only stare at her gore-drenched form transfixed, before he thought to raise his crossbow and warn his fellows.

It seemed like they all turned at once to face her, and Marissa struggled to keep her entire body from shaking as she kept moving. The slavers pointed their crossbows at her, while the Captain drew a cudgel similar to the one she had around her waist. He held it, oddly, by its wooden head.

The scales only stared at her in disbelief.

The fear that radiated off the men was palpable, spectral even. They stared at her mortified, like she was the Reaper himself, their eyes darting behind her to where the hatch lay wide open with no one joining them.

"My name is Marissa de Cantor y Castile, Exactor of the Jasian Enclave, and I am claiming this ship and all of its cargo under the sovereign control of the Citadel. That includes the woman standing next to the scales. Defy me, and face the same fate as the rest of your crew."

The Ayjub captain didn't even blink at her words. "Kill her."

The nearest man raised his crossbow, and Marissa's gut tightened. Crack! Marissa jumped with a start. She stared at the slaver who targeted her with his crossbow. He had not pulled the trigger. In fact he looked intensely confused.

The other men stared at him in disbelief, and then the slaver's eyes rolled into the back of his head and he collapsed to the ground, the handle of a cooking knife sticking out of the base of his skull.

Eyes drifted up to the top of the aftcastle. There, standing on the rail looking like she ruled the seas, was the gnome, "Oi! The lady warned ye!"

"Anyone else?" Marissa asked mirthlessly.

The other slavers looked to one another, terrified. Marissa nodded to the gnome, who smiled with glee. "Now, me pretties!" the little woman bellowed.

Dozens of feminine voices roared in unison as women of all ages, races, and ilk charged forth from the hatch towards the confused slavers. The men directed their aims at the new threats, unsure of what to do. Above the din of raging women, she could hear the roar of the captain's voice: "Kill them! Kill them all!"

CHAPTER FOUR

Marissa de Cantor y Castile

Marissa screamed with the other women as she swung her cutlass at the nearest slaver. It alarmed her how easily the curved blade could part flesh with so little resistance. The weapon slid across his belly so simply, she wasn't sure she even hit him. Then, she looked into the man's eyes. They bulged in disbelief, glazed in intense pain. He pitched over, trying desperately to hold his organs inside him, while his life's essence painted the deck.

"Mari!" Isa yelled from behind her. Instinct made her duck.

Marissa heard the twang of a crossbow and the scream of another woman, caught by a bolt that was meant for her.

She spun to face this new adversary while he was reloading, but already found the orc pouncing upon him like a savage cat. The orc slammed his face against the deck over and over, raking at him with her filthy, blood-caked nails. Marissa gawked in disbelief as the boards splintered under the orc's ferocity.

Relatively safe for the moment, Marissa twisted back around, looking for Isa. She found the woman wrestling frantically with the scales, as he tried to bite her with venomous, dagger-like teeth.

"Isa!"

Marissa charged through the ensuing chaos, swinging her blade in wild and uncoordinated slashes to keep the slavers at bay. The scales, so intent on subduing his slave, did not see Marissa approach him from behind. She swung the blade down for a decapitating blow, but instead she rebounded in pain as the blade ricocheted off the scales' thick bony ridges. Fire raced up her hands and forearms, and she realized with horror that she was too malnourished to have strength enough to pierce all the way through the reptile's scaly flesh.

Her hit was far from useless. The slave-buyer recoiled in pain and pulled away from Isa, one clawed hand swiping towards Marissa, while the other went to where she struck the back of his head. His fingers came away wet with blood.

"I am going to rip out your throat!" he hissed.

Marissa backpedaled away from the scales, raising her cutlass. Behind her, she could hear the cries of women in pain. Who was hurt? Was that wail from the orc? The spriggan? If she looked, even for a second, she would be dead.

The scales drew his yataghan, and the sight of that cruel weapon tightened the scar along her back. He swept the blade forward, Marissa just barely catching the deadly weapon against her own. The swords collided in a loud clang, sparks erupting from steel against steel. His strength was enormous! Marissa yelped as the reverberation pounded at her joints, almost causing her to drop the sword.

"You are as pitiful as a child," the scales said in delight. "You are no Enclave warrior."

The scales' sword swung with skill and precision, and Marissa fought with panic and desperation, narrowly managing to block all attacks that came, but still giving up ground. Always giving up ground.

Then the yataghan breached Marissa's guard, slipping like a graceful dancer underneath her lumbering block and sliding upwards to slice across her left shoulder. Marissa cried out, her fingers going numb in her left hand, while her shoulder grew hot and wet. She backed up, striking the railing of the ship.

Beneath her, angry waves rolled and crested, eagerly awaiting her plunge into the abyss.

Marissa looked away from those hungry waters and back at the scales. His malicious smile told her that he knew he was victorious. She was either going to be impaled, or plummet into the cold maw of the Ire ocean.

Or neither.

Marissa's eyes flicked behind the scales, and that glance caused the creature to hesitate for only a heartbeat, but it was enough.

Isa roared and jumped onto the scales' back, gouging at the sensitive membrane that served as the creature's ears. He hissed in surprise as Isa buried her fingers deeper into the soft tissue, deafening him.

Like a liquid hand of the Maker swatting at insects, a powerful wave kicked up over the prow, washing over the deck, and soaking everyone. Those caught unaware were sent sprawling – Marissa, Isa, and the scales among them.

"Is this a bad time to let ye guys in the know? I killed the yokesman like two minutes ago," the gnome squealed in delight.

Another lurch, and more water doused the decking, sending more scrambling. Marissa was pulled away from Isa and the scales, tumbling in an opposite direction.

She went sliding along the wet deck until she grabbed at sodden rigging. Catching her breath, she pulled herself to her feet, her left arm burning from brine in her wound. "What's that even mean?"

"It means no one is steering the ship," the spriggan replied, seeming to materialize out of nowhere at Marissa's side. Marissa looked down to see the creature's blonde quills fully erect and glistening rose-colored in the dying light.

Suddenly, the ship pitched hard to port, throwing everyone wildly. Marissa held onto the rigging for dear life. Much to her amazement, she watched the spriggan dig her claws into the decking and ride the wild buck of the ship out. Beneath them the ship shuddered, and wood cracked and groaned.

The spriggan sniffed at the salty sea air and pointed east. "Storm is coming fast. We need to end this." She looked at Marissa with her large golden eyes. "I can man the yoke, but that leaves you one less sword arm."

Marissa was about to comment when a cry of pain from a familiar voice tore through the clamor of battle. She looked up in time to see the scales pull his yataghan free from Isa's right thigh, and a surreal gout of blood follow the sword.

"No!" Marissa cried.

Marissa left the spriggan behind, racing at the scales on the uneven and pitching deck. Her sword lost to the waves, she reached for the cudgel at her hip, not knowing what she could even do with a blunt weapon against the hard hide of the lizard's flesh.

It didn't matter. All that mattered was Isa.

Marissa roared as she charged the reptile, her voice an equal cry of anger and agony at the sight of her fallen friend. She closed the gap, swinging wildly at the scales, but he blocked her attacks easily. And he laughed at her – laughed! She caught only a glint of it, before she was sent flying once more by a backhand across her jaw. Blood welled in her mouth.

She rolled with the blow and clambered to her feet, her world a wobbly mess, and not just from the rocking ship. She could see the scales stalking forward proudly, confident of his skill. Behind him the women battled the remaining slavers. Many were on the ground bleeding from bolts in their bodies. More than a few stared lifeless at the sky, their frames listing bonelessly with the rocking ship.

They were dying.

They were all going to die.

Marissa's eyes fell to Isa, her skin already as pale as snow. Isa's hands clamped the wound on her leg closed, but it didn't stop the ceaseless flow of blood that ran liberally between her fingers.

Marissa felt her own hot blood dribbling down her chin and running down the side of her neck. Her world collapsed to a pinprick. Just her and the scales. If this would be how she died, then so be it.

Her fear vanished in that instant. All the terror, all the cowing and trepidation she felt since becoming a slave, it all fell away in a wash as clean as the saltwater coursing over her toes. She found courage in her heart. It was small, only a speck, but she latched onto it.

Hefting her cudgel, she now stalked forward towards the scales. His alien eyes widened as he saw the change in her. The loss of her fear. The loss of his edge. It caused him to hesitate, and it saved Marissa's life.

The ship lurched hard, pulled by another brutal wave, and Marissa stumbled forward out of control. The scales equally staggered backward, his yataghan slicing through the air, glancing off her right cheekbone. One step closer and it would've taken her in the throat.

But the scales' grip on the weapon must've been tenuous because it went flying away, lost in the violence of the rocking ship. Marissa recovered and brought her cudgel down across the scales' extended forearm. There was a crack and he screamed in pain. Whether she broke his arm or not, she didn't know, nor did she have time to find out as he grabbed her by the throat with his good hand. She weighed nothing but a feather to him as he hefted her from the ground. Claws sluiced into her water-logged skin, biting into her neck. He squeezed.

Marissa couldn't breathe! Panic ate at her resolve. She tried to hammer more blows on him, but her angle was terrible. Her strength was virtually non-existent when this melee began, and now what little she did have flagged. She managed one last hit, striking uselessly against the side of his bony horns, and then her weapon slid from her grip. She caught it only by the strange metal mechanism just under the wooden ball of the cudgel itself.

Light began to fade, as darkness threatened to swallow her. She managed one last look at Isa, a pale angel lying on the deck swathed in rivers of red. The gnome next to Isa was trying desperately to tighten something around Isa's leg. The small woman was looking at Marissa and mouthing strange words.

"Sot Im," it appeared to Marissa in her waning consciousness. "Scoot Him," it came again a little clearer. And then Marissa remembered the way she saw the captain holding the cudgel. By the wooden end.

"Shoot him!"

She understood in that final moment. It wasn't a cudgel at all. Marissa squeezed her grip on the wooden end, laced her finger around what she now knew was a trigger, similar to a crossbow, and lifted the metal cylindrical end up... and up... until she rested the barrel of it right next to the scales' alien eye.

It twitched in surprise, looking down the barrel of a gun.

"Die... you... son... of... a... bitch..." she wheezed. Marissa squeezed the trigger.

She saw the metal hammer drop into frizzen as her vision faded to nothing. Then there was light. Bright light followed by a peal of thunder right at her fingertips. Marissa felt herself pitch and drop hard, jarring her legs as she tumbled to the deck. Instinctively she took a deep breath. Mercifully, wonderful air filled her deprived lungs, and before she could celebrate this new discovery that she was no longer choking, bitter acrid smoke replaced it.

She began to cough violently. As she did, her vision swam to the surface once more. Her eyes took in the sight before her in all of its gory splendor.

The scales was lying next to her, one eye staring vacantly at her. The other was gone. Utterly obliterated. To Marissa's revulsion, she realized she was looking through that empty socket and beyond to the remaining battle on deck.

She watched something thick drip in that cavity, and she felt the bile rush to her throat. "Oh Maker, that's disgusting." Fighting down the desire to vomit, Marissa pushed herself to her feet, surveying the battle.

The deck was littered with the dead and the dying, Ayjub slavers and slaves alike. As Marissa absorbed it all, she realized with amazement that those that were still standing ... were all women.

The orc was walking around with a harpoon, stabbing every man on deck in the chest to ensure he was dead.

They did it.

They won.

Before the joy of this startling revelation could sink in, Marissa's gaze landed on Isa. The gnome had her leg in a tourniquet, but both she and Isa were shrouded in crimson waters. The gnome placed something under the back of Isa's head, propping it up slightly. Marissa could see her best friend's eyes were glassily staring at her.

"Isa!" Marissa cried, stumbling across the deck. She collapsed at her childhood friend's side, her hands reaching desperately for Isa's. She twined her fingers with Isa's, and they were so cold. So unbelievably cold.

Isa seemed to feel the sensation, and her glassy eyes fell to Marissa, her lips turned into a weak smile. "Mari, you fought."

Tears began to blot Marissa's vision as she turned to look at the gnome. The usual wild gleam in the gnome's eyes was replaced with a somber expression. "Do something!" Marissa pleaded, "Gnomes know magic – heal her!"

The gnome's mouth compressed into a thin line. "That's a stereotype, Brains. Suren' a lot o' us are creationists of some kind, but not all. I'm no mage, or sorcerer, or whatever other pretty title ye want to give it. I canna perform magic. I'm sorry."

Marissa felt the tears tumble from her eyes, rolling down her cheeks. "But we're supposed to save her."

"Mari."

Isa's voice was a fading whisper, "Mari, look at me."

Marissa's lip quivered as she looked down at her lifelong friend. "It's okay, Mari... It's okay."

Marissa shook her head violently, and she squeezed Isa's hand tighter. A growl formed in her throat, "No. No, it's not okay."

Isa looked away from her, and up to the sky, "Yes, it is Mari, the Maker calls me back."

Marissa shook her head more vehemently, "No. No, it's not fair."

Isa looked back to Marissa, "Go home, Mari, make peace with your family, and take care of Cassy for me... she'll have no one to look out for her."

Marissa sniffed. She could feel the presence of the other women gathering behind her. "Yes, Isa. Of course. I'll look after Cassandra. By the Maker, I swear it."

"Good," Isa breathed as she closed her eyes. "Good. My sister could use a friend like you. I love you Mari."

"I love you too, Isa. I always have."

A smile formed on Isa's lips, and Marissa felt Isa bringing her head down to Isa's own. Their lips touched, and then Isa fell still. It took Marissa a full second to realize that Isa was no longer breathing. Marissa squeezed Isa's limp fingers. "Isa?" Isa's other hand slid from her hair.

Panic welled inside Marissa, "Isa?" She let go of Isa's hand and it tumbled bonelessly to her side. Marissa grabbed at Isa's shoulders and started shaking her, "Isa!"

"She's... gone, mate," the gnome said quietly. "She's gone."

"No!" Marissa wailed, pulling Isa's head to her heart. "No, no, no!"

A ripple of thunder ripped across the sky, and Marissa could feel the first cold drops of rain pelt across her skin. Marissa loved the rain. She always had, but this time it did little to lift her burdened soul.

She failed.

She failed to save her best friend.

"Jasian." The orc said to her quietly. "Jasian, I am sorry for your friend. She died a warrior, but *we* need you now."

"You don't need me." Marissa replied. "I'm no fighter. I couldn't even save Isa."

"Her death was an act of honor, to save you, to save us. Do not waste it."

"Brains, the tusker is right – all of this was possible because of ye."

Marissa looked to the gnome, and then up to the orc, who was nodding her agreement. Behind the orc, the other women were nodding as well.

"Ye've given us a chance at freedom, Brains, but we not be done yet."

Marissa sniffed and looked at the women around her. "What are you saying?"

The gnome smiled sadly, "I'm saying if we're for tryin' ta sail a ship, we're fer needing a cap'n."

"Captain Mari," the orc said.

"Cap'n Mari," the gnome corrected.

"Aye, Bloody Mari!" a woman said from behind the orc.

Murmurs of consent rippled through the group of women.

"Eh, Bloody Mari! I like it!" the gnome agreed.

Marissa looked around at the women before her. All of them were counting on her. She cradled Isa's head to her chest once more, before looking down at the woman she had known for her entire life.

Delicately she put Isa to the deck and closed her eyes. Marissa would mourn Isa, she would mourn the loss of her friend, the hole in her heart, for the rest of her days. But Isa would want this, above all else. Isa would want Marissa to save these women. Marissa could do that for her. She would do that for her. But first, that meant she needed to lead them.

Marissa took a deep breath and stood up. "I wish we could celebrate this moment. Get drunk on sour wine and stale bread, but a storm comes quickly, and we have work to do."

"And what be that?" a human from the back cried out.

Marissa looked around at the deck. Drizzle began to tumble from the sky more readily. "We earn our keep, our right to survive."

The women around her murmured their assent, including the orc and gnome. "And how are we going to do that, Brains?"

Marissa looked down at the gnome who posed the question, "By the Maker, lass, we sail."

"None of us knows how to sail," a voice cried out.

"I can," the gnome declared.

Marissa was becoming emboldened. "Then we learn from her! I for one am not going to die in a shipwreck after so many women just died to give us this chance at freedom! I am going to try, dammit!" Marissa looked in turn at all the women before her, then continued, "And in doing so, we will get home to our families. By the Maker, we will not end here!" Bolstered, some of the women began nodding and looking to one another. "We all will work hard day and night if need be, and we will travel down the coast. I will deliver each and every one of you back to your homes.

"Be it in life," Marissa added as she looked down at her dearest friend, her conviction ironclad, "or in death, I will take you home. This I swear."

When it was evident that Marissa had no more words, the gnome bellowed, "Well, what are ye doin,' ye layabouts? Ye been sittin' on ye arses for months in that hold, just stinkin'!" She pointed at a group of three women who seemed stouter than most. "Ye, ye and ye, man the riggin'."

"It's about to storm."

"Then ye's gets a much-needed bath!" the gnome yelled. "I ain't fer bein' lost at sea right after we takes the ship!"

The women flinched at the mad gnome, and soon those with assignments were scurrying across the deck, either learning their jobs, or teaching others if they had some rudimentary skill.

Marissa stood on the deck with the orc and the gnome, unsure of what to say next. Another clap of thunder, and Marissa watched an arc of lightning cut through the sky.

"Rusalka."

Marissa looked back at the orc. "Excuse me?"

"Friends share their names, right?" she said. "My name is Rusalka."

The gnome held out her three-fingered hand to Marissa, "Nure Onna, but Onna's fine."

Marissa took the small calloused hand in her own, "Mari, and the pleasure is mine."

Another lance of lightning cut through the sky, momentarily blinding them, before the horizon returned to indigo. "Well, Cap'n, I think fer taking the ship was the easy part."

Marissa gazed at the deep purple skyline and the wall of approaching rain, thinking that Onna might very well be right.

PART II
CASTILE

INTERLUDE

Don Fernando Cantor

To his most noble, Veer De' Storm,

KIND SER, IT'S RUMORED THAT YOU FOUGHT IN THE Fermanian Civil War with my beloved daughter, Marissa. I say this, because I once received a letter from her dearest friend Lady Isa Marin saying that my Marissa was quite smitten with you. She bade me not to worry because she said that you are an elf of great honor. If this is true, I must beseech you in my desperate time. Dark forces plot against the Lefhym in the absence of a newly appointed viscount, and I find I have little interest nor care of such politics. Politics, I might add, that should be of the greatest of importance to me. It is because my chest is hollow, ser elf. When Marissa left my home, and my name, she took with her, my heart.

Gone she has been for over five long winters. She left but a girl in mine eyes, and I know, deep down, she must be a woman grown now.

I am told that she is a traitor to the Jasian Enclave, and that she betrayed a direct order while under her fealty. I am told to disavow her as my offspring, to forget about her, as if she never existed, for my benefit, and the benefit of my house and family.

But I cannot.

No matter what it does to my family name, I shall never disavow her from this house. I will never take away her home. She will remain heiress apparent, no matter how much it besmirches the family name.

But that is not why I write you, good ser. It is for what they do not say to me that I seek answers. What they dare not tell me – is her fate.

Please ser, I implore you, the Jasian Enclave has severed all communication between Marissa and my family, and the Seafarer's Caucus of Fermania will not answer my queries. You are my last hope. Can you tell me, were you at the battle near Gnomelaneum when she vanished? Was she taken? Injured? Can you please tell me if my daughter even still draws breath?

We are a family torn asunder by loss. I am merely an old man, seeking some form of closure, with a girl whom I dearly failed as a father. Any word of her would be welcome, even the heartbreaking.

For a broken heart is better than no heart at all.

SINCERELY,
Don Fernando Cantor

FERNANDO PUT DOWN THE QUILL AND MASSAGED HIS SORE eyes. It was getting harder to focus as he grew in the winters. It was especially hard for him to focus when the subject was his beloved daughter. He looked at the vellum before him. There were no words. No words in the world that could communicate what her loss felt like.

She was his baby.

She was his princess.

She was his ondine.

Fernando knew he would give up all he had – titles, lands, all the wealth in all of Castile – just to see her again. If only he could tell her that he was sorry. That his words were spoken, not in malice, but in the heat of the moment. In a fleeting instance of passion, where his rage drove a wagging tongue, not his logical mind. That he was an old fool, an even older fool now, and that she had every right to be who she wanted to be; not who he thought she should be.

He would tell her all of this, but mostly he just wanted to tell his little girl that he loved her. Fernando desperately longed for the days when she was but a tiny waif, hardly larger than a sack of grain. He could still feel how she would wrap her arms around his legs and beg that he play with her, or the weight upon his thighs as she ambled into his lap to look at whatever it was that he was doing. She didn't care what it was, what he was doing, so long as they did it together.

Fernando took a deep shuddering breath. How often had he turned her away? How often had he been too busy for his daughter? How quickly those moments burned away, as frail as crumbling ash, and now they were gone forever... and so was she.

Marissa.

A clamor at the study door brought him back, "Don?"

Fernando rubbed at his eyes and nose once more, making sure

they were free of moisture. Clearing his throat, he called back, "Yes, Javier?"

"Don Fernando, I beg pardon for the interruption, but there is a woman here to see you. She says that she lives on the Cantor lands, and that Don Benecio y Gasset is claiming that the family's farm is on his lands, and that they owe their taxes to him immediately."

Fernando could hear the woman plaintively crying in their native tongue on the other side of the door. He grabbed the bridge of his nose, getting the gist of her plight before Javier even translated her words. "She claims that the Torro family has already paid taxes to you, of course."

"Of course," Fernando muttered. "Damn you Benecio, you greedy little bastard."

Fernando took another deep breath, stood up straight and walked to the door. He would handle this matter as a man of gentry. He ran his coarse thumb over his creased cheeks to make sure there were no tears on them, and then opened the door.

The sight of the woman cowering behind Javier gave him a start. "Javier, what have you done?"

The woman was young, close in age to what he would imagine Marissa to be today. Her dark tresses were disheveled and filthy, as if she were drug roughly across the floor. Her simple tan peasant's dress was torn and speckled brown across her collar and breast. Sleep-deprived brown eyes looked at him through bloodied, swollen cheeks. Her lip was split and still welling a small stringer of blood down her chin.

"It was not me, Don Fernando – she showed up at the gate like this."

Fernando reached out and took both her hands, bidding her inside. The young woman sniffled, barely withholding the tears that wanted to stream forth from her wounded face. He guided her gently down to the settee. "Tell me, dear, how did this happen?"

She hiccupped away another sob, before she spoke. "Don Benecio's son, Rafael, and his men did this." She refused to look in his eyes. "They said next time it will be worse, and they'll do a lot more than just beat me. My sister, too. Please ser, not my sister, she is only twelve."

Fernando's blood boiled at the sight of this poor woman scarcely a day over twenty winters. How terrified she must've been at the hands of those men. How fearful of what they would do, fearful for her life if she didn't comply. And now they threatened to do worse? His stomach tightened at the very thought.

Fernando's nostrils flared. He and Don Benecio had territorial disputes in the past, but it was never taken out on the people, and never anything as extreme as this. Don Benecio was a greedy prude at times, but violence towards his wards? No... it must be his sons' doing. Rafael enjoyed conniving with ruffians and vagrants. His rebellion to his father gave him a false illusion of power. Fernando should just talk to Benecio and be done with it.

Fernando stood and paced over to his desk. He glanced down at the words, almost dry on the vellum. But what if it were his little girl that came to him in this state? Would he just sit idly by and say he'd take care of it? Send transcripts and notaries to spread the message to Benecio to tell Rafael not to do this again? No. They were making an example of this poor girl to others, a power play. A play against Fernando and his people. Seeing how hard he could push. Fernando, in turn, needed to barter with them in their own coin, for that was what they best traded with, after all.

Fernando straightened and looked at the mantle above his fire-place. Long had he retired it there, but as he felt the anger puddling in the center of his chest, he knew that his prized blade would come down from its hallowed place and bite flesh this night.

He grabbed his cutlass from the mantle. "Ser, what are you doing?" Javier's voice carried a lilt of panic to it.

"Making things right," Fernando growled. "I will not have my subjects beaten like unruly dogs!"

"You cannot! If you strike down Rafael..."

A smile touched Fernando's lips at Javier's concern, "Relax my friend, he shall feel my sting to be sure, but the only permanent wound will be to his pride. The boy needs a dose of humility, and my subjects need to know they are safe."

Javier wasn't convinced. "Don Fernando... you are not such a young man..."

Fernando gazed upon the beaten woman, alone and afraid on his settee. "I needn't be for this. Fetch my armor Javier – Cantor rides this night!"

FERNANDO CANTERED OUT OF THE BARBICAN SLOWLY, HIS steed long accustomed to his unusual riding times. The evening song of wildlife and flickering torches barely discomforted the horse at all, only noticeable by the occasional flicker of its ears.

Javier, also on horseback, sat erect in his saddle on Fernando's right side. He shifted, far more uncomfortable in his seat than the mare beneath him. "Lady Miranda will not be pleased with this decision."

Fernando looked to his aide, expecting to see his face etched with worry and concern, but what he really saw was an aged and frail man beneath the morion helmet. The flat brim did little to shadow the deep creases that lined his cheeks and jowls, or hide the sharp crow's feet wrinkling the corners of his dark eyes.

His steel breastplate, engraved with the twin horses standard of Cantor, seemed loose and ill-fitting on his emaciated frame. Still, Javier held the shield at his side solidly, and the weight of the spear resting across his thighs seemed not to wear him down.

But the fact remained: Javier was old, and so was he.

"Then it is a good thing that Lady Miranda set out early on this eve to the Citadel. With the Maker's blessing she won't catch wind of tonight's events until our wounds are healed, and our lands are safe," Fernando remarked about his beautiful wife. "Though 'tis likely she shall cause all manner of new wounds once she does catch the tale."

"I shall fear for your safety even greater then."

Fernando looked over to Javier, to see the glint of humor in his eyes. The don smiled back at his aide and longtime friend. "I know you don't agree with what I am doing, so thank you for being here."

Javier looked away from Fernando, and towards the wooded horizon, blackened in a blanket of starless night. "It's not that I don't agree with the justice, Don, you know I do. It's that I'm afraid you are trying to hold on to something that doesn't exist."

Fernando should've been offended by such a remark, but he was long past such frivolities and he and Javier had known each other a very long time, "I feel older every single day."

Javier looked back to him, almost pleadingly, "Then let our young men handle this task. We can call for them at first light. My son Vicente can head the line if you wish – he has become an astute soldier. Or you can just send a letter to Don Benecio, let him rein in his impertinent son. It doesn't need be you to do it personally, right this instant."

Fernando looked down at the Torro girl, her swollen and bloodied face reminding him so much of his lost daughter. Her eyes, full of concern for her family, looked up at him, her desperation visible in every movement she made. "Yes, Javier," he susurrated, "yes it does."

Javier huffed in obvious agitation before declaring, "I will, as always, follow you, Don Fernando."

That was good enough for Fernando. Still he felt he owed Javier more. "Your son has become quite the soldier though."

At those words, a smile did crease the weary aide's features. "That he has, my Don. That he has."

They set off down the hill and towards the woodlands. It was small for a forest, just a pocket of coniferous trees that separated them from the farmlands and vineyards on the other side. It was a nice respite and often acted as a form of seclusion, keeping those in castle Loja de Cantor out of sight from the more curious locals.

Resting on one of the higher hills of the Shemma peninsula provided Fernando with a wondrous view of all of Castile to his southwest, and of the farmlands northeast of his holdings. Beyond the small forest and farmlands, the massive Shemma woodlands loomed tall and dark on the horizon, a long black smudge blurring against the indigo night.

The Shemma was the largest forest in the known world, and not just by acreage. Its scope was vast. Elders, trees of unimaginable scale, rose from the earth by the scores. They stood as wooden titans that dwarfed the tallest buildings that Fernando had ever seen. Within those woods dwelled predators so massive that they made the largest saltwater crocodile seem like a gecko in comparison. And living up within the trees, risking those apex predators, dwelled the Lefhym, the Wood Elves. They were the true owners of the Shemma peninsula and the woods they called home. Fernando was but an honored guest, as was all of Castile. His duty was to ensure no one ever attempted to cut down an Elder tree, as they were revered by the Lefhym. In return, the humans of Castile acted as port and trade for the Wood Elves. It was an amicable arrangement, set up between the Jasian Enclave, for whom Castile represented, and the ruling High Chieftain of the Shemma.

Fernando shook those thoughts as his view of the lumbering wooded giant disappeared before the much smaller, more intimate conifers. Cedars, junipers, larches, and pines began to vault up around him, reducing those dark-shaped elders into memory.

They walked for a time, enjoying the rich scents of the softwoods all around them. Fernando listened to the crunch of pine straw and cones beneath the horses' hooves. He heard the snorts and heavy breaths of his horse. He watched the flick of its ears, felt the swish of its tail at his back, the crackle of fire from his torch.

Fernando began to slow down, his mind turning over in understanding. His steed snorted in agitation. Fernando watched the ears twitch again, the long hairs of the horse's tail slap his back. He heard the thud of it against his steel breastplate.

Javier took point, the loud crunching echoing through the trees. Where was the sound? Where was the wildlife? The creatures that were alive at night? He should be hearing bugs chirp, owls hoot, and the cry of a fox. There was... nothing.

Fernando looked down at the girl walking beside him, she glanced up once at him and then away, looking around. When she still felt his eyes on her, she looked up at him again. "I'm sorry," she whispered, "but they have my sister."

And all at once, he understood.

"Javier!" Fernando roared, grabbing the reins to wheel about.

Javier began to turn towards him, when a whoosh cut through the air. Fernando turned back at the sound. He knew it all too well. "Javier!" he called again.

Fernando heard a thud, and with terrible understanding he looked to where his trusted aide had last stood.

Laying at the shuffling feet of his mare was Javier's body. A bolt, perfectly shot just beneath the brim of the morion, was embedded in the right cheek of his beloved aide. Javier's glassy eyes stared into the abyss. Dead, before his body had even hit the ground.

Fernando hoisted his shield, intent on wheeling back around to shield the girl, when more hisses permeated the still of the night. Javier's mare cried as it was cut down, and Fernando could only watch in horror as a dozen bolts peppered the helpless Torro girl.

She collapsed into the crunching pine straw with her unuttered scream still upon her lips.

"Hold," a voice cut into the maelstrom.

Fernando looked about, adrenaline coursing through his veins, but he was night-blinded by the proximity of his own torch. He had not expected such a violent attack so near to Loja de Cantor – such an attack to Castile was unheard of.

He began to make out figures in the woods, moving closer. Torches flared to life, and he could see several forms, all of them hooded.

One of them, a burly monster of bundled muscles held a strange crossbow pointed directly at him. He couldn't make out any details, except that is it was larger than standard crossbows and there were obvious protrusions sticking out at forty-five degree angles, on both the left and right side.

He looked down to the young girl, her wide eyes staring blankly into nothingness. Her life seeped into the straw bed beneath her, turning it black.

"Don Fernando Cantor," that same voice that called out 'hold' said to him. A lone figure emerged from the rest and strode forward between the trees. Cowled like the others, the figure came forward, close enough to stand in the amber light cast from Fernando's torch.

It was not Rafael, nor was it his father Benecio. It was someone altogether different. "It was you!" he hissed. "You did this to my people!"

The man before him had an almost bored expression. "Yes."

"Why?" Even as Fernando asked the question, it still hadn't really set in that his lifelong aide, Javier, was dead.

If the man before him heard Fernando, he made no sign of it. "Join us."

Fernando could hardly believe what he was hearing, it couldn't be. "What?"

The man clicked his tongue as if perturbed by Fernando's ineptitude. "Join us... or die."

His eyes took in the other figures around him, each one having joined the man before him. The dons of Castile, almost one and all, having signed their own fate to the Defiler.

"Never!" he spat, "I'll never join you."

The man shrugged as if it didn't matter. "Death then." He turned away.

Fernando laughed, "You can kill me, but Cantor will live on!"

The man half-turned back to Fernando, a smile playing at the corner of his mouth, "Ah, yes. I assume you mean your wife, safe behind the Enclave's walls?" He tapped a gloved hand at his mouth. "Or your estranged daughter, who has been denounced by the Jasian Enclave itself?"

He reached within his cloak and pulled out a single brooch. He tossed it to Fernando's horse's hooves. Fernando cast his light upon it, the twin prancing horses of Cantor reflecting back to him. It was his wife's brooch, and it glistened a wet crimson in his orange light.

"Your wife said no, too."

Rage and pain consumed Fernando all at once. His vision became swollen in red, and he could barely even hear his own words as he roared, "Monster!"

In a single motion he threw his torch into the pine straw and drew his family's cutlass. He galloped towards the hateful man, who only stood a handful of steps away. No one else could stop Fernando in time. He closed the gap and swung his sword, intent on taking the heretic's head.

The bastard wore the same smug smile.

The last sounds Fernando ever heard were a dozen shrill whistles. His chest exploded in pain, he was falling, and then he found himself at the man's feet. He looked up at that awful smile, but he didn't register it, not really. Pain blotted out all else, save one thing... Mari. He would never be able to tell her he was sorry. Sorry for everything. He could never look into those large brown eyes and tell her how much he loved his baby girl, his precious ondine.

A huge mass of what Fernando assumed was another person approached behind the man above him. One final click pierced through the veil of agony and sorrow, and then there was nothing more.

CHAPTER FIVE

Rusalka

Six Months Later...

"JUST GIVE IT A MOMENT, RUE!"

Rusalka looked at Marissa, who wore an ever-growing infectious smile. "I still don't see what the big deal is. They are cliffs. We've seen many now."

Rusalka's comment caused Mari to grin even wider. "Not like this you haven't."

Rusalka folded her muscular arms over her chest, "They're just rocks."

"Bringing her to port!" Emmell, the spriggan, yelled over the crashing waves. "She'll be in view any moment."

"Ye heard the spriggan, ye worthless layabouts, she ain't fer doin' all the work!" Onna bellowed at the remaining dozen women on deck.

Rusalka turned to grab the rigging, when she felt Mari's hand against her forearm. "Not you, Rue. I want you to see this."

Rusalka huffed, "I should work."

"No," Mari corrected, "you need to take this in."

A growl escaped from between her tusks, and she turned back to the bow. "This had better be good."

"Oh... you'll see."

Mari leaned against the rail, waiting expectantly, smiling. Rusalka folded her arms once more over her chest in defiance. There was nothing that could possibly... her mouth fell open.

"This is impossible."

Mari laughed.

As they wended around the bend Mari called Capo Hoorn, Rusalka could see tiny, colorful houses packed closely together, all clinging like babies to the rugged cliff face. They sparkled against the brown stone like gemstones. As more of the view opened itself to her, the cluster of pastel houses fastened to the steep ledges of the cliffs seemed to go on and on. She was dumbstruck.

The bright little homes glittered every vivid color on the spectrum. And the ocean acted as a prism, fracturing the light of the sun and dancing it across the cliffside.

These rainbow houses appeared as if they were stacked one upon the other, yet these homes weren't ramshackle. This wasn't the work of the destitute building homes from flotsam and jetsam, just trying to survive.

No, there was a wealth here, not one of lavish abundance, but more of happiness and comfort. These people did not want for much, there was a sense of harmony to the rolling waves of chromatic seaside homes.

Spaced out amongst the rising crests, and sitting atop each tier of homes, like a mother hen upon her nest of bejeweled eggs, was a castle.

Though Rusalka couldn't be certain, judging by her distance, she knew that the castle, all of the castles actually, had to be immense. She could make out a double line of military walls that meandered over the granite terrain. She could see the promontories clearly at the top of the hill of houses. Not every castle was the same in look, or color, for they were as vibrant as all the homes nestled beneath them, but there were similarities.

For instance, unlike other castles Rusalka noticed when her orc tribes passed closely to human lands, these castles each only had a single tower. These lone towers were crowned with merlons of brilliant red, bronze, and gold that were pyramidion. Even at her distance, she could tell there were exquisite engravings on each of the solitary turrets. Her eyes swayed across the vibrant landscape, taking in each. There were so many! The panorama stretched as far as she could see, until it finally disappeared around the bend of the cliffside.

She looked at Mari, who was smiling radiantly at her. "Welcome to my home, Rue. Welcome to Castile, the city of castles, Prism of Sowle."

A SHORT TIME LATER, RUSALKA WATCHED IN CHILDLIKE wonder as their spriggan sea artist deftly navigated the large galleon between the small sloops and sailboats of fishermen, who casually cast their lines into brilliant, clear waters. If the sailors were concerned with the massive cargo ship, they didn't show it.

While she took over for Onna in giving orders, Marissa left Rusalka to gawk at everything. Never in her wildest dreams did Rusalka ever think she would lay eyes upon such majesty. Orcs were never welcome in places such as these and were generally attacked on sight by pretty much every race on Kuldarr. Rusalka didn't blame them either – her people were like locusts. They travelled in huge tribes, and everywhere they went, all they did was destroy, consume, and desecrate. Rusalka herself would have been no different if she hadn't...

Her eyes broke away from the mesmerizing city of Castile in all its multicolored splendor and sought out Marissa once more. Had six months among these women really rid her of such base desires? Did it change her? Perhaps it was too early to say, though she was grateful to Marissa in being so accepting of her. Were it not for Marissa, she doubted many others aboard the *Bella Dahlia* would've been so receptive.

Rusalka heard the anchor splash and felt the ship slow as she watched the women redirect the rigging, so the sails were against the wind. They had grown into proficient sailors in the last several months – those who were left, anyhow. This was the last stop of the *Bella Dahlia*. All the remaining women here had nowhere left to go. Either their families were gone, deceased, or had moved on without them. Some were just too ashamed to return home. Marissa, being some form of royalty, promised a place for all of them in Cantor lands, even Rusalka. So Rusalka followed her just like the remaining humans, the gnome, and the spriggan.

Rusalka wondered just how accepting the rest of the people might be to have an orc in their presence, upon their lands, or if she would be the first blamed for any little problem the humans may suffer? A pestilence on the crops? Blame the orc. Livestock killed? It's the savage! Worse, if anyone were murdered, she would likely be the first – and probably only – suspect. How long until she was the subject of a witchhunt? A month? A week? Maybe only days? But where else could Rusalka go? Her tribe was destroyed. Most, if not all, the orc men were put to the blade and axe, the older women also slaughtered, as were the orcish children that were too young to be useful. No one wanted an orc slave to raise; their only use was to fight and to die.

She and a handful of other women that were just old enough to be useful, but not so old as to not be brought to heel, were kept alive so that they could be used in gladiator pens across the Scorch-glass Archipelago. Those women separated from her long ago. She was the only gladiator left aboard the *Bella Dahlia*. The Ayjub hoped to capitalize on her death in some arena in the dry deserts of Oganis.

It still would've been a better life than she had amongst her tribe. She couldn't, wouldn't go back to her people. To be a woman in the tribes of orcs was not a life she wanted. Not then, not ever. Not since knowing that there was something different for her now, no matter how short it might last.

Rusalka took in the splendor of Castile again. She thought she had seen more than most orcs when she was a gladiator, but now she knew there was so much more of this world to see. Perhaps she would stay as long as she was welcome by the Cantors, but the moment it began to wane, she would be gone.

The *Bella Dahlia* sluiced through the translucent waters, and the orc stared in wide-eyed wonder as the city dominated the horizon. As they sailed into the docks, Rusalka craned her head back, and back, to see up to the tops of the pointed castle towers that jutted so high into the sky she thought they might pierce the clouds. How could humans build such structures, into the side of a cliff no less? It didn't seem possible. Raised amongst her people, she witnessed the ruins of old forts and castles from the confines of her pen. Nothing like this. Nothing so... alive.

The yelling from Marissa and Onna was drowned out by the tumultuous clamor of dockhands and the roar of a vibrant, living, breathing city. Rusalka was suddenly bombarded by intense fragrances of lemon and sage. And the colors! Her eyes never beheld anything as bright and vivid as the bougainvillea.

Now only a few dozen strides away, she could see a maze of alleys and steps that climbed up the cliff, all with small shops displaying products of local crafts. This only intensified the undisputed beauty of the landscape. Little humans dotted this elegant vista before her, adorned in fresh linen dresses and leather sandals, all as colorful as the architecture around them.

The clangor of the gangplank echoed, and Rusalka turned to see only a trio of women battening down the ship, while the rest disembarked for their new life. This was going to be the last Rusalka ever saw of the *Bella Dahlia*. She would have a new life the moment she crossed that thin plank of wood. A better life.

Marissa, Onna, and Emmell joined Rusalka at the prow, and Rusalka could see the anticipation sparkling like a sunrise on morning dew in Marissa's chestnut eyes. "Ready?" her captain asked, nearly unable to restrain her giddiness.

Rusalka nodded, but she felt the first knots tie in her belly. She was not afraid, no. There was little she, or any orc, ever truly feared. But this was different. This was a reluctance to let go. The moment she crossed that simple strip of oak, all of the acceptance she found amongst the women on this ship would float away like flotsam after a storm. They were going their separate ways – not immediately, she knew, but soon enough. For what did a gnome, a spriggan, a human, and an orc really share once they left this galleon? Rusalka knew that answer too well. There was nothing to tie them together after this.

Rusalka took a deep breath, pulled up the hood of her cloak over her head and shoulders, and gave Marissa her most stoic expression, hoping to hide the hurt she felt inside. "Let us go to your Cantor lands."

Marissa clapped her on the shoulder, with a wide smile, "It will be wondrous and beautiful, I promise you!"

Her captain looked at the other two women. "And my father

will turn none of you away." She looked back at Rusalka. "By this, I swear."

As soon as they crossed the ramp onto the docks, Rusalka heard Onna ask Marissa, "Who will handle the selling of the *Bella Dahlia?*"

"My father will handle it," Mari answered. "Unless he may have need for a cargo ship. I do not know if the vineyards have prospered such that they may need a galleon to add to their fleet of cogs."

"As long as we all get our share," Onna grumped.

Before she could even get a response, though, Marissa was running down the deck, unable to contain herself anymore. The raven-haired human cried in glee as she launched herself from the side of the pier and landed into the salt-white sand, grasping at it as if terrified to let too much sift away through her fingers.

Rusalka had never seen this in Marissa before. She looked from her down to the gnome by her side. Onna merely shrugged and said, "Must be an Enclave thing."

"Jasian, pick yourself up from the sand. People are... looking," Rusalka chastised.

Noticeably ignoring Rusalka, Mari threw the crystalline sands in the air, shouting, "I'm home!" She laughed and spun as the powder fell all around her. "I'm finally home!"

"Jasian!" Rusalka hissed. She tightened the cloak around her shoulders, though she knew it did little to hide the nervous glances flitting her way from the dockhands.

"Ah, let the Cap'n have her fun, tusker," Onna said beside her, waving one of her small pudgy hands in dismissal. "It's been winters fer the lass since she came to these shores."

"She's drawing unwanted attention."

Onna looked up at Rusalka. "No one is gonna bother her."

Rusalka narrowed her eyes at the gnome. "It's not her that is going to be bothered."

She watched as Onna began to take in the dockhands around her and their fretful stares in the quartet's direction, primarily at the towering Rusalka. "Ye makes a good point, tusker." The little gnome turned and hopped off the dock after Marissa. "Okay brains, rein it in a bit, huh?"

"But I'm home!"

"Ye ain't home yet, lassie. Ye's about to get locked up as a looney and likely get Rue and me lynched."

"I'll be thrown in a stew!" Emmell added.

Rusalka watched Onna help Marissa to her feet while nodding at Emmell. "Besides," Onna said, "it's far too early fer a lynching. Everyone knows the best lynch times are at sundown. Makes everything more dramatic. Tides shifting, setting sun casting vibrant hues, and dark shadows. Very colorful, and poignant, with an air o' mystery. Early afternoon lynching's, you contend with a bright over-bearing sun. There's lots of squinting, not really seeing whose getting lynched. That's just embarrassin' fer a gnome of me caliber."

Rue rolled her eyes. "Can we get this procession moving please? Emmell is probably the smartest one of us here, in thinking they will cook her."

"Aye, a spriggan, a gnome, and an orc pull into a port – sounds all kinds of like a good tavern joke," Onna added with a laugh.

Marissa finally looked up at her, and Rusalka could see recognition slowly sinking in. She straightened and said, "Right, well there is only one road from port up through Castile, and it will be littered with people transporting wares. It'll give you the best view of the city as we will be travelling through the heart of her, where you can see all the bustle of life, the splendor of the streets." Rusalka knew that Marissa could read the expression on her face plain as day, and changed her tone. "But... I'm guessing you don't want to take that."

Rusalka nodded in agreement.

Marissa sighed, "I guess we can take the cliffside path and avoid most of populated Castile. It cuts through a wedge between two districts. No one should even pay us any mind, at least until we hit Cantor lands. We'll have to cut through the vineyards there, but no one should bother us until we get to Loja de Cantor."

"I'm fer that one," Onna said.

Emmell nodded. "I concur."

Rusalka didn't need to respond; the answer was obvious enough.

"Well then," Marissa remarked, straightening her salt-stained tunic, "at least we can feast with my family this night, and I guarantee they will show you the utmost hospitality, regardless of your complexion!"

Marissa cast her most charming smile, while Rue sighed. "One step at a time, Jasian. One step at a time."

"Right," Mari agreed. "Quickest way to the path around Castile is this way!" She turned and began to walk down the beach. Onna and Emmell ran to catch up to Mari, their little legs pumping.

By the time Rusalka cleared the dock, Marissa was coming back up to her.

With an embarrassed glint in her eyes, she nodded to the other side of the dock, and the beach beyond. "Actually... it's that way."

Rusalka sighed again. It would be a miracle if she made it to Loja de Cantor without the entire city going up in arms.

Three hours later, they were walking along the cliff's edge looking down at the glittering city below. Rusalka could see Marissa's confidence in her memory of the land growing with each step as she navigated them towards the Cantor vineyards. Down below, in the heart of Castile, Rusalka was awestruck at what she heard – they were singing. Not just one voice either, but many voices, all across the vibrant cityscape. Beautiful voices carrying up the mountains, all singing in unison, even though it was likely they were blocks, or even entire sectors apart.

"What is that?" the spriggan inquired.

"The Ballad of Vanity Shoal," Marissa answered. Rusalka watched her captain's back as she began to swing in rhythm to the song below them. It was nothing like the music of her people, which was aggressive and guttural with heavy use of drums. Nor was it like the drunken pirate shanties she'd heard, locked in her cage as a slave. This was sweet, and melodious, and yet there was a hint of sorrow. She heard Marissa humming along.

"What are they saying? I've never heard this language," Onna asked.

Marissa laughed. "It's my native language of Castellan. As far as I know, we are the only humans with a dialect like it."

"That doesn't answer the question though," Rusalka said, afraid to talk over such beautiful sounds from below. "What is the meaning of the song?"

Marissa didn't answer her right away. Rusalka was about to ask why she was being ignored when she realized that Marissa was waiting for something. She could see it in the cock of her head as she listened to the harmony below. After several seconds the chorus died away but not the beautiful sound of pipes. That harmony continued, and Marissa picked up her humming once more. Rusalka was startled by Marissa's ability to harmonize to the tune, when suddenly her captain began to sing:

SING ME A SONG OF MY LASS THAT IS GONE,
    Goes by the name Vanity Shoal
    Bonny of spirit she sailed on a lark
    O'er the sea of Sowle.

. . .

WINE ON THE STERN,
    Rum on the port,
    Spice on the starboard bow;
    Vigor in bloom glowed in her heart:
    Where is that vigor now?

SING ME A SONG OF MY LASS THAT IS GONE,
    Goes by the name Vanity Shoal
    Bonny of spirit she sailed on a lark
    O'er the sea of Sowle.

GIVE ME AGAIN ALL THAT WAS PURE,
    Give me the sun that shone!
    Give me my heart, gone into the Pale,
    Give me my lass that's gone!

SING ME A SONG OF MY LASS THAT IS GONE,
    Goes by the name Vanity Shoal
    Bonny of spirit she sailed on a lark
    O'er the sea of Sowle.

SURGES AND SWELLS, DEEP IN THE SEA,
    Peaks of glitter and song,
    All that was good, all that was gold,
    All that was me is gone.

                        .   .   .

WHEN SHE WAS FINISHED, MARISSA'S VOICE FELL AWAY, AND all Rusalka could hear was the dying melody of pipes against the backdrop of a crashing surf.

Silence reigned for many seconds before Emmell finally spoke up. "So, this Vanity Shoal – What was she sailing? A sloop or something?"

Marissa turned to look at the spriggan quizzically. "Excuse me?"

Emmell shrugged. "I mean, she went deep out to sea, right? Did she go alone? If not alone, how big was the ship? What about the rest of the crew? No consideration for them? Was she the captain?"

Rusalka gawked at the small creature.

"Did ye totally just miss the fact that Mari sang like... like an angel?" Onna barked at the spriggan.

With a start, Emmell asked, "What do you mean?"

Onna ground the palm of her hand to her head. "Did we just hear two different things?" She pointed at Marissa. "Ye dinna hear that beautiful voice?"

"Of course I heard her voice. How else was I able to decipher the nature of the meaning of the ballad?"

Onna groaned. "By the Defiler's teats, Em, compliment the minstrel on her performance first afore ye go dissectin' her song."

Rusalka watched Marissa's usually caramel cheeks flare a deep crimson. "It...it's fine," she stammered. "Really. It was a crude translation into Trade Tongue."

"Nay it is! Ye got real talent, Brains!"

"Onna really, it's okay. In case you haven't noticed, everyone in Castile can sing. It's what we do here. We produce Juglares and wine, and that's about it," Marissa said merrily, before directing her gaze to the small blonde-headed spriggan. "Ask my father tonight about the ballad of Vanity Shoal. I'm sure he'd love to explain every nuance of the chorus with you."

Emmell nodded. "I'd love to know more about it. Especially why they focused on this Vanity woman. Really, if they were transporting goods and such, I feel it must be a merchant vessel lost at sea. Who was the sea artist? Clearly not a good one to perish in those placid waters. Likely. they never had to sail in a storm on the Ire!"

With a roll of her eyes, Onna looked toward Emmell hopelessly. "Ye just can't help it can ye? Gotta tear it to shreds. I bet yer the type that asks questions in the middle of stage plays."

"Of course. Why wouldn't someone?"

"I'm pretty sure there's a special place in the hells reserved for people like ye."

Emmell shrugged, "It's a good thing I don't believe in your gods then."

"What!"

The two degenerated into an argument about gods and science. Rusalka, not wanting to be thrust into something she knew absolutely nothing about, moved quickly to walk beside Marissa.

She watched as Marissa shook her head and rolled her eyes. "Those two are going to drive mi papa nuts."

Rusalka didn't know much about Marissa's father, or anything really of the wonder that was Castile surrounding her. She cocked her head to the side again, listening to the music. "I have never heard of music quite like this. It sounds so... frail, and yet it is very pleasing to listen to."

"Orcs don't sing?"

Rusalka snorted. "Most of my people can barely form enough words together to speak, let alone attempt something like the feat you just pulled."

"It was..."

"Beautiful," Rusalka interrupted Marissa before she could

shrug it off yet again. "It was one of the most amazing things I've ever heard."

Marissa blushed again, and looked ahead, "How is it that you speak so well, Rue? I know little of your people, and I was afraid to ask much on the ship with all the women around who were not like you. I didn't want you to feel isolated."

"Gladiator pens," Rue answered. "That and my original slave owners. When I was... retrieved from my tribe, I was still very malleable."

"You were a child?"

"No," Rusalka answered a little too brusquely. "They had no need for children. They killed the children and the elderly. I was one of the few who was at an appropriate age to fight."

"That's monstrous," Marissa commented. "Was it... my people that took you?"

Rusalka didn't bother to look at her, but nodded. "Do not burden yourself with the whys of it, Jasian. I do not blame you, nor any other woman on the *Bella Dahlia* for the actions of those humans. Had they not taken me, my life would have hardly been better by my own people. Women are little more than slaves amongst the orcs as well."

"Really? What..." Marissa began but never finished. A scream cut through the crisp seaside air. For a moment, Rusalka was sure someone noticed what she was, and that they were about to be attacked, but then she saw them. Men, several of them, had a young woman by the hair, dragging her to the cliff's edge. To toss her off into the rocky coast below? Rusalka shuddered to think of it.

"Hey!" Marissa yelled as she caught sight of the men. "What is going on here?" Marissa ran, and Rusalka followed quickly behind her, remaining close enough to Marissa that she could move in to protect her at a moment's notice, but otherwise staying out of immediate sight. Unfortunately, she knew she was leaving her two short-legged compatriots behind her.

As Rusalka closed the gap, she saw that there were eight men, all of them armed and armored. Five manhandled the girl, getting ready to pitch her over the edge, while three of them stood back holding crossbows. The hairs on Rusalka's neck bristled. These weren't hooligans or slavers like she had dealt with in the past. These were guardsmen of Castile.

"You, soldiers, I demand to be answered!" Marissa ordered, her hand resting calmly on the butt of the flintlock at her belt.

"A peasant cannot give orders to the likes of us," one soldier with long black hair, much like Marissa's, barked back at her. "This girl has been found stealing grapes from the vineyards and poaching swine from the farms."

"Surely such a meager crime doesn't befit throwing her from the cliff into the shoals below. There must be a more just form of punishment?"

The guard looked up to them, noticing their numbers for the first time. Rusalka did her best to hide her skin in the folds of her cloak, but there was no hiding her bulk.

"These are the viscount's lands, strangers. I suggest you be on your way before I have you arrested for loitering," the guard replied.

Marissa stood tall. "You are wrong. The borders of Cantor began not but half an acre back." She nodded her head back to an ash tree behind her. "That tree marks the border there. If she has been poaching from these lands, she falls under the jurisdiction of Don Fernando Cantor, and as such must answer for her crimes underneath that banner first, before being judged by the viscount of Castile."

The man stepped away from his colleagues. Rusalka could see the tension building in the man as his gauntleted hand felt to the grip of his sword.

"Jasian..." Rusalka whispered.

She watched Marissa subtly shake her head.

The guards lip curled in disgust as Onna and Emmell caught up with them, "Tell me, peasant, why is it you keep such disreputable company? Is that a rodent and a weeble you have with you?"

"I am no peasant," Marissa growled. "My name is Marissa de Cantor y Castile, and you ser, are on my land."

Rusalka watched as the guards around their leader began to exchange dubious glances with one another.

"Well, well, well. If it isn't the long-lost scion, returned from the dead. Welcome home, Doña Marissa de Cantor," He drew his sword in a single smooth motion.

"Kill these vagrants."

CHAPTER SIX

Rusalka

"And this is why we should have let Rue bring a sword!" Onna yelled as she dove into a roll.

Rusalka couldn't disagree with the assessment as she stared at the three crossbowmen who were now turning their way to open fire on Marissa. She knew that only surprise could hope to stall the men now before they cut her captain down, so Rusalka did the only thing she could.

She flung back her hood and roared.

"It's... it's a bloody orc!" one of the guards who had the woman at the cliff's edge yelled in surprise, and they stalled for a fraction of a second.

That was all that Onna needed. Like a blur the little gnome threw three knives into the air. Rusalka heard three thunks, and gurgles of alarm. All three crossbowmen had those knives buried to the hilts in their throats. They grasped uselessly at the weapons as they collapsed to the ground.

Rusalka charged at the cluster of guards holding the girl, her intent only on protecting Marissa. She heard the sharp crack of Marissa's pistol as it fired. Someone cried out in pain, and out of the corner of her eye she thought she saw the talkative lead guardsman clutch his abdomen. The smell of flint and burnt powder seared her nostrils.

Then she was upon them. The shrill echo of swords leaving scabbards sang a new song in her ears. This was a melody that she knew well. This was a song that Rusalka could appreciate.

One of the guardsmen lifted his sword against her. He was a puny thing for a human, small and narrow, not much larger in stature than Marissa. The chainmail gambeson hung limply on him and she knew that he hardly had the strength to swing his weapon, let alone stand against her.

The fear that radiated from his flesh was as bitter in the air as the smoke from Mari's flintlock. His eyes were wide and terrified as he swung at her.

By the angle of his tightly controlled swing she could tell that the guardsmen of Castile were trained. He wasn't wild in his attack, he didn't flail. But training didn't count for as much as actual combat experience.

Rusalka sidestepped the blow and backhanded the arcing blade. Her strength and the already swinging momentum caused the lad's stance to swing wide. She gave him no quarter, lancing out with her forehead, slamming it into the nose guard of his helmet. She felt the metal and bone give way against her thick-hardened brow. The guard had little time to cry in pain before he was crumbling to the ground, either dazed, unconscious, or dead. Rusalka didn't have time to learn which.

Two other men came at her now, one swinging what she guessed was a castellan-issued sword. The other one wielded a warhammer – she chose warhammer next.

Using the piercing tip of the weapon, he tried to use its range to thrust her into the other guard's swinging blade. She wouldn't give him the satisfaction. As the thrust came forward, she reached out and grabbed the head of the hammer. Using all her strength, she pushed back, stopping the guard's forward momentum and driving him off balance as he was suddenly heaved violently backwards.

To keep that balance, he did the worst thing he could have – he let go of the hammer. Not even bothering to worry about correct form, Rusalka grabbed, pivoted, and swung the hammer, handle first at the incoming blow. Sparks flew as the blade collided with the metal shaft of the warhammer. The reverberation of the colliding weapons shimmied up her wrist and forearm, a welcome feeling, one she hadn't felt since they had taken the boat so many months before. She felt, more than saw, the now weaponless man behind her try and come for his hammer again. She kicked out her foot to connect just under his chin, and his head snapped back so violently she could hear the snap of his neck. It sent a shiver of exaltation down her spine.

She now turned to face the swordsman, salivating as she deeply inhaled the pungent aroma of dread from this... coward before her. Anxiety creased his pink face beneath that ludicrous helmet he wore. She wanted to taste that horror. She wanted to revel in his terror. She wanted to be his nightmare.

She smashed down with the handle again, and his sword sailed away. He stumbled backwards, and she drank in his trepidation. Soon she would coat her mouth in his blood. She would feel the hot essence of his life lining her throat. Her tusks would plunge into his heart, tearing at the muscle.

There was another whip-crack in the air, another cry of pain. The smoke burned at Rusalka's nostrils, momentarily driving away her impulse. It didn't last long.

The man raised his hands in surrender. Rusalka didn't want to show him mercy. There was no mercy for him other than glorious death. She flipped the hammer over, so she was holding it the right way, then rose it above her head, ready to drive it into his skull. To smash bone and brain and metal and destroy that once smug face to nothing but pulp and puss would give her such satisfaction...

"Rue!"

She swung at him, wild, uncontrollable. He doubled over, barely escaping her. She was in a rage now, and her vision pulsed in shades of red.

"Rue!"

That word bounced around her head; she barely could recognize the speaker. The throb of her own hungry heart beat loudly in her ears, drowning everything else in near silence. She growled and pushed forward. She could smell blood all around her. It pierced through the burnt smell of discharge and it fueled her.

Another guard swung a sword at her, but she barely felt its puny sting in her shoulder. She thrust the spearhead of the warhammer forward, catching the man in the chest. His eyes registered shock, and then she watched in ecstasy as the light of life died from them.

Rusalka yanked the weapon free and faced her prey once more.

"Please..." her quarry mumbled in fear. "Please, I yield."

No, the desire in her growled. She would not accept submission from the worm. She was starving for this. She would taste of his entrails. She bared her sharp tusks in anticipation and raised the hammer once more, and the man stumbled backwards and fell over, a scared little hare. His hands rose up in a pathetic defense. This time she would not miss. Her muscles coiled and knotted, her grip tightening on the slick handle.

Her whole body quivered, ready for this moment. She roared at him and brought the hammer down.

"Rue!"

And there was a hand, so soft, so gentle on her shoulder, then her face. She had felt that touch before, one of compassion, of friendship.

The Jasian... her captain.

She redirected the blow and it crashed down hard, next to the man's head. Rock shattered under her impact, and Rusalka heaved in great breaths of air.

What had she done?

She looked around, terrified. How many? How many dead? How many did she kill?

"Rue! Rue, it's over. You need to calm down," Rusalka vaguely heard Mari say, over and over again.

Rusalka took several labored breaths, a growl escaping her lips at every exhalation. The desire was still there, the need to glory in the kill. To feast in it. It wasn't gone. Not like she thought. In one fight, she undid the entire last six months. All that time changed... nothing. She may talk pretty and wear a human's clothes. She may encircle herself in other races who say that they didn't care where she came from. But it didn't matter, because at the end of the day, she might try to mask who she was, but she couldn't change what she was. She was a consumer of flesh. She was a desecrator. She was a destroyer.

She was an orc.

CHAPTER SEVEN

Marissa de Cantor y Castile

"Well that was exciting!" Onna cheered as she removed her throwing daggers from the throats of the deceased crossbowmen. "We haven't even been here a day and already yer peckin' a fight with the guard. Stayin' classy, Mari."

Marissa turned her dark glare on the diminutive gnome, while still trying to keep her large friend subdued. "This is not my fault. They attacked us." She watched in disgust as Onna used the tabard of one of the deceased guards to clean her throwing knives. "And stop killing people!"

Onna held her small hands, tinged red, up in defense, "Aye, what'd ye want me to do to stop them from shootin' ye, use harsh language?"

"You know what I mean."

Onna shook her head defiantly, "Nay Brains, fraid I don't see things the same way as ye."

"Well, that's obvious, or there'd be a lot less blood everywhere if you did," Emmell agreed, as she stepped up to the lead guard who was clutching his stomach. "Let me see the wound; you still might be salvageable."

"Get away from me, *ratón!*" the guard hissed, and then groaned, compacting his body in pain.

Emmell looked up to Marissa, "Was that polite? It didn't sound polite. What's a *ratón?*"

"It means mouse."

"Huh?" Emmell looked to him and shrugged, "Guess you can die then."

"Emmell!" Marissa looked at her sea artist in outrage. "Help him!"

Emmell put her hands to her small hips, "Why? You shot him. It's not my fault he'd rather die than be aided by a spriggan."

"Seriously, Brains, we gotta do something about this. I told ye, when you pull the trigger, aim fer the chest or the head. Gut shots are messy. Ye' make a fine cap'n an all, but yer a lousy fighter," Onna commented. She walked over to the wounded man clutching his belly. "What'll it be, ye guttershite? If ye won't let Em look at that hole puckering in ye belly, than shall I?"

"I'll have no weeble near me!" the man hissed the derogatory term for gnomes up at Onna. His hand reached for the sword he dropped. Marissa watched the gnome raise an eyebrow, her fingers sliding along the smooth surface of a throwing knife.

"Onna..."

The gnome held her hands up in the air, "Okay, okay I won't kill him. He's all yer's ta deal with then."

She walked away, kicking the fallen sword away from his grasping fingers. He fell to his side in defeat.

"I just can't leave Rue," Mari said, alarmed.

"I'll be fine," Rusalka returned. "Just... I need to be away from this."

"Aye, come with us tusker!" Onna smiled. "Ye need ta tell me how ta do that trick where ye caught a swinging hammer!"

"And I can look at your shoulder," Emmell added.

Marissa glanced down at Rue's left shoulder to see her green skin now painted scarlet. "Are you sure you'll be okay?" Marissa asked with concern.

Rusalka stared down at Marissa, refusing to break eye contact, "I don't want to talk about it. Not... yet."

Her fearlessness while facing Marissa was just as unnerving as the demons Marissa could see she was clearly fighting inside. Marissa didn't know what was going through Rusalka's mind in this moment, but she did know that Rusalka was almost lost to that same rage she witnessed when they fought for their freedom, a rage that wouldn't benefit them now. Nor would Onna's apparent disregard for life. Marissa wouldn't say that Onna was equally as bloodthirsty as their orc counterpart had displayed, but instead it seemed as if she treated the lives of others as inconsequential. Perhaps Marissa didn't know these women as well as she thought?

"Very well," she said to Rusalka. "Get yourself looked at by Onna, see if she can do something for that shoulder."

Rue looked down at her red-coated arm. "It's only a scratch." With that, her large orc companion joined the two other women, and gave Marissa and the remaining Castile guards the space they needed.

The lead guard was coughing blood as she squatted before him. "Do you want my aid?"

He sneered at her, "You consort with monsters and animals."

Marissa looked from the man to the young girl who was now standing off to the side, looking at her in awe. "Funny, we weren't about to throw a child from the top of a cliff. From where I'm standing, I'd say you seem more like the monster to me than they are."

The guard wheezed, and spit blood in her face. Marissa closed her eyes and slowly wiped it off. "What are you trying to accomplish exactly?" she asked. "Do you want to die? I can help…" She stopped midsentence and pointed to the women only a dozen paces away. "We can help save you. Both the gnome and spriggan are well-versed in medicines."

"Go to hells."

Marissa stood. "Who is it that you serve so faithfully, that you refuse my aid knowing it means a slow death?"

"Don Augusto Cruz," a voice answered her. Marissa looked up to see the guard she had saved from Rue's fury now standing before her. His weapon still lay on the ground, but she could see her crew just on the edge of her vision ready to charge back in the moment the man tried anything.

"Augusto…" Marissa murmured, her thoughts taking her back almost seven winters before, when she was just a young love-struck girl.

"Shut yer mouth, ye idjit," the wounded guard hissed.

Marissa snapped out of her reverie and looked from the fallen guard to the standing one. He was thin, but not skinny. His skin was pale, far paler than someone traditionally of Castile, or anywhere in southern Gurgen for that matter, and his eyes were an enchanting shade of blue that seemed to change green depending on how the light hit them. He was far different from the dark-eyed, caramel-skinned people of Castile. That difference alone made him striking. "Who do I have the pleasure of addressing?" she asked.

He stood straight and aligned his arms, over one and other, striking his chest once in formal salute as if he were addressing a Don. "Alférez Bevan Ó Cuana at your service, Doña Cantor."

"Ó Cuana, I order you at once to kill this woman," the guard on the ground interrupted.

"Ó Cuana…" she murmured.

"It's Halsbrenian, milady. My parents immigrated to Gurgen

before I was born. My father was a member of the Jasian Enclave, and my family was lucky enough to get assignment here, a few winters back. We met once in the Citadel, though I doubt you'd remember me," he said with a smile.

"For Maker's sake, you moron, she doesn't need a life's story, she needs a blade in the chest! Kill her, or so help me..." The guard on the ground degenerated into a fit of wet coughing.

Marissa didn't remember him, though she knew it wasn't the time to rack her brain in the hopes of catching a glimpse of him in there somewhere. Instead, she focused on what was truly important at the moment. "He doesn't sound good."

"No," Ó Cuana answered. "Whatever you did with that wand of yours hurt him."

"Wand?" Marissa asked, confused. He carefully motioned with his head to her hand.

Onna burst out laughing. "This fustilug is about as smart as ye, Brains! Ye thought it was a club, and he thinks it be a magic stick!"

Marissa looked down to her hand and realized she was still holding her flintlock in one hand. Instead of trying to explain the nature of the spriggan-made weapon, she quickly holstered it, and squatted back down to the guard on the ground. Bevan joined her. "We need to do something to treat his wound, control the bleeding and see if the ball is still inside him. If it is, one of the Enclave's curates will have to try and remove it and heal the wound."

"That, er a sawbones could do it." Onna added, pointing a thumb to herself.

Marissa watched Bevan Ó Cuana look at Onna suspiciously. "The gnome is right, alférez," she said. "It was one reason the slavers didn't have her locked up with the rest of us. She's a surgeon," she told the man, biting her lower lip in nervousness, "of sorts."

Marissa watched as Bevan thought it through, momentarily

looking at the three dead crossbowmen that Onna had so quickly dispatched. His eyes then fell on the two other guards Rusalka had killed, and finally those bright eyes looked at her, "If your gnome friend doesn't help the teniente, will I be able to get him help in time?"

"Don't let that *puta* near me," the teniente groaned.

"Now that's just rude," Marissa snapped. She looked at Onna. "Well?"

Onna shrugged, "Hard to say. How much longer ye gonna flap ye lips? If the man leaves now, he might be able to get help in time. Anymore jaberjawing though, and this pile o' shite there on the ground is as good as dead. What ye think, Em?"

Emmell nodded. "I concur with that assessment. He's definitely a pile of shite."

Marissa rolled her eyes.

"Well then, that settles it." Bevan said. "If I can get the man aid, I shall endeavor to do so. Saving his life, after all, is of paramount importance."

"The... women," the teniente groaned.

Bevan stood. "Right you are, ser." Bevan looked to Marissa, and extended a hand. She stared at it wearily before taking it, and he pulled her upright, with one dip of his head in respect. "Doña Cantor, I'm afraid that I must arrest you."

The women to her right shifted and scoffed at him.

"Under what pretenses Alférez Bevan Ó Cuana?" Marissa asked. "You attacked us."

"Well, in our defense, you look like brigands, and at this time if you really are Doña Marissa de Cantor y Castile, we have no way of verifying that."

"You just said you remember me from the Citadel."

He nodded, "But my voice won't carry far. Where have you been that could justify such an absence? Most in Castile believe you dead, Don Cruz among them."

"I was a slave, held aboard a ship for months." Marissa protested.

"And who could corroborate your story?"

"I believe that'd be us, mate." Onna declared.

"No offense, but I'm afraid an Orc, a gnome, and a... spriggan, I believe you called yourself?"

Emmell nodded.

"Yes, well around here that likely won't hold. It would be the safest and most prudent way of course to arrest you all now until this is clear. Don't you agree, teniente?"

The man groaned.

Marissa wanted to yell at Bevan, but he continued before she could. "Seeing though, as I have to retrieve aid for my superior officer, I... find myself at an impasse. I cannot arrest you and hope to save him. So, if you all would be good ladies and... stay here until I return with medical help, then I'm sure we can clear up this whole matter."

"That's ludicrous!" Emmell barked. "Why would we stay here? Why would he leave after–" the spriggan yelped as Onna jabbed her in the ribs. "Why'd you do that?"

"Yes, well." Bevan said nervously. "As I said, rendering aid to my teniente is priority. I must see to it at once." His piercing blue eyes met Marissa's. "Doña Cantor..." His stall made her raise an eyebrow. "You have my sympathies."

Bevan saluted Marissa once more, and then quickly ran down the way they had come.

"I'm lost," Emmell said.

"Clearly," Onna agreed. The gnome turned to Marissa, "What'd he mean by his sympathies? Cuz ye was gone a slave all this time? Or because he was supposed to arrest ye?"

Shaking her head, Marissa answered, "I have no idea." Then she said it again more slowly, clearly lost in her own thoughts, "I have absolutely no idea."

It took Marissa a moment before she realized that the girl was still standing nearby. Marissa waved her over, speaking in her native tongue, *"Hola niña, está bien ahora. Estás seguro?"*

The young woman's eyes widened and she looked over to Marissa's compatriots. *"Pero son monstruos,"* she replied.

"No. Ellos son mis amigas."

"Eres amigas?" she asked.

Marissa nodded, *"Sí."*

"Um, not to sound ignorant, but what are ye sayin' ta each other?" Onna asked.

"I'm trying to convince her that we're friends."

"Well, can you do it as we move? We know gutshot ain't dead, and I'm pretty sure Rue dinna kill all of them. I'd like to be gone a'fore help arrives, or they wakes up and we has to kill em again," Onna stated matter-of-factly.

Marissa nodded at the gnome, "Okay." She turned to face the young lady once more. The girl was perhaps twelve, maybe thirteen-winters-old at most. She asked her for her name.

The girl looked at Marissa sheepishly before answering, "Elena de Torro."

Marissa bowed her head slightly, *"Bueno Elena de Torro. Hablas un idioma de intercambio?"* she asked the girl, hoping Elena spoke the common Trade Tongue.

Elena answered, *"sí."* She then held her hand up flat, facing Marissa and tilted it back and forth slightly, adding, *"Un poco."*

A little.

"Are you really Doña Cantor?" Elena asked.

Marissa nodded, "I am."

Immediately Elena dipped into a curtsy.

Marissa smiled. "That's not necessary. My friends and I are going home to see my family. Where is your family?"

Upon mentioning family, Marissa watched the light die in the young woman's eyes, only to be replaced with shadow and grief. "*Muerto.*"

"Dead."

"Who's dead?" Emmell asked Marissa. "The guards? If so, then yes, Onna is very effective at rendering life signs moot."

"Hey!"

Emmell blinked her large eyes slowly. "Just an assessment."

Marissa shook her head. "No. The girl, her name is Elena and her family is all dead."

"Oh." Emmell replied. "Perhaps she should come with us then."

"Aye," Onna agreed, "we need to move along."

Marissa saw the spriggan nod before adding, "On this, I concur."

"Bring the tiny human," Rusalka said flatly, her voice still distant.

"Ye call that tiny?" Onna asked. "Em must be a speck in ye eyes."

Marissa watched Onna's comment momentarily elevate Rusalka from her sulking. There was a glimmer in her eyes, and a quirk of a smile at the corner of her mouth. "Yes, but she's a useful speck."

Marissa turned her attention back to Elena again to invite her to come with them to her family's castle, but the girl was already bolting away like a startled doe.

"Hey!"

Marissa moved after the girl, but Onna piped up, "Ah let her go, Brains. She ain't fer wantin' ta be seen around us, and I fer one can't be blamin' her. They were willin' ta throw her from the cliff for poachin'. Imagine what they'd do ta her if they added murder ta the charge."

"Which is what is added to our charge I might point out," Emmell added tactlessly.

Onna didn't even take offense. "Right, but we can defend ourselfs, even Brains can, though barely," she added with a wink to Marissa.

Marissa felt torn as she watched the small form disappearing on the horizon. While she wanted to go after Elena, protect her and comfort her, she knew that Emmell and even Onna were right. They needed to get to Loja de Cantor. The deaths of these guards would put a mark on their heads. They had to get behind the safety of the walls of Loja de Cantor, and the protection of her father. Then, with Bevan's help, Maker willing, they'd be able to work out this... mess. With a weight like a sack of salt upon her chest, she turned to her crew. "Let's go."

CHAPTER EIGHT

Rusalka

After everything Rusalka witnessed that morning with the city of Castile, she thought that Marissa's home, too, would be like the castles that sat like den mothers upon their charges. She was wrong. The castle that Marissa called Loja de Cantor was not like the others of the City of Castles that Rusalka had yet witnessed.

It stood alone, on a highland hill overlooking the sea of Sowle, and the swooping city of Castile against the rocky face. It was a guardian to a different sea altogether. Vast rolling hillocks of wine vineyards lined the east. North of Loja de Cantor, the world seemed to disappear into the massive, towering sentinels of the Shemma woods.

To Rusalka, this structure was more on par with what she remembered. Not the bloated structures that sat fat upon colorful homes beneath it, but a bastion of defense with tall stone walls, ramparts, and towers that were far less ornamental, and had utilitarian function to them. In short, Loja de Cantor was a castle built for defense amongst a city built for splendor. It sat alone, a warden to the unknown.

This solidarity didn't make that different though. Even from the base of the hill Rusalka could see where several paths wound around the hilltop of the castle. At an opening in the wall, she saw both single turret, thick wall battlements and railings, and the same crown of a pyramid-shaped merlon upon that turret as in the city below, just less colorful. Where it wasn't as beautiful, nor as ostentatious as its city-dwelling cousins, it hadn't lost all of the Castellan flair that seemed to resonate through the city. It was just muted.

Rusalka didn't say much to the others as Marissa led them up one of the paths. She didn't need to. Emmell had become quite the chatterbox the closer they got to the castle. It seemed she was fascinated with the humans' choice of design in the building of the castle and how wholly "wasteful" it all seemed.

Marissa didn't speak much, either, since the incident with her people. Rusalka didn't blame her. Her people died, and Rusalka in large part was to blame for that. The combat made the beast toiling within her awaken. She thought that her comradery with Marissa, Onna, Emmell, and all the other women aboard the *Bella Dahlia* tempered it, but instead it had merely slumbered. Not once did she enact violence amongst the women in the entirety of the six-month journey. Not once since their liberation did she draw the blood of another. Not once did she kill.

And yet now she stood, at the very gates of Marissa's home, not but a score of hours from departing the *Bella Dahlia*, and already she was slipping... becoming what was ingrained in her very species – a savage.

As they proceeded up the trail, Rusalka could see that the original energy of returning home was gone. Like a familiar cloak, apprehension was wrapping around Marissa once more.

It was so obvious to Rusalka in Marissa's mannerisms; the

buoyancy of her walk gone and become rigid. She looked around more, nervous. Even her odor changed, though Rusalka doubted that anyone else would notice such a thing. Orcs, though, could smell fear as clearly as smelling the sweet scent of a flower, or the earthy odors of barley. Rusalka could taste anxiety on her tongue and it was as familiar as that of an animal's flesh. Many things indicated Marissa's disquiet as they moved closer to the barbican. Rusalka could hear her breathing quicken, could see the perspiration growing at the nape of Mari's neck, and in the lining of her soiled blouse, near her armpits.

When Marissa reached for the giant throw ring on the gate of the barbican, Rusalka could just make out the slight tremor of her fingers. Really, Rusalka was quite impressed that Mari managed this much control. While she didn't quite understand where this tension was coming from, she knew that Mari was a fearful creature.

The old Rusalka would see that as a weakness, something beneath her that only deserved scorn. Yet six months among them taught her that fear was not the same as cowardice. Marissa could be afraid, and that was okay, because she confronted her fear, understood it, and then went forward anyway.

As Rusalka came to understand this, she thought she might even respect it. Why Marissa was fearful of a reunion with her family, Rusalka had no idea. Orcs didn't really know family in the sense that Mari or even Emmell spoke of it. There was only the tribe, and of the tribe, there were only the hunters – the men – and their objects – the women. She felt her own lip sneer at the thought, and she quickly quelled that anger growing within. Now would not be the time for rage.

Rusalka heard the knocker strike the hard wood – once, twice, thrice. Her sensitive ears could pick up the quickening breaths of Marissa as she stood in apt anticipation.

They stood...

And they stood...

And they stood...

Marissa stared puzzled at the large wooden doors of the barbican. She reached up and hammered the striker home harder.

Again, nothing.

"Perhaps ye family is about in the city?" Onna offered.

Marissa shook her head, "No. We may not be the richest castellan nobles, but we do have our share of servants. My father's aide, Javier, should at least be around."

Rusalka could tell by the scrunched expression on Onna's face that the gnome didn't quite agree with Marissa's assessment.

Emmell's large eyes, however, took it all in, and she innocently voiced what Rusalka knew was on all of their minds. "Maybe something changed. You've been gone a long time."

"Not so long," Marissa shot back harshly, as she reached up and violently slammed the striker home several more times.

Again, they stood on the hill in a growing hush. The only sounds were the resonating crash of surf on the rocky shores and the distant melody of music on the air. But the castle of Loja de Cantor was as active as a corpse.

Marissa slammed the ringed striker down so hard over and over that Rusalka could see fresh indentations in the well-worn divot of the wooden door.

Rusalka reached out and gently put a hand on Marissa's forearm, stopping her from banging the knocker anymore. "Jasian, no one answers."

Marissa looked at her, confusion tinged with a new fear in her wide brown eyes. "It hasn't been that long," she whispered weakly.

"Five and one-half winters is a long time to be gone, Mari," Onna agreed. "Too much can happen in that time."

"I concur. Perhaps your parents moved, or maybe they went looking for you?"

Rusalka watched Marissa shake her head. "My father would

never leave. He was too embroiled in the politics here. It's part of the agreement that the Jasian Enclave has with the elves in the Shemma. He'd never abandon this place."

"Not even fer his little girl?" Onna queried.

Marissa looked away from the door and down to her sodden feet. "Not even for me."

Rusalka noted the sun starting to dip down in the sky, and asked, "What do you wish to do, Jasian? I doubt we can make it back to the Dahlia before the sun sets."

"I'm sure the folk around here are quite the ruckus, tis a party place fer sure," Onna said with an over-emphasized wink.

Emmell sighed, "Yeah, great idea Onna, mingle with locals right after being charged with murder of their guard."

"It was self-defense!"

"You killed three before weapons were even drawn!"

"Pre-emptive self-defense!" Onna put her hands on her hips. "I stand by that, I do!"

"More like premeditated..." Emmell muttered, quite loudly.

"Now yer arguin' semantics..."

Rusalka growled, startling the two, "Really? Do you think this is helping Mari right now?"

A single look at Marissa showed the worry etched on her face. Rusalka continued, "We need real answers, not humor or sarcasm."

"No, Rue, it's fine," Mari cut in with a look back to Rusalka. "You're right though, we do need answers."

Rusalka watched Marissa scan the wall to her own family's castle as if looking for something. "What are you..." she began before Marissa interrupted.

"Onna, do you think if we got you over the wall, you can lift the doorbar on the other side?"

Rusalka looked at the expansive distance from the ground up to the top of the wall. She had no real way to measure it yet;

both Emmell and Onna were trying to teach her numbers for the last several months, so she was beginning to understand scale.

"As long as yer not planning on havin' tusker throw me over, aye, I can do it."

Emmell's shoulders slumped slightly, "Shame, I'd like to see that."

"You're not thinking of breaking in?" Rusalka asked.

Marissa looked from the wall back to her. "Yes, I am."

Onna coughed into her hand, drawing Rusalka and Marissa's eyes down to the gnome. "While I'm all fer a little B and E, Brains, ye used to live here. Didn't ye like ever sneak out to slouster with boys or sometin'?" Marissa's ears flushed red. "Ye did!" Onna chided. Clearly, she had not missed their captain's embarrassment either.

"What's slouster?" Emmell asked.

"It's not important," Marissa countered before Onna could answer.

"Well if sloustering will help us get in, I say we do it!" the small spriggan agreed with her hands on her hips.

Marissa's cheeks joined her ears in a crimson hue.

"I really don't think that's something ye wantin' ta be doin' with Brains," Onna said in a chuckle.

"Why not? If it'll help, we should do it," Emmell queried.

"Yes, clearly I too am missing something," Rusalka added.

Marissa cleared her throat, "Slouster is another term for kissing. A somewhat derogatory one, Emmell."

"Huh?" the spriggan replied.

"Oi! It's not just kissin' Emmell. Gotta get all them fluids involved. Ye gotta get dirty and make it messy!" Onna added.

Emmell's large eyes opened wider, "Oh. Is that what humans do to sneak in and out of places? It seems time consuming, and potentially noisy. I really don't see how that helps."

"It absolutely does not help in any way," Marissa deadpanned while looking at Onna.

"Then why do humans do it?" Emmell pressed.

Onna jumped at the opportunity before Marissa could reply. "She would sneak out, Em, so that she could then slouster with boys in secret. Humans, especially Jasians, frown on girls gettin' naughty with boys 'fore they're married."

Marissa sighed loudly. "There is truth to that. Now can we focus on the task of breaking in?"

"Yes, let's get back to that, shall we?" Rusalka heard something above them, looking up quickly as a loud click followed. Above, she could see an armored man looking down on them all, a large crossbow pointed directly at her. "I swear you lot have to be the stupidest, loudest, and most uncoordinated bandits I have ever seen."

CHAPTER NINE

Marissa de Cantor y Castile

Marissa stepped back and looked up at the sentry above. She could just make out the man, but his features were obstructed. Her eyes burned from the reflection of intense light the dying sun cast off his morion helmet. "You there, ser, please lower your weapon. We mean you no harm."

The guard made a chuckling, snorting sound. "You expect me to believe that, do yah? I find a lady, a gnome, a savage, and..." he paused as he looked at Emmell, "some sort of pet on my doorstep. What is that, a dog?"

Emmell stared up at the lone crossbowman indignantly, not as hampered by the intense light due to so much time manning the helm on open sea. "First I'm called a mouse, and now a dog! Your people lack any social acumen, Captain."

"Aye," Onna agreed, "there's no about fer calling Rue a savage either."

"Agreed," Marissa replied, looking to all of them before

directing her attention back upwards towards the guard. With her hands on her hips, she declared loudly for any in the courtyard that might hear her, "My name is Marissa de Cantor y Castile, and you are in my family's estate, upon my family's lands."

Again, the guard let out a snorting cackle, "And I'm the Don Cantor reborn. Marissa is dead by now, lost to the war in the east like so many others. I'll tell you what, lass, since you rabble are the most ridiculous lot I've seen yet, I'll give you a full thirty seconds afore I unleash death upon you, starting with your green-skinned brute. One..."

One phrase stood out over everything else he said to Marissa. Those words tightened the feeling growing in her belly. "What do you mean, 'reborn'? Where is my father?"

"Four..." he continued, "Like you don't know. The Cantor line is dead. Doña Cantor's ship drifted too close to the Pale, and was lost at sea, and Don Cantor was waylaid by brigands not six months past. Both he and his... aide... were found with a young woman, all dead."

"All dead..." Marissa could hardly understand the words she was hearing. Her parents were... how was it possible?

"Now, where was I?" the guard said with an uncomfortable cough, "Ah, yes, five. Six."

Marissa's eyes filled with tears as the realization began to take hold. Emmell was right, five and a half winters was too long. Too much changed in that time. What if it was true? What if her family was gone? If they were dead?

"Ugh, Brains, he's still countin'. Mayhaps we might fallback and reevaluate our strategy a touch?" Onna said quietly. She then quickly added, "I mean, I'd kill him if you like, but he's a bit too high up for my lads to make it."

"Lads?" Emmell queried, seemingly oblivious to the count-down to their deaths.

Onna fingered her throwing knives.

"You gave them boys' names?"

Onna shrugged, "Seems fitting. Men always name their toys after women. I figured I'd name mine after men."

The guard continued to count as the women lingered, "Fourteen, fifteen, sixteen..."

"Mari, we should go," Rusalka whispered loudly.

Marissa shook her head, "This is my home. Where else could we go?"

"...nineteen, twenty." The guard looked up over his crossbow, "You really are some dim lanterns," he heckled. "It's okay. I'll be creating openings in your heads soon enough to let the light in those empty things."

Marissa watched him focus his aim on Rusalka once more. She held up her hands in the air. "How can I possibly convince you that I am who I say I am? I mean there has to be someone in there that remembers me. I haven't changed that much." She looked down at her troupe. "Have I?"

Emmell shrugged, "Couldn't say. I didn't know you five winters ago."

"Tis sometin ye should be focusin' on with the guy with the crossbow, I'm fer thinkin'," Onna added.

Marissa wiped back the few tears that surfaced and looked back up to him. "So, what say you, guardsman? I don't recognize you, and you don't recognize me. But there has to be someone there that was present five winters ago? You said Javier was with my father and another. Where has the rest of the staff all gone?"

"Twenty-seven, twenty..." the guard waivered, "I never told you the aide's name."

Marissa put her hands on her hips. "You don't need to. I grew up with the man in my life for my entire childhood. Wiry man, hawk-like beak of a nose, favored a spear on horseback for hunting free range boar with my father. They had a tendency to leave for the Shemma every now and again."

There was a stall, and Marissa noted how the guard was no longer counting. She held her breath; if he resumed now, Rue was as good as dead. The guard didn't need to be a good shot at this distance, and his elevation ensured he likely wouldn't miss more than once.

"What was Javier's surname? Do you remember?" the guard asked.

Marissa did remember. "Corredor."

She heard the man stifle a near sob. "He... he had a son."

Marissa was nodding now, but this was a little harder. In her youth she had been a spoiled girl, and rarely took time to know her father's servants' children's names. Still Javier had been around her so much that she'd heard the boy's name mentioned at least a few dozen times. It was Vigo, or Vincent, or...

The guardsmen hefted up the crossbow as he took aim once more.

"Vicente!" Marissa bellowed upward suddenly as she remembered. "His name was Vicente."

She could feel the guard looking down at her. For several long moments they stayed that way, the light stabbing painfully at her eyes. Finally, he lowered his crossbow, reached up, and removed his morion helmet.

As the bright light pitched away, Marissa refocused her gaze on the guard above. She could see the same gaunt features, rich, black curly hair and swarthy skin that she remembered. A similar beaklike nose, and intense dark gaze took her in as well, as if he finally recognized her. The sight of him brought her back to her childhood, to the days of sitting in her father's study. She was looking at a spitting image of Javier Corredor, only much, much younger. "Vicente?"

The guard looked among Marissa's friends, still uncertain, before finally meeting her gaze once more. "Mari, where in the hells have you been?"

Marissa's fingers traced along the familiar contours of her father's signature. As a child she thought he had beautiful calligraphy. Each sweep, each curve distinct only to the man she knew as Fernando Cantor III. She met many fine calligraphers over the last few winters, but she always thought of her father's as the best. Marissa's lip began to quiver, and she felt her face scrunch as she fought a losing battle to keep her tears down.

So, she stopped fighting, and collapsed into her father's well-worn leather chair and let them come. Vicente hovered nearby. She knew he was still unsure of her, still questioning. Marissa realized that the sight of her in this state was unbecoming of her station, but she couldn't help it right now. Her papa was gone. He was really gone.

Her mother was gone too, lost at sea, apparently, during a routine journey to the Citadel to issue the bi-annual report between the Shemma and Gurgen. It was a trip they sailed dozens of times in much smaller ships. Why would her mother charter a vessel and then go so close to the Pale? It didn't make any sense. But with her there was still hope, however slim. Her father, however...

She slid her fingertips over the glossy ink, feeling its distinct, smooth, almost cool texture at odds against the coarse vellum. Just the very brush of it against her skin brought with it a fresh influx of tears.

"You mustn't blame me for doubting, especially in your current state, but... it really is you, isn't it? Marissa de Cantor y Castile," Marissa heard Vicente say quietly behind her. She nodded and straightened, attempting to gain some measure of composure. It was a miserable attempt. "What happened to you? How are you..." he gestured with his head outside the study where she knew Rusalka, Onna, and Emmell were waiting out on the parapet, "with them?"

Wearily, she looked at the young man, "It's a long story, Vicente. Just know that I am alive because of those women out there, and many more like them. They are owed the same Cantor respect we would give any honored guest."

Vicente's lips were tight, obviously not liking his question brushed aside. Marissa appraised the young man. He was younger than her, but if her memory was correct it was only by a winter, maybe two at most. She remembered her father trying to get her to play with the boy, but back then Marissa would have none of that. She was the daughter of a Don. She would be respected as such. Further, with no male heirs, Fernando declared her heiress. She was to become a Doña one day, and the most Vicente could become was, if he were lucky, the boatswain of a ship. There was nothing for Marissa to gain in consorting with lessers.

She realized now how naïve and foolish she'd been, how her father treated Javier as an equal, even though their station dictated otherwise. Fernando honored and respected Javier, spoke so highly of him, and tried time after time to get Marissa to understand the importance of those around her, not just the importance of her own self.

Marissa saw that she was still making that same mistake, even now. Vicente shouldn't be forced to wait – he would just question more, when she needed him the most. She needed him to see that she was truly Marissa de Cantor y Castile without a doubt.

"Could I give you the abridged version for now?" Marissa asked, "I don't want to keep my friends waiting."

Vicente visibly relaxed at those simple words. Perhaps her father had taught her something after all? She began, "Isa Marin, I'm not sure if you remember her?"

"I remember the lady," he replied with a nod. "You two were best friends, did everything together."

Marissa blushed, "Not... everything, but yes that is true enough. When I left, it was because Isa convinced me to go to the Citadel and become a purist."

Vicente scoffed.

It caused a small smile to grow on her lips and was the same look his father had when she boldly declared those very words, five and a half winters before. "We were going to be the first ever women purists! Women warrior priestesses that fought side by side, for honor, justice, and the Maker."

The very memory of Isa's energetic eyes as they sailed to the Citadel for the next chapter of their lives made her smile grow just a little more, and the lilt of her voice take on a stronger tone. "All my life, the Juglares would tell wild tales and sing merry songs of the strong and brave Purists. Men of valor, whose integrity was implacable. How they drove the Dark Elves into hiding over the River Koba, or how a contingent single-handedly drove the darkness of wizards into quiet exile in their towers. I remember, as a child, hearing of one man in particular, a purist Commander named Aodhfin Bray."

"I've heard of him," Vicente commented quietly. "He fought a demon or something like that?"

Marissa chuckled, "So the Juglares say. They say he fought off hundreds of the northern wilders, battled a reincarnated warlord from our ancient past, and removed one of the foulest sorcerers to ever walk the earth – all while saving the broken soul of an exiled woman, whom he loved."

Vicente nodded, "I think I heard something like that as well."

"No matter how wild it sounds, if he accomplished any one of those feats it would be truly remarkable. I admired those stories of him greatly."

"So, you wanted to meet this man? Go to the Citadel and be saved, just like the woman?"

"What?" Marissa said with a cocked eyebrow, "No." She shook

her head vehemently, "I wanted to do the saving. I wanted to be the hero, not the damsel in distress."

"Oh," Vicente said, a little embarrassed.

"For too long, Isa and I would be told these wonderful ballads, and watch these plays, and the theme was always the same – hero saves damsel, boy gets girl. If you were a princess, or a dame, or in Isa's and my case, the daughters of Dons, we needed saving by our purist Encantador. Isa and I were fed up with the same routine. We were going to go out and change the world. Castile needed women heroes too."

"What happened?"

Marissa looked back at the large cherry table with all of her father's things still untouched. "The Jasian Enclave does not make women purists. We could enter the church as clergy, become priestesses, abandoning our nobility for the glory of the Maker... and clean the chamberpots of men, all while wearing rather tight-fitting dresses," she finished bitingly.

Marissa glanced up to see Vicente nodding, as if he'd known about the limitations of such things, and perhaps to her realization he had. Could Vicente have had similar aspirations growing up, only to be told because he has no noble blood that he couldn't ever wear the title of purist?

"So why didn't you come home then?"

At this Marissa laughed loudly, "After the explosive way I left my family? Personally disavowing them in public, and telling them I was my own woman and would live my life without the Cantor name? I couldn't just crawl back to papa, not like that." She looked away. "Besides, Isa had other plans, and I couldn't leave her."

"What other plans?" He asked, drawing her gaze back to him.

"We became Exactors."

"Mercenaries for the Enclave?" Vicente asked incredulous, "I thought they were a myth."

Marissa gave him a patronizing glare, "Come now Vicente,

we're close enough to the Citadel to know the Exactors are real. It's just that we rarely know when we're dealing with one because of the stigma that follows them. Actually, they aren't all that bad, most of them at least. There was this spriggan that could be rather infuriating at times..."

"A what?"

"Spriggan, like Emmell. The one you called a dog." The tone in her voice was a little more bellicose than she meant it to be.

"Ah..."

When nothing more was forthcoming, no apology for his confusion, or for the insult whether direct or indirect, she glared at him. Still he held his ground in being unapologetic for his actions. Marissa mentally tallied that in the back of her mind. It was either ignorance, or arrogance – she didn't know enough about him yet to judge – so she continued. "Anyway, the purpose of an Exactor is to do something that the church cannot take credit for, but still needs doing. We don't necessarily work in the shadows, per se, though there were enough of us that did do that sort of thing, or so it seemed."

Marissa shifted uncomfortably, not sure exactly how much she should be saying. Vicente was a stranger to her after all this time, and Exactors were under oath never to reveal what it was they did, let alone openly declare whom they work for. Marissa supposed it was the Enclave who turned their back on her first, but again, she didn't know Vicente – she only knew the man his father was.

Marissa changed course a bit as she continued. "Isa was a natural sword fighter, and I... not so much. But I supported her, stood by her in all things. She may not be a purist, but we thought we could still do heroic things together, working for the church. Tasks of world-shaking importance."

"And did you?"

Marissa took a deep breath, quelling a repressed anger that was beginning to boil in her belly. "In a manner of speaking – yes."

"A manner of speaking..." she could hear the condescension dripping from his voice. It only served to flare the growing anger in her more.

"They dispatched us to put an end to the Fermania Civil War."

"Who, like the whole unit you were in?" Vicente asked.

Marissa shook her head. "No. Just Isa and I."

Vicente snorted. "Just – two women?"

Her glare at that moment withered the smug expression that was growing on his face.

"Just two women," she said flatly. "Isa was a force to be reckoned with when she had a sword in her hand. I knew nobility, etiquette, and I can sing. So, we went in disguised as Juglares, and we were tasked with a mission of great importance."

"And?"

Marissa shook her head, not wanting to answer the obvious to him.

"And?" Vicente pressed.

"And what?" Marissa found herself snapping, "My first mission out, I was captured by the rebels. I couldn't even get being a Juglar right after spending my whole life around them. If not for Isa, I'd be dead. She convinced them that they couldn't kill me, that we were both quick with child. It also prevented them from using us for their... other ends. Since the rebellion was fighting with guerilla tactics, they couldn't afford the burden in their camps of pregnant women, and since the majority of them were still Maker serving men and women, they wouldn't just kill me and condemn an unborn, sin-free child. We'd be better served as slaves. And so that was what I became. We were sold more times than I can remember, each cheaper than the last. We passed so many hands so quickly in the beginning that being quick with child carried us far longer than it should have.

"Isa always said we'd be free as soon as an Enclave ship found us. She never gave up hope. At one point I managed to gather a tabard from one of the battlefields. I thought, maybe, just maybe, someone would see the tabard on me, and it would be my salvation.

"That day never came. It went on like that, week after week, month after month, and then finally winter after winter, until one day we found ourselves, half-starved, wounded, infected, and near death, and we were sold to Ayjub slavers for next to nothing. They nursed us back to health just enough for them to turn a profit. They were taking us to Jaës to be sold to the scales that have a very particular palette for humanoid flesh."

Vicente's eyes widened in horror.

Marissa continued, "Six months ago, the opportunity finally arose. When I thought all was lost, those women out there, from all walks of life, from many different races, broke their shackles, and liberated this world of the filth of one slaver crew."

A long silence filled between the two of them, until finally Vicente asked the question she knew he would. "And Lady Marin?"

Marissa's eyes misted. Even after six months, that wound was nowhere close to healed. "She died saving my life." She sniffed and wiped the tears from the corners of her eyes before they could be allowed to tumble anew. "She became what she always dreamed of becoming – a hero. And I became what I rallied against for so long – a damsel in distress."

Vicente was silent for many minutes, watching her. Slowly Marissa collected herself, ridding herself of the last vestiges of emotion. "Anyhow," she said, "that is the quick version. I will regale you with the longwinded version another time, but I'm afraid I'll need a lot of wine, rum, or whiskey to give such a full accounting." Marissa stood and tried to flatten out the rumbled rags she was wearing. "Do you think we can let my people in now? Am I who I say I am enough, in your eyes?"

Vicente's gaze narrowed at her as he bit his lower lip in thought. Finally, he came to some sort of decision as he set about. He walked to the fireplace where an empty mantle once held her father's sword.

He reached behind it and removed an envelope that had no seal on it. Handing it to Marissa, he said quietly, "This is the last thing your father ever wrote. It was written the night he died to someone he thought you knew. I think you should know that he never gave up hope on you, not once, not ever, not even when all those around him told him to move on with his life, and to declare a new heir to Cantor lands. I think you should read it."

Marissa pulled the envelope from his hands and slowly removed the contents within. As her eyes began to rove over the words quilled to the vellum, she clearly heard Vicente whisper, "There are things you need to know, Doña Cantor."

CHAPTER TEN

Don Augusto Cruz

She was screaming. They always screamed. Which is not to say he didn't appreciate her overwhelming enthusiasm. It was an intense motivator to be sure, if only to enforce his own needs and desires. But this felt a little over the top, even for some of the loudest of women he knew. He had no time for play-acting.

Shoving away from her, he drawled, "This is hopeless."

She looked between her legs at him with surprise bordering on horror. "Please," she groaned, "I'm so close!"

"You may go," he commanded, ignoring her plea, "I've lost all desire."

It wasn't exactly a true statement. He still felt the pressure very keenly against the folds of his pants, but he would get a servant or someone else later that would sate him. In the meantime, he cared little for her company any longer. The noises she made sounded reminiscent to a sack of drowning puppies.

"But... Augusto," she complained, sitting up as Augusto Cruz wrapped a sheer robe around himself. He walked to a window overlooking the bay below.

She pointed to herself, her flesh, hot and enflamed, biding his attention. He waved her needs away dismissively. "I'm sure someone else can pick up where I left off."

As if on cue, the door burst open and a large, well-muscled woman barreled in pulling one of the city guards roughly with her.

Behind them another guard trailed behind, yelling, "Hold on, Ma'am! The viscount doesn't want to be disturbed."

Augusto merely snickered at the mountainous woman's timing. "Osprey, I trust you justify this intrusion with news of monumental import?"

The woman named Osprey's eyes darted to the exposed lady on his bed, before looking back to Augusto. "You need to hear what this Halsbrenian has to say."

Augusto's gaze fell to the man as Osprey let him go. The pale-skinned man stumbled slightly, straightened, and offered Augusto a formal salute, "Alférez Bevan Ó Cuana at your service Viscount, ser."

Augusto waved his hand for him to continue, but before Bevan could speak, he noticed the young lady in his quarters was beginning to pull a sheet over herself. "Did I say you could cover up?" Augusto demanded.

The young woman immediately slid the sheet off once more, exposing herself to everyone in the room.

"Better," he breathed with a smile before directing his gaze back to the soldier. "Continue, Alférez Bevan Ó Cuana."

Bevan coughed, clearly uncomfortable. "Yes, ser. Well, today our company was performing a routine perimeter sweep of the old Cantor lands, when we encountered a troupe that made claim to Cantor and its people."

Augusto raised an eyebrow. "Really? And what man makes claim to my lands? Is someone claiming to be Fernando's bastard?"

Bevan shifted uncomfortably, his blue eyes momentarily dancing to Osprey, and the naked girl, before falling back on Augusto. "It was Marissa, ser."

Augusto's eyebrow raised higher. "Are you certain?"

Bevan nodded to him, "Yes ser, I met her once, at the Citadel. It's her."

Augusto scrutinized the Halsbrenian. This was a sudden burr in his plans. The resurrection of Marissa was too convenient a blockade, an awfully ironic piece for someone to play. Who would use Mari, of all people?

Internally he stewed; it was a puzzle he would need play, but play it he would. Augusto was a master of putting intellectual puzzles together. Besides, his own puzzle already had more than enough pieces in place. This was a practical problem that deserved a practical solution.

He threw his arms in the air in grandiose fashion and smiled disarmingly. "The heiress returns!" His eyes met Osprey's as he continued, "She's a spoiled brat, and a whelp who couldn't tell the pommel of a sword from the blade. She cares about etiquette, courtly fineries, and looking adorable." He nodded nonchalantly to the woman in his bed. "This girl could better her."

"Tell him," Osprey ordered Bevan.

Bevan exhaled slowly. "Her troupe bested my company ser, everyone but myself and my teniente are dead."

Augusto dismissed the comment. "I wouldn't be surprised if your men were high. Chasing the dragon is popular at the moment. Where is the teniente if he still lives? He should be reporting this, not you."

"He is in a critical state with the curates. My priority was to save him, and report what I saw. Marissa used some sort of weapon on him, something I've never seen before, and it – shot – him."

"Shot? Like an arrow or crossbow bolt?"

Osprey held up a small ball for Augusto to see, it was

lacquered in blood and left a crimson smear on the large woman's fingertips. Augusto laughed. "That little thing? How could that hurt anyone?"

"It's hard to explain, ser. I thought at first that it was some sort of magic, like a wand," Bevan explained. "But one of Marissa's group, a gnome, implied it was something more."

"Like what?" Augusto was curious now.

Osprey answered, "I believe it might be a small version of a demi-culverin."

Bevan nodded. "It was round, and barreled like a cannon, and there was a thunderous roar after she pointed it at the teniente, and smoke."

"A hand cannon?" Augusto could barely fathom such a device. "Who could craft such a thing?"

Osprey looked to Bevan. "Tell him what you told me. Tell him about the group that this Cantor woman surrounds herself with."

"Yes, do tell."

"She has three companions with her, all females, all foreigners to these lands," Bevan said. "One was a gnome like I mentioned before. Another was an orc..."

"An orc?" Augusto said, alarmed. "She has a pet beast?"

Bevan nodded, tight-lipped. "Nearly as large as Osprey ser, and just as strong."

Osprey's cheek muscles bulged at the comment.

Augusto turned and looked out into the bay at all of the ships in port. "So Marissa comes home with a gnome, an orc, and a third?"

"I never saw anything like it before, ser. It was short, shorter than a gnome, and it had this... tail. It didn't wear shoes or anything, and had these little clawed feet, and three-fingered hands. What's more was it had these huge eyes. Like four or five times the size of ours, and in place of hair it had quills like a porcupine. But it was smart, real smart-like, ser."

"It was a spriggan," Osprey told them.

"A spriggan?" Augusto rubbed at his chin in thought. "I thought spriggans were from the far-east, and they were insular."

Osprey nodded. "Insular and advanced. They work with technology that is leagues ahead of what we can do. If anyone could miniaturize a culverin, it would be them."

Augusto mulled it over. "Yes, well, at least they should be easy to spot, I'd expect. Good work in this report, son. Consider yourself field promoted to teniente in the absence of yours."

Bevan saluted Augusto again, "Thank you, ser."

"Dismissed."

Osprey nodded to Augusto and turned to escort the soldier back out, when another thought came to the viscount. "Teniente?"

Bevan turned back to face him. "Ser?"

"Gather yourself a small company, twenty or thirty able-bodied men, and bring me Marissa de Cantor y Castile and this 'hand cannon' of hers."

Bevan grimaced, and nodded, "Yes, ser. I shall set out immediately."

Augusto held up a finger. "Give it a night."

"Ser?"

"Let Doña Cantor visit Loja de Cantor, I'm sure she'll find her home not quite like she remembers it. In the morning head to Tosa de Marin. That's where she will head next."

"I'm going with him," Osprey said flatly.

"Of course you are." With an easy smile he waved them all away. Marissa has returned home, has she? His mind wandered back to their time together as curious teenagers and found himself almost longing... almost. He turned back to the woman on his bed, his last image of Marissa imprinted on his mind. "My dear, I find myself suddenly rekindled. Where were we?"

CHAPTER ELEVEN

Rusalka

R usalka looked back at the two guards stationed at the large oak doors. They stood stone still, their hands casually holding their crossbows at a downward angle towards the floor, their expressions full of clear distrust as they stared vehemently toward the three women.

"I don't like this," Onna piped up from behind her. "Cap'n been in there fer far too long."

Rusalka looked away from the guards down to the two diminutive creatures trying to play a game of cards on a table that was three times too large for either of them.

"I'm not sure what you expect," Emmell replied. "They were about to shoot Rue, until Mari convinced the large-nosed human that she just might actually be Marissa de..."

"...Cantor y Castile, ya ya. Fer the life o' me I canna unnerstand why these Castellans have such long surnames. Ye know what I mean?" Onna interrupted.

Emmell looked up from the guards, directly at Onna, and said in all candor, "No. I see no problem with it."

The gnome rolled her eyes. "Course ye don't. Maker forbid ye agree wit me fer anything." She put down her cards and pointed at herself, "I am Nure Onna. Ye see how simple that sounds? New-Rey Oh-nuh," Onna said drawing her words out as if explaining it to someone who didn't understand their language. Onna jabbed a thumb Rusalka's way. "Rue's is even easier. Rue-Sal-Kah, that's it. Done. Nothing else to add, nothing else to see here."

"What's your point?" Emmell demanded, as she resumed looking at her cards.

"Yes, what is the point?" Rusalka wanted to know as well.

"Point is, why the long name? It doesn't make any sense. We call her Cap'n, or Mari, Rue calls her Jasian, or Brains."

"You're the only one that calls her Brains," Emmell pointed out.

"Irrelevant," the gnome added, "Point is, Mari is easy. But this long-arse name, Mari essa de hakuna these tatas or whatever she calls herself, it's too much."

"That sounded absolutely nothing like her appellative and you know it," Emmell countered.

Rusalka watched a perplexed expression wash over the gnome's face. Finally, she asked, "What's an apple-a-tive?"

"I'm not even going to deign to answer that," Emmell returned, laying down four of her cards. "Read them and weep."

"How in the hells?" Onna mumbled in disbelief as she stared at the cards.

Rusalka was growing impatient. Her fingers fidgeted, looking for something to do. She was used to holding rigging or manning the jib. This... lull was hard on her, and the ground was too still. She meandered to the balcony edge and stared out into the growing night sky.

In the distance she could hear the crashing surf upon the shores of the cliffs, and beyond, the merry banter of music, much louder in the evening. It was so very different here, so indescribably beautiful. Her people would never be able to just sit back and take it all in. No, they would want to conquer it, crush it, and waste it until it was all gone.

Rusalka pushed away the memories of her past. Instead she thought of the other women of the Dahlia, and if they were enjoying themselves in the city itself. Would they wander into Cantor lands at all, or would they forge new lives for themselves in Castile, and beyond? What were Badger, Jocquotte, and Anne doing? Getting drunk, probably.

As she took in the horizon, she saw more from this new vantage than she had the previous day. Castile was, to her at least, the largest gathering of people she'd ever seen in one place. Lights sparkled beneath the cliffline, and they seemed never-ending, twinkling gold, orange, and amber, illuminated from what appeared to be the ground itself.

Rusalka was no stranger to fire, and burning villages was something her people did far too often. The light of massive fires was often muted in the sky by the thick billows of black smoke that would emanate from whatever was being burned, be it buildings, carts, or even bodies. This though, cast very little pollution into the sky, letting the brilliant moon also add its light to the great expanse of undulating sea.

Her eyes fell to a curious blot on the vast rolling waters just to their south. Rusalka concentrated on it, staring at the strange phenomenon. She squinted at what appeared to be a dense fog that slowly crept forward across the water. Tendrils of white mist slithered out like river snakes across the surface of the water, pulling itself inexorably towards the shore. She knew that they were a great distance away from the obscuring mists, but to see it move in such a way was alarming. It was an unnerving sight with such unusually clear and magical waters all around her reflecting the dazzling intermixed colors.

"What ye's looking at is called the Stonewall Pale, or just the Pale fer short."

Rusalka looked down to Onna in surprise. She hated that the gnome was deft enough to sneak past her senses every time. Pugnaciously, Rusalka responded, "what happened to your game?"

Onna gestured with a thumb back to Emmell, who was smiling gleefully as she raked in her meager winnings. "Got demolished. Little bugger twas cheatin', I feels it in me girlie bits."

Rusalka shrugged, she had yet to get the hang of the card games they played, but Onna constantly liked to tell her she had a great stone face, whatever that meant.

"What is the Pale?"

Onna pulled herself up on a neighboring crate next to the railing, "Truthfully? Nobody knows. Plenty o' rumors and superstitions about it though," the gnome pointed a chubby finger to a dense rise of mountains to the west. They dominated the sky like massive wedges of shadow. "It starts out there."

"How far away is that?" Rusalka wondered aloud, looking at the dominating dark forms.

"Couple hundred leagues easy," Onna answered. "That's the Impassable Range," Onna declared. "Tallest known mountains in all of Kuldarr."

"Why is it called Impassable Range?"

Onna laughed, "Because no one's cleared ta the other side and ever returned ta speak of it!" She guffawed at the obviously confused expression on Rusalka's own face before continuing. "Every winter, some genius thinks they are going ta be the first ta cross the range an' come back. No one's ever come back."

"How would anyone know if they succeeded?"

Onna shrugged at the question, "Well, people might've made

it to the other side. Fer all we knows, it may be a bountiful land an' they just dinna want to return. Or there may be nothing but death beyond those mountains, or worse... the end o' the world."

"We are at world's end?" Rusalka asked in wonder, looking at the mountains so far on the horizon.

"World's end enough fer ye an me that's fer sure," Onna agreed. "No one sails into the Pale."

"Why not?"

Onna shrugged, "Some say that the Pale is just an extension of the Impassable Range, and that there are towering rock barriers hidden in the fog. Others say that there be a volcano within and that it's constantly bubbling lava out, and that it's steam, and one will sail into the maw and plummet into a sea of magma to burn alive."

Rusalka crinkled her nose at the idea.

"Many others think it be haunted waters. That all the dead who tried to cross the seas, or the Impassable Range, have wound up in these waters. That the mists are these lost souls ready to pull ye in and make ye one of them.

"The fog acts as a boundary, or a warning if ye will. It stops everyone from being stupid enough to sail ta the other side. Jasian Enclave used to call it the Defiler's Breath, in hopes of getting devout Jasians to keep away, but the name didn't stick. The Pale was just catchier soundin' me thinks," Onna concluded with a wink.

"So, no one goes in there at all?" Rusalka asked. "No one dares to venture into this Pale in the hopes of seeing what lies at the end of the world?"

Rusalka saw Emmell's ears perk up at the comment, and she too made her way to the ledge. "End of the world, did you say? That sounds fascinating."

Onna rolled her eyes, "Now ye did it, Tusker, Em's gonna be askin' me questions all night."

Emmell put her little hands on her hips and said, "There is nothing wrong with learning all you can. Besides it's not like we can do anything else."

"Agreed," Rusalka said, following a similar line of thinking. "What if somebody continued further south at sea until this Pale ended, and then just sailed around?"

"Oh... I like this question. Good one Rue," Emmell said with a nod, looking at Onna expectantly.

"Doldrums," Onna answered simply.

"Ugh," Emmell replied, her quills rippling in agitation.

"I don't get it," Rusalka said. "What are doldrums?"

"It's a period of stagnation," Emmell answered before Onna could. "It's a low-pressure area where there are no prevailing winds. It's as if they disappear altogether. No wind means nothing to push the sails, and you've got a trapped ship for days, even weeks."

Onna nodded, "It's like the desert o' the sea, Rue."

Rusalka's face scrunched as she tried to think of what that might mean. She didn't have to wait long as Onna continued to explain.

"We've really only been within a day or so's travel to the coast-line, so all you've ever really seen is unrelenting storms, a couple of really tall waves, and howling wind. But there are parts out there," Onna explained with a wave of her hand, "of absolute stillness."

"Still how?"

"Nothing," Emmell replied "Utter nothingness, just flat water for leagues around. It's like a boat sitting on a plate of glass."

"More like a mirror. Doldrums are probably one of the hottest places in the world," Onna added. "The sun reflects off the water, and it becomes like a fiery beam from sunrise ta sunset. Time seems to stand still. Nothing on the horizon even remotely changes, it's as if ye were trying to make yer way through the Malten desert itself."

"Well, you could at least fish if you had to, I guess," Rusalka said, "so it's not like you'd starve to death."

Onna once more shook her head. "The water is hypoxic."

Rusalka's face contorted at the strange word. "Is that a gnome term?"

"It means that the water doesn't support marine life," Emmell answered. "There's no fish."

"Aye, no nothing in fact," Onna said. "Gnomes have figured much o' this out with our steamships and all, an' there are a number of such places that the water is inhospitable to life. Dead waters, if ye will. South of the Pale is one. Because of that, no gnomes want to risk bringing a steamship all this way to see if it can make the journey around the Pale, through the doldrums. Besides, coal takes up too much space and is too precious to try and guess a variable distance."

"What about a Scales longship then? It has oars. You can row through these doldrums," Rusalka replied.

Onna opened her mouth to speak, but then quickly closed it as she thought about it.

Emmell clapped. "Very good, Rue, excellent deduction. You are a testament to your species."

Onna shook her head. "While it is a good thought, I give ye that Tusker, I'm not fer thinking it would work."

"Why?"

"Well logistically, I be thinkin' it fer requiring a bit too many people. Think of the mouths ta feed, the increase in the weight o' the ship, and that's afore the cargo of food, water, spice, on and on. Bottom line, too many people, and their needs taking up too much space, all fer the chance ta see what 'might' be on the other side."

"I for one think it's worth the risk," Emma declared.

Onna pointed right at her. "And ye wouldn't be rowing worth a spit anyhow – ye'd make Tusker do all the work. Still though, Rue, good thinkin' on ye part."

Rusalka nodded as she looked back out once more to the tentacles of miasma that slithered and swayed out on the still, moonlit sea.

Behind them, the double doors groaned as they slowly opened.

IT WAS OBVIOUS THAT MARISSA CRIED ALL TOO RECENTLY AND Rusalka did not want to be the first to bring it up. She was sure that Marissa had her reasons; perhaps she had learned more about the fate of her family.

Next to Mari, the human male, Vicente, approached the women, "Mari has told me all that you have done to aid her in getting her here. I thank you for bringing her home."

To Rusalka's surprise, he saluted the three of them, much in the same way as the guard had saluted Mari.

"So, are we still held at crossbow point then?" Onna asked.

Vicente looked down at the gnome. "No, senorita, you are not. I needed to confirm that she was indeed who she claimed. I feel confident that she is now."

"Yeah, and how'd ye go about doin' that? Did ye have to confirm the strawberry shaped birthmark on her derriere, to the one ye remember from yesterwinter?" Onna added with a malicious grin.

"Onna!" Marissa declared in horror. Rusalka found it curious as to how red the Jasian's face was becoming.

"I find this would be an acceptable way of helping confirm an identity," Emmell replied. "It makes sense to denote birthmarks on persons of royalty for this reason. We should've done this at the gate, as it would've saved time. Go on, show this man your bum."

Marissa buried her face in her hands.

Vicente coughed into his fist. "That won't be necessary. I am fairly confident that she is indeed who she claims to be."

"Ah!" Onna declared, holding up a finger in the air, "She's got other beauty marks then. Are they like a treasure map to her more intimate bits?"

"I don't even know why I let you off the boat," Marissa murmured.

"Because she'd find a way to sink it if we left her alone," Emmell proclaimed.

Rusalka just looked back and forth at the growing discomfort between the humans, and the bitter smell of pheromones filling the air. All of these strange customs definitely had her at a loss.

"I would not sink 'er!" Onna declared indignantly. "Besides she's moored – how much damage could I do?"

Emmell's large eyes sparkled, "Oh... knowing you, you'd find a way."

Rusalka didn't want this conversation to linger, as she had a pressing one to start of her own. "Does that mean I am free to wander as well?"

Vicente glanced back to the two guards at the door, who clearly shifted uncomfortably at her comment. Before the man could answer, Marissa composed herself from Onna's remarks and said, "Of course Rue, you are my honored guest here. I know it will take the men a bit to adjust, but in time they will find you as welcome a friend as I do."

Rusalka saw Vicente's eyes shift nervously away. "Yes," he vouched quietly, before trying again more confidently. "Yes, it is as Marissa says. You are welcome, but please understand it will take some time to adjust. We are not used to... to..."

Rusalka crossed her large arms over her chest, causing the guard to break off midsentence. She wanted to display a sense of ire to the man, but within she felt a bizarre flutter of anticipation. She knew she clearly was not as welcome as Mari promised.

"... just please, I ask for time, senorita Rusalka," Vicente finished, clearly changing his train of thought. "There is a lot happening, I'm afraid, and the remaining people on Cantor lands are already very confused as it is. To see... well... uhm..."

"An orc?" Onna said flatly.

"Yes," he admitted. "To see an orc freely walking about will surely raise levels of concern. I ask that you try to perhaps limit where you go, or who you travel with."

"That will not be a problem," Marissa interrupted, "as Rue will be with me."

Vicente blinked in surprise. "Marissa, you've just returned... the people..."

"Will have to adapt," Marissa finished firmly. "Rue is as welcome here as any other human we would invite formally, Vicente. End of story."

Rusalka could tell by the momentary fire in his eyes that this Vicente was not used to being ordered in such a fashion.

If Marissa saw the slight rebellion in his eyes, she ignored it. "Vicente is right about a few things, however," she said, turning to Rusalka. "A lot has transpired since I've been gone. Many people will be very confused at my return. With the loss of my father, and the disappearance of my mother, almost all control of the Cantor lands went to Don Cruz. From all of what Vicente has told me, there is a lot that is... not promising."

"What's not promising? I don't understand," Emmell asked.

"Technically, Don Cruz is in control of the Cantor lands, at least until no less than two witnesses of noble decent declare that Marissa is who she claims she is," Vicente told the group of ladies.

"Well, that's not so bad," Onna added.

"Isa's sister will vouch for you, yes?" Rusalka put in.

Marissa nodded to her. "Cassandra? Yes, she should. Like Vicente, it has been many winters since we've seen each other. She was only a child when I left, and now she is a young woman. I hope she will recognize me, and I her."

"Well, we count that as one fer now," Onna declared optimistically. "So, who else do ye think ye canna get on yer side?"

"I don't know," Marissa replied honestly. "I never thought I'd come home to have to defend my title."

"So, what kinda timetable are we lookin' fer here? We have a few weeks?"

Vicente just shook his head in reply.

"Few days?" Emmell asked.

Marissa held up two fingers.

"Two days!" Onna blurted. "Aye, talk about bad timing."

"Or good timing," Emmell countered. "We could've been delayed after all."

"Fair point," Onna conceded.

"So, what is it that you need to do, besides find another who will vouch for you?" Rusalka asked Marissa.

"There is an Adjutant here that maintains the security of the port of Castile, and a great matter of political affairs that have to do with the Jasian Enclave's overall authority within the city and neighboring lands."

"His name is Beneford Love," Vicente told them. "He is the one who holds the deed of the land as well as a duplicate of Don Cantor's will and testament."

"Do you know this Adjutant Love?" Rusalka asked Marissa.

She nodded, "He was a purist commander when I left. I always found him to be a fair and reasonable man. I don't see why, with the appropriate signors, it should be overly difficult."

Rusalka saw the scowl back on Vicente's face. "You don't agree?"

Vicente shook his head. "Marissa has been gone a while, and her view of purists has always been slightly... colored in their favor."

Marissa's cheeks pinked.

"She hasn't seen some of the changes yet. Things have become different in her absence. I hope that she is correct, and soon these lands will be at peace knowing they still hold the Cantor standard. But... Adjutant Love seems to be pushing this a little too hard. Miranda Cantor, Marissa's mother, is only missing, not dead, and yet they are immediately declaring her as such. There is no sign of wreckage washing up on shore. No one has been dispatched as of yet to the Citadel, or Sentinel's Barrow, to see if she might be there. There have been absolutely no survivors, the ship is just gone, swallowed into the Pale."

"Which is very odd," Marissa added. "Ships that have ventured near the Pale have wrecked before, and flotsam has always inevitably made its way to the bay."

Vicente nodded and continued, "Another thing – Don Cantor's will clearly stated that control of Cantor be handed to Marissa in light of his passing, and she too was not declared dead, but missing. However, in that defense you were gone five winters so it is easier to discount you."

Marissa nodded, not arguing with the man.

"Aye not to be a rotten apple, but six months missing is a long time missing, still," Onna pointed out. "Eventually someone'd hafta make a play."

"You're right," Vicente agreed. "In a usual circumstance such as this, one of the other families would be named a place-holder..."

"Which they have," Marissa interrupted.

"Which they have," Vicente said in agreement, "but where is the next of kin demanding an investigation of Miranda's where-abouts? The allocated time that Jasian nobility can remain in limbo is usually around a winter depending on how easy it is to travel, and sometimes it can be as long as two winters. After such time if there is no successor either through Last Will and Testa-ment, or through nomination via the Citadel, the Jasian Enclave itself would usually seize all holdings and then redistribute them to the next noble family in line, or to an adjutant or bishop that is responsible for the area."

"And it's only been half that time," Emmell said.

"And no one is really trying all that hard to find the Jasian's mother," Rusalka posited.

"It just feels... too convenient," Vicente told them. "I've already explained to Marissa that relations with the Citadel were strained because of Don Cantor's refusal to give up on her."

Rusalka looked to Mari, who gave her a tight-lipped nod.

"But Castile as a whole loved the Cantors. They brought jobs to many families and kept a very easy peace with the elves of the Shemma, even with Don Cantor's eccentrics towards the end."

"Which proved to be well founded," Emmell pointed out flourishing her three-fingered hand at Marissa.

"So it would seem," Vicente agreed.

"It's also why there seems to be nobody here," Marissa added.

Vicente agreed with her, "Only a token force stayed behind to hold this place off from bandits and such, and most of the staff of Loja de Cantor were redirected to other occupations. I didn't want Don Cruz getting hold of this place any sooner than legally allowed to."

"That's why ye gave us such a hard time at the gate," Onna said.

"One of many reasons, yes," Vicente agreed, eyeballing Rusalka once more.

"You keep saying this Don Cruz name – where have I heard that before?" Emmell asked.

"Alférez Bevan Ó Cuana mentioned him," Marissa said.

"Yes, the guard," Emmell said snapping her fingers. "That's where I remember the name."

"Why not go to this Don Cruz guy? Did ye know him?" Onna asked Marissa.

Marissa nodded, "Augusto Cruz. I knew him fairly well, yes."

"And what are ye thoughts of the man?" Onna queried.

Rusalka watched Marissa as the woman's mind swam to the past. "Augusto was... arrogant, but at the same time he exuded confidence, and power." Marissa's eyes lit up as she said the words. "He was attractive because of it, and he knew it," she chuckled. "Augusto knew the things he wanted and he simply took them. In short, he was what I thought noble men should be. Everything my father wasn't."

Vicente shifted uncomfortably.

Onna squinted at Marissa. "You were taken with him."

Once more, Marissa's face turned beet red. "I was a young girl and rebelled against my father. Augusto wore his heredity as a point of pride. My father always seemed to downplay his, preferring the people over pomp." Rusalka noticed Marissa's eyes dart to Vicente only briefly as she made the comment.

"He's who ye'd sneak out fer!" Onna added.

"That past is irrelevant," Marissa said. "And long gone."

"Maybe, maybe not," Onna countered. "If ye had a past, suren he'd recognize ye now. He could be yer second." After a moment's silence, she added, "Unless he was ye first," she winked.

Rusalka didn't think Marissa could get any redder at this point.

"While this girl time is all well and good, you are asking Don Cruz to relinquish Cantor lands, on good faith," Vicente asserted. "After what Marissa just told you, do you think he would give that power back?"

The silence grew as they thought about it. Finally, Marissa shook her head, "No, he wouldn't. Ours was but a fleeting moment, and one that didn't end on the best of terms."

"Exactly." Vicente turned to regard Onna. "Don Cruz is still exactly as Marissa described him to be, a man who takes what he wants. Takes, not relinquishes."

Rusalka on the other hand was not thinking of this Don Cruz

person, but of someone very different. "Why not use the Jasian Enclave?" she asked.

"Well technically I'm an exactor, so my name is forsworn," Marissa disclosed.

"But the adjutant would recognize you, right? Get the Exactor thing annulled and be Cantor again. Why can't he be your second?" Rusalka asked.

"Aye, good thought Rue," Onna said. "Use Adjutant Love!"

Rusalka smiled as she could see the wheels turning behind Marissa's dark eyes. Slowly a smile crept upon her face as well. "That could work," Marissa said with a nod, "I'm last in line, they would have to annul me from the Exactors. Plus, Beneford Love is a noble, albeit barely, and the rules do stipulate that it has to be someone of noble descent. Since he is a purist, and they fall underneath the domain of the Jasian Enclave, he may very well be the second noble as long as Cassandra's testimony on my behalf holds."

Radiating with joy, Emmell smiled up at Marissa. "This is promising – we may have both people already!"

Rusalka's nose crinkled. She sniffed once and noted there was something a hint more bitter in the air. She looked to Vicente, whose odor had changed. "You don't agree."

Vicente blinked at her in surprise. "What?"

"You don't agree, I can tell."

Vicente looked at all the women, especially at Marissa, before directing his gaze back to her. "But I didn't speak or move or anything."

Onna chuckled at him. "So afraid of the big, scary orc, but ye dunna know a thing about em' do ye?"

"What do you disagree about?" Rue asked. "Is it the thought of Marissa going to the Adjutant on her behalf, or... is it that you want her yourself?"

"What? No," Vicente scoffed, "it's not that at all." He looked to them all, and then at Marissa as she walked over and stood next to Rusalka. The orc tried not to tower over her, but it couldn't be helped.

Marissa put her hands on her hips, "I trust Rue's instincts. What is it, Vicente? What is it that you are not saying?"

Vicente ran his fingers through his hair as he looked back and forth between all the women. In the back the guards were becoming restless. Finally, he sighed and dropped his arms to his sides, "Look, it's just for the last six months, I've been in charge here, and we've held this place at bay from the clutches of poachers, thieves, Cruz and his lackeys, and other village idiots. Now all of the sudden a Cantor is back, after missing for winters – I'll admit, it's still hard for me to wrap my head around that. I mean, it's been five winters... And to top it off, she's brought friends." He waved his hands at them. "Castile may be a port, but every one of you is a rare oddity in these parts, especially you," he finished, pointing at Rusalka. "Whenever orcs appear, it's either to attack the elves in the Shemma or burn our crops, and now here you are, all friendly... I didn't even know orcs could be civil!"

"Careful lad, Tusker be one of us," Onna warned.

Vicente, nodded, "Look it's not meant to be an insult, just Marissa returns, and now is making all these decisions without listening to anyone who has been here for the last several winters, and I mean you are rushing into making really dumb decisions..."

"Dumb how?" Marissa demanded.

"Yeah, we only have two days," Emmell added.

Vicente pointed out at Castile, "First you want to go to Cruz? C'mon, this is the guy who is taking your lands."

Marissa scowled, "I never said Don Cruz was a good option, he was only a thought by the crew."

"Now instead of trying to appeal to other nobles, you want to use Love?" Vicente retorted.

Marissa's voice took on an edge, "who still answers to the

Jasian Enclave. It's a quick solution. It's not exactly like I've been blessed with time here."

Vicente shook his head in disgust. "Beneford Love is political now. I'm telling you, he doesn't care about you, or Cantor. He's in it for himself. What does he gain by annulling you? He could just ship you back to the Citadel and be done with it."

"He's an Adjutant with the Jasian Enclave; they're above such petty things like corruption!"

"Yeah, okay, sure, Marissa. This is the spoiled child I remember. Once you have your mind made up, that's it. You're letting the Juglares' tales warp your mind again."

Rusalka could tell Marissa was thrown off by the offhanded comment. "What the hells is that supposed to mean?"

Vicente threw up his hands in the air, "You know what? Forget it, you're the Doña now, do what you think is best. In the meantime, I'll hold this place from Cruz and his lackeys for as long as I can, though Maker knows why I care. Your father's dead, and everything good about this place died with him!" Vicente turned from them and stormed into the night, disappearing around the nearest parapet.

"Wow, and they say women are emotional," Onna said.

Rusalka was more than a little perplexed at the sudden change of mood in Vicente as well. Only moments before he was being very helpful in identifying the problem laid out before the four of them. Now he was having a temper tantrum.

"Your kind acts very peculiar here," Emmell noted.

Rusalka watched Onna tug at Marissa's sleeve, directing the Jasian's hot glare away from where Vicente stormed off. "C'mon, Brains, forget Big Nose – let's work on this plan some more."

"What?" Marissa said, clearly having trouble shaking away the ire that bubbled to the surface so quickly.

"We needs ta figure out exactly what to say to both Cassandra and this Adjutant Love tomorrow. I fer one want to see ye become this Doña, if only fer enjoying the laps of luxury that bein' chums with a noble will bring!"

"And Onna is back to thinking of herself," Emmell added, standing next to Marissa. She leaned over and sniffed at the Jasian once. "Also, might I recommend a bath, and perhaps a haircut?"

Marissa's hands reached up to her head, feeling the strands of her raven mane. "What's wrong with my hair?"

Rusalka looked away from the women as they quipped, and peered back out to the open sea. Castile was not turning out how Marissa promised.

She felt a twinge of sorrow for the Jasian. The joy she had when they first came to shore was now marred with the prospect of losing everything she knew. While Rusalka herself had never had anything more than she had now, looking around at the castle she could feel that sense of home that Marissa held for the place. A ground for her roots, so near to being taken away.

Absently, as her thoughts trailed off, her gaze fell once more upon the Stonewall Pale, reaching tendrils of fog slithering across the surface of the water, just waiting to pull the unwary within its deathly hallowed clutches.

CHAPTER TWELVE

Marissa de Cantor y Castile

It was very early morning when they set out for Tossa de Marin, and it took them over four hours to traverse the open lands on horseback, backtracking to one of the Castile mounds of homes that the late Isa's family controlled. Marissa stared at the back of the ostentatious castle. Tossa de Marin was just as bedazzled as all the other Castellan castles, except this one was the closest thing to a second home Marissa had.

As a child she didn't recognize all the resplendent gilding that lined the parapets as being gaudy, but as identifying who and what they were – nobility. Yet slavery, and a brief life at sea changed that view now. She looked at the tiled mosaics decorating the tower, the sparkling precious stones glinting in the growing light, and she only could think of how ridiculous it all seemed.

The solitary tower's crown merlon was a cascade of brilliant blues, silvers, and gold. Across the top of the tower was the bold engraving of the Escudo de Marin – azure tiles crested around a golden dolphin, posed in fess and swimming on a sea of silver. It was beautiful and regal, and so much more "noble" than her family's own coat of arms, twin steeds facing one another, one black, the other white. With the absence of her father creating a hollow in her chest, Marissa realized now that she really did love her heraldry. It was just as much a part of her as her surname.

When had she changed so much? When had she no longer accepted the glitz and glamor as something that she was entitled to, but instead saw it as a shallow shell she used in the vain defense of that which she rightfully was owed? Was it war? Slavery? Maturity? Or was it Isa? Her thoughts lingered on her best friend. How she missed her. Now at the Marin estate, enroute to pass along Isa's last wishes, the impact of her loss was once again hitting her. Marissa reached up and tried to loosen the collar at her neck. She was suddenly so hot...

"Stop messing with it, Brains," Onna quipped in front of her.

She looked down at the small gnome, "I can't help it, it's all so tight. I haven't worn clothing like this..."

"...In five winters, we know!" Onna said, interrupting her. "But ye need to look the part now, right? Gotta be all nobley-like?"

"Nobley-like?" Emmell queried from in front of a heavily clothed and helmeted Rusalka.

Marissa glanced from Emmell to Rusalka. She felt for Rue. If she was hot, the orc had to be roasting alive in the thick layers of padded armor, cloak, and morion helmet with full cheek guards. A chainmail hood hung from the helmet itself. At a casual glance one could easily confuse her in her current outfit as a very large man. Of course, a closer look, especially at her face, where they would see her green skin and protruding tusks, would be an obvious giveaway that she was no common guard.

Marissa still hoped that Rusalka would be able to walk around Cantor as openly as she did on the Dahlia. Perhaps she was just being naïve. Rusalka nodded at Marissa, "Jasian."

"She looks good, don't she?" Onna countered Emmell, "That's nobley-like. Ye should learn yer term-oh-ah-logy."

"And you should learn proper Trade Tongue," Emmell fired back.

"Ladies!" Marissa barked. "You are the ones that suggested I dress as I did before so I could be better recognized." Onna started to protest, but Marissa continued over her. "You also suggested that it would be more believable to be seen with me if you were dressed as servants."

"Right," Emmell agreed, "as we are." She motioned to the children's serf clothing they were in that they found in the servant's quarters.

"Servants don't bicker and fight in the presence of their lord or lady," Marissa said.

"Aye, but ye are Cap'n – there be a difference," Onna said with a mischievous glint in her eye.

"Right now, I'm Doña Cantor, Onna. If we hope to pull this off, they need to believe it, Cassandra needs to believe it," Marissa said sternly. Already she could feel the apprehension growing in her belly. It didn't help that Vicente never returned to her for the rest of the night. She didn't like the niggling feeling in the back of her head that maybe, just maybe, he was right and her idea was dumb. Still, what could she do? With only a day and a half left, she was pressed for options.

Besides, what she really thought was that Vicente was having a hard time taking orders from a woman. He held a deep respect for her father – that was obvious – but he barely even mentioned her mother, let alone addressed her as Doña. Even more telling to Marissa was that he didn't even refer to her as Doña. Not that she was looking forward to being Doña, not anymore. But she couldn't let Don Cruz take her lands, her people, her home. She just couldn't. She needed to fight for them. She needed to fight for the women around her to whom she promised Cantor would be their home.

"Sorry, Mari," Emmell apologized.

"Aye, we'll b'have, Brains," Onna added.

"Doña," Rusalka corrected. "Jas- Doña Cantor is right. We need to address her as Doña."

Onna nodded. "Awright. But when were done, I'm callin' ye Brains for the rest o' the winter!"

Before they could canter the rest of the way up to the barbican, Rusalka dismounted, and moved Onna to her horse, behind Emmell. Marissa could see the gnome's fervent desire to make some snide and lewd comment, but mercifully she managed to refrain.

Rusalka then took the reins of their horse and began to lead them in, a respectful distance behind Marissa. Marissa took a deep breath – this was it, a moment of truth. They passed under the barbican and the same coat of arms just above the gate to be stopped by a guard on the inside of the outer bailey. "Mi'lady, are you expected by the Lady?"

Marissa held her head up high, leaning on the memory of her mother whenever the woman was questioned in the absence of her father, "No, but Lady Cassandra Marin will want to see me. I bring news of her sister, Lady Isa Marin."

The guard blinked at her in stilted silence for several long moments. "I see," he said at last. "And who shall I say brings this information about Lady Isa?"

Marissa looked down at him, her eyes never leaving his, "Doña Marissa Cantor y Castile."

"I don't think they're fer letting you in... mi'lady," Onna said almost forty minutes later.

They were dismounted and their horses were stabled. The women themselves were forced to wait within the inner bailey while the Lady of the house "prepared" to meet her guests.

This left the four of them to stand around and ponder what might be going on in Cassandra Marin's head, or worse, what she might be telling the guards at this moment. They also knew they were being heavily scrutinized by the dozen or so guards that were positioned all around the bailey and ramparts.

"They've doubled the guard," Emmell commented dryly.

"Glad I can't count that well, yet," Rusalka muttered, "but I did notice there were more of them."

"I think we need to be prepared ta run if need be, Doña," Onna said as she looked about. "I'm feeling like a sitting duck just... standing here."

"Just give her more time," Marissa said, trying to keep the pleading tone out of her voice and remaining hopeful. "Cassandra is probably just readying herself, as appropriate to a woman of stature. We have no idea what we may have interrupted upon our arrival."

"Aye, but if someone recognized us comin' in..." Onna suggested.

Emmell nodded, "We are still wanted, Doña." The spriggan looked to the growing number of guards, "Perhaps word has spread? A word of warning to the nobles?"

The twin oak doors, stained with salt from many winters against the sea, groaned as it opened behind them. Marissa turned, hopeful to see Lady Cassandra, or at least an orderly with Cassandra behind in tow. Instead, a guard stood there, his hand resting casually on the pommel of his sword.

When he spoke, his voice was rough like a dog's bark. "Which one of you is claiming to be Marissa de Cantor ye Castile?"

"Doña Cantor," Emmell reported to the man, looking up at

him indignantly. "Seeing as no one wants to bother to search for her mother."

Marissa reached down and touched Emmell's shoulder. She watched the spriggan's quill's flutter in slight agitation. "Forgive my aide; she is most distraught over recent events, but what she says is true. Unless my mother resurfaces, I am Marissa de Cantor y Castile, and am the acting Doña."

The gruff soldier looked her up and down, sizing her up. It amazed her that no one at all seemed to recognize her, but truth be told, she didn't know this man, either.

"Very well," he said. "Remove all weapons upon your person and enter."

Onna began to grumble as she reached for her throwing knives, when the guard told them, "Only Doña Cantor. The rest of you wait out here."

Onna opened her mouth to object, but Marissa quickly said, "If that is Lady Cassandra's will."

Onna glared up at her with a 'you can't be serious' expression on her face.

"It'll be fine," Marissa told them. "Isa was my best friend. This was basically my second home. Someone is bound to recognize me inside."

"Aye, maybe. A bolt may recognize ye just as suren," Onna said angrily.

"I agree, Doña," Rusalka said quietly. Marissa could hear the orc fighting hard to bottle the growing concern in her voice. "This is not a smart decision. We shouldn't be separated." Rusalka nodded her hooded head towards the ramparts and the increasing number of guards.

Marissa bit her lip as she eyed them warily. She knew Rusalka and Onna were right, and perhaps maybe they should try the adjutant instead? She knew purists, knew how to deal with them. In the end, though, she knew she couldn't. She made a promise to Isa to watch over Cassandra, and Cassandra was her best chance of holding on to the Cantor estate.

"I will be fine," she told the three of them. The guard turned away from them impatiently, and Marissa lowered herself to Emmell and whispered, "You may want to check on the horses though, make sure their conditions are well and good, and they're being adequately cared for."

Emmell's eyebrows arched. "Why would we do that? The horses are probably being treated better than we are, I'd imagine."

Luckily, Marissa didn't have to spell it out for the spriggan, for Onna understood. "Aye, Doña, we'll be checkin' on ye horses. Making suren they are right and cared for."

Marissa could read the confusion on Emmell's face, and only hoped that Onna would explain it to her discretely as she stepped into the threshold and let the double doors close behind her, severing her from her friends.

"This way, Lady Cantor."

Marissa ignored the derision in his voice. She was beginning to come to terms with the fact that she no longer appeared to be the girl that they remembered.

The guard led her down long roughstone passages that she recalled fondly as a child. She used to play all manner of chasing and tagging games in these very corridors with Isa and a stumpy-legged little Cassandra, when their fathers were busy at the viscount's estate politicking. Little had changed in the halls since those times, with the exception of there now being a very large number of candles burning all around them.

As she was directed through rooms that invoked memory after memory of a different time, the candles and incense seemed to intensify. Finally, Marissa's curiosity overcame her. "Why all the candles?"

The guard glanced back at her, somewhat mystified. "Excuse me?"

She directed her hand around the room. "All the candles. What's with them? I feel like I'm walking through an Enclave cathedral."

The guard turned back away from her. "That's because you basically are," he answered her.

"What?"

"Lady Cassandra has taken a vow of celibacy and joined the Jasian Enclave as a priestess. She serves here at home in Castile as a diplomatic envoy. As such, the land that Tossa de Marin resides upon is now consecrated soil."

Marissa was dumbfounded. "What does Don Marin have to say about all of this?" she asked, looking once more at the flickering amber rooms.

"I'm sure he would be very proud of his youngest child," the guard answered tartly.

Marissa stumbled as the guard stopped abruptly in front of a set of ornate mahogany doors. She looked at him confused. She thought for sure that he was going to escort her to one of the flower gardens where Isa's mother used to meet dignitaries, maybe the solar for a private, more intimate meeting, or even quite possibly her father's cabinet if the Don wanted to have a word about Isa as well. Instead, Marissa found herself directly in front of the antechamber doors that would lead to the room before the great hall and the Don's personal bed chambers. She stared at the guard confused as he opened the door.

"You will wait in the antechamber until called for, Lady Cantor," the guard directed.

Marissa nodded dumbly and stepped inside the well-lit, cylindrical chamber in the center of Tossa de Marin. She turned and looked back at the guard, "Why am I in the antechamber?"

He looked at her once more, "Because you have requested to speak to the lady of the house." He closed the door on her, and she abruptly heard the lock audibly click shut on the other end.

"Just lovely," she sighed.

Marissa looked about the antechamber while she waited. Like many antechambers in the castles of Castile, it was a waiting room. Armchairs and lounging chairs were dotted throughout the room to allow guests to be seated while waiting to be received by the castle master – in this case it would be Cassandra now.

Marissa knew that traditionally the wait was more or less long, but she was hoping that Cassandra wouldn't play the social games with her, and just go straight to demanding to know about her sister. Still, she knew the truth of the matter. It was likely to be a while.

Marissa sat in one of the armchairs and really took the room in. She was in the second antechamber of the noble apartments, if her memory served her right. The Maker's Eye Antechamber. She gazed up to the circular window that brought light into the room on the southern side.

Looking at the startling rays of golden light that cut a line through the room, her mind was thrust back to when she was only seven-winters-old. The room she sat in was originally divided into two by a partition wall and was composed of the antechamber and the Don's chamber. Frustrated by the small size of these rooms, which could barely contain all the courtiers in attendance from morning to night, Don Marin decided to knock down the wall and combine the two rooms into one. Above them a gallery was installed to look over the awaiting dignitaries and courtiers below.

Her eyes fell to the double doors on the north portion of the room. Somewhere beyond that point was where the apartments began.

Marissa once asked her father why the Marin's apartments were so close to the grand hall and he told her, "The Maker's Eye Antechamber occupies a strategic position in Tossa de Marin, for a key reason. To the north it leads to the Don's chamber; to the west, the tall glass doors open directly onto the Great Hall of Light, enabling courtiers to enter and leave the Don's apartments or the Great Hall alike. A door in the southern wall to the right of the windows leads to the Doña's apartments, while a staircase in the eastern wall leads to the Ladies apartments on the ground floor. It also serves another very important function."

"What's that, Papa?" she remembered asking.

"If ever attacked, both the ladies' apartments, the Doña's apartments, and an emergency escape from behind the great chair in the Hall of Light, all meet up below and run through a tunnel that emerges into one of the servant's houses."

"Really Papa?"

Her father smiled and nodded.

"How come the Don's chambers don't have a staircase as well?" she had asked.

"Because Don Marin is a man of great honor. He would stay behind to ensure his family escaped..." Her father paused for a moment before adding, "And so would I."

Marissa wiped a tear from her eye as she thought of her father. How many times had she run circles as a child around these very chairs, or ran up and down those stairs? How many times had he yelled at her when she placed her palms and face against the glass doors to get a better look at the Great Hall of Light, leaving smears against the impeccable glass? She thought then that he was cruel, but really he was teaching her, molding her into the woman he'd hoped she'd become.

Marissa looked at the Maker's Eye, wondering if that streamer of light held her father looking down upon her. "I hope I haven't disappointed you too much, Papa."

Marissa took a deep breath and balanced her feelings out. She recognized all the things that were still the same. Those brought a smile to her face, but if it was true that Cassandra was now the Lady of the house, then much that did change must've been altered in Cassandra's new taste.

With Don Marin she remembered rich marble decorations abounding in the room, mostly statuettes of the mythological women of the sea – the Sirens. She remembered vaulted, painted ceilings in fresco of those maidens of the oceans. Now this antechamber was replaced with white ceilings and gilded wood-work. All the marble statues were gone, and a frieze depicting the very children's games she had thought of while traversing the halls ran along the cornice. She smiled ruefully at the small girls in that frieze.

"Lady Marissa de Cantor y Castile," A voice called from above her very punctually. It was a deep, husky voice, but still decidedly feminine. Marissa stood up and turned to look above her. Though she was standing in a well-lit area, the galleries above were cast in shadows with only a few flickering candles casting orange flashes against the shrouding darkness.

"I am," she answered, "who do I have the pleasure of addressing?"

She heard the shadows scoff, "You lie – surely, Marissa is dead. Step into the light of the Maker's Eye."

Marissa glanced over to where the beam of golden light struck the floor. She walked over to the center of the beam, feeling the warm radiance kiss her skin. She held up both hands for the woman in shadows to see.

"Turn around," the ghost bade.

Marissa feigned amusement as she turned slowly around. "Shall I sing for you next? I've heard the Ballad of Vanity Shoal recently, so it's fresh in my mind. Sing me a song of my lass that is gone, goes by the name Vanity Shoal..."

"Enough of that!" the throaty vociferation exclaimed.

"Enough indeed!" Marissa said back. "You see me now. Please address to me who you are."

"I am Lady Marin."

Marissa blinked in surprise. True, Cassandra was only a young teenager when she left, but her voice seemed so... stout now. "Please, I ask that you show yourself."

Slowly the woman stepped forward and the blankets of inky shadows pulled away. If her voice had thrown Marissa off before, the woman before her now stole every word from her lips.

Before her, leaning with proper lady's etiquette against the baluster above was a woman just as strapping as her voice. The tight white priestess's garb of the Jasian Enclave cleaved to a thick torso and muscular arms. She was in finer fighting condition than Isa ever was. This was a woman built for battle, not diplomatic affairs.

"You've... grown," was all Marissa could muster.

"I've had to in the absence of my sister," the robust priestess returned.

Marissa looked down at her feet. "Yes, about that..."

Cassandra interrupted her. "I hold no illusions about the fate of my sister. I've heard it from bishops and adjutants alike within the very Citadel itself. Isa became a mercenary and died, betraying the very people she was sworn to protect."

Marissa's eyes shot up in surprise. "What? No! That's not what happened at all."

Cassandra held her head up haughtily. "Since Isa's abandonment of her family, I've had to take to training. With no Don in this home any longer, I've had to look to protecting myself and my people, guarding us from a villainy that has grown thick as a sea of thieves."

"Suren you can see that it's me, Mari, and not someone of disrepute?" Marissa asked, still reeling from what she had been told of Isa. Had they really labelled her a traitor? She was doing exactly as they had ordered! Was this what Vicente wasn't telling her?

Cassandra shrugged, seeming to read her very thoughts. "Even if I were to believe you were Marissa, that still makes you a traitor to the Maker for your actions against the Enclave, and a criminal. You've had your fun and you've wasted my time. Remove yourself from this castle posthaste."

Marissa was flabbergasted; this was all happening too fast. She needed to explain herself, she needed to tell Cassandra about Isa, about her words. Marissa looked up to the Lady of Marin and folded her arms over her breasts. "I'm afraid I cannot do that Lady Marin. I promised Isa that I would look after you."

Cassandra was agog. "Look after me? Look after me?" she snapped. "Let me tell you about Marissa de Cantor y Castile, you little puterelle. Marissa was nothing but a prissy little 'lady' who thought that she was above everyone, even her best friend, MY SISTER!" Cassandra was yelling now. "She convinced Isa to give up her virtuous, Maker-loving ways to become a deserter and a hypocrite to the Maker's name! She caused Isa to shame this House!"

Marissa acutely felt the point of something sharp pierce through the back of her dress and poke into her ribs.

"As you can see, Mari," Cassandra sneered from above, "Tossa de Marin has all the protection it needs."

CHAPTER THIRTEEN

Rusalka

Onna tossed Rusalka a brush.

Rusalka looked down at it confused. "What am I to do with this?" the orc asked.

"Brush the road out, of course," Onna replied.

Rusalka looked at the coarse bristles sticking out of the flat wooden paddle. She looked back to Onna, who was now dragging a crate over to their position.

They were in the stables like Marissa suggested, with all the barding and saddles nearby and ready to throw on the horses at a moment's notice. Now, they were waiting.

Rusalka's eyes looked from Onna and the crate back to the brush, and to Emmell, who merely shrugged at her in equal confusion. Tentatively, Rusalka reached up and pulled her own hair from under the morion helmet. She began to run the brush through her knotted black locks.

"What in the hells are ye doin'?"

Rusalka froze and looked up at Onna, whose face was screwed

up in a befuddled expression. Her eyes drifted to Onna's small cherubic hand which held another brush that was currently resting against the flank of their mare.

"You didn't specify who we were brushing the road out of," Rusalka said, feeling misled.

Tentatively she removed the sharp points from her clumpy hair, and she shifted it to the mare's neck. Rusalka saw from the corner of her eye Onna watching her speculatively, before she resumed brushing down the side of the horse.

Rusalka imitated the gnome's movements, noting the strands of black hair she was leaving on the thickly muscled neck of the tan mare.

"How long do you think this will take?" Emmell asked after only a minute of brushing in silence.

Onna shrugged, "I'm fer thinking this be politics of the gentry now. We be out of our element."

Rusalka's nose crinkled as she smelled the tension and fear on the growing number of guards outside. "And are all those men outside also politics of the gentry?"

"Nay," Onna answered, "they're here because of ye."

Rusalka stared at Onna who brandished a large smile. Despite a snort of disdain, she couldn't help but find herself snickering as well.

"Seriously, the prejudice of these people is ridiculous," Emmell remarked. "I thought it just might have been the Ayjub slavers, but since we've been here, I've been called a rodent numerous times."

"And a dog," Rusalka reported.

Emmell held up a claw. "And a dog."

"I dunno," Onna said as she patted the horse on its rump. "Only one has been disrespectful ta me so far, and I'm fer thinkin' its cuz Mari filled his belly with lead."

"That's because you look more like them – it's not so bad,"

Emmell pointed out. "Minus the fact that you're, well, minus a digit on each hand and foot from them, you could pass for one of their children, I'm guessing."

"It's cuz we gnomes hold our youth so well," Onna added with a larger smile.

"I've seen gnome men. I do not agree with that choice of words," Rusalka returned.

"The orc is correct," Emmell agreed. "I grew up in Spriggei. Our neighbor was Gnomelaneum just around the bend of Mount Secundus, so I've seen gnomish men too – they're balding when they're only teenagers!"

"Only the best-looking ones!" Onna shot back. "What are they fer needin' hair on their heads fer anyway? It's the beard that's important. It's character-defining. Long, thick, and good fer pullin'!"

"I... I don't think I have words for that," Emmell answered flatly.

"Small miracle," Onna said clasping her hands together as if in prayer. She nodded over to Rusalka, "What about ye, Tusker? I know spriggans ain't exactly attracted to each other the way gnomes, humans, and elves are."

"Spriggans are communal – we do what's important for all of our people," Emmell protested. "We love our men, no different than you do."

"Aye, mayhaps. But we 'love' our gnomish men, if ye get my meaning," Onna declared, wiggling her eyebrows. "Like humans, it's not merely an act o' makin' babies. We do it fer fun too!"

"And that's why your species breeds like rabbits," Emmell said, putting her small hands on her hips. "At least you are good at controlling your own numbers, seeing as how your kind constantly are blowing themselves up."

Onna went to remark, then closed her mouth again. "Point for the spriggan." She then shifted her focus back in Rusalka's direction. "What do ye like in yer brutish he-orcs, huh? They look like savages to us, but something has to draw ye green-skinned women to em' time and again. Is it the tusks? You like them curved and hard? Or all the bulging muscles? Do you like when their backs look like a topographical map of the Broken Teeth Mountains? All ridges and peaks?"

Emmell looked to Onna. "Wait, you know what topographical means?"

Onna waved her away. "Don't distract me, I wanna ere' what Rue has to say."

Rusalka looked away from her compatriots and focused on brushing the horse. "I really don't want to talk about it."

"Why not? I told you what I find attractive in a man," Onna declared.

"It wasn't as if she had a choice in that matter," Emmell defended.

"Don't tell me orcs are like spriggans, and only breed to make baby orcs?"

Rusalka shook her head. "Oh no, I think most orcs are a lot more like how Emmell describes gnomes to be."

Out of the corner of her eye, Rusalka saw Onna jab Emmell in the ribs, a big dumb smile splayed across her face. "See, another race that knows how to have fun. Ye should take lessons from us, Emmell. It's why gnomes and humans get along so well. If we knew orcs liked to romp so much too, I bet we'd never have wars!"

"No, just really bizarre orgies," Emmell commented dryly.

Rusalka tensed at the words.

"Look, I really don't think Rue is comfortable with this," Emmell said.

"Why not, we're all grown women, even you, Emmell," Onna said proudly. "We've just spent six months on a boat together. I mean, really, we have no secrets anymore, or not too many at least."

Rusalka thought about how easy it was for Onna to kill, almost as easy as it was for an orc to kill. "We all have secrets," she murmured.

"What's that supposed to mean?" Onna asked.

Rusalka froze. Dimly she could hear Onna launch into a small tirade about her comment, but that wasn't what had her attention. No, it was something else, something distant. Above the clamor of the bustling harbor city, the hawking of merchants, and the ever-present singing of people Marissa called juglares, she thought she caught the sound of shifting armor. A lot of shifting armor.

Her head turned towards the stable doors at the two men who were watching them bicker. They were obviously tense at the presence of Rusalka, and with Onna's big mouth they knew she was an orc by now, but there wasn't an expectant tension. It was as if they knew something was about to happen. Rusalka sniffed, their pheromones pungent in the air – no, this was nervousness coming from them.

She sniffed again, there was something more. Was it... oil?

Rusalka turned away from Onna's barking. "Emmell, with me."

"Wait? What?" Onna said, clearly confused. "Where are ye going? Awgh come on, Tusker, I dinna mean it!" Rusalka heard the two ambling after her as she quickly approached the two men standing station at the stable entrance.

"Am I allowed to enter the bailey?" Rusalka asked the men.

One of them nodded, "Yes. You just can't enter the castle proper or any other buildings, other than the stables." She could tell by his perspiration that her very presence was making him even more nervous. The other guard twitched and she kept her hands far from her weapons.

"What about the ramparts? Are they off limits?"

The two men looked at one another as Emmell came up, panting from behind. "Doña Cantor asked us to make sure the horses were comfortable. We shouldn't go anywhere until we know everything's okay."

Rusalka looked back at the horses and she saw the lead mare's ear twitch nervously. She felt it too. "Everything is not okay." She looked to the two guards, "Well?"

"N... no," the talkative one stammered. He pointed out the large doors to the right. "Stairs are over there, just don't try and get into the castle that way."

"We won't."

"I still don't understand what's going on?" Onna asked.

Rusalka was hardly listening to her, though, moving quickly. As she followed the instructions of the two guardsmen, she could see the dozen or so other Marin protectors beginning to mobilize and move with her. She tried to force herself not to run, but the clank and rattle sound in the distance dominated all of her thoughts.

She took the stairs two at a time. At one point she watched one of the guards going for his sword in alarm. "We're guests! We're guests!" Onna squawked behind her, and the man stalled just enough to let her pass. After several minutes she was at the top of the ramparts facing southwest and looking down at the city spread out before her like colorful pebbles spread out on the shore of a pond. Down below, just in the bay, she could see the *Bella Dahlia* swaying slightly in the barely undulating waters.

It momentarily gave her a sense of longing. She never felt so alive, or like she truly belonged, as she did in the months at sea. She shook the thought away.

Onna was panting heavily behind her, "Okay Tusker, what in the hells is it ye're looking fer? If it was only to escape having ta answer me questions about ye men..."

"Shhhh!" Rusalka hissed. She tried to follow the grating and clomping she heard from the stables. Her eyes drifted down the steep angle of the cliffside city. She caught a glimpse of her horror between a yellow roofed house, and what looked like a bakery of some sort. Light sparkled and glimmered, again and again from that spot.

"There!" she said pointing in the general direction.

Onna moved forward and squinted. "What is it that's got ye knickers in a twist, Tusker? I ain't fer seein' nothing but a big ol' city."

"Where?" Emmell asked, producing a small cylinder with a piece of glass on each end.

Rusalka leaned over and pointed to the best of her ability to where she saw the flickering light. She watched as Emmell brought the contraption up to her large eye. "Oh, blimey," the spriggan muttered.

She reached over and handed the unusual ocular device to Onna, who did the same as she. "Blimey is right."

Onna pulled away and handed the strange leather-wrapped cylinder to Rusalka. She had seen both the gnome and spriggan use it before, especially when Onna was in the crow's nest on the Bella Dahlia, but Rusalka had never touched it.

"Helps if ye close yer other eye, ye won't feel so disoriented." Onna said as Rusalka carefully took it and held it to her eye.

Instantly everything grew larger and closer by a magnitude beyond Rusalka's understanding. She saw what she heard, there marching its way up the steep cobblestone road towards Tossa de Marin.

Soldiers. Many soldiers marching directly towards them, all heavily armed and armored. Rusalka reached with her free hand for her weapon. Instantly she felt the small pricks of Emmell's nails as she clamped down on her hands. "No, they're not as close as you think they are!"

Rusalka turned away from the looking glass to look down at Emmell, who nodded with her head back to the city below. "Look without the glass," she ordered.

Rusalka did and saw once more the glittering armored specks making their way forward, now on a direct line for the castle. She held her eye up to the looking glass, and the lead guardsmen materialized before her; Bevan Ó Cuana. And next to him was a towering figure shrouded in an armor that Rusalka had only seen once before – in the coliseum. It felt like they were only a few feet away. She could almost touch them. With her other hand, she reached up and tried to do just that.

"Oh fer the Maker, put that thing down, ye look like an idiot," Onna ordered.

Bewildered, Rusalka lowered the glass and the man shrank back down to the size of her thumbnail. "Amazing," she breathed.

"I'll explain how it works later. We've got more pressing problems," Emmell said.

Rusalka couldn't agree more.

"How in the hells did ye know?" Onna asked as they swiftly made their way back down the ramparts.

"Platemail grates," Rusalka answered.

"Wait, ye mean ye heard that, over everything else?" Onna asked bewildered.

"It's not a sound you ever forget," Rusalka closed her eyes, trying not to think about the last time a large contingent of heavily armed and armored men marched into a fort she was in. Though she didn't view her kind very highly, she'll never forget the slaughter she witnessed that day. The children... no species deserved that, not even hers.

They made their way back to the stables, and the two guards who were stationed by their horses looked at them uncomfortably once more. Onna ran to their mares and started throwing the saddles on the two beasts' backs.

"Onna slow down," Emmell protested. "We have to find a way to alert Mari first."

Onna looked at the spriggan, "I know, but did ye see them, Em? Looked to be about twenty at least."

"Twenty-six," Emmell responded calmly.

"Aye, and the guard who we let go was leadin' the pack! And the biggin', looked like they had their own orc with them."

"I noticed that as well," Rusalka added.

"I be thinkin' Bevan said what he said, just to save his own skin. Pullin' on the Cap'n's heart strings."

"Doña Cantor," Emmell corrected.

"Bugger that, she may be the only surviving Cantor, but she won't be if we don't get moving!"

"And how are we going to go about that?" Rusalka asked. "The moment I get near a door to the castle, they'll attack," she finished with a nod of her head to the guards.

"And I'm guessing if we try and just leave while Mari's inside, they'll detain us, or attack us as well," Emmell supplied.

"And they're gonna attack if we do nothin' afore all them troops get here. They's lookin' fer a reason to get at Rue, each and every one of us be's knowin' it fer what it is, cept Mari."

Rusalka wanted to object, wanted desperately to defend the Jasian, but she knew the truth of Onna's words. Marissa was an idealist who was either blind, or blatantly trying to ignore the vitriol around her for Emmell and Rusalka.

Onna threw the saddle on the lead mare and began cinching the straps, "I'm not talkin' cross bout the Cap'n, I love her just as much as both of ye, but we be knowin' the truth of it. Mari'll be far better off than ye two will in the next five minutes if ye don't be tryin' to get out of here."

Rusalka folded her arms over her chest. "You want to just leave her? We can't!" She was astonished – she knew Onna was capable of a lot of things, but abandoning Mari just seemed too far.

Onna stopped what she was doing and ran her fingers through

her hair. "No, I dunna, but what else can ye do? Can ye fight off the Marin guard and twenty-six heavily armed soldiers?"

Rusalka scowled at Onna, but she knew the truth of it. She couldn't. Even if she were consumed with fury, she couldn't hope to defend herself against that many, let alone protect Onna and Emmell. One, if not all of them, would die, because the humans would not treat them as civilized people needing to be detained. They would be treated as animals, as monsters, and they would be put down.

But Mari alone...

"I don't like it, but in this regard I do think Onna is right," Emmell stated, expressing Rusalka's very thoughts. "We will not survive this. Not even with your skill and strength, Rue, or Onna's cunning. We should leave."

"And go where?" Rusalka asked. "Where is safe for us right now? If Mari gets captured here and now, we can't just amble back to Loja de Cantor. They'd never let us in, and even if they did, we'd be right back in the same position we are now. We can't do anything here, without Mari."

Both women realized Rusalka was correct; she could read it on their faces and smell it by the shift in their pheromones.

"Bella Dahlia," Emmell remarked. She looked up. "We need to get back to the ship. The three of us can control her, at least to take her out of port and stick to the coast."

Onna shook her head, "Not much more than that though, ye needs a crew if ye are pursued. And we three ain't no crew for the Dahlia. A sloop, maybe."

Emmell looked rejected, but Rusalka knew that they had few options. "No, this is a start, a good plan. We take the Dahlia and pull from port, then we find a way later to put to shore, then go to Loja de Cantor and see if Mari made it back."

Even at this, Onna was shaking her head. "She won't. She'll be arrested. She ain't fer being killed like ye both will be, but no, she'll be arrested."

"It was your idea to leave, and now what? Are you saying no?" Emmell asked.

"That's exactly what I'm sayin,'" Onna said. "I don't plan on goin' anywhere, but the two of ye, ye need's ta go to the ship and get her ready.

"And what are you going to do?" Emmell asked.

Onna gave them both a lopsided grin. "I'm gonna get the Cap'n." Rusalka stepped forward and Onna held up her hands, "I'm fer knowin' ye wants ta protect Mari, but face it, Tusker, ye and Em stick out like a couple o' sore thumbs. And we know the humans will have no qualms about killin' ye, no justification needed. Me though, it's exactly as we talked about. I can pass fer one o' they kids, right?"

Rusalka's scowl grew at the prospect of not just leaving Mari behind, but now Onna. She was looking at Emmell who she thought would be sharing the same sentiment. The spriggan was not. In fact, she was smiling. "You have a plan?"

Rusalka looked back at the gnome, who pulled out Mari's flint-lock pistol and black powder. "As a matter o' fact, I do."

CHAPTER FOURTEEN

Marissa de Cantor y Castile

"Cassie, please you're making a mistake!"

The hard woman who Marissa no longer recognized stared down at her. "I think it is you who is mistaken, whoever you are. Marissa de Cantor y Castile is dead. I'll accept no charlatans here who claim otherwise."

"But Cass..." Marissa began, but grunted as the blade pricked a little deeper through the fabric of her clothing.

"No, Mari. It's time for you to leave." Cassandra called down in finality.

She felt the tip dip further and could feel the back of her garment growing wet, whether from her sweat or blood, she didn't know. Marissa looked back to the guard that held her at sword point. The guard was very slender for a man, dressed in the same Marin gambeson and leather breeches as all the others she had met outside. He was sporting the same morion helmet as all the others as well, but unlike the other guards she had met, this helmet had a special full facemask of the same steel shrouding their identity.

Only a pair of dark orbs glittered at her under the light of the Maker's eye. Very curious.

Marissa sighed, shaking her head as Cassandra turned away from her. She took a first step towards the door muttering angrily to herself, "Wear a dress they said, you'll look regal, they said." The short sword twisted against her skin. "Yeah, yeah. I'm going."

Marissa moved towards the door, through the scattered array of obstacles before her. As she maneuvered around a wide, uphol-stered chair she felt the sword tip leave her back, as the guard bumped into the chair with his hip.

Marissa capitalized on the moment, spinning away from where she knew the last position of the sword to be. She grabbed the chair the guard bumped into and heaved it with all her might. Already off guard, the swordsman stumbled forward, his weapon sliding between the wooden slats of the chair and dipping into a cushion deeply.

Marissa didn't miss how easily the sword cut through the fabric. She reached down and twisted the legs, wrenching the weapon free from the guard, and tearing a long seam through the chair to launch downy white feathers all around them. The feathers drifted through the light of the Maker's Eye like snowflakes.

Now unarmed, Marissa moved in on the guard to take him out of commission. Though she was terrible at fighting, she figured that the small-framed Marin guard couldn't weigh much more than she did. Plus, she had the luxury of training with an orc while trapped aboard a boat for the last six months. She had to have learned something... right?

The guard tried correcting himself awkwardly, valuing the sword over all else. Marissa, however, was more concerned with not taking a life. She wanted Cassandra to listen to her, to take the time to see it was her. She doubted the Lady of Marin would give her that time if she killed the guard in front of her.

As the guard reached for the sword, Marissa dropped the remains of the chair, hiked up her skirts, and kicked out. She caught the guard in the stomach, driving all wind from the person in a startled cry.

A distinctly feminine cry.

Marissa didn't waste any time thinking about this startling predicament. She reached over and grabbed the wide brim of the morion helmet with both hands. Growling, she wrenched it forward, tearing the leather chin strap from the guard's head. The woman stumbled forward, falling to the ground. As the helmet tore away, a cascade of brown locks broke free of the shackles that held them at bay.

The petite, curly-haired woman turned around and faced Marissa in astonishment. She couldn't be a day over nineteen winters, but it was her dark eyes that seared with an intensity Marissa recognized all too well. Atop the gallery, Marissa heard the audible click of a crossbow locking in place. "One more move and I will kill you, puterelle!" the woman from above hissed.

Marissa glanced up to see the large muscle-laden woman holding the crossbow level at Marissa. At that range, the woman couldn't miss. Winded from the momentary ordeal, Marissa dropped the morion helmet to the ground, and raised her hands in the air.

"No!" the guard called up to the archer. Marissa could tell by the way the curly-haired young lady looked at her, just like so many others before her, as if recognition finally set in.

Tentatively, Marissa lowered her hand and held it out to the woman. The guard took Marissa's outstretched hand, and Marissa pulled the young woman to her feet.

"Hello, Cassandra."

PRIESTESS CASSANDRA MARIN SAT ON THE CHAIR ACROSS from Marissa, weeping silently into her hands for several minutes. She was still dressed as a guard. Marissa tried to remain stoic, but she too felt herself misting up once more for the loss of Isa.

Finally, Cassandra sniffled one final time, and cleaned away the remaining tears with her left thumb. When she looked up at Marissa again, her eyes were red and puffy, but she was composed. "I'm sorry," the young woman confessed, "here I am crying over someone who I thought dead for the last three winters, and you... you've come home to find your whole world in shambles."

Marissa reached out and lightly rested her hand on top of Cassandra's. To her surprise, the priestess turned her hand over and gripped it tightly. "It's okay," Marissa confessed. "I had a good long cry last night with Vicente, and to be honest at this point I'm too overwhelmed for it to really set in just yet."

Cassandra sniffed, "I'll bet." She looked up at Marissa, and Marissa was alarmed to see how much Cassandra had grown since she last saw her – not just into a woman. - In her eyes, there was wisdom there now. The kind that was hard-earned. "Have you spoken to Augusto yet?"

Marissa shook her head, "I came to you first. It was Isa's wish that I look after you. It was the last thing she asked of me."

Cassandra squeezed her hand tightly. "Of course Isa would say that. She always was such a big sister." She let out a laugh at the thought. "But how she adored you!"

"And I her," Marissa admitted.

"I was always a little jealous of the bond the two of you had. It was as if from the moment you met, you became inseparable."

"Isa loved you very much, too."

Cassandra waved the comment away. "I know she did. It was just foolish jealousy of an adolescent girl. Anyway, it's good you've come to see me first then, though if I'd known you were back, I wouldn't have orchestrated..." she motioned to the state of the room, and her own dress, "all of this. I hate armor, it's so heavy."

Marissa snickered and nodded up to the balustrade. "Why did you set this up? Why did you want me to believe that woman was you?"

"Things have changed around here, Mari. I can't tell you how many times now, someone has come back claiming to be Isa returned from war. It has gotten so tiring. This was the first claiming to be Marissa de Cantor y Castile, though."

"Vicente actually mentioned something similar, since my father..."

Marissa could tell her words didn't surprise Cassandra in the slightest. "While you and Isa were off playing purists-in-training, charlatans have multiplied in the land like roaches. Privateers have come to port more often, bringing with them vagrants of every type."

"I don't understand, isn't that what the adjutant is here to stop, or at the very least the viscount?" Marissa exclaimed.

"Your old beau has levied himself into the position of provisional viscount."

Marissa blinked in surprise, "Augusto is the viscount?"

Cassandra nodded, "Vicente didn't tell you?"

Marissa flushed, "No, we kind of fell into an argument before he could mention it, I suppose."

"I see."

"Things have been a little awkward between us, I'll admit," Marissa posited. "But you were saying about Augusto – he really is the viscount?"

Cassandra nodded once.

"How is this possible?"

"Right," Cassandra said with another nod, "you need backstory. Our last viscount, I'm not sure if you remember him, Don Raphael de la Torga?"

Marissa shook her head.

"Oh, well he was a kind man. Anyway, he passed, from what most believed was some sort of heart complication. To temporarily fill his place, Adjutant Love placed the crown jewel of Castile, Augusto Cruz, in the spot until a proper vote could be levied amongst the Dons to properly fill in a new viscount. It was no surprise to anyone really. Older Dons like my father and yours never sought such a position out, and Augusto seemed almost bred for courtly politics. He's dashing and regal, charming and well-spoken, with just the right level of cruelty and lack of compassion that allows him to make decisions that would feel impossible to some. Besides, even Adjutant Love suggested that it was time to put someone with youth and vigor in such a position, instead of the curmudgeonly old bastards that occupied the position for the last fifty winters out of some type of secret dons club seniority."

Marissa raised an eyebrow.

Cassandra smiled. "His words, not mine. Adjutant Love went on to say that until a proper ruling from the Citadel could be established on who would properly take the title, it was to be a... temporary position."

"Okay, I confess, I'm unfamiliar with this. About how long does something like that take?" Marissa asked, genuinely confused.

Cassandra shrugged. "Like you, I've little interest in a life at court. Generally it seems mostly about gossip and currying favors. So, I paid it little mind at the time. It wasn't until my parents died that I took notice. And to answer your question, it's usually completed in about one winter, sometimes less."

Marissa nodded, wanting to know about Cassandra's mother and father, as they had once been like second parents to her, but she withheld, patiently waiting out Cassandra's tale. "So, they're a bit overdue."

Cassandra nodded, "Yes, about two winters overdue in fact, and while it can happen, I'm sure. The play of events that have transpired up to now has been a little too conveniently in Augusto's favor."

"Please explain."

"Aside from becoming the provisional viscount, Cruz has been either buying out the other Dons directly or absorbing their lands through unusual passings of Dons and even Doñas."

Marissa looked about the antechamber, seeing how little it resembled what she once knew. She knew this was the best segue she was going to get. "Is that how you lost your parents?"

Cassandra stared over longingly to what Marissa knew was her father's old quarters. "Truthfully? I don't know." She shook her head in dismay and turned to look Marissa in the eyes. "I'd love to be able to blame somebody, anybody, especially Don Cruz, but I can't. Not with any certainty, anyhow." She held up her hands in a passive gesture, and continued, "It wouldn't be proper as a priestess of the Maker to harbor ill will towards the man."

Marissa wanted to reply with something snide. She often heard such rhetoric amongst the exactors, but she kept her mouth shut.

"The fact remains, they're gone, and they are not coming back. The Pale took them, just as I am told it took your mother."

Marissa bit her lip. "How long now?"

"Almost two winters to the day. The anniversary of their disappearance is two weeks from today. There will be a feast, and dancing, and some juglares re-enacting how my mother and father met and fell in love. You should come."

Marissa smiled, "I will."

There was a moment of uncomfortable silence as the two digested each other's news before Marissa asked, "With your parents gone, you were what, seventeen winters old? How is it you kept your lands?"

"I have given no one, not even Augusto, room to take them. By swearing fealty to the Jasian Enclave and becoming a priestess in their name I was able to keep these lands untouched by Cruz, having them consecrated as holy ground." She motioned to all the unusually large number of candles that had confounded Marissa earlier. "As long as I stay a priestess for the Enclave, swear away marriage, and vow to remain chaste, neither Cruz nor any other can hope to steal these lands away from my family, legally or otherwise – not even the Enclave itself."

Marissa whistled. "You gave up all of that for your lands?"

"For the people, Mari. Castile needs to have hope. Tossa de Marin provides it. All these guards are here by choice. To protect this place from what they fear Castile is becoming. Maria up there, is from the Citadel. Like Isa, like you, she aspires to serve as a guardian for the Maker."

Marissa leaned forward and whispered, "Is she an Exactor?"

"She is my aide, and my protector," Cassandra declared. "Her role in the Enclave, however, is not spoken."

Marissa nodded – she got the gist. "Why hasn't the Jasian Enclave stepped in if they suspect some form of wrongdoing? Why hasn't Adjutant Love recanted the nomination from Cruz, if he has despoiled Castile so thoroughly in the last three winters?"

"Because there is no ironclad proof of any means of ill-repute," Cassandra replied. "Cruz's purchases and claims have all been within the bounds of legality. He's doing what dons do; he's simply more aggressive, better prepared, very successful, and ridiculously lucky in timing. But he has done nothing wrong. For all I know – and I do know so very little – Augusto might be merely a puppet."

Marissa snickered. "For someone desiring to stay out of courtly gossip, the mention of a super-secret shadowy backer sure feels... gossipy."

"Perhaps you're right," Cassandra confessed. "Perhaps I'm still just a girl wishing that the death of her parents was part of some huge conspiracy, and not because they carelessly sailed too close to the one thing they warned me all my life to stay clear of."

Cassandra stared back at her father's chambers for several long minutes, before turning back to Marissa once more. "So... outside of my sister's decree of 'watching over me', what does the resurrected Marissa de Cantor y Castile plan to do now?"

Marissa shook her head with a sigh. "To be honest, I don't know. I've spent so long just trying to get all those women home, and then get home myself, I never planned what was next. But... now I've returned to find my home isn't really home anymore. My father murdered, my mother lost at sea, and the only explanations I have for any of it come from a bitter young man who I neglected in my childhood, and who somehow blames me for all these terrible disparities."

"Mari... I am not siding with Vicente, but can you not blame him for distrusting you?" Cassandra pointed out. "He lost his father too, much as we all have too frequently lately, and every noble he's had dealings with has had ulterior motives that would leave both he, and those he cares about, destitute. Loja de Cantor is all they have left, and he's about to lose it all to either a cruel and arrogant man, or a girl who was little more than a spoiled brat to him as a child."

Marissa looked down to see herself wringing her own hands. "I'm... different now. Winters of slavery have changed me from the child I was before I left." She unknotted her hands and pointed out towards the door she came in from, "I have friends out there who are counting on me to sort this out. I have promised them homes, homes that won't exist unless I can find two people to vouch that I am me within the next day."

Now it was Cassandra who reached out and pulled Marissa's hand to her. "And you will have them, Lady Cantor."

"You... you will vouch for me?"

Cassandra's eyes twinkled with excitement, "I'll do you one better. I will file on your behalf myself. I am a priestess, it is within my rights here in Castile. Though you will still need to see Adjutant Love, I will appeal to the few remaining dons left that I can count on. You will not lose Cantor, Mari." Marissa's eyes began to water a little, and Cassandra continued, "But, that is the easy part. It is you that will have to earn Vicente's trust, and the trust of the vassals beneath you. Being a Doña is not easy work, Mari – I don't envy you."

Above them, Maria called down urgently, "Lady Marin!"

Both women stood from their chairs, Marissa immediately fearing the worst for her friends.

"What is it?" Cassandra asked.

"The viscount's guard. mum," Maria replied, her eyes darting to Marissa then back to Cassandra. "They're here to arrest Lady Cantor. They're callin' her a murderer."

"What of my friends?" Marissa said, distraught. "Where are my friends?"

Maria looked back to Marissa, and Marissa could read the distrust in her eyes.

"Tell her, Maria." Cassandra patiently ordered.

Maria nodded, and started to explain what was happening in the courtyard.

CHAPTER FIFTEEN

Rusalka

The courtyard was, in fact, in chaos.

"Onna has the worst plans," Rusalka yelled down to the spriggan in her lap.

"Agreed!" Emmell agreed loudly over the screaming and pandemonium around them. "From now on, Mari makes all the plans."

"Agreed!" Rusalka mirrored.

Thunderous crackling erupted on the rampart they had been on minutes earlier, quickly followed by screams of surprise and panic. Seconds later, Rusalka could see plumes of smoke and fire.

Rusalka looked down at Emmell to make sure she was holding on tight, and instead she found the spriggan admiring the growing smoke and licking orange flames.

A guard ran in front of them, and Rusalka pulled hard on the reins to get their mare to veer away from the man at the last moment. The sharp yank brought Emmell's eyes forward and holding onto the mane for dear life.

Rusalka rushed the horse forward towards the back gate that they entered in. The large gate was firmly lowered baring her way.

"Onna..." she heard Emmell hiss.

Rusalka didn't slow, instead pushing the horse forward towards the gate, hoping the little gnome would arrive in time to open it. If she slowed, it would give the guards a chance to realize what she was doing.

They moved closer and closer. Rusalka considered her next move should things not work as planned, when the gate began to raise. *How does she do it?* Rusalka thought in wonder.

Rusalka hunkered over and put more speed into the horse – if she caught it perfectly, Onna could lower the gate as soon as she was through. As the gate came high enough, Rusalka could see clearly to the other side. Her spirits plummeted.

A line of guards stood on the other side, these bearing the same symbol that she saw marching up the street with Emmell's special glass. She could only assume they were with Bevan. They held large tower shields and spears. Apparently, this guard was more prepared for a rear escape than the Marin troupe was.

Rusalka pulled back mightily on the reins, causing the horse to stop and rear up on her hind legs. They would not be able to make it through a line of spearmen on horseback. She had seen that folly too often in the coliseums.

She wheeled the horse about and began to ride another way.

"This isn't the plan!" Emmell yelled.

"We won't survive the plan," Rusalka snarled back.

A scream of alarm behind her brought Rusalka's head around to see the gate crashing back down as the spearmen were entering. They scrambled back, nearly getting crushed by the large thick iron. Apparently Onna realized what happened, too.

"What are we going to do, then, charge the line of guards out front?" Emmell asked, incredulous.

"Did they have spears?"

"I didn't see any, but I didn't see those guys either," Emmell admitted.

"Point taken."

More crackling and more smoke and soon Rusalka came upon large thatches of burning hay.

"She's gonna use up all of Mari's black powder," Emmell remarked.

Rusalka couldn't disagree. Onna was burning right through it. Soon there would be nothing left for the Jasian to pack her pistol with. "I'm sure Mari will make do."

Emmell scoffed. "She fights with the skill of a three-legged drunken cow."

"C'mon now, you don't need to insult the cow."

A shrieking whoosh flew past Rusalka's ear, cutting their conversation short.

"Archers!" Emmell cried a second later.

Rusalka wheeled the horse towards the entrance of the inner bailey where she could see Bevan and his men pouring in. A number of them with crossbows fanned out.

"I count eight," Emmell yelled in response to Rusalka's unspoken question. Rusalka panned around – they needed to make it to the outer bailey if they were to hope to have any chance at all.

"Ditch the horse?" Emmell asked.

Rusalka shook her head. "Not yet." There was no way Emmell could outrun any human on foot. She may be lithe, but she wasn't faster than the long gait of a human. Nor did she have the endurance to outlast one in a flat-out run.

Rusalka could do it, but Emmell had no chance. She needed this horse. Rusalka angled the horse towards the steps of the ramparts. She was surprised how well the horse reacted under the violence around her. She was used to animals panicking around her kind – at least until she became a gladiator. Those creatures were trained to be tamer around such bedlam. Whoever Mari's father was, he had a similar standard for the mares as well, and for that, Rusalka was grateful. The horse followed her direction without hesitation and took the stone steps up to the top of the ramparts.

"There will be no steps down to the ramparts for the outer bailey," Emmell told her as the horse began to race along the edge at a harrowing speed.

"I know," Rusalka answered.

Crossbow bolts slammed into the stone behind them, launching jagged shrapnel chips and thick white dust in their wake.

"Well, Onna was right, they certainly don't care about keeping us alive. I'm really starting to dislike humans in general... the captain excluded of course," Emmell remarked.

Rusalka didn't even try to reply. Her breathing was already labored in directing the horse, her heart hammering in her chest. She could feel violence within her churning, desperate to be released. It vibrated in her chest like a living thing clawing through her, trying to escape. She wanted nothing more than to turn the horse around and charge into the swaths of men, to tear at them with her bare hands, to rip them into puddles of liquid and viscera.

How the spriggan could remain so calm while being shot at, whilst riding on the edge of a thirty-foot sheer drop into a tumble of extremely solid and colorful homes below, was beyond her. Emmell's safety was the only thing keeping the beast within Rusalka firmly locked away.

Rusalka risked a glance down to the inner bailey to see half the men now charging into the castle itself. The Marin guards scrambled between trying to put out fires and trying to stop Bevan's troops from harming anyone... well, anyone human, apparently.

In the center of the maelstrom stood the barbaric woman in gladiator armor. Her horned helmet was some kind of skull from an animal Rusalka did not recognize. She was massive, larger than even Rusalka herself. Corded muscles, braided thick like ship rigging, held the largest crossbow Rusalka had ever laid eyes on.

The woman was drawing a bead on them, and Rusalka could see the woman was just as calculating, just as meticulous as the spriggan in her lap. She would take her time, and she wouldn't miss.

Rusalka urged the horse faster, and hunkered low, leaning with the turn to make it smoother.

"Are you just going to run us in a circle?" Emmell shouted up at her as they began to wend the way back around towards the castle proper.

Rusalka, though, was looking for her opportunity, and it was in that moment that she spotted it. The one thing that all old castles seemed to share was that they were always in some state of constant repair. Rusalka saw this from when her tribes would take over derelict castles and rotting fortresses. Rotten, wooden scaffolding would be dotted about, fixing the stone that would inevitably become loose from time, wear, weather, or battle. Though Rusalka was nowhere near as smart as Onna, or Em, or even Mari for that matter, she figured that seaside castles must too take their share of weathering thanks to the salty sea spray.

She was glad she was not wrong.

On the outside of the inner bailey, constructed against the stone itself, were layers of wooden scaffolding. It hung suspended by dozens of ropes and was perhaps only a handful of feet below them. Another handful of feet below that were the outer bailey ramparts.

"Rue, please tell me you're not thinking what I think you're thinking?"

Without responding, Rusalka angled the mare toward the suspended scaffolding.

"Rue, basic math lesson. If a scaffold can hold about twenty-five stone, and a horse weighs seventy-nine stone, how much more does the horse weigh than the scaffolding can hold?"

Rusalka smiled. "Don't know, I haven't quite made it to ten yet in counting."

She felt Emmell brace against her, "Then a physics lesson perhaps? The weight of something falling is..."

Emmell's lesson morphed into a scream as Rusalka launched them out over the empty space towards the slowly swaying wooden scaffolding.

Rusalka felt triumphant as the front hooves struck hard against the planks of wood. She felt even better as the horse's hind legs also landed gracefully. She had done it!

That attitude changed half a heartbeat later, as the momentum of their jump swung the scaffolding wildly forward, further away from the inner baily ramparts and out further towards the openness of a thirty-foot plummet. Such a thing wouldn't have concerned her so much except for the groaning and snapping she heard in rapid succession as she realized all of the pulleys holding the scaffolding in place broke at the same time due to the sheer force of the load that was now upon it.

She propelled the terrified mare forward, fighting against the inexorable pull of gravity as the wooden scaffold began to decant away, pitching them at a terrible angle.

The mare leapt once more into the openness around them, but it was a weak jump, and the wall was fast approaching them. Rusalka didn't think they would make it to the outer bailey, so close, yet just a breadth too far away.

Then she felt something slam into the side of her head. She figured one of the pulleys must've bounced off her morion helmet, but the pressure stayed where it was. It was annoying to be sure, and in fact it was beginning to ache more than a little. Rusalka wanted to reach up and see what it was, but she knew she had to hold tight to the reins, especially on the slim chance that they somehow cleared the fast approaching wall. Yet when she looked down, she saw that her hands already reflexively let go of the reins, and that the horse and Emmell were fast leaving her.

It was with a growing horror that she realized she was leaving them. Something knocked her off her trajectory.

Her world seemed to slow down to the speed of dripping molasses as she watched Emmell and the horse get further and further away. She watched as the front hooves cleared onto the rampart of the outer bailey, but the hind quarters of the horse missed its mark and hit the wall. The horse fought and ambled with a terror of its own, its hooves grinding and railing against the stones, ripping away pieces of wall as it fought to find some semblance of a perch.

Miraculously, it found it.

The hind hooves found a small outcropping of stones, and it heaved its massive frame onto the outer bailey ramparts. Without direction, the horse took off at a dead run, intent on fleeing the danger around it. Emmell was holding on for dear life, unable to take the reins.

Emmell would be safe, Rusalka mused in that strangely bloated moment of time. She wondered idly what caused her to let go of the reins. Her grip was solid up until that very point.

As she turned her head, she could briefly see the beastly woman with the crossbow. She was lowering the massive hulk of a weapon, and a smile played about the bottom of the skull helmet. Rusalka understood. She had been shot off of the horse. Shot in the head and knocked off the horse while it was jumping through the air!

It was a strange realization to have in that final moment as gravity took hold of her body, and yet it was the only one she could clutch onto as she fell helplessly away to the bevy of very solid, very painful-looking multicolored buildings below.

CHAPTER SIXTEEN

Marissa de Cantor y Castile

M arissa had no time to formulate a plan as the thunderous sound of platemail hammered through the long corridors to the antechamber that she and the priestess Cassandra stood in. Within moments, over a dozen men charged into the room brandishing all forms of weapons meant to inflict maximum harm upon her. She was almost angry now that she was forced to leave her flintlock pistol and dagger back with the mare. It was so unfair. Why was she the only one that was apparently playing by the rules? Hells, she wasn't even quite sure what the rules were.

"Put those weapons down!" Cassandra ordered. "There will be no bloodshed in a consecrated house of the Maker."

None of the guards moved. Marissa looked up to see that Maria was surrounded, swords leveled directly at the stout woman's midsection. To her credit though, she didn't even acknowledge them, but kept her crossbow firmly leveled at Marissa.

"Lovely," she muttered sarcastically.

Then to her astonishment, Bevan Ó Cuana walked into the antechamber.

"Alférez Ó Cuana!" she said in alarm. "What's going on?"

"Actually Doña, it's teniente now. Don Cruz promoted me last night," he answered her.

She raised an eyebrow, "Um, congratulations I guess?"

Bevan dipped his head to her. "Thank you, Doña."

"So, why all of this?" Marissa asked of the men brandishing weapons at her.

"I told you yesterday that you were under arrest, did I not?"

"Well... I suppose, but then you sort of ran away," she answered.

"I had to save as many lives as I could."

Cassandra looked over to Marissa intently. "What is this man talking about? Why were you under arrest?"

"You didn't tell her?" Bevan asked, mildly surprised. "And here I was going to charge her with sheltering outlaws."

Marissa looked over to Cassandra apologetically. "Yesterday on our way to Loja de Cantor, we encountered some men trying to throw a young girl off the cliffs."

Bevan's posture stiffened. "She was a wanted poacher and was resisting arrest."

"You were going to throw a teenage girl to her death!" Marissa snapped.

"It was the teniente's orders," Bevan pressed back.

"So, you killed them?" Cassandra asked in shock.

Marissa shook her head. "They attacked me first, specifically after I told them who I was, while on Cantor lands!"

Cassandra turned and scowled at the men, and Marissa was alarmed to see so much of Isa in that expression. "Is this true, teniente? Did she identify herself as Lady Cantor, and then your men still attacked?"

Bevan's posture did not wither under her scrutiny. "Senorita, how many charlatans have you seen yourself claiming to be long lost kin? If you would've seen her yesterday, in the bedraggled shape she was in, with the company she keeps..."

"And yet you recognized me," Marissa spat, "and you verily said such to me."

"Of course," Bevan replied. "My unit was down. People were dead, and the teniente was in terrible shape. I had to think of their survival."

"So, you played along but didn't believe me?" Marissa said in growing disgust.

"Doña Cantor... you are making this unduly difficult for everyone," he said slowly. "As I told you yesterday, come peacefully, and we can get this all worked out."

As he said the words, Marissa could hear screams of commotion outside, and what sounded to her like multiple tiny pistol shots. "It doesn't sound like you want to take me peacefully."

"I agree with the Lady Cantor on this one," Cassandra agreed. "What is going on in my courtyard?"

Bevan's eyes glittered with ire at Marissa. "Her friends are... resisting, and at this moment trying to escape on horseback." He quickly composed himself, adding, "Though both entrances are fully guarded, the effort should prove itself to be rather trite, in short order."

"And then what, you'll capture them?" Marissa asked.

"Don Cruz specifically asked for you, Doña. The fate of your companions – who are not by nature, civilized people – I cannot say."

"You son of a bitch. I should've let Rue kill you!" Marissa barked as she lunged forward. She was surprised to see Cassandra's arm holding her back.

"No violence in the house of the Maker," she repeated calmly.

"Doña Cantor, please," Bevan pleaded, "I harbor you no ill will. I am trying to do my job."

"By killing innocent people?"

Bevan grit his teeth. "By enforcing the law."

"And what law is that?" Marissa asked. "What law says it is acceptable to kill people because they don't look like you, or act like you? Rusalka has done nothing here but try and survive and at every turn she is chastised, threatened, or accosted simply for being who she is. You assaulted us first, and she defended me, you know this is true."

"Even if I were to overlook the fact that your companion is an orc, Doña, the viscount has ordered your detainment. His command must be followed. That is not something I can say no to."

"But the adjutant's order supersedes that of Don Cruz, does it not?" Cassandra asked.

Bevan had to think about it for a moment before nodding. "Yes priestess, in this I believe you are right."

"So, could Adjutant Love absolve Marissa of her accused crimes?"

Bevan shrugged. "I don't know, to be honest, but if you come with me peacefully, I can see what I can do."

"Then I will go to Adjutant Love and explain what is happening, including the injustice of all this." Cassandra gestured around the room and at Don Cruz's guards before turning to Marissa. "But you must go with him to show good intent."

Marissa looked at her in shock, but quickly saw the logic in what she was proposing. She faced Bevan and raised her chin. "Call off the apprehension of my friends and let them go, and I will come with you."

Bevan relaxed a little. "A wise choice. Thank you, Doña." He turned to face one of the nearby soldiers, "Tell Osprey that I order her to desist, and if Doña Cantor's companions are already rounded up, tell her they are to remain here in the safety of Tossa de Marin." Then he looked to Cassandra. "Is this okay?"

Cassandra nodded in approval.

"Doña Cantor?" he asked.

Marissa took a deep breath, "I agree to these terms, and will wait to hear that my friends are safe, but if any harm comes to them..."

Bevan shook his head and looked about the guards in the room. "You are hardly in any position to threaten me, lady, but very well."

"Oi! I'll save ye lot the trip, and rest assured that I is in a position to threaten ye," a voice called from above.

Marissa looked up in as much surprise as everyone else. There on the balustrade, balanced perfectly, was Onna, with one of Marissa's flintlock pistols pointed directly at Bevan. It was a lengthy distance for the pistol to make the shot, but Marissa had already witnessed Onna's accuracy with her throwing daggers alone. If anyone could make the shot in this room, it'd easily be her.

And the look on Onna's face was murder.

"They shot Rue."

"What?" Bevan and Marissa yelled up simultaneously.

"Is she alright?" Marissa asked, feeling the terror building up in her.

Onna's dark orbs looked once at Marissa, and she could read the pain in those eyes. "Shot her offa the horse, and she fell o'er the side o' the ramparts."

Marissa's gut clenched at the thought of her friend falling like that. There was no way she could survive that kind of fall. Sure, thirty feet didn't seem like much, but if she were already shot, such a fall would likely break bones, even an orc's.

Marissa wanted to buckle over and cry at the indignity of it all. She felt Cassandra's hand against her, still stopping her from... she didn't know what. Collapsing onto the floor in tears? Screaming in pain and frustration? Or... she looked back at Onna. Or attacking them all in unbridled fury.

Onna leapt from the balustrade, gracefully landing on a chair and hopping off to wind up standing directly between Marissa and the guards. Her aim never left Bevan, and now only separated by a dozen steps, she wouldn't miss.

"Confirm the gnome's claims," Bevan ordered the guard that was still standing there. Then he turned to Marissa, a pleading look in his eyes. "Doña Cantor... if this is true... I... I am sorry."

"Oh, it's a little too late for that, I'm fer thinkin'. One o' are own is dead, fer no other reason than bein' different than ye," the gnome declared. "Explain to me why I shouldn't return the favor?"

Bevan scoffed. "Because we have you surrounded? Because there is only two of you? I've seen firsthand what that weapon in your hands is capable of, gnome, but I'm pretty sure, like a crossbow, you only have a single shot. Otherwise Marissa would've used it on more than just the teniente."

"Very perceptive, Ó Cuana. What ye failed to miss though, was why ye was busy ramblin' at ye mouth I packed all o' ye boots with black powder. Now if ye'll kindly take a look at each other's feet ye'll see what I'm sayin' is true."

Marissa couldn't help it; she, like so many guards, stared down at their feet. There, tucked between the sabaton on their feet and the padding beneath, were over a dozen small bundles of cloth. They were the wads she needed to pack her pistol with, and they bulged with the black powder used to charge her pistols. It wasn't enough to, say, blow up the entire house, but with the curvature of the sabaton, and all the powder being beneath it, if something were to discharge, it would definitely blow off some toes at the very least.

A small line of cloth ran from all the men on the ground floor and connected to Onna's servant blouse. She reached down and plucked it off, holding it up for everyone to see. Cocking back the hammer, she placed the twine against the frizzen of her pistol.

"One shot kills ye, and makes all o' them cripples, just like that," she said to Bevan.

Bevan's expression was hard.

"Go on, test me resolve, lad."

Onna was about to do something very, very stupid. And Marissa found that she didn't want to stop her.

"This is a house of the Maker!" Cassandra declared loudly. "This needs to cease this instant. Already someone has died – do we need to aggravate the situation further?"

"Just an orc," one of the guards muttered, but Marissa heard it clearly, and that was enough. She looked down at Onna and saw the butt of her other flintlock sticking out of the top of her breeches. Quickly she reached down and plucked the weapon free, cocking the hammer back. She pointed it towards the general audience of guardsmen where she heard the voice.

"For Maker's sake, Marissa, think!" Bevan exclaimed. "You are surrounded, with a dozen crossbows leveled at you. Even if the gnome were to shoot me, and ignite the thread, you would be dead, the gnome would be dead, and it pains me to say that likely Lady Cassandra would be shot down at the very least for your foolishness as well. Is that what you want? To bring others down with you?"

Marissa bit her lip in thought. She knew Bevan was right – any misstep right now would likely wind up with Cassandra dead... the exact opposite of what she promised Isa. She looked to her friend's sister, who at this point could offer her no answers other than surrender. "I'm afraid I've placed you in terrible danger."

"Yes, well, we all have our lows, I suppose," Cassandra replied, attempting to sound coy in the tense situation.

It was the words, though, that meant something more to her.

Cassandra was trying to tell her something. Something that she should know, and exploit.

Then it came to her.

"Onna," she hissed.

"Aye, Cap'n?" the gnome replied without looking back.

"Get ready."

"Get ready for what?" Bevan demanded. "What are you planning, Doña?"

She looked right at Cassandra. "I'm dreadfully sorry about this."

"About wh..." the priestess began. Marissa grabbed her by the arm and spun her about, pinning her arm like a chicken wing behind her back, and putting the barrel of the pistol to Cassandra's temple.

Maria above gasped. "Let me take the shot!" the woman bellowed.

Cassandra held up her one free arm. "No! No violence."

"Marissa, what in the blazes are you doing?" Bevan demanded, and Marissa thought that at that moment he very much looked like a deer caught in torchlight.

Marissa began to walk Cassandra back towards the Hall of Light. She was hunkered behind the woman for fear that Maria might actually take the shot anyway, knowing it would kill all of them. "Please tell me in your remodeling you left the High Chair as it was?" she whispered into Cassandra's ear.

Cassandra turned her head slightly, "What? I don't..." Then she stopped and slowly nodded once.

"Marissa, please don't! I don't want it to be like this!" Bevan pleaded.

Marissa's hindquarters bumped against the glass door that led to the Hall of Light. Directly at her side was Onna still holding the twine, though it looked as if her blouse was beginning to lose a great deal of fabric.

"Let me shoot her!" Maria demanded from above, "Let me protect the Lady!"

"Where's the key?" Marissa whispered.

"Around my neck," Cassandra all but breathed out the words.

Marissa glanced at Cassandra's collar and could see an ornate silver chain dip beneath the neckline.

"Marissa, you give me no choice, if you persist any further then I am going to let this woman take the shot," Bevan declared.

"Aye, and ye all lose quite a bit o' ye tootsies, not to mention ye spiritual leader. Great plan Bev's," Onna rubbed in.

"Give me a reason to push you away," Marissa whispered like a breeze against Cassandra's neck.

Cassandra's hand was still up, and she gave no reply that she understood, but instead called out, "Maria, don't! Marissa is just... she's just very confused. She's not well in the head and needs help. Serious medical help!"

Marissa looked at Cassandra, taken aback. "I'm not a blimey loon! That's a downright unkind thing to say!"

With her leg, she kicked the door open. She spun Cassandra back around and wrapped her hand around the chain at Cassandra's neck. With a heave she pushed the woman back, the chain broke free, and as the priestess stumbled backwards, a blackened-iron key slid free from her neckline and dangled in Marissa's hand. Cassandra tumbled to the floor, out of harm's way.

Marissa aimed her pistol to the ceiling above Maria and the guards, "Onna now!"

Onna flipped backwards into the room, and Marissa dove through the doorway after her, kicking the door shut as a dozen crossbow bolts hammered into the glass wall of the Hall of Light. Much to the consternation of the guards, the glass did not shatter under the hail of bolts. Instead the bolts barely stuck in the glass, some causing a couple of spiderweb cracks.

Marissa quickly stood and drove the key into the blackened

iron lock on the door. With a turn, two large iron door bars locked against the thick tempered glass. She looked through the walls at Bevan, whose face was completely agog. With a smile from the corner of her mouth, she saluted Bevan and turned away from the perplexed guards. Cassandra was yelling at them to open the doors, and screaming that Marissa was a traitor.

"Good girl," she whispered, before looking to Onna. "You all right?"

Onna dusted herself off. "I'm fine. How'd ye know the glass'd hold?"

"My father helped design it," she said. "Quickly now, help me move the High Chair."

"Why?"

"There's a secret entrance there that will lead down to an escape route into the city below, near the base of the Marin holdings. If we're lucky, maybe we can catch up with Emmell before they catch her," Marissa said.

It took only seconds for the two to move the great chair and reveal the trap door underneath.

Marissa looked out into the room beyond once more to see Bevan, who was just shaking his head at her in bewilderment. Four guards were beating against the glass with the butts of their crossbows, causing an odd reverberating sound throughout the Hall of Light.

Onna nodded. "It's really a shame."

"What is?" Marissa asked, fearing she was about to bring up Rusalka. Now wasn't the time to mourn – not yet.

Onna held up the twine of her blouse now broken away from the rest of the string on the floor, "I was really hoping to blow all of their damn feet off."

CHAPTER SEVENTEEN

Rusalka

It was awfully noisy in the afterlife. There was a lot of screaming, and ordering about, and there were horses running down cobbled streets. As an orc, she didn't have a preferred deity of worship, but she always thought that once you were dead, everything wouldn't be quite so... loud.

Or painful, she realized, as aches began to develop across her body. They were mainly focused in two areas: the side of her head, and her right leg, mostly by her ankle and hip. It was strange – she should be without a body now, right? Didn't the Jasian mention something about a soul? Did the soul still feel the body after it was gone from it? Was this some sort of ghost pain she was feeling, the last moments of her life that she would be forced to carry for eternity? If so, she'd rather have no faith, and have the option to disappear into oblivion.

The next thing to assail her was the scent. The acrid smoke of burning hay and wood smelled of fire, of destruction. Great, now she had to suffer an eternity of fire because of the sins of her people. Maybe this was some version of orc afterlife? All war and strife and fire… it seemed appropriate.

But the yelling – it didn't sound like orcs. It sounded like men, foreign men speaking an odd tongue. What was the language… Castellan?

Slowly, Rusalka opened her eyes and found the world completely turned upside down. The city of Castile was laid out before her. All rooftops of multiple colors that tiered further and further upwards. As she continued to look up, she was alarmed to see the glittering Sowle Sea sparkling viridian in the sunlight. Boats sailed lazily on the surface, all of them facing the wrong way, the sails pointing downward.

She shifted her focus and began to look down. A brilliant blue sky, devoid of any clouds, came into focus. Soon after it was filled with the dark grey and black of rolling smoke, and then the slate grey of a wall.

Hanging from that wall was the shattered remains of scaffolding with pulleys and ropes dangling every which way but one. One was very taut. She followed it, and much to Rusalka's surprise she found one of the pulleys fastened tight around the sabaton of her right foot.

Okay, the world wasn't upside down – she was. Somehow her boot and sabaton got caught in a pulley as she fell, and she struck her head against the wall and passed out. But for how long? And how far had she fallen?

She looked up once more, expecting to see a long fall to the roof tops. Rusalka blinked several times to try and clear her vision. No, that couldn't be right. She reached out and with barely a stretch, her fingertips grazed across the tile surface of one of the homes. Rusalka missed hitting the roof by only two feet.

So, she knew where she was, and that she was alive, but how

long had she been like this? Hours? Days? She heard the clopping of a horse off to her right and looked up – or down, rather – at the direction of the sound. In seconds, a familiar mare went soaring by with a terrified spriggan holding onto its mane for dear life.

"Minutes then," she groaned.

She heard the sound of a woman with a deep voice, clipped and harsh, shouting... orders? In another minute, Rusalka heard other horses galloping and she craned her neck to see a team of horses, complete with armed riders, off in pursuit of Emmell. They would be passing above – well, beneath – her in a matter of minutes.

It took considerable effort, but Rusalka reached up and pulled at the pulley. Even with her strength, she could not get it to budge. In the distance, she was very aware of the quickly approaching horses. Instead of fighting against gravity, she decided to give in to it. Rusalka angled up and found the clasp that held her sabaton in place. She pulled against it, and it sprang free. The next thing she knew, she was falling once more.

She struck hard against the tiles, driving the breath from her lungs, and she heard several things crack. Hopefully, it was simply the tiles. Rusalka rolled over onto her stomach and began to take in measured breaths. Already the pain in her hip and ankle were diminishing, but the ache in her head remained a constant throb. She would have to address it later, she was sure.

Rusalka pulled herself to her feet, trying carefully to maintain balance against the shifting tiles beneath her feet. It was like walking on a den of writhing snakes. She made it to the edge of the roof and could hear the heavy hoof beats growing closer. A quick glance revealed she was next to some form of underpass that ran through the cliffs beneath the castle's outer bailey above.

Then the first morion helmet appeared as the lead horseman galloped in pursuit of her friend. Rusalka flared her nose, taking in all the aromas she could. She was well versed in the scent of horse flesh, and the lather of their sweat. A quick inhalation told her there were six in total, which was about right from what she remembered was in the stables. She smiled ruefully for a moment. She was glad Emmell taught her to count to ten.

The second and third passed beneath.

Then the fourth.

And fifth.

She heard the galloping steady in the distance. She felt the rumble of its heavy gait against her outstretched hand on the rampart wall. She could smell the last closing quickly toward her.

She heard his heavy breathing as if the horse were breathing on her own neck. It was so close. She tensed, mentally ticked off a two count, and then jumped.

The horse's head appeared beneath her feet, and then a completely surprised guard as she landed directly behind him on the horse. He reached for his sword, but Rusalka was quicker and had better leverage. She grabbed his sword arm and curled her other large hand around the gap in his plate cuirass at his neck. She heaved with intense strength, ripping the man from his stirrups and sending him flying off the horse to careen into the cornerstone of a home with a resounding clang.

Rusalka grabbed at the reins and corrected her seat atop the steed. *I hope he's not a Marin guard*, she thought – *otherwise, Mari is going to kill me!*

THE PURSUIT WAS ON. RUSALKA HELD THE REINS TIGHT AS she rode after the remaining soldiers that were quickly gaining on the mare with its childlike occupant.

Rusalka held no reservations on what they would do to Emmell as soon as they got to her. While she witnessed the spriggan fight bravely for her life aboard the *Bella Dahlia* during their liberation, she knew that alone, against five armed and armored men, she stood no chance. These guards were trained with their weapons, and thus far seemed to hold no compunction about being willing to end a person's life.

The cobblestone roads wound downward steeply, forcing Rusalka not to ride as recklessly as she would like. Furthermore, the confines of the small road were narrow as she blurred by white, pink, and yellow homes. Several times she ducked under netting that was meant to screen out the sun. Other times, she didn't turn sharply enough and smashed into small corner boutiques selling bright scarves, flowers, or hats. Worse, she was at the tail end of the chase, which meant that more damage was happening ahead of her. What would become of Emmell if she wasn't fast enough?

She kept the fifth guard always in view, and gradually she closed the distance. People all around scurried and screamed in surprise – how daft these people were! Why would they try and come back into the road after six horses had already stampeded past? Rusalka really thought they would be more cautious. Still, on more than one occasion she was slowed down by either having to jump over some fallen civilian or swerve around them.

Finally, the gap closed, and she found herself nestling up to the side of the guard. The cobbled path was narrow, but it afforded enough space to allow the two of them to ride side by side, at least until the next cart shop materialized on another turn. These roads were never intended for horses, let alone a chase.

The guard glanced over at her, expecting to see his comrade riding side by side with him. Rusalka grinned wildly at the startled expression on his face as he realized he was next to an orc. Without giving him too much time to process it, she lanced out with both legs, kicking him off the horse while simultaneously shifting over to the new animal. The man flew limply from the steed and crashed into a cart selling some sort of sweet pastries and hot chocolate. The thick melted chocolate splashed up, painting the white walls of the home behind it. Rusalka recovered quickly, though, and released the reins of the other horse she was holding, confident that the guard wouldn't be getting up anytime soon.

They rode on, winding down the narrow road, and gradually all the screams of alarm and panic were beginning to be overtaken by the ballads of the juglares and the crashing surf. Salt spray manifested itself as she descended into an area where white stains marked the streets and the corners of homes. She was going to reach the bottom of the winding path soon, and then everything would open up to docks and beaches. There, Rusalka knew the remaining soldiers would catch Emmell.

She whipped the reins and kicked at the flank of the horse to make the beast go faster. And faster it went. She caught up to the next unaware guard even quicker than the first, but found that this time she wasn't going to be able to just sidle up to him as she had the previous. The gap was considerably narrower.

She was going to need to jump onto his horse. Rusalka held the reins tight as she slid her knees up underneath her bottom. Slowly, carefully, she pushed herself up, balancing precariously on the hardback saddle. She brought the horse up right behind the other, and just as the guard finally looked back to wonder at why his partner would be doing something so unnecessarily risky, she leapt.

She crashed into him sabaton-first, right into the back of his cuirass, raising a din of scratching and grinding metal. She dropped behind him, much like the first rider, but the path here was so narrow that she had nowhere to throw him off.

Instead she grabbed him by both shoulder pauldrons and slammed him back and forth into the passing buildings. He clanged and clattered, but had no time to scream before uncon-sciousness took him. By the time the path opened up again, he slid from the horse bonelessly, tumbling back behind Rusalka in a plume of startled cries and dust. She slid into the seat and pressed on.

As she turned another tight corner, the whole area opened up to reveal a marketplace. Rusalka realized they were virtually at the bottom of the mound of Marin homes now. She needed to act faster.

She leaned to the side of the horse, reaching out to feel smooth wood slap into her hand, and she yanked fiercely. The Marin banner tore away from its base under the combination of her strength and the speed of the horse.

She eyed her targets in front of her. Now that the marketplace opened up, the two guards rode side-by-side. They each were brandishing their swords and she could see the lead guard now, just behind Emmell. They were almost upon her!

Without thinking, she rolled the Marin standard across her chest, angling the stand so that the pole ran horizontal to her. She looked ahead of all the guards and saw that soon the gap would be narrowing once more. She had little time. Using the standard as a balance beam, she held it up and pivoted around in her seat so that she was facing aft. She had to look over her shoulder as they closed in. It was going to be close.

The horse galloped forward putting every ounce of speed into his run. As Rusalka saddled up between the two guards, the horses moved naturally to let their compatriot in. Rusalka held the banner up high so that as she slid between them it passed over both of their heads. She glanced back once to see that the narrow path was only a few strides away, then turned back at the startled guards getting ready to cut her down.

Lowering the banner in front of her, the walls came to loom before her on either side. Rusalka let go of the pole just as the two buildings caught it. Half a breath later, unable to stop their forward momentum, both guards clotheslined into the pole with bone-rattling force. They tumbled backwards, flipping head over heels as their brandished swords went flying away. The horses, unaware they lost their riders, stayed with the pack, racing on behind Rusalka. She smiled a feral smile – the rush was exhilarating!

She rolled around in the saddle once more to face forward and grabbed the reins to catch up to her final quarry. She could see him just ahead. He was a scant handful of feet behind Emmell, and he had his sword up high, ready to slash down on the unsuspecting spriggan.

Rusalka let out a berserker's roar and pushed her horse until it was snorting and gasping for air. She closed the gap inch by bloody inch, but she knew she wasn't going to make it in time. All she could do was cry out when she saw the guard swing down on her friend. Rusalka tried to reach out, hoping by some miracle that she could will away the horror she was about to witness.

The sword cut a perfect arc through the air and slashed directly into the saddle... except Emmell was no longer there.

Quick and canny, the small spriggan fell to the side of the horse hanging on by her claws and boring into the leather of the saddle. As the guard recovered from his slash, he pulled back his arm in preparation to strike at the nimble creature again. But Emmell was faster.

Her prehensile tail wrapped around the guard's wrist, and Rusalka watched as the lithe woman released her grip on the saddle and swung underneath the outstretched arm like a harvest mouse. She swung up and over onto the horse behind the guard, the quills on her head now fully erect. She scrambled up the guard's back like a crazed spider monkey and proceeded to slam her head into the back of his neck, between his morion helmet and cuirass, over and over again. The scene before her was violent, twisted, and horrible, but somehow Rusalka couldn't look away.

All three horses slowed to a canter, and by the time Emmell

was done the guard slid from his saddle into a puddle of his own blood, lying on the ground very, very still.

Emmell breathed in heavy, ragged breaths, a feralness in her eyes that Rusalka never saw on the spriggan before. When Emmell recognized Rusalka, she straightened. "Oh, Rue," she said rather sheepishly, reaching up to wipe the blood from her face. When she was done, she looked a little more confident, though her skin was still smeared with pink residue. "It's about time you caught up." The spriggan then cocked her head and looked at Rusalka oddly. "By the way, did you know there's a crossbow bolt sticking out of your head?"

Before Rusalka could even process Emmell's words, a door slammed open just to the right of them, and two bedraggled women came running out, panting just as hard, and lathered just as thickly with sweat, as the horse Rusalka was on.

Rusalka looked at the two of them and her heart skipped a beat.

"Rue!" Marissa exclaimed in pure, unfettered joy. "You're alive!"

———

THE NEXT SEVERAL MINUTES WERE A DAZE AS RUSALKA TOOK Onna on her horse, and Marissa joined Emmell on the former guard's steed. They made their way down to the docks as adroitly as possible, all the while trying not to be suspicious or make more of a scene than they already had. It didn't take long for Bevan's company to mobilize a quick pursuit, and by the time they abandoned the horses, the quartet was running down the pier frantically.

All of it was giving Rusalka a dreadful headache, and she was beginning to feel more than a little lightheaded, but she said nothing about it. The women in front of Rusalka ran up the gangplank, and Marissa began barking orders to the three of them. "Onna, unfurl the sails. Rue weigh anchor, and Em..." Rue watched as Marissa quickly sucked on her finger and stuck it in the air; when she was confident, she pointed south. "Haul wind."

"Aye!" the three shouted in unison, and Rusalka ran to the lines and began untying the hefty rope from the pier. She stared down the long length and saw the guards entering the docks. One of the dockhands looked confused and pointed in their direction. Rusalka worked faster.

A loud clap let her know that the sails had dropped. As she came up the gangplank, Marissa was already shouting for Onna to square the rigging. Onna in turn bellowed back, "Boom about!"

Rusalka ducked low as she made her way to the capstan. With a loud groan the boom swung over her head. Seconds later, Onna yelled that the rigging was belayed. Rusalka set to work on the capstan, and the chains began to clink up one by one winding in the anchor. It wasn't long before the chains darkened with water, and then sand and silt began to cover them, as well as a few barnacles. Rusalka swept them off with the back of her gauntleted hand, careful not to cut herself on their sharp, calcareous shells.

The ship rocked forward as the sails snapped full of wind. Rusalka held on and looked down the docks. She could see over a dozen armored men running down the pier. It was almost comical seeing men in that much platemail trying to move swiftly, like a head of tortoises making their way to them. One however was not impeded, nor wearing heavy platemail, and she was a threat as she brandished her massive crossbow. She stopped and took aim – directly at Marissa!

"Shot across the bow!" Rusalka yelled. Like women trained at the sail for the last six months, all three ducked low just as the massive woman pulled the trigger. There was a loud crack and Rusalka could see a crossbow bolt jutting from the railing by Marissa's head.

Blimey, that woman is a good shot, Rusalka thought in awe.

"I'm not fer thinkin' they want to parley!" Onna yelled.

Rusalka looked again and the team of tortoises were closer now. Even with wind in their sails, leaving port was a slow prospect for the most trained yokesman. In less than a minute the guards would be on them.

Another crack echoed about and Rusalka could see another bolt only inches from the first. Marissa cursed in a very unladylike fashion. Rusalka looked up at Marissa hunkered downed behind the rail. There were slats in the rails to let water run off, but if the archer managed to get a shot through...

"Ye know we would be going much better if we had like six more hands!" Onna barked as she struggled to hold onto the rigging wrapped about a cleat.

Rusalka ran to another open rigging line, painfully aware that if the archer switched targets, she was a sitting duck. With a bang that startled her, the top hatch came open, and one of the women that they had sailed with stuck her head out, "Oi is the boatswain calling fer hands?"

"Ye damn right me is!" Onna said in jubilation, "get your worthless arse up here, Badger, you pretty puterelle."

Rusalka was surprised not only to see Charlotte Badger emerge from below deck, but Anne and Jocquotte as well. Marissa almost cried with joy at the sight of the three women, but another crack at the rail and the shower of splintered wood that covered her prevented it.

"That beast of a woman is a right bitch," Onna remarked angrily. Rusalka wasn't sure if it was because the large archer was shooting at Marissa or because she was such a good shot it was keeping the captain low. Probably both.

Emmell muttered something to Marissa, and then Rusalka heard Marissa yell, "Reset eighty degrees left!"

Now with multiple experienced women there, the five of them

quickly did as they were bade. The *Bella Dahlia* heeled heavily, and spray kicked up over the deck from the normally placid waters. Rusalka looked back, a growing smile taking to her face. She watched in triumph as the vessel pulled away from the pier, catching favorable wind, and thrusting them out to sea.

She made eye contact one last time with the archer who stared at her down the length of her massive crossbow. They glared at each other for several long heartbeats as the ship slowly bucked up and down. Finally, the woman lowered the weapon, and turned to begin speaking with Bevan in a manner that said that she was most displeased.

"Oi!" Badger asked after they were far away from the pier. "Anyone mind sharing with me why ye were running from the local constabulary?"

"It's a long story," Marissa told her.

"I'm right fer hearing it then."

Marissa nodded. "First thing's first, and I'm grateful and all, but why are you three on the ship?"

Badger, Anne, and Jocquotte all looked at each other before looking back at Marissa, "Well, when we disembarked yesterday and saw the city, even with what coin we had, we just..." Badger began.

"Sailing is what we know," Anne finished. She was Halsbrenian, like Bevan, but her accent was so thick that even Rusalka had trouble understanding her most days.

"Right," Jocquotte, a dark-skinned Ayjub agreed. "To be honest, Cap'n, we haven't quite got our 'land legs' back, and were just more comfortable on the Dahlia."

"Well I'm damn glad you were here," Marissa admitted. "We wouldn't have gotten away without your timely additions."

At this, Onna put her hands on her hips. "And why was ye down below decks bein' nothing but some quisbys when ye heard us strugglin' up here?"

The three looked at each other once more, before a noticeable twinkle formed in Badger's eyes. "We captured a stowaway!"

IT TURNED OUT THAT "STOWAWAY" WAS A VERY SUBJECTIVE term to the three women. "I thought they'd be larger," Rusalka confessed.

The three women beamed with pride at their catch, showing it off inside their empty rum bottle. It fluttered and slammed angrily against the glass, muttering a litany of disparities at all the eyes that stared down at it.

"Is that what I think it is?" Onna asked in obvious wonder.

Jocquotte nodded savagely. "It's a faery."

At this, the tiny creature halted, and they could clearly see it looked very much like a small girl with blurring, colorful insect wings. She folded her little delicate arms over one another in angry defiance as she shouted, "I'm not a faery! I'm a kållråden, you dumb ogres!"

"Faeries are real?" Rusalka asked, feeling more than a little embarrassed.

"This one is!" Badger said excitedly. "Found it pilfering some of that spice we picked up in that gnomish port."

"Aye, the stuff that makes me arse all pucker up when ye put it on stuff," Anne added.

"Melegueta pepper?" Onna offered.

"Grains of Paradise," the little voice from the bottle chirped up at them with a sigh of delight.

Everyone looked down to the tiny thing who was clearly in a dreamy state at the mention of the spice. Onna twisted her face in confusion. "Faeries like spicy food?"

The small winged woman shook herself of her daze, "Not. A. Faery!" she bellowed.

Onna turned up with wide-eyed glee at Marissa, "I like it! Can we keep it Cap'n?"

Rusalka could see the concern on Marissa's face as she eyed the creature trapped in glass. "Keep it contained for now, I have to think."

PART III
RHOMBUS

INTERLUDE

Marissa de Cantor y Castile

T en Winters Earlier...

"CASSIE HURRY UP!" ISA YELLED BEHIND HER AT THE SQUAT eight-winter-old girl. Marissa watched impatiently as the little girl's legs pumped hard, trying to catch up to them. She twisted and fidgeted, hopping up and down in barely contained excitement. Isa squeezed her hand to get her to calm down, but instead Marissa tried to pull Isa closer to the front of the congregation. "We're going to miss it!" she pleaded. "Just leave her with the Corredor boy."

"No!" Cassie wailed. "I don't want to miss it."

"Marissa de Cantor y Castile, you are not going anywhere without Cassie and Vicente, am I understood?" Don Fernando ordered as he walked slowly behind them with his aide, Javier Corredor, and their blacksmith, Corey Johns.

Mari's ears turned scarlet as she looked to her feet, "Yes Papa."

When the Corredor boy and Cassie finally made their way to her, she scowled at the peasant. "I don't know why I should have to wait for the likes of you," she hissed at him in a whisper so her father would not hear. "I'm going to miss everything because of you two!"

Cassie's eyes began to water, but to Mari's consternation her father's serf son didn't look the least bit cowed by her noble decree. It only riled her more that she had to be seen sharing space with this bumpkin.

Isa squeezed Mari's hand reassuringly. "Everything will be fine. We'll make it to the front."

Just then, the sound of trumpets cut through the air. "The fanfare!" Mari cried, all thoughts of having to stand with Vicente washed away in the excitement of Purist Commander Love's triumphant return home. Marissa pulled Isa through the crowd of nobles, pushing through brilliant crème, yellow, gold, and pink summer dresses. The voluminous fabric blocked her view of the first line of bellators that were marching forward.

"Move!" she growled as she pushed through the aristocratic women, hoping to catch the eye of the valiant purists so recently returned from their latest engagement in the Fermania Civil War. Behind her, she heard Cassie squeal and cry as she and Isa left the little girl and the Corredor peon behind, sacrificed to the gods of textile.

Mari and Isa barged their way through, finally reaching the front of the patrician pile just as the first file of bellators blew by. Mari stared at them in wonder. Young men, scantly older than her, marched through the streets from the Jasian Enclave's heart – the Rhombus – all the way towards where she was now, at the Palacio de los Vizcondes. She stood just at the base of the whitewashed steps, at the edge of the cobbled streets. The Viscount of Castile waited at the top, seated in a light oak chair awaiting the exultant return of the Purist Commander.

It was a monumental day for Castile. With the Jasian Enclave's involvement – namely Purist Commander Love's Castellan fleet, they scored a stunning victory against the gnomes who had been harassing the trade lanes between Buckner, the capital of Fermania, and the Citadel itself. Love's victory, Mari was told, was a crucial turning point in this war.

Soon the procession of young bellators was finished, and the cream of the noble crop began to march past – the purists. Mari and Isa stared in wonder at the magnificent soldiers. They stood tall, their silvery plate cuirasses polished so finely that the men glittered like precious gems in the brilliant sun. Each man was regal, almost angelic in Mari's eyes. True heroes, just like the juglares told. These were what real men were like – noble, honorable men of strong faith and integrity.

Vicente pushed forward next to her, bringing Cassie with him. Marissa's nose crinkled in disdain at the lesser that was now polluting her moment.

Cassie seemed not to notice as she looked up in wonder at the brilliantly marching men. Then Isa was tapping her shoulder and pointing excitedly. "There! There he is!"

Mari turned to look where Isa was pointing, and she saw him – the Purist Commander, Beneford Love.

"He's amazing," Mari swooned.

And verily, it was true. Taller than his purist brethren around him, Beneford Love was a powerful soldier of the Maker. His armor, a brilliant bronze, shone like it was its own sun. He was a titan with a barrel chest and broad shoulders. Mari thought those shoulders alone could bear the entire weight of the fleet upon them.

He walked by, as proud and regal as they come, and his strong black tresses, only slightly peppered with grey, made him look handsome and distinguished. His jawline was firm and accentuated with a sharp beard that came to a point on his strong chin.

As he strode by the three girls, he bowed his head to them. "Ladies," he said, and his voice was sonorous, smooth like fine silk.

Marissa's ears burned as he passed by them. Purist Commander Beneford Love was the pinnacle of what Mari believed a hero looked like, what he should be, and he had just spoken to her!

"He... just... spoke to us!" Isa squeaked in jubilation. Mari and Isa interlocked arms and bounced up and down in delight.

When they were done, Mari watched as the viscount awarded Purist Commander Love a medal for extreme bravery, then began to speak loudly of his accolades. Isa sighed next to her. "One day, Mari that's going to be me."

"Us, you mean," Mari corrected.

Isa's eyes lit up. "Yes, us! First women purists ever! Ballads will be sung of our heroics just like Love."

Next to them, the Corredor boy scoffed, "Like that will ever happen."

Mari's lip snarled in disgust. "What would you know, peasant?"

Isa tugged on Mari's arm. "Ignore him, Mari. He probably can't even read."

Mari laughed at the boy and then rose her head haughtily so that she was looking down her nose at him. "You're probably right, Isa. The most he could ever hope for in his pathetic life is to be someone else's servant."

With that, she paid the boy no more attention. Instead, fantasies danced across her mind, internal ballads of her and Isa marching across the countryside, the twin banners of Cantor and Marin billowing in the wind. She could hear the praises of kings and queens thanking them, the first two women purists that would scour the earth and rout out evil – just like Love.

CHAPTER EIGHTEEN

Marissa de Cantor y Castile

The present...

MARISSA HELD THE YOKE WHILE EMMELL AND ONNA WORKED on Rusalka, trying to get the morion helmet off her head without further aggravating the bolt.

"This is not something that should be done on open deck," Emmell chastised the gnome.

"Don't be lookin' at me, it's Rue who wants to be up here."

"If this thing kills me, the last thing I want to see is the sky, not some soggy arse boards," Rusalka quipped to Emmell.

"Ye ain't gonna die, ye big baby."

"I dunno, that bolt looks really deep," Emmell offered, neutral. "If you do the slightest thing wrong, it might kill her at best."

Marissa eyed the spriggan. "And what could be worse than death?"

Emmell shrugged, "Well if it's deep enough and Onna fumbles it bad, she could turn Rusalka into a vegetable."

"Like a cabbage?" Badger asked, looking over from the rigging.

"Is it a magic bolt then?" Anne wondered aloud.

Marissa could see Emmell shaking her head. "No, like it will make Rusalka dumb."

"Oh, that's not good. She just learned ta count ta ten," Jocquotte said. "Don't be wanting to take that away."

Emmell shook her head. "Worse than that. By dumb, I don't mean she can't count. I mean she won't be rational at all. We'll have to feed her, change her clothes, bathe her, and even wipe her if she soils herself."

"So... like Badger then?" Anne asked. Jocquotte snickered at this. Badger eyed them all maliciously.

"Kind of," Emmell agreed, much to Badger's bewilderment. "Except Rue won't know she's doing it. She won't know much of anything because nothing will be processing right upstairs," She touched her head. "She'll be alive but not even really know she's alive."

"So best not to mess up then," Marissa added to the discussion."

"Sure Brains, no pressure now," Onna added, slowly working the helmet off.

Marissa felt terrible. She blamed herself for bringing her friends into all of this. Most of all she felt awful for Rusalka. For a short while she believed her friend dead, and now when she found out the orc was alive, it might only be short-lived. The fact that she managed to stay alive so long with a crossbow bolt lodged in her skull was amazing in and of itself. But now... they might simply lose her to blood loss, or infection.

Marissa wanted to be at her side, wanted to assure Rue that it would be all right, even if it wasn't going to be. She wanted to hold Rue's hand if she needed to. Watching Isa die was hard enough – she'd lost her best friend. But for some reason when she looked to the orc, and what they accomplished together in such a short time, she felt like the large muscle-laden woman was a little sister... a really big, little sister.

Marissa tried not to think about it. While Emmell and Onna tended to the orc, she managed the yoke. Badger might've been able to do it for a short time, but she could easily have them fall prey to the Pale that was just off their port bow.

Marissa wanted to get them away from potential pursuit and taking them near the Pale was the easiest way to do that. Though she didn't want to get too close; she wouldn't want to wind up like her mother.

"So, Tusker, this woman that shot ye in the head, ye ever seen anything like her afore? She was as big as ye are." Onna asked. Marissa knew it was to distract the orc from what was happening on her head.

"I have," Rusalka said, though her words were a little slurred. Marissa hoped it was due the jarring motion of Onna trying to remove the helmet and not due to any brain damage.

When Rusalka made no more effort to respond, Onna said. "Well, are ye gonna share it with the rest o' the class?"

After another bloated pause, Marissa heard Rusalka say, "She was a wilder."

Anne let out a whistle from the crow's nest above, while Marissa looked up. "Did Rue just say wilder?"

"Aye," Onna answered, "what's a wilder? Is it like another kind o' orc o' something? Couldn't see much with her skull-like helmet."

"No, they're human, mostly," Anne answered.

"Frequent around these parts then?" Emmell asked.

"They aren't frequent, anywhere but the Wilds, and sometimes in Halsbren," the Halsbrenian in the crow's nest answered.

"But more accepted than Tusker here, I see," Onna said, a little bitingly.

"Well, wilders are human," Anne replied. "Just really big ones."

"And why is it they are so big?" Emmell asked, fascinated.

"No one really knows," Marissa answered, "but like everything around here, the juglares have stories."

"Rue, do you know?" Onna asked.

"No... clue," came Rusalka's voice after a moment. "I've seen them though, in the coliseums. Brutal warriors. They can take a lot of punishment before they go down."

"Lovely, and it looks like Bevan gots one."

"More likely Cruz," Marissa remarked.

"Okay, Brains, tell me the story of the wilders then," Onna said.

Marissa took a breath, "Okay, but like I said before, it's a juglares tale, so a lot of it tends to be larger than life."

"Well if Rue doesn't have more to go on, I'd rather hear a story then nothing at all."

"Very well." Marissa thought of the tales she heard before and tried to find a way to condense it as best as she could. "Wilders are the result of a dark pact made by a great Warlord of old named Zad, and a demon."

"A... demon?" Emmell asked in disbelief.

"It be an evil creature in the Jasian religion," Onna explained to Emmell. "Not many others believe in them 'cept the Jasians."

"I thought you wanted to hear this?" Marissa said, a little miffed at the comment.

"Aye, I'll try not to interrupt anymore," Onna promised.

"I will make no such promises," Emmell added.

Marissa rolled her eyes and continued, "In exchange for his

promised soul, Zad imbued his human armies with a dark curse, granting them unnatural size and ferocity. He then pitted his altered humans against the most savage lands in Kuldarr – the Wilds. There his men turned into a brutal army and marched across the southern face of Kuldarr, conquering humanity in his name. During his reign, his army sired many progeny, continuing the darkened curse from one generation to the next."

"And this is true?" Emmell asked in bewilderment. "This warlord formed this monster army and took over your kind?"

Marissa nodded, but it was Anne who answered, "Warlord Zad was real. Before his wilders marched across the craggy hills of Gurgen and the dunes of Malten, all of humanity fell under one nation: Malten. After the reign of Warlord Zad, humanity splintered into the three nations that occupy the southwest here today, Halsbren, Gurgen, and what remains of Malten."

"So ye blame the size o' the woman on... magic?" Onna asked, nonplussed.

"And what would you say? You saw her yourself – she made Rusalka look like a spriggan in comparison," Marissa said.

"Good point," Onna conceded.

"Well I think it was genetics," Emmell said. "Living in a savage land, one would need to adapt. Maybe size was the evolutionary result."

"It hasn't been more than five generations, Em." Marissa said. "Does the spriggan theory of Evolution work that quickly?"

Marissa saw Emmell was about to make some sort of scientific retort when Anne yelled from the crow's nest above, "Blimey, that scary lookin' fog is movin' ta us!"

Marissa looked to the port to see long tendrils of white reaching towards them like a kraken's tentacles. She turned the yoke and directed the ship further away. They weren't too close yet, but closer than Marissa would've liked to be. She became so distracted with the wilder she wasn't paying attention.

Within several tense minutes they were away from the deathly grip of the Pale. Marissa let out a breath that she hadn't realized she was holding. She looked up to thank Anne for her quick eye but saw her staring with Em's spyglass into the Pale.

"You're supposed to be looking for pursuing ships!" Marissa yelled up to the blonde woman.

"Aye, aye," Anne agreed. "Nery a ship in sight, at least none o' the war cogs we saw."

Well that's good news, Marissa thought. Bevan hadn't pursued them out to sea. A wise decision, seeing as they came burdened in heavy armor. If they engaged the *Bella Dahlia* in a foray at sea, many of those men would have sank and drowned, unable to swim in such ridiculously heavy armor.

Marissa saw that ugly sight once before during the Fermania Civil War. It was horrible to watch the one thing meant to protect men during combat be their undoing out at sea. As she thought about it, she looked down to the thick layers of armor on Rusalka. No matter how strong the orc was, should the *Bella Dahlia* suffer the same fate as those ships she witnessed off Gnomelaneum Bay, Rue would cut like an anchor through the blue.

A shrill whistle from the crow's nest got Marissa's attention. She looked up to see the woman studying the Pale intently once more. "Me sees something in that freaky mist. It looks like islands, maybe two o' three of them. Doesn't look like it's too far in. Maybe we should hide in there while Onna and Em work on Rue?"

Marissa shook her head. "The Jasian Enclave named them the Li Galli. But we in Castile have another name for them – the Sirens."

"Oi? Why is that?" Badger asked.

"Because they tempt you," Marissa replied. "They lure you in, either by curiosity, or comfort, or need, and then you are never seen again. That is why they are allowing you to see them now. They sense our need."

"But... they're just islands?" Anne called back in confusion. "I see them. It'd be easy to get to."

"Nay, Brains is right on this, lass," Onna added. "I heard o' the Sirens. I'm suren' fer thinkin' the isles be fine, but they are a temptin' song and when ye in the mist, it's what's in the Pale that's gonna get ye. I'm fer believin' this more than demon's curses makin' the wilders."

Marissa was about to interject about the curse when Badger asked, "What's in the Pale?"

This was something Marissa knew she could better answer. "That's the real problem – no one has ever been able to find out. Any ships that sail in disappear and the flotsam makes its way to shore, generally within the week. Either on the coast of Castile, the Citadel, or Sentinel's Barrow, but it always makes it to shore, almost like it's a message. And there are no survivors."

Badger scoffed, "Sounds like another children's folk tale like ye wilders, made up to scare ye away from the big bad fog."

"Except that we know this one is true," Marissa remarked. "I saw it all too frequently as a child growing up. So, no. We are not going into the Pale. Not to escape, or explore, and certainly not for Li Galli."

Marissa could see Anne scrunching her face in disapproval, but she'd made her decision. Seconds later, they heard the dull thunk of the morion helmet falling against the wet planking.

"Well, we got the helmet off!" Onna declared, but there was something in the tone of her voice that Marissa didn't like.

"So... what's the problem?" Marissa asked.

"Bolt went through it quite a bit and it's definitely in her skull," Emmell reported.

Rusalka snorted, "I could've told you that."

Marissa strained to look down at them on the deck, but she couldn't see anything good from her angle. She did see Emmell shaking her head at Rue. "We were hoping for something superficial, maybe only the tip embedded in your skull by an inch or something. Something we could withdraw clean, sew up and call it a day."

"This be worse, I'm fer fearin'. It might be in ye brain cavity," Onna added.

"What's that mean?" Rusalka asked.

"It means I canna do anythin' here fer one," Onna began. "And that when I do remove it, there's gonna be a hole directly to ye brain, which is not good. I need to cover it, preferably with something as hard as bone that ye skin can heal over."

"Like a metal plate?" Marissa asked, thinking about the field medicine she saw in the civil war.

"Exactly!" Onna called up. "Needs to be tempered and shaped to her skull though, which means we need ta get her to shore and seen by someone who could do it."

Emmell walked up to Marissa on the aft castle and offered to take the yoke. Marissa stepped aside and let the sea artist have her place. "How long do we have?" Marissa asked the spriggan in a quiet voice.

Emmell shrugged, "Hard to say really. I'm surprised Rue can function as well as she can, and that the pain hasn't rendered her unconscious. Let alone handling rigging, riding horses, and kicking the shite out of people like she has."

This made Marissa smile a little. "Well, she's a tough orc."

Emmell nodded, "I don't know enough about them or how they work, but a human, a gnome, even a spriggan wouldn't be able to keep going like she is. I can't give you a solid estimate. Couple days, maybe a week, tops. Delirium will set in very soon, especially since now that the helmet is off and the area can swell, which is fine – we can deal with that. Eventually bleeding inside her head is going to be a big problem, but we shouldn't remove the bolt until we can do something about the hole."

"If we changed course now, we could make the Citadel in four days," Marissa stated.

Emmell looked down to the orc lying on the deck. Marissa followed her gaze and heard Onna trying to make jokes about Rue being so hard-headed. After a moment she nodded. "Four days is reasonable," Emmell declared. "We could try, but we'd have to find a smith who would be willing to shape the plate for an orc. How long would that take? Not to mention, didn't Onna say you're a criminal in the Citadel for disavowing being an Exactor or something?"

Marissa looked out to where she knew the Citadel lay – even across the glittering sea of Sowle, she could see the tips of the pearlescent spires on the horizon. It was a massive city, policed by purists and clergy. If Cassandra was correct, if even one of them recognized her things would get complicated. She could stay on the ship and let Onna and Emmell handle it, she supposed. The Citadel wasn't as xenophobic as Castile was. She offered that suggestion to Emmell.

"I could, I suppose," Emmell agreed. "Though I doubt we could navigate the place like you could, even with directions."

"I could draw you a map," Marissa offered.

"Oh?" Emmell asked, "Are you a cartographer?"

Marissa shook her head. "No. But it'd be something, right?"

Emmell shrugged, "I guess."

Marissa knew by her voice that the spriggan didn't sound very optimistic. Onna walked up to them a second after that. "Me thinks delirium is beginning to set in."

Marissa looked in alarm down at Rusalka, who was laying on the deck grasping at something in the air. "What's she doing?"

"Trying to catch butterflies," Onna muttered quietly.

Marissa looked harder, trying to see what it was that Rusalka must be seeing.

"Don't bother," Onna said. "They ain't there."

"Looks like we have less time than my original forecast," Emmell added. "I knew delirium would be soon, but not this soon."

They heard Rusalka begin mumbling to herself in a deep guttural way that didn't make an ounce of sense to any of them.

"I think she's growling at the butterflies now," Onna suggested.

"What happens if she gets too far gone?" Marissa asked. "Could she attack one of us?"

Emmell nodded. "That's a logical assumption. At some point, the delirium will set in so badly that she won't be able to recognize that we are friends."

"In other words, she'll go back to bein' an orc," Onna explained.

Marissa bit her lip. "We'll never make it to the Citadel, will we?"

Emmell was shaking her head, "No, I don't think we will. You should prepare yourself, Marissa. Rusalka might not make it."

Marissa looked at her friend on the deck. Frustration swelled in her like a budding storm and she could feel moisture building in her eyes. Not Rue. She made a promise to the orc. A promise that she'd live safe on Cantor lands.

Marissa turned and looked starboard at the kaleidoscope of color that was Castile. It was only a few hours away, and no pursuit was obvious – Anne was right. Plus, she knew her way around the town better than anyone else. And, she knew a black-smith that might be able to help.

"Turn about," she ordered.

"What?" Onna asked, incredulously. "We just left there, and if ye ain't fer noticin,' they was none too friendly."

"I'm aware," Marissa said, her expression firm. "But Rue needs help, and that's the best place we're going to find it. If not a black-smith, then a Jasian curate."

Emmell began to turn the wheel, and as she did, Onna

observed the direction change and called out for Jocquotte and Badger to adjust the sails. The two women scurried into motion. Onna looked up at Marissa, "Okay, so we're heading back to a place that wants Em and Tusker dead, and I'm fer thinking they really don't want ye in charge of Cantor, Brains. I'm more fer thinkin' they want ye to dance a hempen jig."

"Why would they want her to dance?" Emmell asked.

Onna rolled her eyes.

"Onna means they want to hang me," Marissa explained.

"Oh. Yeah, that big one, she definitely wants you dead. Though I'm thinking she'd rather it be by arrows or bolts, not by a noose," Emmell said as she thought about it. "Unless she made a weird noose on the end of a bolt and shot it over your head somehow. Then she could use it like that. I guess? But then..."

"So, what's the plan?" Onna interrupted, stopping Emmell in her bizarre, gory logic. "How do ye plan on making this work?"

Marissa looked down at Onna, "You, Badger, and I are heading to the Enclave this time. You and Badger find the supplies you need. I'll talk to a blacksmith that was loyal to my family, and then I will speak with Adjutant Love in the hopes of getting a curate as well. Also, I want answers."

"And if they try and arrest ye again?" Onna asked.

"We are going to the Jasian Enclave. The viscount has no authority within Enclave grounds. Besides, I thought Love was a good man before I left, so why should that change now that he's an adjutant?"

Onna remained silent, clearly objecting.

"Is this because of Vicente?" Marissa questioned bitterly.

"The man is fer havin' fine points, most of which have been accurate so far."

Marissa nodded. She couldn't argue with that. Cruz did seem to want her dead, and Bevan was not as trustworthy as she had once hoped.

"Why are ye fer thinkin' this Love is any different?"

Marissa shook her head, "I have to. He's a member of the Enclave, a high-ranking member. At one time I was sworn to them."

"And look how that panned out," Emmell observed.

Marissa bit her lip, knowing too well the truth of that statement. "Rue is the priority first and foremost," she finally said. "If getting to Adjutant Love proves impossible, then it's impossible. But if I can talk to him, reason with him, then he's the best chance we have for Rue, and for getting Cantor back."

"Ye not fer thinkin' Cassandra can do it?"

"I don't want her affiliated with us any worse than she already is."

Onna nodded, "Okay Brains, I canna get behind that, but don't ye think it's gonna be hard to pull the *Bella Dahlia* into a port we just raced out of whilst being shot at by a giant woman?"

"We need a safe harbor," Emmell said.

Marissa thought about it for a moment, and she realized that she had one. "I know a cove that we can stow the ship in that is big enough to put the Dahlia where no one will look for it right away. It'll be tight, but I know you can manage it, Em."

The spriggan nodded.

"And no one will be there?" Onna asked.

Marissa blushed a little. "Oh people will be there... its where, um, young couples go to have... dalliances."

Onna raised an eyebrow. "What kind of dalliances?"

Marissa's cheeks and ears grew hot. "The 'I don't see what you're doing if you don't see what we're doing' kind."

"So, you want us to hide the ship where you used to slouster the very man who wants to kill you?"

Marissa hunched her shoulders. "Um... yes? I think."

"I like it!" Onna said with a gleeful clap of her hands. "Let's do it. Emmell, take us to Get that Booty Bay!"

"It's not called that!" Marissa protested. "It was very romantic. They call it... Cuddle Cove."

"Booty Bay!" Onna said more firmly.

"Aye, I'm fer agreeing with Onna on this," Badger said. "That definitely sounds more like a Booty Bay to me. How much cuddling did ye really do?"

Marissa sighed and shook her head, not wanting to make eye contact with anyone in that moment.

"Way Booty Bay!" Jocquotte agreed. "Look at Mari's face!"

"All the Way Bay!" Anne added. "Way to go Cap'n!"

"Someone definitely found their way into ye cove!" Badger... badgered.

"That's why she wanted to cuddle afterwards o' course!" Onna snorted, and all the women laughed at Mari's expense. All but Mari herself, of course, and Emmell, who didn't quite understand what they were talking about.

"I hate you all..." Marissa said, shaking her head in embarrassment. Still she was smiling.

"So where are we heading then, Cuddle Cove or Booty Bay?" Emmell asked, clearly confused.

"I think ye got em backwards, Em. First its Booty Bay, then Cuddle Cove," Onna said with a guffaw.

"Depends on how good he was? It might have been right to Slumber Strait!" Jocquotte added, bringing on more laughter at Mari's expense.

"Unless he made it a Blasé Basin!"

Mari ignored the ongoing jests and looked down to Emmell instead. "I'll guide you."

The spriggan nodded, "Thank you, because I'm completely lost. I don't see why we didn't go to any of these places to begin with."

Marissa had to give the spriggan credit as usual. When she first saw the sharp coral reefs on both sides of the cove, she thought that she might have misjudged her memory of the place. The opening seemed so much larger when Augusto brought her here with his family's sailboat winters before. But as the galleon closed the distance, the once wide opening seemed dreadfully puny compared to the bulk of the three-master.

A quarter of a league out, the humans all began to look at Emmell nervously, and then back to Marissa, waiting for her to change course. But Emmell held steady. At only two dozen meters away, Emmell called for point reefing, and Onna enforced that call, yelling loudly and sending the three human women into action. They scrambled at the rigging and reduced the area of the mainsail by partially lowering the sail. This effect drastically cut their forward momentum and they coasted easily through the narrow gap of the sharp coral reefs.

"Damn, you're good," Marissa whispered, not wanting the spriggan to lose her concentration.

"Yes, I am," Emmell answered, never once staring any other direction but straight forward.

"We need a berth," Marissa called to Anne. The Halsbrenian nodded and scurried up into into the crow's nest.

"Got one," the woman replied, followed by the coordinates.

Soon, Emmell had the *Bella Dahlia* sitting calmly in the cove, a myriad of smaller sailing ships lounging all around them. Marissa knew curious eyes were looking at who it was that would dare bring such a massive cargo ship in their private little love pond.

"I thought ye said they wouldn't stare?" Badger said as she came up to Marissa on the aftcastle.

"No, I said they wouldn't say anything."

"Aye, they're all in little monogamous love ships and we just pulled up in an orgy yacht," Onna said, waving a three fingered hand at a couple who were gawking up at them slack-jawed as their little ship casually ambled past them, propelled by the *Bella Dahlia's* wake.

"How much time ye think we have, afore someone grows bold and tattles?" Onna asked.

Marissa waved a hand at the scant ships free floating in the cove, "This will double by nightfall, and everything about this place is a huge sin according to the Jasian Enclave and the eyes of the Maker. I don't think anyone is going to report this to the guard or alert the Enclave purists, until morning at the least."

"Mayhaps," Onna told her, and Marissa could see she didn't believe it. "How many actually know about this place?"

"It's the most widely known secret around. Everyone knows this place exists. Teenagers of this age think it's theirs, just as in my time I thought we were the only ones to know, and I'm sure it's the same with my parents, and even grandparents," Marissa explained.

"So, we're in the open, is what yer saying," Anne asked.

"We needed safe harbor and a place close enough that Badger, Onna, and myself can get help for Rue. This is enough of one for now."

"Aye, lass, true enough. I shouldn't be complainin' and we ain't fer havin' the time to scuttlebutt. Let's get ashore and get Tusker some help," Onna added.

Marissa looked at Emmell, Anne, and Jocquotte who were going to stay aboard. "Keep the ship ready for departure, and if it looks like anything larger than a schooner is going to try and make its way in here, make a break for it."

Emmell nodded.

Marissa looked down at Rusalka, now wrapped in blankets and shaking on deck. She refused to go below deck, again claiming she wouldn't die in a box – she wanted to see the sky. "Keep an eye on Rue too."

Emmell nodded. "Go, get help, we'll be fine here."

"What about the stow-away?" Jocquotte asked looking around. "Want to let her go here?"

"Let her go? That's our faery!" Onna protested.

"I'm not a faery!" They heard a surprisingly loud voice call from the Captain's quarters.

Marissa shook her head, "Not yet. We'll figure out what to do with her soon enough."

Jocquotte nodded. "Aye, Aye Cap'n."

With their plan ready, Marissa, Onna, and Badger disembarked. It was a modest hike through crags and rocks, not wanting to be overly obvious in taking the pebbled beach. By the time they arrived, the sun was waning in the sky, and the lights of Castile were coming alive. Music filled the air.

"Ye know, if we weren't such outlaws already, this place seems like a real hoot," Onna commented.

"I'm the only outlaw at the moment," Marissa replied. "They know I'm travelling with a gnome, but little else. If you left now, Onna, none here would be the wiser."

"Bevan peeped me pretty good."

"Perhaps," Marissa agreed, "but I also think that if you walked by him on the street tonight he wouldn't look twice at you."

"Even after I threatened to blow em' up?"

"Even then." She turned to her friends, suddenly very serious. "Onna, Badger, if you want to go now, if you want to live your lives, I won't stop you. Hells, I think it'd be the smartest thing you can do. My world here is turned upside down. Nothing is as I thought it was going to be. I can't promise you anything anymore. I don't know what tomorrow is going to bring except for one thing – if you stay with me, as of right now, you'll be labelled a criminal. An outlaw. This is your best chance to walk away."

Onna looked at her with rare intensity. "And what about Tusker?"

"I will do everything I can to save her," Marissa exclaimed.

Onna shook her head, "Not what I mean. I know ye'll do yer best. And if ye save her, then what? Way I sees it, as long as ye is an outlaw here, they will be comin' after Rue all the same."

"Then after I save her, I'll take her wherever she wants to go to be free."

Onna turned away from Marissa and looked into the streets of Castile. "I'm fer thinkin' that Rue ain't very safe nowhere, except at ye side. So that's where I need ta be."

"Onna's right, Mari," Badger spoke up. "I've no family left, no friends back in Fermania. Civil War took me town, Ayjub took me body and made it a slave fer others' entertainment. But you, and Onna, and Rue, ye saved us. Ye freed us that day, and as far as I'm concerned, ye made us a family. Only family me gots now. And ye stick by yer family, even the big, green, grumpy ones."

Marissa's heart swelled at Onna and Badger's words, and she couldn't help but wipe the tears away from the corners of her dark eyes.

"There ain't no time fer that, lass," Onna decreed. "Cool the waterworks."

"I don't deserve you guys."

"Perhaps, but yer stuck with us," Onna said with a smile.

"Aye, Cap'n. Onna's right," Badger added. "We ain't fer goin' nowhere."

Marissa nodded, a newfound respect for her friends. She pointed to a diamond-shaped structure near the base of the water, where two lookout towers flanked the structure out in the bay. They sat on what looked like two large rocky outcroppings.

The structure itself was squat and unassuming in comparison with the multi-tiered villages crowned with colorful castles. It held no colorful stone or massive stained-glass windows. It was a construct of steel and reinforced stone.

Marissa knew the outer structure was very disarming, because it was far more complex within. Excluding its rather large mezzanine, in which a massive statue of Jasia stood in center, the building divided within into four concentric diamonds, or "rings," with several spoke-like corridors connecting the whole thing together. They called it the Rhombus, and there were many such Jasian Enclave purist fortresses elsewhere. Its design was made so that it was possible to mobilize purists, and by extension exactors, and they could reach any two points within seven minutes. Unseen to the public eye, there were two docks, a paddock, and stables, though the last she always found rather self-defeating.

The design served a religious function, too, with the building's four corners perfectly aligned to form a directional compass. It was a symbolic gesture to indicate that the Maker's gaze reaches all ends of the earth. Most traditional Jasian Enclave cathedrals were designed in a complete circle, their roofs coming together like a great dome with five brilliant spires jutting from the top. But, since this wasn't tactically sound for a defensive structure, as they didn't need massive stone pillars collapsing on them and killing their own troops or civilians during battle, the purists opted for the less auspicious design of four corners instead of the need for towering spires.

Still, every true Jasian Enclave structure was designed to create a *circumpunct,* the holy symbol of the Enclave. The building was meticulously measured, so that if someone really wanted to test it they could theoretically draw an arc from point to point on the building and it would form a perfect circle. And like a circumpunct, if you were to then draw another arcing line inside the center-most structure, you would then create another circle, and thus a true circumpunct. Marissa had no idea if this was true of the Rhombus, but it sounded quite impressive.

"There is where we need to go," Marissa whispered.

"Ye got to be kiddin' me. That's not an Enclave, Brains – that's Fort Ain't-No-Way-in-Hells."

Marissa looked down at her gnome counterpart. "We're not going to break in, Onna. We're going to walk in."

"Well, that feels rather anticlimactic."

Marissa was not amused. "The Enclave is separate from Castile and the viscount's power. Think of it like its own separate little nation. Within those walls, Cruz has no power over us."

"So why don't all criminals just run there then?" Badger asked.

"They... just can't," Marissa explained weakly. "I, however, am an exactor, and we're known for being criminals."

"I don't know, Brains, that feels awfully weak."

"Look, somewhere in there is all the medical supplies you could ever need: a curate, my family's old blacksmith, and Adjutant Love. If you have a better plan, I'd love to hear it."

"Help!" Marissa screamed as she ran forward, towards the gate to the Jasian Enclave, cradling a heavy weight in her arms. "Help, they're trying to take my baby! Please! Please help me!"

The two purists at the gate reacted immediately, opening the gate to allow her admittance. "Thank you! Maker bless you," Marissa gushed.

"Who... who, ma'am? Who is after your child?" the lead purist asked.

Marissa sobbed, "I was walking on the beach with my daughter and my sister, and these... these... jackboots appeared and grabbed for us."

Marissa produced tears and let them stream down her face. "My sister, Charlotte, they took her... they had a schooner. I bit one of them, look for the bite! Please help her!"

"Check it out," the lead purist instructed. Immediately the other nodded, drew his sword and headed swiftly in the direction that Marissa had come from. The other purist unable to leave his position, motioned her inside. "Please, ma'am, head inside to the mezzanine, tell one of the curates what happened, and they will help you. We'll try to help your sister."

Marissa bowed repeatedly. "Thank you! Thank you ser!" After a fair amount of groveling, she scampered through the solid double doors of the Rhombus.

Once inside, she made sure no one was watching, and she set down the heavy burden she held. Onna scorned up at Marissa, "Really, Charlotte was taken? Couldn't stick to the script could ye? Ye had to be more melodramatic?"

"What?" Marissa objected. "Men always fall for the damsel in distress routine. The child bit wasn't enough – I needed to improvise."

"The plan was fine," Onna scowled. "Now we have no way of getting Badger in here, because there are going to be search parties all night looking for a woman named Charlotte."

"Badger will be fine; she's resourceful. Besides you told her that if we couldn't get her inside, or we get apprehended, to go into Castile, get what supplies she can, and head back. She'll lay low and wait for us for a bit longer and then do as you said."

"Right, with a bunch of men screaming fer Charlotte?"

Marissa dismissed it with a wave. "Aw, hells, she probably doesn't even remember her name is Charlotte anymore. We never call her that."

"True," Onna admitted. "But I'm not fer liking when ye change plans like that!"

"Okay, pumpkin," Marissa jibbed. "Mommy's sorry."

Onna held up a stubby finger. "Don't ye dare. We never talk about this, do ye hear me? Ye know what this would do to me reputation?"

Marissa bit back a smile and hunched towards Onna. "Whatever you say, my little snoochie boochies."

Onna, however, continued to hold up that finger. "Not. Another. Word," the little gnome seethed.

"As you will, master strategist. Think you can handle snagging the medical supplies you need on your own now?"

Onna nodded. "As long as ye can convince the smith." Onna handed Marissa a folded piece of vellum. "I measured Rue's skull and took a diameter of the bolt and how much I am going to have to cut away. Ye need to get the smith to make ye the plate at those exact specifications."

"Got it."

"Exact specifications," Onna reiterated. "I'm serious Brains, it needs to be precise."

Marissa nodded. "Got it. Johns is good, he can do it."

"Ye're sure?"

"Yes, it's how my father lost him to the Enclave in the first place," Marissa explained.

The words seemed to put Onna at ease a little. "Hopefully ye canna speak with Adjutant Love and this won't even be a problem. Now just stick to the rest of the plan okay? No more improv work."

Marissa nodded. "Go." And with that, the gnome was gone.

Marissa looked up at the massive statue of Jasia, the only true sculpture within the entire visible chamber. Aside from the Maker himself, she was the cornerstone of the Jasian faith. The statue was carved as a beautiful human woman, though bearing certain features of every devoted race. She had the high cheekbones, almond eyes, and slightly pointed ears of an elf. Long flowing hair that fell over her shoulders and down her back tied into two indi-vidual, thick-woven braids reaching just above the small of her back. This was a staple style of the gnomish people. She also had about a dozen or so more noticeable traits that could be tied to other races, but the humans, elves, and gnomes were the iconic three followers. Jasia's height and physical stature were just neutral enough that she could resemble a taller, lithe gnome, or a slightly buxom, elven woman. To accent this, she wore only a simple full-length garment cinched tightly around her waist to reveal her womanly figure. Robes were standard to every race, and so did not gravitate to merely one style alone.

To finish off her design, Jasia's hands were clasped together in reverence, for her father above. For as long as humanity could remember, humans put their hands together to pray, no matter the god. .

In her left hand, she bore a string of pearls, each engraved with a different leaf, identifying all the elven races that followed her. On her right hand, she bore two heavy rings, one bearing a hammer, the other a cog. This signified her attunement to the forge and steam, a mainstay of the inquisitive picayune.

This was the mortal daughter of the Maker, the one he had chosen to show the world that Creation is the will of one god, not many. It was a hard road, discounting multiple civilizations' ingrained beliefs in so many different deities. Jasia had picked up followers – disciples – who believed in her teachings, and had performed feats that bordered on the miraculous, even in such magical times. In the end though, she was a martyr, sacrificing herself for her beliefs. That sacrifice solidified the true birth of her religion, ultimately turning her fledgling belief into one of the most influential empires on all of Kuldarr – an empire Marissa once faithfully served.

Marissa knelt in front of the statue and whispered a quick prayer to the daughter of the Maker. "Please," she bade the marble construct, "please help me to save my friend."

With a quick genuflection of the five points of the Jasian faith, Marissa stood and headed for the smithy.

CHAPTER NINETEEN

Marissa de Cantor y Castile

Marissa looked at the small, slightly curved and paper-thin piece of steel sitting in the palm of her hand. It was still warm from its time on the forge. "This is it?"

"That's it," the gruff, white-bearded old man answered. Marissa looked up to Corey Johns, who was in the twilight winters of his life. Canyons ran through his skin, and Marissa was well-versed on the rivers that made them by the stories she was told as a child. Johns had not had an easy life, one of constant conflict and tragedy, but he had endured. He was a living font of wisdom now, and probably her last real connection to Castile, aside from Cassandra Marin.

Though stress and sun may have weathered Johns to craggy leather, Marissa couldn't deny the strength the old shark still bore, both in spirit and in body. His forearms rippled with ripcords of muscle taut from constant use. He not only survived his profession; he embraced it as a lover. As far as Marissa knew, Johns had never taken a second wife, ever since losing his first and their daughter to the sea long before Marissa was even born.

"Thank you, Johns," Marissa whispered. "You may have just saved my friend's life."

The old man snickered, his ivory beard cast orange by the forge light. "It seems that is the one thing I make above all others since I left your father's service."

"Plates?"

Johns nodded. "Or rods. Soldiers are always hurt, Mari – it is the way of our world. It matters not what god they serve, or nation, or man, or morals, or agenda. People still get injured."

"But the Enclave has the curates..."

Johns shrugged. "I have witnessed their magic, and it is impressive. But nothing heals the body, ultimately, except itself. Magic might speed the treatment along, but the body is still responsible for its own mending. It will either work, or it will fail. So, unless the injury is extremely life-threatening, curates often do little more than numb the pain."

Marissa took the news in stride, realizing that it would likely be Onna that would be responsible for Rue's very fate.

"Mari," Johns' deep voice resonated quietly. Marissa looked up from her reverie. "By now, you've heard things I'm sure, about your mother and your father. How they died?"

Marissa nodded solemnly.

"Don't believe any of it," Johns said venomously. "Fernando had too much guile to be taken down by brigands, and your mother was too smart to even let a foolish Capitan venture near the Pale."

"What are you saying, Johns?"

The old man sighed and ran a scarred hand through his white hairs, leaving behind dark streaks of soot. "You know, just this morning I was watching the ocean, and with every new wave, I came to the realization that another must make way for it. When the former viscount Don Raphael de la Torga's benevolent hand on Castile loosened, I thought that Don Cruz's tyrant's grip was what was in store for Castile. It was the new wave, replacing the last. But then on this very morning, running across the docks like a lunatic, I see this woman in a dress, and a band of merry misfits."

Marissa smiled – she supposed they did make quite the sight running along the planks earlier that day. Johns continued. "I figured it was perhaps more privateers who just committed some larceny upon my beloved town. And then the woman in the dress turns... and I see just for a glimmer of a moment, the lady of Cantor – Miranda."

Johns looked away from Marissa suddenly, and when his eyes came back, they were surprisingly full of tears. "I served your family not only as smith, but as friend and counsel for many winters. When I left... it was the hardest decision of my life. To hear that your mother was lost at sea! It broke my heart. I loved her like a sister, I did. So, for that first instant, I thought Miranda was home. But I knew... deep down, I knew it wasn't truly Miranda, but there is no mistaking it now, Mari. you are her daughter." Marissa smiled at, what for Johns, was a deep compliment. The blustery smith continued, unabated. "I also saw in that mere fraction of a moment that the true wind of change was upon us. The lost child of Cantor, gone for how many winters now?"

"Five," Marissa said quietly.

"Five winters..." Johns shook his head, "Now you return, just as Cruz is about to take seat as permanent viscount. No, this cannot be coincidence."

"What has happened, Johns? Why is Augusto suddenly so bad? That doesn't seem like the boy I once..." she trailed off.

"Loved?" Johns finished with a broken smile. Marissa was stricken in surprise. Augusto and her affair was a secret. Clearly, Johns could read this on her face. "I knew. Hells Mari, we all knew. Did you think we were all so blind?" Marissa didn't even know how to answer. Johns shook his head. "Your father was certain the two of you were going to be betrothed. He didn't care for Augusto much, but he understood that it wasn't for him to decide who you loved. Then you became a soldier of fortune."

"It wasn't like that."

"Oh, I know!" Johns said with a laugh. "But that is what happened. I've spent enough time here, Mari. I hear things. I heard that you and Isa became exactors. I knew what that meant."

Marissa looked up, worried. "You know then that I've been... disavowed?"

Johns nodded, and grumbled a little, "Exactors always seem like they have this..." he looked down at his hands rolling his fingers into claws, "this great power. They are elusive, granted amnesty to do unspeakable acts in the name of the Maker. They get to break all the rules and suffer none of the punishments."

Marissa nodded.

Johns looked from his hands and stared Marissa in the eyes. "But the truth is, exactors are extremely fragile things. They are nothing more than flickering candles. Sure, they can burn you, burn you quite badly in fact, if you are not careful. Even one well-placed candle has the ability to burn down a village. Yet, exactors are but a single puff of air away from annihilation. A touch of wind and all their strength, all their might –" he fanned his scarred fingers out – "nothing but insubstantial smoke. And like smoke they fade into nothingness, hardly remembered at all."

In the quiet, Johns stoked the coals of his forge, sizzling and popping filling the absence of his voice. "Are you going to turn me in?" Marissa asked.

Johns' broken smile returned. "No, Mari. I have watched you fade into this world; I do not desire to watch you fade out. In truth, I think Castile needs your candle right now. For candles can also burn brightest in the darkest nights. The people need your light now as a beacon of hope. They need it to light the fire that will burn away the blight of Don Cruz."

Marissa shook her head, "I've heard so much vitriol against Augusto. Vicente, Cassandra, and now you, Johns. I need to know what it is that he has done that is so..."

"The word you are looking for is evil, Mari," Johns said with no preamble. "To understand it, just take a look at your own land."

"Cantor? What about it?"

"Where are its people?"

Marissa shrugged. "They left. Vicente said that they moved on when my father died."

"And where do you think they have gone?"

"I don't know, new lands? Back to Gurgen? I haven't exactly been graced with large swaths of time to look at my surroundings."

"Cantor may not be the largest fiefdom, Mari, but it had the most difficult duty, and it employed the most people. A people of that number does not simply disappear. Let me ask you this one instead, and think very hard, my dear. What have you seen predominantly since your return?"

Marissa had no idea what Johns was talking about. Since her return? Well, mostly what she saw was nothing but weapons pointed at her in one fashion or another. She'd seen a ton of armored faces, all filled with hate and contempt for her friends. No one seemed to want to even give them a chance, let alone her. They were angry guards bent on killing a young girl for simply trying to live. Guards willing to kill a child. Guards willing to kill her friends. Guards...

Marissa looked up. "Where are all the regular people on the outlying lands? The field hands, stablemasters, farmers... the working men, women and children? I saw none of them on my way to Cantor."

Johns smiled much smaller now, his eyes full of sadness. "Where indeed Mari? Where indeed?"

MARISSA WALKED QUICKLY TO THE WIDE, ORNATE DOOR IN front of her. It took several minutes of backtracking and redirecting to get here unnoticed, but she was sure now that she had at least a few minutes before any purists or clergy would show up. She was now following the second part of the plan as Onna laid it out – much to her discomfort. All she had now was a few minutes to get much needed answers.

She looked at the doors before her, doors she remembered fondly from her childhood. Currently closed, the large door was cast in bronze and was intricately worked into eight different panels. In each panel there was a relief within that somehow depicted the trials and tribulations of Jasia and her disciples. The quality of the work was astounding. Unlike many pictographs that ran from left to right, top to bottom, the story of Jasia on the door ran from right to left, bottom to top. This was to represent her ascension into heaven. Marissa vividly remembered her father telling her of the importance of the door, and that all the doors to Jasian Cathedrals in major provinces were often as elaborate. Whenever she came to a door of this nature, she should be aware that once she crossed its threshold, on the other side she would be speaking directly to someone who was verily a retainer to their lord the Maker, and that she owed him her utmost fealty.

She took a breath and walked to the door, immediately hearing voices on the other side... somewhat raised voices. Marissa found herself leaning her ear against the door to hear what they had to say.

"My decision still stands," a male voice said. It was a deep sonorous voice, peaceful and soothing in its way, one of those voices that you could relax, close your eyes, and just enjoy listening to. Marissa recognized it from her winters at Jasian sermons – Purist Commander, now Adjutant, Love.

"That's impractical to say the least," a far higher, more feminine voice retorted. This one too, she recognized, but not as much from childhood, since puberty changed it, but from the fact that she heard it earlier in the day. "You won't even give her a chance then?"

"She tried to kill you," the Adjutant proclaimed loud enough that Marissa hadn't even needed to press herself against the door to hear him.

"It was an act," Cassandra defended. "She needed to get to her friends."

"It did not look like an act to me," a third, also feminine voice, answered.

"That would have to be Maria," Marissa mumbled.

"She also killed several men the day before," Love continued, "fled from the authorities twice now, and created a huge public scene resulting in untold damage and countless injuries to more Castellan guardsmen."

Marissa winced at the proclamations. It wasn't sounding good.

"The guards tried to kill her before she even made it home!" Cassandra argued.

"So this woman says," the adjutant huffed. "I could see if she came forward publically, so that we could address her, and maybe my opinion might change. But really Cassandra, how can you be sure it's even her?"

"That sounds like a cue if ever there were one," Marissa whispered aloud. She took a deep breath, opened the door and stepped inside. "I don't know, Adjutant, how about you tell me?"

Three startled faces looked at her. Marissa was impressed to see Maria already had a hand on that crossbow of hers and was drawing it out. Marissa raised her hands. "I'm unarmed. I'm just here to talk." Still, Maria raised the crossbow and aimed it at her chest. Marissa sighed and shook her head. "This again."

As Marissa hoped, the chamber looked very much the same as

it had when she was only a teenager. The room was fairly cylindrical, not a true circle, but that was only because of the adjoining
corridors on the sides that ran to the other spokes of the diamond.
No, this was a circle in further representation of the circumpunct,
and she was told once that this room was in the very center of the
Rhombus, the inner circle itself. Marissa had no clue if that was
true or not; she always got terribly turned about in here and lost all
sense of direction.

Within, there were three divans where the adjutant would
listen to parishioners, and the center of the room held a thick, long
rope. Marissa gazed up at a narrow passage that no human, barring
a small child, could ever hope to fit through. It was up there where
she knew a bell lay. It was for the adjutant to ring in case he was
attacked, a large bell, almost like those found in cathedrals, and it
could be heard throughout the Rhombus. A single ring of the bell
would have purists on her in less than a minute. Sure, the Adjutant
might be dead by then, but she would have almost nowhere to go.
There were no other exits that she could see, but she wouldn't be
surprised if the adjutant didn't have some means of escape.

"Mari!" Cassandra squeaked in surprise.

"Bless the Maker," Adjutant Love said in shock. "It looks just
like her."

"I told you," Cassandra said with a smug smile.

"A little malnourished to be sure, and the winters certainly
haven't been kind to that face. Her bum seems oddly thick
compared to the rest of her, but I'll be buggered, it looks like her,"
he continued.

"Excuse me?" Marissa replied astonished. "You haven't exactly
aged like a delicate flower yourself. Your own arse looks like it's
hanging out the front of your doublet now."

At this, the adjutant barked a laugh. "If it's Marissa, she
certainly has found spirit from the child I remember."

In the few winters of elevating to the position of Adjutant, he'd let himself go more than a little. Gone was the powerful soldier of the Maker that she remembered, shining in his well-polished armor. Gone was the titan with a barrel chest and broad shoulders that seemed to hold the weight of the entire Gurgen fleet upon them. His hair had thinned significantly from the strong black tresses it had once been, when it was only slightly peppered with grey. Marissa had found that mix handsome and distinguished. Now it was papery-thin and combed loosely over his head. Jowls replaced his once firm jawline and strong chin, and though his shoulders were still broad, and his chest still barreled, there seemed to be a few extra barrels firmly lodged in his gut as well. In fact, she doubted there was any armor that could fit that frame and have any hope of protecting him. It would be like trying to armor a manatee.

Marissa, by contrast, knew she had lost all traces of her baby fat, and she was whipcord thin now, all sinew and muscle thanks to the labors of the open seas. If losing all the plump of her noble life of pomp made her look... old, then she might have to invest in the occasional bender of some pastries every now and again. Pastries the old adjutant could surely do without.

Adjutant Love looked Marissa up and down for several long, pregnant moments before a huge white smile lit up his pudgy face. "Young Lady Cantor, it really is you!"

He held his arms out wide, and she fell into his swallowing embrace. She felt his breath warm on her face, and she could distinctly smell the scent of cinnamon and red wine coming from him. Marissa never remembered the man to be a drinker. Maybe it was just one more thing she'd turned a blind eye to as she wallowed in the self-indulgence of her own noble bubble.

There was a momentary pull at her skirts, and a draft between her legs, and had the adjutant not had both hands firmly placed on her shoulder blades she would have thought the man tried to plant a hand on the bum that he had so blithely assessed moments before. As it was, he smiled at her in a fatherly way, true in form to the pious man she remembered.

He pulled back and offered her his hands with twin rings. They were the same rings that all adjutants, bishops, and even the Supreme Pontiff himself wore – the rings of Jasia. Marissa obediently bent down and kissed each one. He grasped her hand in his own, and she could feel the once hard callouses of the sword now soft in her own vice-like grip.

"Wow, strong hands," he commented.

"Rigging is hard work, Adjutant," Marissa returned.

With grace that defied his large stature, he guided Marissa to another divan that was situated between where both he and priestess Cassandra were sitting before her unannounced arrival. There was no seat for Maria.

As she glanced at the hardened woman, Marissa could see the lady still held her crossbow firmly leveled at her. "Oh for Maker's sake, calm down, Artemis," Marissa exclaimed, referencing her as the mythological goddess who protected young girls with a bow. "Can't you see there's a truce here? We're all friends for the moment."

Cassandra motioned for Maria to lower the weapon, but the woman held steadfast and did not budge.

"Language..." Adjutant Love counseled.

Marissa sighed. "I've spent the last six months surrounded by sailors, sorry."

Marissa sat with the rest of their little delegation with burning questions for Beneford Love, questions she needed answered, but she knew she needed to be diplomatic. She needed his alliance, if anything for Rusalka's sake.

"Before your surprise arrival, Priestess Marin has spoken much of what you've been through, and how you've survived all of this time." He reached out to take her hands in his once more. "Child, I am truly sorry for what you have endured."

"Thank you, Adjutant, I am grateful for your condolences, but at this time I am forced to put that past me, for I have issues of a more immediate concern."

"Your titles," Love replied simply.

Marissa nodded slowly, "Yes, that among other things. While that is indeed important, seeing as I have only one day left before the lands become Viscount Cruz's, I now have a matter that I feel is even more pressing."

"Oh?" Adjutant Love said in surprise, "Something more pressing for a noble lady than the return of her status and lands?"

Marissa chuckled wryly. "I have been gone a long time. Sometimes I still forget the priorities of where I come from, but yes, something more important to me."

"Well dear, let us hear this momentous matter that would cause a lady to place her material and godly wealth firmly behind her," Love said, and Marissa wondered if he was mocking her. Did he really believe she was who she said, or did he still believe her a charlatan? She didn't have time to think too deeply into it.

"This afternoon one of my friends was dreadfully wounded, shot in the head by Don Cruz's wilder associate."

"Osprey," Maria said between the three of them, giving name to the wilder.

"And she lives?" Love sounded amazed.

Marissa nodded. "She's rather hard-headed." She smiled at her own personal joke. "But the truth is, it's bad. The bolt has pierced her skull and is in her brain cavity. Please don't ask for details – I know little. I'm only relaying the information from my sawbones."

"You want a curate," Love stated, rather than asked.

Marissa nodded again.

"You are indeed asking for something rather momentous," he reported.

"How so?" Cassandra queried. "One of the Maker's children is hurt, and it is our sworn oath to aid where we can do the most good."

"The rub is at the last part of that statement, Cassie," Adjutant Love said, and Marissa did not miss the personal nature of it. Cassandra must at least have faith in Beneford Love if they were willing to be so informal with each other. "Right now, Marissa is a wanted fugitive, as are her compatriots."

"So what?" Cassandra pushed.

"So, if I choose to send a curate to aid Marissa's ally, I am sending a clear message to the rest of Castile."

Marissa found herself bobbing her head as she understood the rationale of his thinking.

"I don't see how that really matters," Cassandra continued to object.

"He's openly choosing a side then," Marissa said before Love could. "And by him choosing a side, the entirety of the Jasian Enclave chooses a side."

Love raised his eyebrows, impressed. "War has taught you much."

"Yeah, and it all sucks," Marissa said as she stood up. "Look, Adjutant, I have a lot of questions." She closed her eyes briefly as all the thoughts of her parents, her lands, the missing men, women, and children ran rapidly through her mind like a raging stampede of bison. "So many questions, but right now I need to know two things. Am I a criminal to the Jasian Enclave? And why? Why has the search for my mother stopped?"

Love paused, and Marissa watched as his eyes darted to the other women in the room. Carefully he began, "This is not something we should discuss with an audience, Mari."

Marissa shook her head; she wouldn't be deterred. "You may speak in front of Cassie, and I really think Maria ought to hear this." That is, if Maria was exactly what she suspected her to be.

Love sighed, and nodded. "Yes Mari, you have indeed become ex-communicated from the Enclave and are wanted as a terrorist."

Marissa could only stare at Love in shock. "And when were you going to tell me this? After I agreed to whatever tricks you have up your sleeve, Love? Were you going to use it as a trump card against me?"

Love licked his dry lips. Marissa could tell he clearly was not liking what he was about to say in front of the others. "Mari, you tried to assassinate Countess Kavon of the Seafarer's Caucus."

"Is that what they're saying?" Marissa hissed.

She looked at Cassandra, who was looking at her feet, Marissa realized that was the story she had been given about Isa too, and why Maria acted with such vitriol towards her. They were fed a lie.

She pointed a finger at Love. "When Isa and I became Exactors, we were tasked with infiltrating Kavon's cabinet on the Supreme Pontiff's orders. We were meant to use what we learned to give it to the rebels. Shit went sideways and we were found out. We fled to the rebellion, to get sanctuary, and do you know what they did?" Marissa didn't wait for Love to respond. "They 'captured' us and held us for ransom against the Seafarer's Caucus. The very side we were supposed to be on was using us against the Caucus. Well, Kavon called their bluff, and we were going to be executed, tying up that little problem of loose exactors for you tidily, I suppose, but Isa saved us by thinking quickly, and we became slaves. Slaves, Love... for three Maker-be-damned winters!"

Marissa was seething. Where Isa had never given up hope in the Jasian Enclave, Marissa always feared that they'd been abandoned because of their status as exactors. They were expendable, and as such when their usefulness was at its end... they were expended. Now Love was telling her that the very mission she was assigned was the reason she was a criminal to them. The hypocrisy was too much. She launched to her feet, and Maria, quick as ever, pointed that crossbow right at her chest.

"You know what, Love, I'm done with the Enclave anyway. So, tell me right now, why didn't you search for my mother?"

Love looked stricken. "Please Mari, you're angry... this should wait until you've had a chance to come to your senses."

Marissa growled, "Tell me!"

Love shook his head sadly, his voice quiet. "Cantor lands are too important to leave unguarded while a dispute rages as to who has legitimacy over them, Mari. You of all people should understand that.

"Do you mean the Elder Accords?"

Love nodded. "We needed the Shemma protected from those that would seek to poach it. That's always been the Cantors' tasking – and every one of you was gone. I couldn't wait. If one Elder was cut down by a lumberer, either one ignorant to the Accord or acting illegally, you know what that would mean?"

Now it was Marissa who was nodding. "The Lefhym would revoke our lands and excise us."

"They would destroy Castile, Mari," Love said flatly. "They worship those trees, believe that their deceased live on within them, watching them from the boughs. To cut down a tree is a heresy and an outright act of war against their religion. While we may consider them pagan in their belief of the one true Maker, we have a peace with them, and it must be held. Cantor has always been the vanguard in maintaining the peace. Fernando and Miranda were gone, you were ex-communicated and thought dead, so tell me, Marissa, what else could I have done?"

Marissa breathed the anger out through her nose, knowing there was nothing he could have done. She should have known that from the beginning. Of course Vicente would find it suspicious, but that was simply because he wasn't made aware of the careful balancing act that Cantor had to maintain. Love really had no choice – he needed those borders patrolled and the provisional viscount was just the man to do it.

"I understand," Marissa said at last, "but I have to go. Rue's life is in jeopardy and I've already stayed too long."

Cassandra stood too. "No, Mari, wait. We'll find a way to help her."

Marissa shook her head. "Really Cass, it's probably better if you don't. All this political shite... it's too much right now."

Beneford Love stood up and reached for Marissa. "Just calm down, my child, please sit back down. Let's at least discuss this. Talk it through. Don't give up on the Enclave. The problem is, you're a criminal now, but if you turn yourself in, we can right this."

Marissa looked at Love incredulously. "What? I can't turn myself in – I need to get to Rue and make sure she survives. She's my priority."

Love nodded his head and took a careful step forward. Marissa hadn't even known she stepped back out of his reach, and closer to the door. "Precisely Marissa, protecting 'your' people, those of Cantor. That should be your highest priority. The Lefhym will slaughter everyone if a single elder is cut down. No one understands this like a Cantor. You can't help them if you are a wanted fugitive. You need to turn yourself in. If you are awaiting a trial, you and your friend's ailments can be treated, both the physical and the spiritual. You and your associates can stay detained here in the Rhombus, not in a Castile prison. I can promise you a full Jasian Enclave investigation, not one by an angry and vindictive guard who only wants revenge for their fallen comrades. We can get this worked out, but you need to trust me, trust in the Maker."

His words sounded good, they really did. So simple. So true. Turning herself in could save Rue, could help everyone, and it might even stall Cruz from taking Cantor. But that was only if she was proven innocent. Right now, her only witnesses were a poacher and her crew, and as far as she saw, the guards tried to kill every one of them at some point.

But she *knew* Beneford Love and she remembered him to be a good man. He would watch out for her. But would he watch out for Onna, Emmell, or Rue? How long had he fought against Orcs? Or even Gnomes during the Fermania Civil War? Would his view be painted as poorly as everyone else's seemed to be?

And then there was his decision in nominating Augusto for provisional viscount. From everything she heard so far, it was the worst possible choice he could have made. But how could she truly know? It wasn't like she was here in the last five winters. For all she knew, his choice in naming Cruz as the provisional viscount may truly have been the best decision at the time. A lesser of two evils. She supposed she could never know unless she was there. She didn't know for certain if Love could really give her the best investigation and trial. It would be better than the viscount's, but she didn't know how deep he was willing to go in finding the truth of the matter.

There also was another bitter truth that both of them weren't even addressing at that moment – the real elephant in the room. She was an outlaw. Not the outlaw named by the Castile guard, but by the Jasian Enclave itself. The Jasian Enclave used her, and she was expended. Her life to them was forfeit. As soon as word of her trial reached the Citadel, they would come immediately and clean up their mess quite privately. She would disappear and her friends would have no chance at a life. None at all. In their little house-cleaning, they would without a doubt kill Rue, or worse, if they thought they could exploit her, they could make her an exactor.

Marissa looked to Maria. "Have you ever known an Exactor to be pardoned?"

Maria blinked, surprised to be asked the question, but then her face went stoic once more and she simply said, "No."

Marissa nodded. "I thought as much."

Adjutant Love shot Maria an angry look, and the woman shrugged. "She asked."

As much as it pained her, Marissa knew that Adjutant Love's path wasn't the right one. No matter how hard they tried, the verdict would not be in her favor. She needed to get back to the ship, have Onna heal Rue, and clear her name her own way, both with Castile, and the Jasian Enclave. The only rub was that she had absolutely no clue how she was going to do it.

"Adjutant... your words are pretty, but we both know the truth," she said at last. "But my crew... they are my charges. They are my people." Her eyes met Love's. "I can help them."

Love nodded at her. "They're family."

"Yes..." she said, understanding the words as she knew the old soldier himself understood them.

Adjutant Love shook his head sadly. "I can't do anything for you, Marissa, if you choose to walk out that door. You will set your own path."

Cassandra looked from Marissa to Beneford, still not understanding. "What's going on? What are you talking about? Why can't you help her?"

"I understand," Marissa agreed, and she did understand. Love couldn't be put in a position to save an exactor. "Do you think you could do one favor for me?"

Beneford took a deep breath. "Mari..."

She would make him hear her terms before he refuted. "Look into where all the Cantor civilians have gone. The place is a ghost town, and yet I haven't seen Castile itself swelling with numbers like it should be."

She could see Adjutant Love thinking about it, and finally he held up the pointer finger on his left hand. "One favor. I'll look into it, Mari."

"Wait, Mari, what about Cantor?" Cassandra asked.

"Marissa's father was very specific on the point that she is the heiress of the title and lands." Love looked at her. Marissa breathed a sigh of relief. "But it won't stay yours for very long. Once the Enclave learns of your return, they will strip you of your nobility and Cruz will get what he wants, Marissa. You are an outlaw of the church. Noble or no, your lands will be seized and redistributed."

"Just not right now."

Love nodded. "Just not right now. It is not for me to decide such matters. That is for the quill pushers back in the capitol of Gurgen to handle."

"Cruz won't be happy."

"I can handle the viscount for now."

"Thank you."

Love shook his head. "Don't thank me, Marissa. I don't know why you are doing this, and I don't think this is the smartest option, but I won't stop you. Unless you surrender, our connection ends right here, right now." Marissa looked to Cassandra. "Her too," he added.

Marissa bit her lip, her promise to Isa coursing through her mind.

Cassandra was shaking her head. "Why are you doing this?" she asked, not understanding. "Stay. Adjutant Love can help you. I can help you. If you try to do this alone, you will lose. You will lose everything! Think about your parents, Mari! Your people!"

"She is," Maria said, drawing the looks of everyone in the room to her. "She's thinking like an Exactor."

Marissa squeezed her eyes shut and felt hot tears rolling down her face. Maria was more right than she even knew.

"Something has changed you, Marissa de Cantor," Love told her. "And I hope to the Maker that it is for the better, because right now I cannot see it."

Marissa shrugged, wiping away the tears. "The Maker works in strange ways..." Reaching for the door, she started to turn away.

Love nodded. "That he does."

"Mari, don't do this!" Cassandra objected, but Marissa made her choice. The bronze door opened to her push, and on the other side, just raising his hand to knock, was Don Augusto Cruz.

CHAPTER TWENTY

Don Augusto Cruz

Augusto Cruz was not having a very good day. Sure, it started out as it always did – a woman in his bed, another on retainer if the first bored him or he just wanted to spice things up. Then, a good breakfast. It was, in his mind, the most important meal of the day, the meal that wakes up the man and invigorates him to carry on the important details of running a massive port like Castile.

Then he received the news: Marissa was spotted heading to Tossa de Marin. Of course she was, he knew. After a night seeing the poor remains of Loja de Cantor, she would go to the next best place she knew. Marissa always was predictable that way. So, he dispatched the new teniente, Bevan whatever-his-name-was, and Osprey to deal with Marissa's ragtag group and retrieve the "hand cannon."

Instead, Osprey returned with news that nearly a dozen of his men were injured, that some might not make it through the night, and that every single one of Mari's crew escaped on her ship! They were gone, leagues out at sea, last seen near the Pale. They would probably be at the Citadel within the week, or if they were smart, they'd head directly for Sentinel's Barrow. So, Marissa and her weapon were gone. Just like that.

It did not please him. Nor did the damage control he now needed to do. Immediately, he dispatched one of his trusted aides to report to the adjutant about the impostor acting as Marissa de Cantor, and all the damage she caused in her wake. While Augusto had no control over the purists, Beneford Love at least listened to him. He knew they would arrest her on sight – not that this was going to happen now that she was gone. Still, it was better to be safe than sorry. He was too close to controlling Cantor now. He needed to see who, and if, anyone was willing enough to vouch as witness to her return. He assumed that Cassandra Marin might, and that would do him no good. He needed to get Adjutant Love to see reason, as he always did, and slap Cassandra's mouth shut before she could sway any of the other nobles that might have a weak spine about their cause. If she did, and Marissa assumed control of her lands now, everything would be set back for months, maybe even winters.

Now, after hours of assuring all the right heads that everything was fine, and that no, that wasn't Marissa de Cantor you saw, he now found himself walking down the spoke-like corridors of the Rhombus, heading to the adjutant's wing, his mind a maelstrom of dark thoughts.

Like a giant silent shadow, Osprey followed obediently behind him. His only solace was that he knew Osprey was no happier about the situation than he was. Osprey was a predator, one of the deadliest he'd seen. She assured him that she shot the orc that allied itself with Mari. Shot the thing in the head, and still it continued to fight on, enough so that it dispatched six of his riders! Wilders were not well-versed in failure. Normally, if they failed it was against something bigger, stronger, or more cunning than they, and they were dead. No, she failed to kill the orc, it defeated soldiers she was allied with, and the orc escaped, seemingly no worse for the wear. Osprey had been one-upped and she would not rest until her anger was sated, preferably with Orc blood.

Tumultuous thoughts echoed in Augusto's mind as he approached the door of Adjutant Love. No purists detained him or Osprey on their way – none ever did, as there was an unspoken understanding that the viscount could go where he liked... even here. So, as he closed his way to the door, his distracted thoughts did not put together the additional voices on the other side of the door. He reached up to politely knock, because even though he was viscount, he was a man of gentry first and foremost. And men of gentry were nothing if not polite, even to a lowborn noble like Beneford Love, for it wasn't his nobility that gave Love power, it was his station. Augusto always respected station.

As his fingers rapped gently upon the chamber door, the barest scrape of knuckles, the door suddenly flew open, and he found himself – impossibly – face-to-face with none other than Marissa de Cantor y Castile.

Marissa blinked those large dark eyes several times at him in equal surprise. Strangely, with everything that transpired that day, his first thought upon seeing this woman was, *she is breathtaking*. However, before he could address her, a large muscular forearm appeared before him, and he was pushed behind the powerful hulk that was Osprey. Now clear of Osprey's path, the titanesque woman lunged forward for the lithe Castellan in a torn dress.

"This is a house of the Maker!" Love bellowed behind the two women. "There will be no violence here!"

Augusto was still trying to piece everything together. *It's Marissa, she's here!* By the time he registered his fortuitous luck, he realized it was going to be short-lived. The wilder held only murder in her eyes for Marissa. She suffered defeat by his ex-beau and her troupe. She failed to strike down the orc – she would not be stopped again. Augusto could only watch as Osprey reached out with both meaty hands to wrap them around Marissa's elegant, thin neck. He knew the truth of what was to come, and his mind was already two steps ahead now, trying to evaluate the damage control he would need to manage. Osprey murdering someone in front of the Jasian Enclave was far above the typical problematic faux-pas. Marissa was a criminal, so that made it easy enough to explain, and it could be assumed that it was in self-defense. The rub was, if Adjutant Love offered her any clemency or immunities before his timely arrival, then Maker help him.

Osprey's thick fingers began to throttle Marissa, and Augusto knew that with a simple flick of her wrist, the massive wilder would break the noblewoman's neck. But Osprey didn't. She froze.

Augusto heard a strange click. Marissa said with lethal menace, "If I so much as even feel your pulse in your fingers, I will blow your womb straight out of your arse."

Augusto carefully stepped around the towering woman to see what stopped the titan dead in her tracks. His eyes went wide as he saw not one, but two, odd cylindrical metal devices pushed firmly into the Osprey's lower abdomen.

These must be the "hand cannons." They were peculiar contraptions. Studying the long barrels, he had to admit that Osprey's explanation of them was rather spot on. They did look like little ship's culverins.

Augusto also understood in that moment that Osprey must know what was placed against her stomach. It would be the only reason she wouldn't follow through with killing Marissa. Were it a blade or crossbow, Osprey wouldn't have hesitated and took the blade or bolt in the gut just to complete her kill. But the teniente that Marissa shot the day before died that morning... very painfully. Osprey feared nothing as far as Augusto knew, but those devices buried against her gut were still such unknowns. His wilder was smart. Osprey wouldn't risk the fangs of a poisonous snake unless she knew she could live through it.

"You said you were unarmed!" Cassandra's aide Maria yelled in angry alarm, her crossbow trained on the both of them.

"Well, in my defense," Marissa growled, "you keep pointing that damn thing at me! What am I supposed to say? Oh, I've got two flintlocks wrapped in the folds of my dress, is that okay?" Osprey's hands were still planted firmly around her throat, but she spoke through with little more than a crack in her voice. "Now, why don't you be a good giant and take your sausages off my neck?"

Osprey didn't move. Augusto watched as Marissa slid one of the strange weapons Marissa called a flintlock up the towering behemoth's abs and drew it beneath her chin. He watched in fascination as Marissa drew back a hammer mechanism and placed her finger on what appeared to be a trigger.

"This one blew a hole completely through a scales' skull at this distance. Do you want to test and see if yours is thicker than his was?"

"Marissa..." Augusto said, finally finding his voice.

"I would curtsey, milord, but I am at the moment otherwise detained," the shrewd woman replied bitingly.

"Osprey, let the lovely lady go," he commanded. The Osprey's wild eyes looked down briefly at Augusto and, after several heartbeats, she obediently pulled her hands free from Marissa's neck.

Augusto could see thick red bands now lined Marissa's sunkissed throat. Osprey's grip was not a delicate thing. "Marissa," he began, hoping to sweet talk the exotic creature before him that once was his lover. Instead, to his surprise, the weapon that was against Osprey's abdomen was now leveled directly in front of his face. He stared at it in surprise, and then glanced at Osprey, who was tensing to move.

"Marissa, my flower, why such hostility? Should you not be

ecstatic to see me again?" Augusto asked, in his most debonair voice.

"Maybe," Marissa said to him with a shrug. She narrowed her eyes, "But when you've taken my lands, chased off my friends, and tried to kill me not once, but twice now, it rather dampens the mood."

"Don Cruz, Lady Cantor, please, do not make me alert the purists. This does not need to degenerate further. How about we all talk like the civilized aristocrats we are?" Adjutant Love interjected.

"What a marvelous idea, Lord Adjutant," Augusto replied. "Perhaps we could have beverages ordered?" He glanced briefly to Cassandra. "And may I add, Lady Marin, what an unexpected pleasure it is to see you here as well."

Priestess Marin looked at him agog for a moment before rolling her eyes. The tribade. It was a shame too, because as Cassandra grew older, she was becoming quite the looker. Such a waste. He instead focused his attention back towards Marissa, more than a little bit leery of the barrel that was hovering before him. He wanted to reach out and touch it – it seemed so peculiar – but he wasn't sure what would cause the thing to discharge, and he was none too thrilled with the idea of having one of those painful looking balls lodged somewhere in his person.

"What say you, Marissa? Put down this weapon of yours and let us speak as nobles. We are not creatures of violence," he bade.

"Tell that to your wilder who shot my friend today," Marissa hissed, "or your men yesterday that were going to throw a young girl from the cliffside."

"Misunderstandings..." he began, but Marissa cut him off.

"My friend is wounded and dying, and you call it a misunderstanding?"

"That's exactly what it is!" Augusto exclaimed. "Marissa, why are you running around like this? You are fleeing like some common vagrant! You know all you had to do was come to me directly. Why didn't you? So much of this could've been avoided. Were you afraid I'd be angry with you still?"

"Angry with me?" Marissa said nonplussed.

"Yes. Your decision to leave affected both of us, Marissa. You know how much I cared for you; you hurt me when you left."

Marissa let out what sounded like a pained laugh. "You cared for me? That's rich. I was in love with you, Augusto, and I was what to you exactly? Part of your stable? Harem, maybe? I think you hurt me far deeper than I hurt you."

"I was a young man, Marissa. I was lustful, and they were youthful indiscretions I thought owed to me for my nobility, but my heart was for you. Always for you."

"That ham-fisted line might have worked on me five winters ago, but not anymore," Marissa told him, stoned-faced.

"And perhaps some of that ire is deserved," he admitted. "But this isn't a discussion we should be having in front of an audience, especially not this 'kind' of audience."

"Agreed," she told him.

"So, what say you? Lower your... what did you call them, flint-locks? Lower them and let us talk."

"I would, as I have some important things to say to you, Augusto, but I am rather pressed for time."

"Because of your wounded friend?" he asked.

She nodded tightly.

"Marissa, let's resolve this. Talk out this quarrel that has seemingly sprung up between us, and I promise that I will endeavor to help your friend," he said as charmingly as he could. Augusto made sure not to look over at the anger seething in his wilder's eyes.

Marissa, however, could be seen easily weighing her options. That was good. This friend's desperate need could be an advantage he could exploit. Finally, she shook her head and leveled the gun right between his eyes completely ruining the moment. "No, I don't have time for this. If you want to parley, we can parley... later. Now move out of my way, Augusto."

"This is a mistake," he said through gritted teeth. "Face it, doll, you need me."

"Actually, *ex*-lover, I have everyone I need." She flicked the gun she had in front of his face to the right. "And I'm not a doll. Now move."

And for the first time since he was a child, Augusto had to obey someone else's command.

───────

After Marissa was gone down the hall, Cruz turned to Osprey and whispered, "I want you on her as soon as she clears the gates."

"And if she reaches the water first?" Osprey asked.

"Use my fleet. I don't care what it takes – pursue her and kill her," he growled.

Osprey nodded and then disappeared down the hall.

"Siccing your pet after your ex-girlfriend?" Cassandra asked bitterly.

Augusto flashed her his most charming smile, though he didn't know why he bothered. "She is a wanted fugitive, Lady Marin, and I believe you were witness to me offering her a chance to explain her actions, and she refused. I have no choice but to apprehend her once she clears Enclave grounds, as I am sure she is under some type of immunity."

"Yes," Love said, "she is a wayward child of the Maker, and I wanted to offer her a chance to explain herself as well."

"And did she?"

Love shook his head. "Not as much as I'd've liked."

Augusto nodded, and looked to Cassandra, smiling once again.

"I thank you for being here as a witness, my dearest lady, but at this time, Adjutant Love and I need to have words."

"And if I am not done here?" she asked.

Love now turned to Cassandra. "My child, I have heard your words, and I will give you an answer soon. Please adjourn now for this eve and go with the Maker. I must speak with the viscount."

"Provisional viscount," Cassandra reminded Adjutant Love. "This is why she's running, gentlemen. Because of duplicity, on both your parts. We could've cleared this up had we taken the time to at least find out why she did what she did. Instead, no, she gets knee-jerk reactions of violence. Come Maria, let us return to Tossa de Marin. I need to figure out how to salvage this."

"Of course, priestess," Maria answered.

As Cassandra passed by Augusto, she curtseyed slightly. "Don Cruz."

"Lady Marin."

Once she was gone and he could hear her steps fading down the hall, Augusto turned on Adjutant Love. "You're not going soft on me are you, Beneford?"

Augusto watched as Beneford Love's demeanor changed from pious priest to the man he truly knew. "Don't be ridiculous, Cruz. Marissa barged in out of the blue. Maker, I don't know how she even got on the grounds! I would've arrested her on the spot if not for Cassie." The adjutant walked over to his bar and poured himself a glass of red wine. He poured a second for Augusto and handed him the glass.

"Is she going to pose a problem?" Augusto asked.

"Cassie or Marissa?"

"You tell me," Augusto said, taking a sip of wine. It was delicious as always. Beneford had impeccable taste.

"I can control Cassie," Beneford said as he walked to his divan and took a seat. "Marissa is a different matter; her very existence now poses a problem."

"So, Osprey will be taking care of that inconvenience shortly," Cruz told the adjutant.

The heavyset man looked over his wine glass with raised eyebrows. "Were you not just professing that your heart belonged to her?"

"True," Cruz agreed with a nod, "but absence will make the heart grow fonder as I am told."

"She hasn't been absent long enough, apparently. Too many people have seen her alive. Vicente and his posse in Loja de Cantor, Cassandra, her exactor, the people of Tossa de Marin," Love reminded him.

"So what?" Cruz declared. "Bandits were a problem before near Loja de Cantor. Vicente could encounter them again if need be, but in greater numbers. Both Cassandra and the exactor can easily be reassigned. Not that Cassandra would leave very willingly, but she'll go."

"So quick to kill your own people?" Love asked curiously.

"Of course not, but we are too close to attaining our goal of a free and independent Castile," Cruz said with fervor. "I will do what it takes to achieve that end, and someday the people will thank me for it."

Love raised his glass in salute. "I commend you, boy, I truly do. What you've accomplished in these last few winters, I didn't think it could be done."

Cruz took a seat next to Love. "And don't you think it's a bit suspicious that Marissa returns now? One day out from my control of Cantor, and absorption of the Elder Accords?"

"You think there are other influences at play?"

Cruz shrugged. "I hope not, Beneford. But it is rather a suspicious thing to find an ex-exactor in conference with an adjutant and a priestess."

Love took another sip, "You are devilishly clever, so I could see how you would draw that conclusion, but when you came to me with this idea of yours, wasn't it I that put your plan into motion?"

Cruz nodded.

"So, would I not have just as much to lose in this as you, if not more at this point?"

Cruz shrugged. "You could be getting cold feet."

"Boy, I have survived thirty-six campaigns against the wilders, not to mention countless naval campaigns during the Fermania Civil War, witnessing all manners of atrocity, all while you were still nursing your momma's teats. Don't talk to me about cold feet."

Cruz yawned. He'd heard this rigmarole before. "Fair point – I concede, my dearest Adjutant. But could someone else in the Enclave have gotten word?"

Love shrugged, "It is possible. Any number of people could have witnessed the proceedings once the pact accords was drawn up. I'm sure they're in triplicate somewhere."

"Please tell me at least that she didn't see the map."

"Of course not. She didn't get the map, Don Cantor's will, the title to her lands, or the pact. All of it is still in the chest, safe and secure, and impossible to get into without the key." Love patted his small lambskin hip satchel.

Augusto looked over his shoulder and saw the ornate chest solidly secure. "And your people are ready then? For after I take over Cantor?"

"They will do their part."

Augusto relaxed as he leaned into the divan. It was still all coming together very nicely. He sipped his wine as he thought about the last few moments. "She was rather incredible, though, wasn't she?"

Beneford took a long drink, emptying his glass before looking over to him. "I assume we're talking about Marissa?"

Augusto nodded.

Beneford studied his wine glass, "War changes people,

Augusto. Sometimes for the better, most often for the worse. Where Marissa lies, I cannot say, but yes, she has certainly found herself."

Augusto thought about this for a long while, as Beneford Love filled and then drained another glass of wine. Idly he realized that Marissa was the only woman to break it off with him. Every other woman, he always discarded first. It was a curiosity, and he wondered if that was why he was feeling the way he was feeling right now. She challenged him. He had yet to have a worthy antagonist, and now, when all seemed like certain victory, a real challenge finally presented itself.

"Pining for the glory days?" Love asked, as he topped off another glass of wine.

Cruz looked over to the adjutant. "Of course not. Just wondering if Osprey has killed her yet."

Love snorted as he slowly rocked and lowered his bulbous mass into the divan. "If Marissa is smart, she'll hover around here for as long as she can."

"Yes, but she's not smart right now, is she? She's urgently trying to find a way back to her friend. She'll break for it, and Osprey will be there when she does." Augusto leaned his head over to look at the adjutant more clearly. "Did she ask about her parents, by chance?"

Love nodded, enjoying his latest pull of spiced wine with a satisfied grunt. "Just why we never searched for her mother," he added after a moment. "She said she had questions for me, but all she wanted more than anything was a curate."

"Not even her lands?" Augusto asked curiously.

"She said they weren't as important as her friend, or something along those lines," Love answered, now slightly besotted.

"Really? That's vexing."

Love laughed, but Augusto could hear it was full of disdain. "Marissa's a soldier now, not some dandy noble – I could read it in everything she did. Her lands, while a little important to her, mean nothing compared to her crew. Something you would know nothing about."

"And for good reason, Beneford. If what you say is true, her attachments to these cretins are what is going to be her undoing," he held up a finger. "If Osprey isn't dismantling her like a broken doll as we speak."

The adjutant's glazed expression took him in with mild amusement. "Even after everything I've just told you, and everything you've already seen, including that grand escape today on the docks, you still think Marissa is the same naïve, love-struck little strumpet from five winters ago, don't you?"

"People don't change."

"No," the adjutant agreed. "They grow. And I think Marissa has outgrown all the expectations you've ever set for her, and that bothers you. She's an adversary you didn't count on, and one you have no way to predict."

Augusto wrinkled his nose in disdain at Love's assessment, but he knew the veteran was right. Marissa was a wildcard here, and if she survived the Osprey this night, he wasn't quite sure what would follow. Part of that thought filled him with anger at the off chance she could ruin everything. But a large part of him was invigorated by the challenge.

Faintly, Augusto heard a very light gong of the bell above him. It was weak, and in any other circumstance he probably would have ignored it. But it seemed so suddenly out of place in the silence of the room, that he looked up behind him out of impulse. To his alarm he caught the glimpse of a tiny moccasin disappearing up into the hole. Augusto quickly shot to his feet, staring up into the dark void. Did he really just see what he thought he saw?

"Cruz, what is it?" the old adjutant asked, and Cruz realized now that Love would have seen it for sure, if something were there.

He was far better trained to ferret out these matters than Augusto. Unless he was drinking that spiced wine for quite some time... in which case, he wouldn't hear a thing.

Augusto looked at the carafe of wine to confirm his suspicions – the damn thing was almost empty. No, he could've imagined it. As his eyes drifted back to the waning portal above them, they passed once more over the secured ornate chest. Except there was something different about it now. The lock was open.

Throwing the divan out of the way with one arm, he ran towards the chest. Cruz slapped the lock out of the linkage and pulled the draw open. The contents within chilled him to the bone.

In a fit of rage, he threw his glass of red wine against the wall, the crystal shattering in a glittering crimson shower and leaving a burgundy swell against the slate grey brick.

"What is your problem, Augusto?" Adjutant Love barked, staggering to his feet.

Augusto used all his strength to tilt the chest to its side. It was a mighty effort, since the adjutant had it laden with lead and reinforced with steel so that no one could simply steal the chest when he wasn't in the room. The lock was among the best in all of Kuldarr, virtually impossible to pick, he had once told Cruz. Breathing heavily, he looked down at the contents that should've spilt out upon the floor. Except there was nothing. Nothing at all.

"What is this?" the adjutant howled, looking at the empty container lined in black silk.

"You said it was impossible to open without a key!" Augusto pointed at the chest, now lying on its side.

"It is!" the adjutant argued back. "It's the work of the elves. Impossible to crack."

"Then how is it opened? Where is the map? Where is everything? You said Marissa wasn't near it!"

"She wasn't!" Love defended, "And nothing could open it but this key!"

The adjutant unclipped the tassel holding the hip satchel shut and thrust his hand in the small pouch to prove his point. Augusto waited impatiently, and then watched as Love's face first went from anger, to confusion, and then to horror.

Augusto tracked his eyes down to the satchel and saw the glint of Beneford's ring poking through the bottom of the satchel. Then he saw as Love stuck two of his fingers through a slit at the bottom of the lambskin.

Once more, Augusto Cruz looked up at the hole in the ceiling. "Tell me Adjutant, who could fit through that hole?"

Love's mouth worked several times before he said, "No one. It's designed that small just so no one could try and sneak in here to kill me."

"A child could fit through that," Augusto said, his mind in a whirl.

"No child could fit through something that small. A toddler maybe, but no child over four winters has any hope of squeezing through that space."

Augusto was already making his way to the door; he already knew who was here, who could fit through a space that small, and who could hide under the folds of a dress unnoticed. Marissa was turning out to be a cunning adversary indeed, and the horror of it thrilled him. "Summon your purists, Love. We have a thief on the premises."

"I'm telling you, Augusto, no human child could fit through that hole."

Augusto wheeled on the inebriated adjutant. "It's not a child, you idiot, and it's not a human. Think! What was special about Marissa's crew? What did she have on it?"

Even as intoxicated as he was, Augusto was relieved to see how quickly Love understood. "Maker help us."

CHAPTER TWENTY-ONE

Marissa de Cantor y Castile

The bell's sonorous clang echoed throughout the spokes of the concourse. Marissa tensed for a moment as several purists drew steel and ran past her, heading for the adjutant's quarters. Clearly Onna was successful at... something. Whether it was getting her titles like Marissa hoped, or just pissing off Love and Cruz, she didn't know. "I hope she didn't kill one of them," she murmured as an afterthought.

Marissa feared for Onna. This was the weakest part of her plan. Marissa knew the bell holes and how they were essentially hollow chambers that ran all along the diamond-shaped structure, with additional holes interspersed throughout, so that the sound would travel to purists at all ends of the garrison, but she had no idea where the gnome could successfully exit. Soon everyone in the concourse was gone, and Marissa wasn't quite sure if she should backtrack to try and find Onna, or press on further and hope that Onna would meet her in the mezzanine.

Turns out, Marissa needn't have worried.

"Defiler's furry funbag, that is loud!" she heard Onna curse from somewhere above her.

Marissa shot a look to the ceiling, but all she could see was the same corrugated dark stone that lined all the walls. "You'd think they'd decorate a corridor? So, at the very least you could tell them apart," she mumbled to herself before jumping into a full mock conversation. "Oh, where are you heading?" Then, she lowered her voice, pretending to sound like a man. "Corridor C, you know the one with the painting of the gnome." Back to normal: "The naked one?"

"Brains?" Onna replied in confusion. "Is that ye? Are ye talkin' to ye soddin' self again?"

Marissa flushed and nodded, and then felt stupid because she realized that Onna couldn't see her. "Yes, I think I'm below you."

"I can barely hear shite wit all this ringing. Where is this other portal ye were speaking of?" Onna asked. "After I climbed in the hole, I had like eight directions to choose from, yet I peeps no other holes."

Marissa looked around at the bland walls, it had to be close, as she could hear Onna. Then she realized that the gnome could be further back and the sound was just carrying, much like the bell. It was possible in that moment that everyone could hear Onna.

Marissa looked around frantically and spotted a hole in the wall, itself hidden discretely behind a pillar. The gap between the two was narrow, but it was possibly just large enough for Onna to pass through. She hoped it would be enough.

"I see a hole!" Marissa called up.

"I can't see anything, Brains – get me some light," was the reply.

Light! Marissa looked around for something she could use. It took less than a minute to locate a sconce against the wall that held a burning oil lantern. With a well-angled twist she broke the lantern free and hurried to the hole. Without worrying about who else might hear or see, she thrust the lantern between the narrow gaps of the pillar and wall.

"I see it!" came a much louder reply, but still no signs of the gnome.

It felt like a lifetime before Onna's small hand first peeked through the opening, and Marissa let out a sigh of relief. She put the lantern on the floor and then helped the gnome through. She could see a rolled-up bundle of documents in Onna's belt.

"It's bad, isn't it?" Marissa hazarded.

Onna looked up to her with sorrow in her eyes. "Aye lass, tis not something ye need to hear just yet though. Just know that sod, Vicente, was right."

Marissa closed her eyes and nodded. Though her heart sank just a little more in the depths of sorrow, she knew it wasn't the time or place to grill Onna on what she overheard. They needed to get out of the Rhombus first, get to the ship second, and save Rusalka third. Everything else came after, assuming they survived. "Any suggestions on how to get out? I don't think we'll be able to do the same trick twice?"

"Nay," Onna agreed. "Ta make matters worse, ye boy toy sicced 'is wilder on ye with orders to kill once ye breech the gates. Me has no doubts that fustilug is skulking about somewheres."

"Simply, lovely," Marissa said with a sigh. "We can't go through the main gate, and with this alarm, there's no way we can hope to scale a wall."

"And we don't have time to hunker down and wait it out," Onna added.

"Yeah," Marissa agreed, exasperated. "So that really only leaves us one option."

"We're gonna steal us a boat, ain't we?"

Marissa looked down at the gnome smiling up at her madly. "Yes, we are."

THE TRIP DOWN TO THE ENCLOSED DOCKS WAS MERCIFULLY devoid of purists or priestesses, who had all elected to respond to either protecting the adjutant or covering the traditional exits. She knew from her training with the exactors that the docks were designed like a bay and enclosed with a set of massive gates that lifted out of the water to allow entry and exit of all naval vessels. Marissa also knew that there would be no way to open those gates without separating, and she wasn't ready to be apart from her ship-mate again – not after the beginning of the day's fiasco – so she had another plan in mind.

"Help me get a dinghy into the water," Marissa instructed.

She watched as Onna looked around at all of the massive warships, ranging from the smaller single-masted flat-bottomed cogs to the massive, four-master ironclad, and scalemade carracks, all docked in the manmade bay.

"We can't hope to pilot any of them, Onna, and now it's my turn to implement a plan. You got us in – I'm getting us out."

As usual, Onna opened her mouth to retort, but this time she closed it and instead nodded. "Where is everyone?" she asked a moment later as they were dragging their dinghy into the water. As the ship floated in the water, Onna threw her satchel in. It now contained all of the documents she took from Love as well as the medical supplies she acquired.

"That's waterproof, right?" Marissa asked tentatively. She hadn't considered the supplies and paperwork when she quickly made this plan.

"Aye lassie, tis quite waterproof, no need ta worry."

Marissa nodded. "Good, because it's going to be floating, and to answer your question, they'll be here any moment, as soon as they realize we aren't exiting out any of the landside portals and that all walls are secure. They're going to be looking to the sea for our craft."

"So then... this fer might no being the best o' ideas," Onna retorted.

"No, we want them to come," Marissa said. "I'm counting on it in fact."

Onna raised an eyebrow. "We stowin' away?"

"Not so much. You'll see." Waist deep in the warm waters, Marissa looked about for what would hopefully be the frontline ship they dispatched. "Thanks for the training," she mumbled to herself. The purists drilled the tactics into her, and for once something good came of it. She saw the ship of the line that would be acting as their pursuer. Reaching in, she slid the oars between the seat boards and then pointed to the cog. "That one."

With Onna's help, Marissa pushed their dinghy up against the cog. Looking about once more for pursuers, she noted that the dock on the other side for visitors was beginning to become quite active. Onna smiled wryly. "What are ye up to, Brains?"

"They're searching the civilian craft – we don't have much time. Take your bag back." Onna reached in and took the bag, and Marissa released a held breath as she saw it bob neatly next to Onna's head and not sink as she feared. "This is going to be the tricky part," she told Onna, flipping the dinghy over so that it was capsized. Onna continued to stare at her in a mixture of curiosity and confusion.

Without another word, Marissa showed her exactly what she was up to as she began to slide the dinghy down the hull of the cog. Moments later the two were panting heavily, their water laden bodies slick with sweat as well as the sea.

"This is absolutely not what I had in mind when ye said we'd take a ship," Onna's voice echoed in the small hollow space.

Marissa looked slightly over her shoulder at the gnome whose little legs were lazily kicking behind her. "I know," Marissa replied confidently.

There was a little space of air in the capsized dinghy and the two had to lay on their backs, their heads only breaking the water by a few inches.

"Brains, ye make some mad decisions, but this be ranking up as one of the higher one's ye's ever did."

Above them they heard dozens of feet begin hammering across the deck. "They're here," Marissa whispered.

Both fell silent as the thundering of steps was followed quickly by a loud groan and then the rhythmic thump as a chain and anchor were removed from the water. There was a great lurch and the water around them began to drift backward. They were moving forward.

"It's working," Marissa said, holding her breath.

"I really hope so, otherwise the barnacles are going to shred the hull and if we're not careful, us as well."

Marissa didn't answer the gnome. Instead she concentrated on what she could hear and what she could see in the water at her chest. What she did notice as they moved forward was a stirring of the sandy floor and a fresh influx of fish. The large gates beneath the Rhombus that led to the marina were opening; and with them, their chance of escape.

A large scraping groan echoed directly above her head and she held tight to both ends of the small dinghy as it slid backwards grating along the flat bottom of the cog that they hid their ship underneath. With a sudden jolt that made Onna squeak like a piglet lit on fire, their dinghy was held in place.

Marissa took a deep breath and plunged her head beneath the water to look back between Onna's pumping appendages. The large stern-mounted rudder was what stopped their motion, as Marissa hoped. It was now holding them firmly in place.

She surfaced back up in their air pocket. "We're good – just don't rock too much, otherwise we'll roll up the side of the cog and probably be battered to death by oars."

Onna spit out a torrent of saltwater and colorful expletives as the water began to lap within, reducing their space even more. "How are we gonna know when we're far enough out?" she asked between the lurching swells of water.

"I think when the ground disappears and the water turns cold, that'll be good," Marissa replied. Though she didn't know how deep the marina was, she felt it had to be shallower than the sea itself, once they passed the towers. It all hinged on passing those towers unseen.

"Ye know," Onna began with a sputtered chuckle, "if we pull this off, that wilder is gonna right get murderous that we got away a second time from her in the same day!"

Marissa scowled at the thought. Hopefully that murderous intent might be directed towards herself or Augusto. Even then as she thought about Augusto, she couldn't deny to herself how good he looked now. Though she knew he was likely to blame for every-thing happening, she marveled at his ability to convey such sensu-ality and emotional range only with his dark eyes alone. She couldn't help but feel a strange longing to run her fingers across his firm jawline, or to tousle his soft, curly black hair. Even in the briefest of encounters, she could see those equal parts machismo and sensitivity that made her fall for him when she was a love-struck teenager.

She shook away the thoughts and looked down into the water. Beneath her, the world faded away into a void of deep blue. "I'm gonna check for the towers. Don't move," she told Onna.

"Hardy, har, har," the gnome replied. "Like me's canna go anywhere right now."

Marissa didn't bother with a response and instead took another breath and plunged herself underwater. She knew she was going to have to be quick, because there was no way she could swim as fast as the rowing men once they got a steady rhythm going. She only hoped she didn't catch a long oar into her skull in the process.

She released her hold of the dinghy and started paddling backward. As the ship lumbered by, she grabbed onto the rudder, careful not to cut her hands on the sharp barnacles. The last thing they needed right now was for her blood to bring in the sea's predators. Safely in the wake of the ship she clambered up the wobbling rudder. She would have to be quick about it because it wouldn't take the helmsman long to realize there was drag on the rudder. When that happened, her gambit would be up.

She pulled herself out of the water and looked about, trying to catch sight of the two towers. She looked up just as massive lights lit up the water. Blinded by the intense beam, she plunged herself back underwater. She held on, listening for any muted screams to look on the stern or rudder, or that she had been spotted. The heat of the light seemed to burn into her, as if they knew exactly where she was. She waited, her lungs aching.

Within a minute the lights turned away from the back of the boat. Tentatively she resurfaced and found the twin towers now a safe five-hundred meters behind them shining their lights on a cog heading west down the coastline.

"Unfurl the sails!" Marissa heard the boatswain order above. A loud snap and crack followed as the sails rolled out. "Stow the oars!"

Marissa turned to see the oars lifting out of the water. That was her cue. It was the best time to get back to Onna. Once the ship caught wind, she wouldn't hope to catch it swimming.

Marissa plunged beneath the salty swells once more and kicked hard off the rudder. Were it any more than a half dozen feet she had to travel, she would have been hard pressed to make it with how fast the cog was moving. The seafaring purists were a well-organized and efficient lot – far more so than Augusto's men.

Kicking furiously, she barely made the short distance and pulled herself back into the small sanctuary they created. She could see Onna had shifted her handholds to the dinghy seating, and Marissa quickly realized why. At the speed they were moving it was too hard to hold on to the ends of the dinghy's frame itself. She emulated her boatswain.

"They've unfurled and are setting rigging now. Oars are stowed, and we're a good distance past the lookout towers," she updated Onna.

"How far at sea are we? Can we hope to row in a riptide or longshore current? Did ye see the swells?" Onna asked.

"Too far for currents, swells didn't seem horrible. If I had to guess, I'd say a little more than half a league."

Onna nodded and listened intently. There was a flapping, almost clapping, sound above them that wasn't coming from the men. "Sounds like the sails are luffing." Finishing her statement, Onna was rewarded with a mouthful of saltwater, which she quickly spit up. "So now what, we just rock free?"

"Yes, as soon as they're on a good run. This way if we happened to be spotted, they'll be going too fast and will be forced to turn about at a great distance or try and back wind."

"Savvy that," Onna agreed.

"We'll keep the dinghy turtled. It'll be harder to see at night. Once they are a distance away, we'll flip the boat."

"And then just row for the mainland?" Onna asked.

Marissa shook her head. "The crow's nest is going to be focused on the shore, so we stay far to its stern and starboard, and follow discreetly. When they pass by Cuddle Cove, we'll take our opportunity to row in and meet up with our friends."

"And Badger?" Onna asked.

Marissa bit her lower lip in thought. "If she's not back with whatever she's gathered, I'll go back into Castile."

"With that monster wilder and her orders to kill on sight?" Onna posited. "Ye canna do everything, Brains. If Badger still be missin,' send Jocquotte or Anne."

"That'll cripple the Dahlia," Marissa stated. "Anyone could fill my position in a pinch, and we need deckhands and riggers. We need our sea-artist. These women are indispensable. If you could do without anyone, it's me."

"Ye think too little of yourself, Brains. A Cap'n is needed just as much as all of those women, if not more so. We be needin' quick thinkin', course plotting, and goals, just as much as Badger be needin' ta hold a rope. Asides, this not be the time fer such a talk."

Marissa wanted to disagree with her on both fronts, for now was such a time as they wouldn't be doing much but drifting listlessly for the next several minutes. But they still needed to get themselves apart from the cog and back to the Dahlia. Then, they could worry about what came next. As she thought of the Dahlia, a pang of pain ran through her core. Her need to see Adjutant Love put them here, and if she returned back, and was too late to save Rusalka...

With a thunderous crack above them, they felt the ship lurch forward, "Sheets are full, Brains!"

"Rock free!"

Marissa and Onna rocked the dinghy as hard as they could, and with a mighty whump the small rowboat lurched free of the rudder. There was a rumbling, tumbling sound as their hull scrapped against the cog's and then the ship became very buoyant as they surged to the surface.

"That was loud!" Onna whispered.

"Don't move," Marissa returned, her heart pounding. "If we're lucky they'll think they hit some flotsam coming in from the Pale."

They both strained to listen for an alerted crew and expected to hear orders to turn about. They waited... and waited. Only the sound of the crashing waves, the bobbing of their dinghy, and their own heartbeats could be heard.

"Let's check it out," Marissa whispered.

Onna nodded and the two left their confines to swim to the surface. There on the horizon, glittering like a topaz in the moonlight, they could make out the lantern of the cog.

"Shite, they caught a mighty header, look at em go!" Onna said with obvious envy. "That's a good crew there!"

Marissa shared her enthusiasm, but not because of how well-trained the crew was. Now, they could row to Cuddle Cove in relative ease under the cover of darkness. "Let's flip this boat and get back to Rue."

THE JOURNEY BACK TO THE BELLA DAHLIA WAS MERCIFULLY uneventful, and as they entered the mouth of Cuddle Cove, no one seemed concerned to see yet another dinghy enter the beautifully tranquil waters. Onna looked about at the vast number of small ships in the flat, windless waters that were all strangely rocking, as if caught in an imaginary gale. "How is it they be rocking so... oh!" Onna stumbled as she realized why the ships were thrashing in such calm waters.

Marissa shook her head, and guided them to the Dahlia, which sat quite alone. Every other vessel was giving it a wide berth, first because they were leery that it might be pirates, and secondly, because the deck of the galleon sat so high that they didn't want anyone to be able to easily see what they were doing in their own boats. Not that the rocking – or odd moaning – wasn't enough of a giveaway.

"Blimey, did you hear that one?" Onna whispered in astonishment. "I didn't know humans had that kind of vocal range."

"Shh!" Marissa hissed.

Onna shook her head. "It sounded like cats in heat. So many octaves..."

Marissa gave Onna a withering glare and the gnome was mercifully quiet for the rest of the short trip. By the time they scaled up the gangplank, the rest of the crew was there to meet them, including – much to Marissa's relief – Badger.

"Badger, I'm so glad you made it back!" she crowed.

Badger beamed. "Took a bit I must confess. After ye two got into the Rhombus, a bunch of purists started calling out me name, and I thought fer sure they'd caught ye and were comin' fer me next!"

Marissa's ears went hot as she felt the glare of her gnome compatriot behind her. "Yes... well... that's odd," she stumbled.

"Very," Badger agreed, "took me a right minute though ta remember me name."

"Badger couldn't remember her name be Badger?" Anne asked confused.

"No," Badger retorted, "me name be Charlotte."

"Oh... right... forgot that, too, I did," Anne agreed.

"Wait, yer name isn't Badger?" Jocquotte asked.

Badger ignored her and continued looking at Marissa, "Charlotte must be a common name then around these parts?"

"Well... you know..."

Onna walked up, her hands on her hips, "None too common."

Marissa looked away, "I'm just glad you made it back alright. I was afraid we were going to have to go back into Castile to look for you."

Badger beamed at them both, "No need, I saw as soon as ye went in that there be no way I be savvy enough to follow ye, so I changed course like Onna mentioned and went in to scrounge provisions. I brought all the hardtack and fresh water I could carry."

Marissa stared at her rigger in shock. "I'm impressed! Good going, Badger."

Badger nodded excitedly. "Thanks, Cap'n."

"So, did they have it?" Onna asked, excited. "Please tell me they had it?"

Marissa watched a small smile curve at the corner of Badger's lips. "Mayhaps they did, mayhaps not."

Onna began to fastidiously rub her hands together. "Come on, don't be pullin' on me heartstrings."

Badger reached into a hip pouch and pulled out a small vial containing numerous small, reddish-brown seeds. It wasn't exactly moisture-sealed, and Marissa could smell a pungent, almost citrus-like scent. She stared at it with interest. "What is that?"

"Melegueta pepper," Onna said reverently as Badger put the vial in her hands. "Me faery ate all of the rest."

They all tensed, awaiting the faery's reprisal about not being a faery, but nothing was forthcoming. Instead, Anne looked down at Onna. "Ye keep those Defiler's shite pellets to yeself, gnome! Last time ye gave it to me, my gas was so bad it'd chase off a wild boar!"

"Meerkat at the least," Jocquotte concurred.

"Aye, couldn't be down wind o' that one," Badger agreed.

Onna stared at them all incredulously. "I'll have ye three be knowin' that this pepper has quite the salubrious effect on yer cardiovascular health."

"Not if Anne's arse whispers be killing us in our sleep," Badger retorted.

"Hardly a whisper," Jocquotte cracked back, "sounds like a gorilla's mating call if ye ask me."

Marissa ignored their banter and looked to Emmell. "How's Rue?"

"Rue's holding up surprisingly well," the spriggan stated proudly.

"Yeah, if ye don't take into account she was trying to eat the barnacles off the anchor chains about an hour ago," Anne put in.

"Or that she keeps chasing singing butterflies," Jocquotte added.

"All standard stages of dementia," Emmell replied flatly.

"Wait, she's up again?" Marissa replied, a hint of panic creeping in her voice.

"We could hardly contain her," Emmell returned, not the least bit put off by it. "She's an orc. She can overpower all of us like infant children."

"Where?" Marissa asked. "Where's Rue?"

"Here, Jasian!" Rusalka called loudly from the helm. "I've almost got them!"

Marissa turned and looked up the steps at her friend. Rusalka's head was swathed heavily in bandages, with the very noticeable protrusion of bolt feathers sticking out the side of her head like some sort of deranged headdress.

Onna pocketed her precious spice. "Sooner we get the blood drained from her skull," she said, "the sooner the pressure will be gone, and she'll be back to normal. Well as normal as an orc canna be, I'm fer thinkin'."

"Yes," Emmell said, "I think we should begin at once. This is not something to tarry on."

"Aye," Onna agreed, and looked up at Marissa. "Savvy?"

Marissa nodded. "Savvy." She looked back to the orc, "Rue, get down here! We have what we need to help you!"

A roar cut through the night air. All the women on the deck spun at once to the ear-splitting sound that muted out the background din of off-key moans.

"Where did that...?" Onna asked, before an interrupting whistle brought them looking southward. There was a brilliant explosion of sparkling white water forty meters from the *Bella Dahlia*. Small ringlet waves continued from the impact site, swelling out like a rock that just skipped across the surface of the water.

Marissa's eyes traced back from the impact point to where the roar first reverberated. Sitting outside the mouth of the cove, port-side facing them, was a War Cog, and even at the distance they were at they could see the titanic figure of Osprey on the deck.

The wilder had found them.

CHAPTER TWENTY-TWO

Marissa de Cantor y Castile

"I'm right fer hatin' that blasted woman," Onna growled. "How'd she manage ta follow us? Ye plan was brilliant!"

Marissa shook her head. "I don't know."

They saw another explosion of light and white smoke from the cog right before the thunderous roar of the culverin carried to them a second later. A scant heartbeat after that was another eruption of white spray, now thirty meters out. Screams of terror and alarm resounded throughout the cove. Marissa looked at all of the small watercraft bobbing helplessly. A single miscalculation by the gunner on the cog and they would kill innocent adolescents.

"Unfurl the sails!" Marissa commanded. The women looked at her in alarm, and she gazed back at each one of them in turn. "We're going to give them a moving target."

The women scattered across the deck, including a very discombobulated orc.

"Not you Rue, sit this one out."

"Cap, we may need er' strength on this," Badger pointed out as she began to roll out the sails.

"She's right," Emmell agreed. "I'm going to be extremely hard-pressed trying to catch a wind in here without the ladies able to quickly jib the sails. No one can do that as quickly or as efficiently as Rue."

"That effort will kill her," Marissa protested.

"*May* kill her," Onna returned, "but rest assured that cannon fire will kill her most definitely."

Marissa bit her lower lip in thought, but only for a moment – they were right, it was a necessary risk. "Rue, man the jib."

Rusalka nodded and shuffled her way across the deck. Onna ran to handle rigging while Marissa quickly moved to the capstan to weigh anchor. She paused in her work, quickly sucked on her finger and stuck it in the air. When she was confident, she pointed south. "Em... haul wind."

"Aye, aye!" the women cried in unison, and Marissa watched her sailors run to the lines, untying the hefty rope. Marissa looked back to the cog – any moment now she expected another shot to be fired. A loud clap let her know that the sails dropped. Without even looking back at the women, Marissa shouted for Onna to square the rigging. Onna in turn bellowed, "Boom about!"

Marissa finished winding up the anchor and wiped the barnacles free. She then ducked low as she made her way to the helm. With a loud groan the boom swung over her head. Seconds later, Onna confirmed that the rigging was belayed. The ship rocked forward as the sails snapped with a small pocket of wind.

Marissa stared intently at the cog. It was an outdated ship compared to the caravels, carracks, and galleons that the scales had designed. Still, cogs and their big brothers, the hulk, were solidly-built transports of cargo, and the predominant means of travel on the Sowle Sea. The model she was staring at now was an advanced build with fore and aft towers, and what looked like twin sets of culverins on the deck.

Under normal circumstances, it wouldn't stand a chance against a fully armed and crewed galleon such as the *Bella Dahlia*, but these were far from normal circumstances, and she didn't have a single hand to spare to even think about using one of the cannons. She was operating with a severe handicap. Her only advantages were that because the Dahlia had three masts to the advanced cog's two, and that it had virtually no cargo and very limited shot, she was going to be fast, especially in Emmell's capable hands.

They only needed to get through the cove's reefs. But to do that, they would be pinned between deadly-sharp sheets of living calcium, while facing the cog's culverins directly.

"Point reefing?" Onna called, standing by with Badger, Anne, and Jocquotte.

Marissa looked down to the small spriggan who wore an intense look of concentration upon her brow. "Em?"

The spriggan just stared at the gap before them.

The cog rumbled again, and Marissa caught a glimpse of smoke rising before Onna screamed, "Shot across the bow!"

Marissa ducked low as the cannon ball ripped across the rails, exploding the oak into deadly splinters. Onna and the three human women all dived for cover from the lethal shrapnel, and Marissa could swear she heard one of them cry out. The ball ricocheted off the mainsail to leave a fist-sized dent in the shaft before careening into the water.

Marissa picked herself up to see Rue hadn't even moved and was holding the rope to the rigging all by herself. Her face was locked in a wide, feral grin, her tusks glinting in the moonlight.

"Like a true orc," Marissa muttered at her utterly fearless friend. "Roll!" she called out to the others.

Onna stood waving a hand, "I be okay."

The other three women also stood up, but it was Anne who stumbled and groaned. Marissa could see a long eight-inch splinter of wood completely pierced through her right shoulder.

"Shite!" Marissa barked and went to move to her friend, but Onna held up a hand. "I got her, Brains; ye busy yerself by bein' Cap'n!"

"Were down two!" Badger exclaimed, pointing out the obvious. "Cap needs to take the riggin'."

"We need a navigator!" Onna objected.

"I'm fine!" Anne growled at them all. "If Rue can suffer with a bloody bolt in her head, I'll deal with this little stick in me arm. Just do something about all of this blood."

Marissa knew she had to make a decision, so she wasted no time. "Put her in. Three hands are better than none."

"It's not the first time ye had a little prick in ye!" Jocquotte guffawed.

Marissa turned back to Emmell. "We need to point reef."

Emmell again scrutinized the narrow gap they were fast approaching and shook her head.

Marissa looked at her little spriggan incredulously, "Em, I know you're good, but we barely squeezed through the first time going slowly. We're moving now at what... three knots?"

Emmell looked at the fullness of the sails. "Four knots."

Marissa shook her head – she never understood how Emmell could figure that out with the fullness of the sails versus a Dutchman's log. Still, four knots was a ridiculous speed to attempt the gap.

Emmell looked up at Marissa with those large alien eyes. "They have approximately two more shots on us before we get through the reef. They've already got bearings on us and are anticipating we'll either point reef, or back wind, and are adjusting to maximize their shots. We're gonna take the hits. We just need to minimize how bad it's gonna be. I can do this,

Captain, but the women need to do exactly as I say. That goes for you, too."

Marissa could only stare back down at the rare creature in wonder. "If we go through at a full four knots, we'll never be able to turn away in time. We'll ram the ship."

Emmell looked back ahead and the quickly approaching gap. "I am aware."

Marissa thought about it for the briefest of seconds – what did Onna say only a scant hour before, that she made the craziest decisions? *Well*, she thought, *let's let another one of the girls have a chance at it.*

"All right, ladies, listen up. We're punching through, no reef sails."

"What?" Onna said in disbelief. "Ye canna be serious?"

Marissa nodded. "This is Em's plan, and I'm confident that she can do it, but we all need to do exactly as she says."

"There's no way!" Badger argued. "Em's fantastic, no doubt 'bout it, Cap, but this is gonna scuttle the Dahlia!"

Marissa pointed to the cog sitting right outside the cove getting ready to fire at any moment. "That ship is going to scuttle us for sure if we do nothing. I say we go for it!"

"Aye, why the hells not!" Onna agreed. "Let's do it!"

Marissa looked down to Emmell. "Em the ship is yours. What are your orders?"

Emmell looked up at Marissa in momentary wonder, before blinking it away and looking serious again. "Man the jib with Rue, Mari."

Marissa put her hand down on Emmell's shoulder. "Aye, aye, Captain."

Emmell's quills ruffled at the statement. "Don't call me that Mari, that's your title."

Marissa didn't object as she scurried down to the jib, taking a long rope opposite of Rusalka. "How are you feeling Rue?"

The orc looked at her in wild glee. "Never better. If I'm to die on this day, it'd never be more glorious!"

"Well, let's try not to die just yet."

Rusalka shrugged and waited for her orders.

Marissa now on the frontsail had clear vantage of the cog that they were fast approaching. The sails were furled, and she could clearly see they were cast irons. This was a common tactic of purists, and yet the bodies ambling across the deck were not in the blue livery of the Jasian Enclave. No, these were Cruz's men.

That fact gave Marissa small comfort. No matter what bad news Onna told her, if they made it out of this, she would at least be happy to know that Love held his word. Against the might of the Enclave, they stood no chance. Against Cruz's lackeys? They were long odds, but better than no odds at all.

They sliced a direct line through the water, and Marissa cringed as the small ships in the cove were thrown in the ship's wake, but it was preferable to the alternative.

Emmell shouted her orders. She spoke loud and fast, and yet was immaculately precise and clear. Marissa and Rusalka worked side by side as a team, just like they had for so many months. Behind them, Marissa could hear Onna shouting out confirmations for direction changes, and moving beams, just as quickly as Emmell was uttering course changes.

The reefs loomed ever closer. The wind buffeted Marissa's skin. Leave it to Emmell to find a headwind in a cove where virtually no wind existed. The sails cracked, snapped, and fluttered wildly with every move they made, with every command they followed.

Boom!

One of the cannons in front of them roared. "Brace!" was all Marissa managed before a hole materialized in the bowsprit sail, and the bowsprit itself disappeared in a flurry of wooden chips.

The oaken missiles peppered above her and Rue like confetti, shredding into the heavy sheets of the foresail.

Marissa looked back to see the shot bury a hole in the aftcastle, through the captain's quarters, and continue to travel out back into the water, taking with it a furor of lumber and a bustle of her undergarments.

"Unbelievable," she muttered.

"Whoo Cap'n, not the first time yer panties be left behind in these waters I reckon!" came Badger's banter.

"One shot left!" Emmell called, seemingly unfazed by the fact that a cannonball just ripped through the ship beneath her feet.

The wind tore wildly at her dark hair, billowing it like a flag behind her head. She'd only ever gone this fast out on the open sea – where was Emmell finding this wind? More importantly, how in the hells were they supposed to clear the narrow and shallow reefs cutting across the water at what she had to guess was almost six knots?

The ship prow lifted higher with less air driving it down now that it was riddled with holes. With the forecastle raised up, it was going to be nearly impossible for Emmell to see over the bow. She was going to be sailing blind and relying on her instincts. It also made it impossible to see the cog's cannons, so they couldn't even begin to guess where the next shot would strike them.

Seemingly undeterred by the series of events, Emmell continued to bellow out course corrections at a rate that Marissa's mind couldn't even begin to calculate. She and Rue only responded to the commands, becoming an extension of Emmell's will, just another facet of the ship bending to her skill as a sea artist.

And then they were upon the reefs. The narrow gap erupted upon them on both sides like the great maw of a shark lunging from the sea to swallow them whole. Sharp, ragged coral slid along both sides of them, glittering in a wondrous array of orange, greens, and pinks. The slightest error in that moment would bilge their hull faster than Anne passed gas after eating melegueta pepper.

The Dahlia groaned in protest on both sides of the ship's hull as it grated on the lower parts of the coral reef. Marissa cringed and gritted her teeth at the terrible sounds echoing out from beneath them.

"That be one way to careen the Dahlia!" Jocquotte yelled over the terrible noise.

"Not really the way I'd clean the barnacles off," Anne hollered back.

"Saves ye both the work then!" Badger added, and to Marissa's surprise she was laughing.

"Mari, drop anchor!" came a yell from the spriggan, and Marissa thought for a moment that she didn't hear that right.

"Drop anchor!" came the voice more urgently.

Marissa looked at Rusalka who merely shrugged. Numbly, Marissa ran forward. She had to hold a rope to get her to the front of the forecastle, which was now lifted so high from the water. If they dropped the anchor at this speed, this close to the reefs, it would send them crashing right into the cliff face and end their mad escape. Still, Marissa said she trusted Emmell, and gave her the bridge. If she mutinied against her ideas now, they were all going to die. Sighing in resignation that this was now the absolute stupidest thing she did in a day of highlighted stupid events, she reached the capstan and released its hold. The bar swung recklessly as the anchor tumbled down and crashed into the water.

"Give it slack!" Emmell ordered as Marissa was just about to lock the capstan in place.

Marissa watched as the chains kept feeding into the water at an alarming rate.

"More slack," Emmell calmly ordered.

Linkage after linkage disappeared over the side of the ship

disappearing behind them with the haste normally reserved for antelope trying to escape a cheetah.

"Now!" Emmell yelled.

Marissa reached in and dropped the catch on the wildly spinning capstan. The lock held, and beneath them they heard an agonizing caterwaul as the anchor ripped across the native, beautiful, and priceless coral reef as it tried to find perch on stone. Marissa braced and within seconds it found that perch.

The chains snapped violently taut, and the entire bow plunged down into the water, bringing the sea in front of them once more into view. Only forty meters away was a scrambling crew trying in vain to unfurl their sails and get away from the barreling galleon missile heading right for them.

Unperturbed by the soon to be ship-rending carnage stood Osprey. She was poised and ready, her arm hovering expertly over the last armed culverin, priming iron in hand. When Marissa caught sight of the wilder, the massive woman smiled from the corner of her mouth, ready to drive the match home.

The explosion was deafening. Marissa could hardly react before the shot lanced through the bowsprit mast, jettisoning over her head with a power that ripped the air from her lungs. The ball continued its destructive wake through the main sail, ripping a gouge across the deck before disappearing into the opposing side of the aftcastle from where the last cannon shot had struck. Her mind was too numb to even register what other unmentionables might be pouring out of the back of the ship.

Then the prow crashed headlong into the water sending a torrent of salty white spray washing over the deck, dousing Marissa. She held on for dear life as the wood suddenly became slick. Before Marissa could even orient herself however, or prepare for the imminent collision, the *Bella Dahlia* listed violently starboard, slingshotting them.

Marissa watched in wide-eyed horror, coupled with intense

fascination, as the Dahlia began an impossible bank. Where the cog was at one time directly in front of them, now it was suddenly parallel to them on their portside. Osprey, too, seemed at a loss for this sudden and unexplainable phenomenon, until Marissa heard Emmell's way-too-calm voice say, "Anchor's away."

Too numb to even think, Marissa reached up and threw the latch once more, watching the last of the chain links fade until the entirety of their anchor chains disappeared into the sea.

And then the cog was behind them, still scrambling to unfurl their sails, while the *Bella Dahlia* was soaring across the Sea of Sowle.

Marissa looked at the little sea artist in rapt fascination and couldn't believe how luck brought the little creature into her life. No human helmsmen in her life would've ever attempted to even try that maneuver, let alone be quick enough to do the mental math necessary to pull off the feat.

Emmell was a small bundle of miracle, and that fact was punctuated adroitly with the next words that came from Onna's sailor's lips. "Fuck me, we cleared it!"

Before anyone could comment on the jubilance of Onna's words, Badger yelled, "We're not out of this yet!"

Marissa, now mentally taxed to her limits, looked to Badger pointing west. Marissa turned to follow Badger's extended finger and couldn't believe what she saw. It was nothing short of a fleet, arranged in a semi-circle, blockading Cuddle Cove. She swiveled her head to the east, hoping to escape around the cape of Cabo Hoorn and make her way away from Castile. Her heart dropped as she saw not one, but two Jasian Enclave war cogs now returning from their patrol.

Even though the Dahlia was faster than any cog, she couldn't hope to outmaneuver the Jasians with only six women. Their complement of sailors was too well-trained, with no less than twenty-eight men on each vessel. There were just too many of them.

"For the love of the Maker!" she cried angrily as she stood up from the capstan. She made her way to the aftcastle, delicately walking around the rut that was now cut diagonally across the main deck. Marissa cast a distressing glance at the large holes in her captain's quarters and could only imagine what was lost into the cove's waters. It was a good thing they really hadn't the time to stock anything, otherwise the losses could be worse. Sighing inwardly, she climbed the steps of the aftcastle and stood next to Emmell. "Thoughts?"

The sea artist didn't answer her right away and instead concentrated on the scene before her. Finally, after several moments, she looked up at Marissa. "I've got nothing. If you don't mind Mari, I'd like you to be Captain again. Getting out of the cove was one thing, but this…" Emmell shook her head, her delicate blonde quills ruffling in the wind. "I can't make this call. It has to be you."

"Fair enough."

She eyed the fleet of seven ships to her west once more – they were dragging irons to keep from moving, and they were positioned so all of their port culverins were facing the exit point of Cuddle Cove. At the moment, they were only a hair's breadth out of range, but that would soon change.

Marissa glanced behind her, and already saw the sails unfurled and the riggers hard at work to catch the same wind that Emmell was riding on. She could make out Osprey, arming her massive crossbow. It was obvious that Osprey and Cruz's men weren't there to take prisoners. Her eyes then fell to Rue, who was looking at her with the fire of combat still alight in her eyes. The orc wanted this fight. Marissa knew that there would be no surrender for Rusalka, only battle and death.

Marissa looked down at Emmell again, and knew that though

surrender was a viable option to the little spriggan, chances were that she too would meet some awful end because the Castellan humans would never recognize her as the person that Marissa saw, the brilliant woman who was knowledgeable in many medicines and alchemy, and who could pilot a ship better than any man she'd ever met. No, all they would see was the floppy ears, the quills, the claws, and the tail. They wouldn't see the person, only a creature.

The Jasians, however...

Marissa looked to the incoming cogs. They, too, would be within firing range in a matter of moments. And even if Marissa bolted with the Dahlia towards them in the hopes of somehow evading the Jasians and escaping around the cape, that would still open her up for a close-range broadside from the cog Osprey was aboard. Marissa wasn't sure how much punishment the *Bella Dahlia* could take.

The way she saw it, she had few options. She could surrender to Don Cruz's people and hope that at least Onna, Anne, Badger, and Jocquotte survived. Or, surrender to the Jasian Enclave, get quickly executed, and hope that the Enclave wouldn't turn her crew into exactors, which was tantamount to slavery once again. Or, fight, in which case they would die very, very quickly. Or...

She looked at her fourth option out on the horizon, and it twisted her gut. This was not a decision she could make lightly, and yet she knew she had no time – a minute, maybe three at most.

"Ladies, huddle up!" she called out quickly.

The women wasted no time gathering around her, even Rue, whose motions were becoming more and more awkward and disoriented as long as she stood up. She was slowly killing her friend, and it ate at her inside. As they encircled her, she looked each and every one of them in the eyes.

"What's the plan, Cap'n?" Onna asked, not waiting for Marissa to try and sugarcoat it.

Marissa nodded ahead, and the women turned to look at what she was looking at.

"Ye can't be serious," Onna declared.

"Very serious," Marissa replied with conviction. "If I surrender, you all will be killed at the least, or returned to slavery. Some of you will be tortured horribly and then killed, all because we are a vindictive, and sometimes very hateful and intolerant, race." She didn't need to say who would be tortured – everyone knew. "We can't outrun them, either. We're pinned to the west, and the Enclave cogs are professionals. They'll shred us the moment we're within range. So, I say we go forward, together."

They all looked at what was slowly creeping forward across the water towards them like a great sea beast. Tendrils of white mist slithered out like river snakes across the surface of the water, pulling itself inexorably closer.

Marissa knew that they were a great distance away from the obscuring mists, but to see it move in such a way across the crystal-clear waters was alarming. "We're going into the Pale."

CHAPTER TWENTY-THREE

Marissa de Cantor y Castile

I t didn't take long for the captains of the cogs to realize Marissa's plan. They immediately changed course in an effort to cut off her escape into the grasping miasma.

"We need more speed," Marissa growled as she watched the redirected Jasians closing in to firing range. "This ship is way faster than any cog!"

"Suren it is," Onna agreed, "when we had a bowsprit, and our foresail didn't resemble pauper's stockings."

"Dragging the sails isn't helping matters," Emmell added as they had yet to cut away the bowsprit.

Marissa watched as Badger moved forward, drawing her dagger to do just that, when an idea came to mind. "Wait!" Marissa cried out.

Badger stopped and Emmell looked up at her. "First you complain we are going too slow, and now you don't want us to speed up the ship?"

Marissa shook her head. "We can use it to deter the chase. We may not have to go far into the Pale."

Onna, who was running across the deck with rigging rope to readjust for wind, glanced up to the aftcastle at her. "How ye figure, Brains?"

"Flotsam," Marissa said easily. "Every time a ship enters the Pale, only the debris comes out."

"If we rush in and cut the bowsprit mast off and let it sail out..."

"Along with whatever cargo we can spare..." Marissa added.

"It'll look like the Pale ate us!" Anne agreed in understanding.

"Aye, all good an' all... as long as the Pale doesn't actually eat us, that is," Badger replied.

A large extension of pale mist rolled out across the waters towards them at an alarming rate. Like a palpus it rushed over the ship before retreating backwards into the undulating miasma almost a league away. The whole event made Marissa shudder. "Let's not talk about the Pale eating us again, please."

Marissa watched as Cruz's fleet closed in, now within firing range. They too found the headwind that Emmell was taking advantage of. Culverins began to bark their calls of aggression at the *Bella Dahlia* and seconds later the sea was wounded as geysers of water jettied where the shot impacted. Salt spray rolled up over the deck, showering the women.

"That was close for a first volley," Marissa said through clenched teeth.

"Very," Emmell agreed.

"How fast are we going?"

Emmell glanced at the sails. "Four knots, which is the same speed as a cog. We're also beginning to list starboard."

Marissa saw Emmell was correct – the horizon rose higher on the starboard side. "Did we bilge on our own anchor?" she asked.

"It's too early to tell, Cap, could very well be the drag from the bowsprit is simply pulling us down."

Marissa thought Emmell's voice was entirely too calm for the situation. "I hope you're right."

"I usually am."

Marissa cast the spriggan a sidelong glance, and then the cog's cannons let out another chorus of clapping concussions. Bursts of brine doused them once more as the cannon shot plunged into the clear blue depths only a scant few meters away. Frothing white waters roiled on the surface of the sea where the iron violated its cerulean skin.

Before them the pale loomed like a ghostly leviathan. The very sight of it brought to mind a song the juglares used to sing of a great sea monster. *What the hell,* she thought, *if I am going to die, I might as well do it with a song on my lips.*

"Below the rumble of the blue deep:

Far far beneath in the great wide seas,

His ancient, dreamless, uninvaded sleep

The Lusca sleepeth where the sunlight flees."

"Shanties!" Onna screamed in delight. "Yes, shanties! Sing that one ye did on the cliff, Brains!"

"Uhm... well..." Marissa stumbled, caught off guard. "It's not really a song for sailing into the Pale."

"So what? If we's gonna die, I'm fer hearin' that one again!" Onna declared.

"Wait, the Cap'n can sing?" Badger's voice cut through the next wave of cannon fire.

"Is this really a discussion we need to be having right now?" Marissa asked. Water, frothy and thick, laced the deck as two more cannon shot plunged deep into the drink only meters away.

"Aye, I think it is!" Anne called out as another swell of water washed over them. She spit out the brine and cried out, "Is she any good?"

"The Jasian has a voice like an angel."

Everyone stopped to look at the front of the deck where Rusalka was operating the jib alone. She looked back at everyone. "Onna's words." Marissa flushed red at the compliment, but the moment was quickly dispelled as Rusalka swiped at the air again. "Blasted butterflies."

Onna slid across the deck, sending the boom in a new direction to keep their heading as the sails slackened momentarily, only to fill once again with gusto. "Come on Brains, give us that one again, what'd it be, the Ballad of Shanty Soul or something?"

"The Ballad of Vanity Shoal?" Anne asked, surprising them all.

"You've heard of it?" Marissa asked, holding onto the rail as the ship lurched hard to port in the suddenly choppy waters, as the beast of the Pale now encompassed the world before them.

"Aye, love that one – sing it fer me, Cap'n!"

Marissa watched as massive tentacles writhed out of the bloated massed of dense fog before them, reaching, always reaching. They came out like an insect's feelers, landing on both sides of the *Bella Dahlia*. Gusts of wind roared in her ears, her midnight hair billowed, and fear clutched at her gut.

We're all afraid, she thought, and song... song was a way of breaking that fear. So, she opened her lips, and she began to sing.

"Sing me a song of my lass that is gone,
Goes by the name Vanity Shoal
Bonny of spirit she sailed on a lark
O'er the sea of Sowle."

The words tumbled forth, as loud and as pure as she could make them. Her fear did not cause her voice to waver. As she began to sing the first verse, another voice entered with her own. It was Anne's, thick and bold.

Marissa smiled as Anne looked her way. The Halsbrenian's own eyes were alight with fear and wonder as she desperately held onto the rigging. It was Anne who started the next bout of chorus, but Marissa's heart swelled with pride as all the other women joined in.

The great maw of the Stonewall Pale encompassed everything now. The wind roared across her ears, pushing the bellowing cannon fire into nothing so much as a distant thought.

Marissa's ears rang, and the floorboards vibrated from the deep soul-shaking rumble before them. The white that wends writhed forward, a warped whorl of effluvium webbing that wrapped about the stern. Marissa momentarily lost her voice.

"Keep singing!" Onna encouraged, facing the waxen wall.

Marissa found her voice then, and she did keep singing. The women followed her lead in song, ship, and heart as they sailed into the terrible pallid gullet of the Stonewall Pale; and they were consumed by it... entirely.

CHAPTER TWENTY-FOUR

Don Augusto Cruz

Augusto stood on the parapet of the eastern tower and watched in disbelief as Marissa sailed her priceless galleon into the mouth of madness. He lowered his looking glass just as the last sprays of missed cannon fire erupted off the stern of Marissa's ship. Seconds later, the bowsprit of the galleon floated out.

The provisional viscount shook his head in wonder. "I can't believe she just did that."

"Hmm," came a noncommittal voice to his right. He looked over at Adjutant Love, who was still staring hard at the Pale, looking, Cruz guessed, for any signs of Marissa's re-emergence.

Augusto noticed all of his ships redirecting their sails to pull away from the Pale's extending tendrils. All except for one cog that stayed a safe distance out. He put the looking glass to his eye once more, dancing over the name of the ship, *The Pandion*, before looking for the crew. He knew who he was looking for, and he found her on the bow of the ship, scrutinizing the churning wan mass. It undulated in front of the vessel, waiting, almost taunting Osprey to pursue.

He knew she would too, but his men would not. She could threaten the captain, even kill him, and the men would not budge. She was strong and terrifying, but the Pale was more so. They would rather die at her hands than die by the Pale. Twice now her prey escaped the huntress.

He placed his sights on the two Jasian watercraft that were heading full sail back to the Rhombus. They would be giving Love a full report. Augusto turned to look at Beneford Love. He wore a very sour expression upon his face.

After several heartbeats Love lowered the looking glass and turned away. The night wind licked at the adjutant's thin strands of hair, pulling it back to reveal the bald pate, not so well hidden, underneath. He harrumphed as he angled his large weight down the spiraling stairs. Augusto, now alone on the parapet, save for the attendant, reluctantly looked back to his retreating ships. Marissa was gone. His chance at a worthy challenge snuffed itself out instead of facing him head on. "Such a waste."

This was not a loss, but it was far from victory. It left him feeling hollow. He followed Adjutant Love down the stairs to the awaiting dinghy that would take them back to the Rhombus.

As Cruz climbed inside, he noted the adjutant's lingering silence with a growing disquiet. Love was thinking, and while Cruz did not like the outcome, he didn't quite find it as disconcerting as the elder adjutant seemed to. A Jasian Enclave soldier – Augusto wasn't sure what purists-in-training were exactly called – rowed them back into the garrison hangars. After they berthed the small vessel, he walked with Love towards the adjutant's quarters. Love stopped him with a held-out hand at one of the spokes that would lead to the end by his room.

"I will adjourn to my quarters alone," he stated.

At this, choler bit at the melancholy of Augusto's mood. He

tolerated much from the lesser noble because he respected Love's station, but he had little respect for the familial line. To be denied a victory celebration despite the desired outcome incensed the young don.

"Did we not achieve what we set out to do?" he asked through gritted teeth.

"No," Love returned. "We did not. We have a very big problem now, Augusto, and I need to reflect on it... alone."

Augusto's jaw muscles flexed. He wasn't even addressing Cruz by his proper appellative, and in front of subordinates no less. He was treating Augusto like a lesser, and Maker be damned, he would not accept that kind of treatment. He pointed his finger at Love. "We are too close to finishing this for you to dare address me as anything less than Don, am I understood, Beneford?" He spit out Love's first name with as much derision as he could.

Beneford Love looked to both sides of Augusto where his retainers were positioned, and with a nod he told them, "You may leave us."

Both purists saluted their adjutant and disappeared down the corridor. Adjutant Love then looked back to Cruz, and all Augusto received for his efforts to rile the surly old man was a raised eyebrow. "So, this upsets you?"

"You're damned right!"

Love nodded. "Good. Because I don't think you understand how close to the brink of destruction we are right now, *Don* Cruz."

Those words took the bluster right out of his sails, and he stared at Love confused. "I don't understand... Marissa is gone, we won. Sure, the paperwork is ruined but..."

"Paperwork is ruined," Love interrupted. That mere interruption pissed off Cruz even more. "Tell me, *Don,* who has the map?"

"No one."

Love shook his head. "Who has the map?" he responded more firmly, and Cruz felt like he was being treated like an unruly child.

"Marissa, or her damned gnome," Cruz all but growled.

"That's right, and tell me, are your sworn men prepared to face the might of the Jasian Enclave or the Lefhym of the Shemma?"

"Of course not."

"Because that's exactly who we will be facing if anyone else other than us gets that map back."

Cruz pointed to the wall, guessing that somewhere in that general direction was the sea, "It is gone, in the Pale, with Marissa! It is gone, Beneford! It is a threat to no one!"

"I do not agree," Beneford Love replied so calmly that it pissed Cruz off even more.

Livid, he all but foamed at the mouth. "That's because you are being irrationally paranoid, old man! The Pale destroys all it touches. No one has ever survived the Pale. Ever!"

"You're right. But what about the ships?"

Augusto disregarded him with a wave of his hand. "None have ever returned either. Usually within a week, the flotsam washes to shore."

Love nodded. "Whose shores?"

"Sometimes ours, but it's mostly..." Augusto froze midsentence as he put it together. "Oh shite."

Love nodded again. "Precisely. This was not a victory, Cruz. It has now become a scavenger hunt, we are going to be searching now... searching for a needle in a haystack. Or, in our quite literal case, a treasure map lost at sea. The map, the will, they are water-proof for the most part... the trade pact not so much, mercifully. But all it takes is for one interested party in the Citadel to find the map and make a little expedition to where it leads, and everything we've worked for will come undone. Worse, imagine if it washes up where the sea touches the Shemma directly. If one of the elves get the map and finds the truth..." The adjutant let the words hang.

"It could mean war."

"It would mean annihilation," Love corrected. "The elves would butcher us, every man, woman, and child. How will that be for your legacy, *Don* Augusto Cruz? The viscount who destroyed Castile and sent the nations of Gurgen and the Shemma into a bloody, brutal war." Without waiting for an answer, the adjutant turned and walked away, letting Cruz brood on the dire possibilities that were now before them.

Augusto couldn't sleep that night. He aggressively lavished himself on his usual women, and even all of his retainers, and still he was not quenched. It was not lust that drove him, but fury tinged with fear. Thoughts of the damnation of all his work ate at him. They chewed through his innards like starving rats burrowing their way through his flesh to feast on his mind.

Obvious reminders danced about his thoughts, like watching the same play over and over again. The sea was too vast to cover it all in the hopes of recovering the wreckage of Marissa's ship. The Pale flotsam washed ashore at night, so the crews would be working round the clock, trying to find a map in the dark. Everything that was proceeding so smoothly was now completely and utterly turned on its head. Not to mention that in day and a half's time he was supposed to finalize the pact and deliver his first shipment, and the only two people that even knew where to go were he and Osprey.

He could imagine the map washing up on shore right into the hands of an adjutant or purist in the heart of the Enclave. He could see it so vividly, an army sailing to the destination, finding out the truth of everything, and then marching upon his very shores to destroy not only him, but his family, and his legacy.

All of this would happen because that bitch of an ex-girlfriend decided to rise from whatever hole she hid in and re-enter his world, only a handful of days before he would be set for life – before all of Castile would be set. True, he'd made sacrifices to reach this juncture, or Castile made sacrifices, at least. But his father always told him that you can't make an omelet without breaking a few eggs. Castile had had to break, and the yolk of its people needed to spill onto the cooking stone before he could mold it into perfection. Along the way, some of it had simply become waste. Stuck upon the shell of old and no use to the new form that Castile was to take. A better form. So, like the shell, they were discarded. It was for the best. Adjutant Love could see it, as did others. Many others. But now this... Marissa and her crew. They were a scourge to his well-laid plan. They were the sharp flecks of shell in his omelet, and the Supreme Pontiff was about to bite down. And should he find out the truth, it wouldn't be just a prick from the eggshells – they would shred his tongue to ribbons.

Augusto pried himself from his pillows and women, draped his sheer silver robes over his body, then proceeded out into the white halls of Palacio de los Vizcondes. The palace of the viscounts wasn't as lovely or as ostentatious as Toja de Cruz where his mother still resided. It lacked the vibrant seaside colors that decorated each and every wall in his ancestral home. Nor did it show any of his father's love of nude busts, or his mother's strange floral adornments in every room, even though she lacked any skill in gardening or caring for anything living, really.

No, Palacio de los Vizcondes was the odd man out of all the castles in the entirety of Castile, save possibly the Rhombus, which was only a castle by the thinnest of technicalities. Palacio de los Vizcondes stood out because the entire structure was utterly white, the pearl of healthy teeth. The whitewashed stone was scrubbed every night by a rigorous staff that cleaned away the salty brine that built up on the castle through constant spray from the bay below. The Palacio was the most prime real estate in all of Castile, and it was owned by no man, but by Castile itself. Whomever was the viscount of the time – or provisional viscount, in Augusto's case – was the resident of this fine structure for his term of service, and he sat directly in the heart of Castile's government district.

The Palacio was a stone's throw away from his very own port, which held a combination of the viscount's ships, and cargo ships from his family. Just east of the Palacio was the Jasian Enclave's Rhombus. To the north, further up the cliff was some of the more important noble families' fiefs, and to his west the main port and merchant district. Everything was within quick reach of the viscount; nothing was out of bounds. And so, Augusto was forced to tolerate his usual lack of finery in exchange for brilliant scarlet wall hangings in the halls that denoted the lines of viscount succession before him, and all the vases that dotted every room, each seemingly older than the one before it, that told of the legacy of the Castellan peoples and of the Jasian Enclave.

One day, if Marissa's meddling didn't ruin everything, and Castile was free and independent, he would decorate the Palacio as he saw fit. Hells, he might even tear the structure down and have a finer castle built in the image he desired. No Castellan alive today or even five generations past would be able to say the same.

The thought filled him with a moment of triumph that was quickly soured once more with the reality of his predicament. He hoped for a challenge from Marissa, secretly coveted the idea, but this... this wasn't a challenge. It was something altogether different. The potential for tragedy was coming from nothing other than a terrible stroke of ill fortune.

He walked the empty halls of the Palacio listening to the sounds of life outside his building. Just outside his walls he could hear the cleaning crews scrubbing the day's brine from the whitewashed stone. Past that, he could hear the life of the port city of Castile, alive and breathing. Songs sung by juglares and their attended friends, families, and fans. He could hear the crash of the surf. And more... he paused. The clangor of crashing of steel against steel echoed to him.

Combat! And it was coming from his own Palacio courtyard. Augusto increased his steps and moved with urgency. Had the Jasian Enclave already found the map? Were the Lefhym here to assassinate him? He had no answers, only questions as he rounded the corner and the balcony to the courtyard that opened up before him.

He stepped out onto the open terrace between the colonnades and looked into the cobbled courtyard below, expecting to see a great battle. Instead, he blinked several times in surprise. There was a battle going on, but it was a single opponent versus four heavily-armed men. A single, quite completely nude, opponent... He blinked again in disbelief.

It was Osprey, fighting four of the men from *The Pandion*. He recognized one of the men as the captain, and he thought the one holding a trident might be the boatswain. The other two, he didn't know, other than that they still bore the livery of Cruz.

For her part, Osprey wasn't armed at all. She stood hunched forward, legs shoulder width apart, with her hands out to her sides, long fingers splayed wide open. The fight was apparently well underway, the captain and one of the men Cruz didn't really recognize both bloodied.

From what he could see of Osprey herself, she seemed uninjured. What did impress him though, was the figure she cut. She wasn't what the Castellan standards for women said was even remotely attractive, yet he was compelled to give credit where credit was due. He knew that the Osprey was strong, not just for a woman, but strong in general because she was a wilder. But this... he had no idea that the female form was able to produce musculature in this way... Some of his best men didn't have the shoulder width that this woman did. Her sea-tanned skin looked like it was chiseled from the same stone as the colonnade next to him. She was all ridges and cuts of muscle along her shoulders, back, buttocks, and thighs. Her mop of red hair, normally held in braids tightly woven to her scalp, was uncoiled and wild against her head. It looked like the mane of a lion.

Men formed a half circle around her. As she pivoted, he caught her in profile – the image he saw was nothing short of stunning in physique. He would never find her beautiful, of that he was certain, but this view of her, utterly naked and feral, was forever burned into his mind.

The muscles of her arms and legs looked like rigging cables made from steel, her stomach as hard and as riveted as the chains of an anchor. Her breasts were lacking in every way he found a woman's should be, but it seemed a trivial contrivance compared to the masterpiece of muscle and sinew that he saw before him. When his gaze inevitably drifted to her other womanly virtues, he decided that it was wholly possible that her very dense thighs alone could probably crush boulders into dust. He averted his gaze back to her face, not out of any modesty on his part, but because the idea of his head exploding like a watermelon between those legs suddenly made him lightheaded.

Her face, too, was just as chiseled as the mountains of beef that she wore over what he imagined was a normal woman's body underneath. In the last two winters of service, he only saw her without the skull helm twice, and both times he marveled at the strange vitium that slashed across her face from the bottom of her left earlobe to the top of her right ear, covering over her eyes and nose like a white mask. He saw the skin disorder before on people, mostly those of a darker complexion, like the islander Ayjub, but not until meeting her did he see the loss of pigment on a light-skinned person before; especially not one that was displayed in such an artful manner. Seeing all of her now, he realized that the ivory veil over her eyes was the only place she suffered the strange affliction.

The sight of her reminded him of his father's nude sculptures, mostly of men to serve as representations of ideal male form. That was what Osprey looked like – an artist's sculpture.

The men came forward, again brandishing their weapons, and the captain and boatswain actually looked like they knew how to use them. Augusto was intrigued to see the outcome, though he knew that either would result in the loss of a valuable resource. Osprey was something akin to one of his tenientes, and the captain, was, well, a captain. They were not as easy to replace as plays made it seem.

Still, he found himself riveted to the display. He knew Osprey was a force to be reckoned with, but he'd never seen her fight without her repeating crossbow.

Augusto's eyes snapped from the Osprey to the captain as he feinted left with his sabre and moved in for the kill with a long dagger, but Osprey was fast. With a lunge, the palm of her right hand smashed into the captain's sabre wrist, numbing the nerves and effectively disarming him. He howled in rage, and then chaos erupted all around her.

Osprey, being larger than the men, was no lumbering beast, even with a superior range of arm. She was a blur. She moved laterally, forcing the fighters to gather to the center and pivot to keep her in sight. They transferred weight to their lead foot, which meant they couldn't transfer their weight into their blows. She rendered their own physicality useless to them.

Osprey kept moving on the men, making all their constant turning cumbersome. She managed to circle around one of the men at a blind angle and lunged, scoring a forceful blow to the back of his head. He crumpled to the cobbled ground.

She continued to pivot, following the direction her prey moved. It was a game of reactions and attrition. She was faster than them, and they knew it. She baited them, drawing strikes out of them, and evaded.

The captain finally managed to pick up his sabre. Dual

wielding was cumbersome at best, and often showboating. It was no different here. The captain lunged at her, his teeth bared like a wild animal. She parried with open slaps of her hands and danced away.

Augusto began making his way to a narrow spiral staircase at the corner of the courtyard. He identified the standard thug stratagem. They employed simple tactics of overpower and dominate quickly. Only the captain was a man of any real skill, wasted now with trying to employ two weapons. He would have been better served with a small shield.

The seafaring men weren't prepared for a prolonged battle. Soon enough, they slowed, becoming unfocused, less keen to take Osprey. Two men eventually gambled and lashed out at her, and she caught both of them from behind, slamming their heads together with a sickening crack. She dumped them to the courtyard with their other comrade, so that only the captain remained. He was labored and bruised from her ripostes, and yet the Osprey looked barely winded, though her body glistened in a fine sheen of hot sweat.

Another circle, another lunge, another riposte. Reaching the stairs Augusto descended the narrow, spiraling steps. He heard the captain yell, "Fight me face to face like a man!"

Augusto came around the final steps, and her eyes looked up and met his own. Osprey smiled at the corner of her mouth. "I think I've shown you very clearly already. I am no man."

She roared and struck at the captain like a mongoose. The captain tried to slash at Osprey's outstretched arms, but with surprising agility for her size, she gracefully pivoted away in a spin, overextending the captain's twin slashes and exposing his back to her. She brought her fist down like a hammer of the gods, driving it into the captain's kidney. He cried out, dropping to his knees, but Osprey offered no mercy. She slammed the heel of her foot in quick succession into his back, thighs, and neck until she drove him completely to the ground. And without so much as a victory flourish, she thrust her knee down upon the base of his skull, dropping all of her impressive bulk down on the man's head. The captain fell still at her feet.

Augusto clapped slowly. "Excellent, my dear."

Osprey turned her head, looking over her shoulder to regard him. Her hair was darkened by sweat and spread out in clumps. The layers of red reminded Augusto of a campfire. His eyes also descended to take in her derriere, which actually looked rather phenomenal at this angle. He heard her snort in disdain when she caught him looking.

"You wouldn't even know what to do with someone like me."

He arced an eyebrow. That almost sounded like a challenge to him. She was not attractive in his eyes, not at all, truth be told. He preferred his women soft and voluptuous. But something about her fighting four men, in the nude, something about the power of that body left him suddenly... wanting it. He feigned indifference. "You're probably right. I did just expend myself on a handful of women. I probably couldn't give you the attention you deserve."

"And I've just played with four inadequate men," she mocked. Osprey stood up and faced him, not hiding anything of herself from him. She towered over him, her bulging muscles taut and slick with sweat. He could smell her excitement, pungent on her lacquered body. Her body had its own way of communicating its desire to him. "This would be a bad idea," she warned. "Tonight, I won't be fulfilled without blood."

"Then we are equally unsated," he agreed. "For Marissa has scored a blow on us both."

Osprey looked out to the sea and growled, "I was robbed of my hunt by cowardly suicide. The hunt is everything."

"And all I've worked for may be destroyed by the week's end," Augusto added, stepping closer to her. They were only inches apart. Her breathing was quickening now, more than in the fight.

"Then what we are has collapsed in on us both," Osprey said as she reached out and pulled the cording that held his robe shut. "We need better release."

She opened his robes, revealing him to be just as enamored in the moment as she was. "I can work with that," she told him.

She began to lower herself to her knees, intent on doing it here in the courtyard, amongst the fallen men. What the hells Augusto thought. Why not? He felt her hot breath on his abdomen, felt her large course hands on his tender flesh, and then her words railed through his mind once more... *collapsed in on us.*

He grabbed her by the hair and pulled her head back to look at him. "Osprey, you are a genius."

Augusto pulled away from her, his mind sated by her answers. He was resolved now. There was a way out of this mess. Not the best way out, but as the plan formed in his head, he realized it was a damn effective one. Let them find the map – he didn't care anymore. He cinched his robe, and looked back at the hot, angry, panting woman. "Get rest, Wilder," he eyed her sweat-slick flesh now distastefully, "and perhaps a bath. Tomorrow we will be very busy indeed, and the day after that, you will have all the blood you desire."

"And then?" she asked, looking down his robes, almost salivating in need.

He eyed her mischievously. "And then, my dear Osprey, we celebrate success."

PART IV
THE PALE

INTERLUDE

Marissa de Cantor y Castile

Six Winters Earlier...

DIAMONDS SPARKLED ACROSS DAZZLING BANDS OF COLOR —
pinks, reds, whites, greens, and blues – slowly undulating across
the night sky. The stars hung bound in the rolling belt like frozen
tears glittering in moonlight. Beneath her, the ship swayed lazily in
crystal waters that reflected the wonders above. It made her soul
feel alive!

"This is beautiful, Augusto," she larked merrily, as she lay
strung out across Augusto Cruz's sailboat, staring into the heavens.

"Not nearly as beautiful as what lies before me," Augusto
bade, smiling down upon her extended, lithe body. Her sun-kissed
skin still hot from spending the day out on the beach with Isa. He

directed the ship in the meager current of air so that it drifted slowly, lazily, through the tranquil waters.

Marissa smiled devilishly up at him. "What are you aiming for?"

His eyes sparkled. "I think you know."

Marissa extended a long caramel leg and ran her foot across his shin towards his inner thigh. "Then why aren't we at Cuddle Cove? I'm sure the view is just as striking."

"And crowded with plebeians with loose lips," Augusto finished. "Any one of them might recognize us – do you really want Don Fernando to find out?"

Marissa scrunched up her face at the thought of her papa. If he knew what she was doing right now...?

"A woman of your beauty, dignity, and caliber should not have to be subjected to going to Cuddle Cove – all of the time."

Marissa beamed at Augusto. His words – the way he looked at her – always made her feel so pretty. So desired. None of the other noble young men looked at her the way he did. To them she was merely the daughter of the "Elder Warden," the mock name they'd given her father, the one don foolish enough to be tasked with babysitting the elves' trees. No noble wanted that responsibility, and so not many paid her any mind – not like Augusto. Her father's arduous responsibilities did not seem to daunt him in the least. It made him all the more desirable.

"So where then, Ser Cruz, are you taking me?"

"Upon sailing today with my father, Don Lorenzo," Augusto said with a glimmer in his eye, "I spied a deliciously small alcove not even half a league northwest of Beauty Rock."

"On my father's lands?" Marissa asked.

He winked at her. "Technically, beneath his lands. And they are your lands, too. Anyway, the alcove looked recent, perhaps opened by this last spring's storms. It was very small, and passage in was no wider than this ship."

"Did you enter?"

Augusto shook his head. "Don Lorenzo was too happy enjoying the fine wind, and verily he did not even notice the small malady upon the cliff-face. So, I plotted that it could be *our* adventure."

Marissa's eyes came alive, "Our own adventure?"

"Our own secluded adventure," Augusto pointed out. "No one has any idea of this spot, Mari – it'll be ours... alone."

Marissa could barely see the cleft in the cliffside, even at a quarter of a league away. "How did you find this?"

Behind her, she heard Augusto laugh as he directed the sails. "Don Lorenzo was adamant about controlling the boom this afternoon, I had little to do but stare at the rocky shore. It was only a fortuitous glance and the right play of sunlight that I noticed the little inlet. When I did, though, my mind devised a plan."

Marissa looked back at him. "And what were you devising, Ser Cruz?"

"Our own Cuddle Cove," he said, and Marissa did not miss the lust in his eyes.

Her eyebrows raised. "Is that so? Very presumptuous of you, Ser Cruz." She turned her head away, taunting him... yet the very idea thrilled her. She was a Maker-fearing girl, her parents raised her that way. She knew the Jasian Enclave's rules for women and what it stipulated – what she was absolutely not allowed to do before marriage. Still, she couldn't deny the desire for this man growing within her. It was feverous, and consumed every fiber of her, every nerve, until her body was tingling. Marissa may have – just maybe – stuck her derriere out a little more, to give him a place to settle those hungry eyes.

Augusto maneuvered the small sailboat deftly between the

slivers of orange rock, dyed cobalt, in the moonlight. A few barnacles could be seen fastidiously holding to the stone just below the waterline, and the first indications of fire coral were just stretching their branchy fingers across the mirror-like surface, but Marissa knew Augusto was right. This cleft was new – no older than a winter, two at the very most.

Surprisingly, there were little dolines in the monstrous walls of the cliff-face, and stringers of moonlight cut through into the opening guiding their way. Carefully, Augusto maneuvered the twists and bends until the wind completely died and the small waves lapped no more. He was forced to pull out an oar and guide the ship off the rocky banks, further and further in.

Marissa worried that they might get stuck, and then what would they do? Abandon the ship? How would she get home? She was a league away from any shore, hours away from home on foot even then. She might not arrive until late morning. How would she ever explain herself to her father if that happened? Apprehension filled her. This might not have been the smartest idea. They should've waited until daytime to explore – at least then she'd have an excuse. She could've brought Isa. But no... she was alone with Augusto. If they were stuck together and had to be rescued, she knew what it would look like – exactly what it was. It might tarnish her papa's name.

Marissa was about to voice her fears when the narrow passage unexpectedly opened up to reveal an underground pond. Above them, brilliant stalactites speared down like pearl fangs. The dolines above cast rays of silver moonlight against the cavern walls. On those walls were hundreds, no thousands, of pink gemstones that glinted in the light. Their scintillations bathed the entire chamber in a muted rose. It stole Marissa's breath. This might be the most romantic setting she'd ever seen.

Augusto's dark eyes were also full of wonder. Marissa could

tell he too had no idea that this was what they were going to find. "I think... I think I see a bank over there."

Augusto brought the small boat to shore. The waters were so still that they didn't even moor the ship, for there was no fear of it drifting away.

At the shoreline, it became evident that the pond continued further in, in the form of a freshwater river. "Should we follow it?" Marissa asked.

Augusto held out his hand for her to take. She did, and he led her deeper within. The blush radiance continued to guide their way as they entered deeper and deeper into the ever-growing cavern.

Then Marissa's feet brushed against something soft and moist – no longer the stony bank and scree she'd walked on for the last twenty minutes. She squeaked in fright.

"What?" Augusto asked in alarm.

Marissa looked down at the ground and she realized that it was a long verdant bed of moss. Slowly, tentatively, she bent down and pressed her hand on it. It was so soft, incredibly soft, like a cradle of feathers.

Augusto squatted next to her, staring at the moss in amazement. It was from that angle, though, that the full scope of the cavern truly came alive, and what was in it. Marissa had no words.

Augusto also looked up to take in their surroundings. "This... this is incredible," he wheezed breathlessly. "I've never seen anything like this."

"It's paradise." Marissa whispered.

Augusto turned to look at her, the hunger in his eyes once more. "It's *our* paradise, Mari. No one knows about this place but you and me. It's ours and ours alone!"

Marissa could see the excitement and power radiating through him. It captivated her. *He* captivated her. She lunged forward and kissed him. It was long, passionate, and ravenous.

When she came away, she was breathless and more than a little lightheaded, and Augusto was more rapacious for her than ever. All her fears, all her reservations, were gone. No further thoughts about what anyone would think, or what might happen to her papa's name. Surrounded in this subterranean wonderland, she let her inhibitions drift into the pond and then finally out into the ocean beyond. Marissa untied the shift of her dress and opened it wide, showing all of herself to him.

His eyes danced across her, devouring every inch of her in eager anticipation. Wanting her. Craving her. Without another word, surrounded in their own personal utopia, entranced by the overwhelming emotion it invoked, she lay back against the mossy bed, and pulled Augusto on top of her. She let him feed his appetite for her, and she sated his desires – completely.

CHAPTER TWENTY-FIVE

Marissa de Cantor y Castile

The present...

"Not that I'm not complaining, mind ye, but how are we not dead yet?" Marissa tilted her head down, following the gnome's voice.

There was little noise to be had within the thick miasma – the only sounds Marissa could hear were the gentle slapping of water upon the hull, and the occasional creaking of the galleon itself. Oh, and her own tense breathing. Other than that, there was absolutely no noise. Not a single sound.

"See anything?" Marissa asked Anne in the unnatural quiet. She couldn't see the woman whom she'd asked to blindly climb up into the crow's nest, but they could still communicate, at least.

"Nay, Cap'n," the voice came back. "This fog ain't fer liftin' any up here, either."

"Tis an unnatural thing," Jocquotte muttered.

"I don't get it," Badger called out in the chalky morass. "I saw islands in here from the outside. Why can't we see anything at all inside?"

"Now you know why they're called the Sirens," Marissa proclaimed. "They taunt you and lure you into a place you can't escape." She faced what she thought was the prow, "You still with us, Rue?"

A snort was all she received in reply. Marissa was dreadfully worried for her friend, but at least she was relieved that Rue was still with them, even if she was in some fugue state.

"Good thing we'd ne'r fall fer such a thing!" Onna called into the silence.

No one bothered to take the bait on that jibe.

"How do we know we're even moving?" Badger asked. "I mean the boat's barely rocking, and I don't feel a lick o' wind on me face."

"I've no resistance on the yoke either," Emmell answered.

Marissa turned about and blindly groped for the rail at the stern. She gazed hard into the murk, but she couldn't see anything beyond the wall of white. Could it be possible that they were only just inside the Pale? If they found a way to turn about, would everything clear away and reveal the Royal Castile Navy and Jasian Enclave ships on the other side, ready to reduce their ship to flotsam? She could take the women in the dinghy and abandon the ship. They'd at least have rowing power. But if she were wrong, they'd be lost at sea with no food, no fresh water, no shelter. She'd be condemning them to a very slow and agonizing death.

Normally she'd drop anchor to try and guess how deep they were to see how close they might be to the islands, but Emmell's trick left them without one for the moment.

What could she do? She needed to do something, and relatively quickly. Every second that passed was one that was bringing Rusalka closer to death. They may have their supplies, and the plate to close the hole in her skull, but Onna couldn't operate blind. She was good, but even this was well beyond her skill.

Marissa needed to find a way to navigate in the unnatural gloom she was in. She needed a way to propel the galleon. It felt like they stopped moving the moment they entered the Pale. "First thing first, Badger is right."

"I am?" the woman called out confused.

"First time fer everything I guess," Anne replied.

"Don't let it get to ye head," Jocquotte called out.

Marissa ignored the comments, knowing they were all just very tense. "We need to find out if we're actually moving. If we are, then we need figure out if we're still heading south. If we're not moving, we need to find a way to move."

"Shouldn't Rue be our priority at this point?" The question came from the small voice beside her.

"Trust me, I desperately want to help Rue, but we can't see. And until we can, there's little that can really be done for her. Onna can't operate blind."

"So, then sight should be the true priority," Onna offered.

Marissa wished she could see the people instead of just dealing with their strange, disembodied voices. "No."

"How ye figure, Brains?"

"We went into the Pale at full sails – well almost full sails since we were dragging our bowsprit. Then after we entered this murk, there's suddenly nothing. No wind cutting across the deck, no crash of waves against the prow, no sound at all. We can't even hear the ships behind us. Did any follow us into the Pale? Did the wilder? Are they firing cannons even now? We've been effectively rendered blind and mute to everything around us. So, we need to know if we're moving. If we are that means we still have propulsion. But where to? Without sight we could crash right into a reef. If we're not moving, then the Pale has crippled us in every way, and that's equally as troubling."

"Could we be dead and not know it?" Anne asked after a moment's silence.

"Well, I'm pretty sure Rue is still dying, so unless orcs have the ability to die twice then I'm reasonably certain we're still alive," the spriggan to her left commented. As cold as the statement was, Marissa couldn't deny the logic of it.

"Okay, so we need to know if we be movin'. Do ye have any idea how ta figure such a thing with nary a sight or sound?" Onna called out.

"No." Marissa admitted.

"Ask the butterflies," a voice called from the bow. It was changed from before, though. It was deeper, more guttural, the words more of a bark then the usual coherence of her speech.

"Her dementia is starting to set in strong now if she thinks she can talk to her imaginary butterflies," Emmell whispered to her. "Seeing them is one thing, figments from the corner of her vision and what not, but conversation? I fear things are getting far along now. Mari. She needs help soon, and by soon I mean within the next few hours."

"Or?" Marissa dared ask.

There was no hesitation in the spriggan's word. "There is no *or* left Mari. She gets help now, or she doesn't at all."

A low growl rumbled from the front of the deck, and Marissa wondered if Rusalka heard Emmell's words... her declaration of finality, so to speak. She needed to think! She needed to find a way out of this... this hells that she took her crew into. Yet every time she put her mind to the problem, it felt lethargic, slow to react to the puzzle, like her head was in the same muddling fog that their ship was in. Was it fear causing it? Stress? She was a wreck.

Wreckage!

Every time a ship was lost in the Pale, flotsam re-emerged. Always wreckage. But if wreckage emerged from the Pale, then that meant there was a way out. A way that brought with it a means of propulsion. "Think..." she muttered aloud. She knew there was an answer to this... a simple one, but her addled brain wasn't helping her.

The growl at the front of the ship continued, and then began to intensify. "Rue?" Marissa called out hesitantly. She received no answer. They heard the creaking of oaken boards as well as the swinging of the rigging.

"Fer the love of the..." Onna began, "Brains, me thinks Rue's moving about. If she falls in the water, we'll be losing her for sure."

The growling shifted another octave, followed by the sudden slamming sound on the deck. BOOM, BOOM, BOOM.

"I think we're in trouble," Emmell muttered. "I think the dementia's peaked. She's orc again."

"Rue, are you okay?" Marissa called out, panic beginning to lace her voice. "Rue, you need to answer us."

The slamming continued – BOOM, BOOM, BOOM. It took a few seconds, but Marissa recognized it for what it was: stomps against the decking. Rhythmic footfalls. Marissa knew how orcs operated, how they used drums and footfalls to communicate to each other during raids. They also used them to inspire fear in their prey, and to rile up their adrenaline before an attack.

"Um... Cap'n, what do we do?" Badger called out.

The footfalls continued, heavier and louder. BOOM, BOOM, BOOM. The rhythmic cadence drowned out what few trickling sounds there were on the *Bella Dahlia*.

"She can't see us," Anne whispered loudly. "If we all stay real quiet, we can just wait until she passes out. Really, how much longer can she stay conscious after all of this? How much abuse can she take? We'd all be dead by now, just from exertion."

Marissa was going to reply, but it was Onna that spoke up first.

"Have ye learnt nothin' about our friend ere'? She's fueled by rage. Driven by blood. Worse, she don't need to see us. In fact, she's the only one here that ain't fully handicapped."

BOOM, BOOM, BOOM. The foot falls continued. Rue's growls starting to turn into low, husky barks.

"What do you mean?" Anne asked and Marissa could now tell by her tone that it was dripping with panic.

"She's an orc," Marissa replied into the murk, mirthlessly. "She can smell us. She knows exactly where we all are."

The hammering on the deck stopped, and everything fell as silent as death itself.

CHAPTER TWENTY-SIX

Marissa de Cantor y Castile

Marissa knew that they all were in very big trouble. No one on board had the strength, speed, or skill to take Rue in a fight, save Onna maybe. Even then, it was highly possible that Rue could rip the limbs off the gnome as easily as she could de-wing a small game bird. Marissa needed to do something to protect her people, but her brain felt so sluggish, like her mind was attempting to crawl through molasses on a cold day. Why couldn't she think? Why didn't she know what to do? She always had ideas. They might be horrible ones, but still they were something. Now though, it felt like she just smoked haze, and her entire mind was covered in a shroud of confusion.

She felt a sensation at her left hand, and she jumped. Was it Rue? Had the orc decided that she should die first, even though she was the furthest away? Then that sensation sharpened into the points of tiny keen-edged claws. Something small... no, someone small was grabbing her hand. "We need to go. Outlast her below decks." Those words came from her side, quiet as a whisper, and yet making sense. Of course, below deck – why didn't she think of that?

She could hear others milling about on the deck now, seemingly as confused as she was. The predator was out there and could track them much better than any of them could move in the dense pale. But it was wounded. Of course, that made it far more dangerous the closer it got to the end.

Marissa nodded into the thick mists, and let the little hand guide her. The white all around her coiled and snaked against her skin like a living thing. It seemed to pulse and undulate in front of her eyes with every breath she took. What was this stuff? What was happening to them? Why could she come up with only questions, but not formulate answers? She was so befuddled.

A growl resonated to her right, and she heard a woman's scream in surprise. There was a sound of scuffle, and then a howl of pain.

"No!" Marissa cried reflexively, trying to pull away from Emmell. Someone was hurt by the predator of the mists.

Emmell was far weaker than Marissa, and the movement arrested her for a moment, but the spriggan was persistent. "First we get you into the captain's quarters, then we figure out what the hells is going on."

"But someone is hurt," Marissa argued. "The creature of the mists got them."

"Creature of the mists?" Emmell said perplexed, "Mari, that's Rue out there. I just hope she hasn't killed any of our friends. Or if so, I hope it was quick at least."

"Rue?" Marissa mumbled as she was drawn blindly forward. She stumbled when she reached the stairs, but the small hand was steady and seemed to know where it was going.

Suddenly a damaged wooden wall emerged before them. She could see a hole in the wood the size of a grapefruit, the opening jagged and raw like the toothy maw of a ravenous tiger shark.

Behind them there was another crash, followed by a roar. "'Ello beasty," a familiar voice modulated in the wan aura. It was quickly followed by another trumpet of fury.

The small figure holding Marissa's hand intoned, "This is so ugly."

Marissa had no words. Her mind was growing more abstract by the moment. The disjointed claws led her into a chamber and quickly closed and barred the door. Outside of that, the brume was just as dense in the small room that they were concealed in. On the other side of the door, she could hear more clamoring as one of the people out there dared to challenge the fiend that hunted them.

Marissa was guided to her bed, where she was forced to push aside numerous sharp, oaken boards before she could sit down. When she was level with the clawed hand, the cherubic, yet alien face of her guide came into view. "Wow you have really big eyes," was all Marissa could think to say.

That small clawed hand attached to the thing with the porcupine quills reached up and grabbed her chin, turning her head left and right. "What's wrong with you Mari? Do you have a concussion?"

Concussion? That word sounded familiar, but it was so hard to understand, let alone communicate. Marissa felt as if the cognitive side of her brain was cut off from her tongue. It was infuriating.

"It's the petrichor," a very tiny voice added into the woolpack that enveloped them. Marissa watched in fascination as the quilled head of her guide disappeared, only to return a few seconds later holding a rum bottle with the most curious thing inside.

The tiny creature was hovering in the center of the bottle, shimmering, translucent, delicate wings fluttering furiously. They resembled something akin to a dragonfly's diaphanous makeup, but were shaped more like a moth's wings. Attached to those luminous, wildly beating appendages, Marissa could clearly see what looked very much like a small girl, except the tiny thing seemed elongated somehow. Warped. Her neck was too long for her head, which housed eyes that were virtually owl-like in scale, and crowned with a wild mane of hair that closely resembled flickering flames. Her torso was stretched, comically so, looking on the verge of malnourishment. She folded her frail, rangy arms, over one another, and flicked a hand dismissively Marissa's way. Her three-fingered hand ended in little claws. "Yup this mortal is done for, crimble, best let her back out there to suffer the same fate as every other mortal that enters the veil."

"Don't call me that," the spriggan replied, "and it's the Pale, not veil," she corrected.

The small winged person made a rude gesture with her finger at the spriggan. "I know what I said, crimble. Veil. Stonewaël Veil."

Marissa stared at the two in fascination, as it became harder and harder for her to think. Outside, bellows continued to reverberate off the walls, as well as a litany of higher-pitched curses. Someone speaking with a thick Halsbrenian accent was hollering from a distance that sounded like she was high in the sky.

"Listen to that baying of pigs out there, crimble. The petrichor of the veil is turning them into what mortals are – animals. Each and every one."

The spriggan responded tersely to being called a crimble again, but through the din outside and the arguing of the winged little person, and the not really much bigger person, Marissa thought she could hear singing. "It's so pretty..."

The spriggan who was in midsentence about the nature of the veil and the Pale turned to look back at her. "What was that?"

"The song," Marissa said, swaying to the sound now that was so much louder than all that unnecessary violence happening outside. "It's lovely."

The woman trapped in the bottle snorted, "She's done, crimble. Cast her back into the water – the nøkken have her, just like the rest of your crew. You want my advice? Let me out of this bottle, get to one of your little boats with the paddle sticks, and I'll direct you out of here. It's the least I can do for my kin, even a crimble."

"Wait," the spriggan replied, catching on, "are you saying it's not effecting me because I'm a descendant of fey?"

"Sidhe," the little kållråden corrected, "Aes Sidhe more to the point, and that's exactly what I'm saying. Stonewaël Veil is a weak point between the planes of the Gu Tur and the Tír fo Thuinn, where our two worlds intersect. I think I've heard a gnome call the planes Mundane and the Nether, if that helps, though I personally think gnomes are idiots. Either way, they are one and the same. The petrichor is result of this plane's air, intermixing with the air of Tír fo Thuinn. It doesn't affect the Sidhe in any way, but a mortal?" The kållråden nodded in Marissa's direction. "You can see for yourself."

The spriggan shook her head, "But... even if she is degenerating into an animal, why is Rue trying to kill everyone?"

"Ah," the kållråden said with obvious enjoyment at the whole scenario. "Well, for that you can thank the nøkken. They're sort of the guardians of the Stonewaël Veil, and they prevent any mortal from passing through into Tír fo Thuinn. They relish in their task, and their results are always lethal."

"Nøkken?"

"Yup, bunch of upstart male daoine sidhe who play enchanting songs on the ghittern. Chances are you've never seen one, or you're not supposed to anyway. You wouldn't have ever seen or caught me, had I not been riding on the Grains of Paradise when you found me."

"I see one!" Marissa said jubilantly, as something darted right by her head. She distinctly saw the vivid beautiful wings of a monarch butterfly. "They're butterflies!"

"Butterflies?" the spriggan answered, and Marissa could see

her eyes light up in understanding. "These nøkken have been entrancing Rue ever since we came back on the ship!"

The kållråden smiled. "Not just her, but everyone who could succumb to the nøkken song. It's a slow, subtle thing, but we sidhe grow easily bored, and a ship full of female mortals is ripe for the taunting of the nøkken."

The spriggan held up the bottle frantically to her face, and Marissa thought it made her face look funny. She giggled while the spriggan pressed on. "How can I save my friends? How can I stop the nøkken?"

"Why should I tell you? You've kept me trapped as a prisoner now for almost two days."

"You were stealing our Melegueta pepper," the spriggan returned.

"How was I stealing it?" the kållråden answered defensively. "It's not like you were cooking with it."

"But it was ours!"

The little creature in the bottle did not budge. "It comes from nature. No one puts ownership on such a thing. It was there, you weren't using it, so I did."

"You little..." Marissa watched the spriggan take a deep breath to calm down. "This isn't helping my friends. We'll talk about this later."

The kållråden shrugged.

"I'll tell you what – I'll release you if you tell me how I can save them. And don't you dare tell me there is no way," the spriggan groused.

The kållråden seemed to think about it. "There is little you can do for their mental faculties while they are within the petrichor, but they could become docile and not try and kill each other if you could convince the nøkken you are worth leaving alone."

"And how can I do that?" the spriggan asked through gritted teeth.

The kållråden put her hands on her hips, "Nope, not gonna tell you. I need payment."

"Payment?"

"The *Creideamh Sí*," Marissa said gleefully, swaying her hips to the lovely music of the nøkken. "It is the 'Faery Faith', a collection of beliefs and practices observed by those who wish to keep good relationships with the sidhe to avoid angering them. It is the custom of offering milk and food." Marissa noticed both of the creatures staring at her oddly. "What? My mother used to tell me that story all the time as a child."

The kållråden stared at her for a moment in astonishment, before closing her mouth, stamping her foot on the glass jar and yelling, "Not a faery!"

"But she is right?" the spriggan asked.

"Yes," the kållråden answered. "The mortal has the right of it. It is amazing she remembered, but it is often the childhood memories that are the last to go in the petrichor."

"Fine!" the spriggan answered. "I will give you another container of melegueta pepper if you tell me how to stop the nøkken."

"You have more?" the kållråden said, suddenly very excited. Desperately so in fact.

"I do," the spriggan answered, "but only as long as Onna out there hasn't been killed by Rue yet."

"Ye stupid fustilug!" came a high-pitched voice from the outside, followed by a crash and a blustering yell.

"Nope, not dead yet, and still surprisingly cognizant," the spriggan said, looking down at the kållråden in a jar. Marissa was transfixed by the two.

"Yeah... gnomes are pretty resilient for a while," the kållråden commented. Marissa could tell she was giving it serious thought. Finally, the tiny thing nodded, "We have an accord. You can repel the nøkken by doing the same thing they are doing to your crew."

"What? Music?" the spriggan asked, startled.

The kållråden nodded. "But not just any music, crimble. It has to be something as beautiful and as pure as their own, if not better, to get them to silence their song and become entranced by your own."

"But... I can't sing – I have no talent for such a thing."

And then the two of them were looking directly at Marissa. She giggled, but their expressions made her childish fit of laughter stop. She looked at them seriously. "What?"

"You need to sing, Mari."

Her question turned to alarm. "What!?"

The little kållråden nodded in the bottle. "Yes... yes... you were the one who sang the shanty song, correct?"

Marissa bit her lip in thought. "I... can't remember."

"You can't remember singing, or the words to the song."

Marissa raised her eyebrows. "Both?"

The little creature threw up her hands in frustration. "There's no hope with these mortals, crimble."

The spriggan shook her head. "I refuse to believe this mist has robbed her of everything already."

"Believe it," the kållråden told her, "she's going to be lumbering around on all fours in the next twenty minutes or so like a monkey... if the green one out there doesn't kill her first."

"Mari, think, think real hard!" the spriggan said, taking Mari's hands in her own tiny clawed ones. "Can you remember any songs, any at all?"

Mari was shaking her head, but before she could speak the spriggan interrupted her. "Listen to me, Mari, right now – all of our crew, all of them are dependent on you, on your ability to sing. Rue, Onna, Anne, Badger, and Jocquotte, they are all going to die if you can't remember a single song. Can you not remember a single melody at all?"

"I... I'm sorry," Marissa mumbled, "but it's so hard to even... think, let alone try and sing."

"But you need to try..." the creature holding her hands pressed. "You need to try."

Marissa was still shaking her head. "I... can't. I don't remember anything that I sang recently... I want to help. I don't want these people to die."

"These people are your friends," the large-eyed thing in front of her said with emphasis, and though Marissa couldn't remember, she believed it.

"She's slipping further," the moth in the jar said.

Big Eyes placed her tiny hands over her face in frustration. She was shaking her head, making those curious pointy objects on her head bounce up and down. "There has to be something."

"There is," the bizarre speaking bottle said to the creature. "You get me the grains of paradise, then you get in a rowboat and you leave. I'll guide you, on my sidhe honor."

The critter sank to the floor next to Marissa's legs, and to her surprise the thing began to shudder. "I can't," it said through sobs. "I can't leave my friends."

"Then you will die, crimble."

The creature nodded, "I guess I'm okay with that."

Marissa felt bad for the creature. She was sorry she couldn't help it with the shanty it wanted, but she just didn't know what it was talking about. She wanted to reach out and pet it, make it not feel so sad and lonely, but she was afraid she might prick herself on that sharp-looking hair.

Instead, she put a hand on its shoulder, and its little clawed hands took hers in reassurance. She began to hum to the little thing like her mother used to hum to her, when she felt scared and alone.

The thing's shuddering stopped, and Marissa watched as the

quills on her head rustled. It turned and looked at her with large, wide eyes.

Marissa smiled dumbly down at it.

"What... melody is that?" It asked her.

Marissa stopped humming. "Just something my mother used to sing to me when I was a tiny little girl, maybe four-winters-old."

"And do you know the words?" it asked.

Marissa thought about it and nodded. "She must've sung me the song a thousand times. I've never sung it myself..." She paused and racked her brain. "At least I don't think I've ever sung it. I don't much care for the song... at least I don't think I did, but it was soothing as a child when my mother sang it."

The animal stood up before her. It was funny to see a talking animal. "Could you sing it?"

Marissa smiled a lopsided grin. "I think so."

The beast took its tiny claws and wrapped them around her hands. "Try Mari. Try hard."

Marissa thought the little critter was cute. She liked cute animals. "Okay, I'll sing for you, bunny rabbit."

"Bunny rabbit?"

"Well, I fear this is going to be the biggest, but most short-lived calamity of your life, crimble. It was fine knowing you," the magic bottle told the bunny. "If you could by chance remove this lid so I can search your corpses for the grains of paradise when you're gone, that'd be great."

Mari smiled at them both.

CHAPTER TWENTY-SEVEN

Rusalka

She could smell their fear, their terror, their confusion, and it thrilled her. She taunted her prey, dragging out each succulent moment. Already the blood of another filled her mouth. She gorged on it, relished in it, devoured its essence, and now the taste triumphantly lingered on, driving her forward.

Constantly there were puny stings from a little thing. It came out of the haze and peppered her with tiny little bites on her legs and arms. She fell over crates and barrels, and twice tripped over a strange furrow on the wooden floor. Once, one of the humans was even clever enough to push the boom into her. That dazed her for a handful of seconds, but none of them were hunters. None of them had what it took to commit to the kill. To desire it. To revel in it.

Through it all, the butterflies continued to serenade her with their violins and their little songs. In the beginning, before she entered the swallowing gloom, she found their incessant nature a bother. She'd swatted at them, tried to bat them away to stop with their odd songs. But here, covered in obscurity, surrounded by a buttermilk sky, she began to breathe in their melody, consume their consonance, and embrace the inflections. They wanted her to be what she was good at, what she knew how to do well. What she was. They wanted her to embrace the hunter. Embrace orc.

It was a long fight, and she was tired of it now. Tired of the strain. When she submitted to the song it gave her new strength. Their verse filled her with clarity of purpose. The rhythm made everything clear when the world all around her was fog. They made her orc once more, and as orc, she had hunting to do.

She licked her lips, still feeling the blood of her first victim hot upon them. Yet while she relished in it, and relished in the taunting, the butterflies' song told her she was ready to taste the next one. Yes, she thought in agreement. Yes, she was ready.

She could smell one of the human mongrels up the pole. That one was easy prey. It was no fun to hunt. The other she could taste near the front of the ship. This one too would be easy prey, and though her head throbbed, and each step seemed heavier than the last, she wanted to tackle her truest game – the gnome.

She crinkled her nose as two other scents drifted to her, another human and a spriggan. They were locked inside their little room, but she knew that tiny box wouldn't keep her out. She would bend and twist the door until it splintered and shattered beneath her might, and then she would consume them as well. She would gorge herself on their entrails, and her victory would be complete. First though... she needed to eliminate the gnome, and her little pricker.

Suddenly, her senses flared as the vermin moved in on her. She reached for it, and was rewarded with a sting across her fingertips, and a howl of banter, something about a bilge rat. She didn't care. She wanted to crush her foe.

The scent faded back, closer to the human once more. Clearly it was trying to lead her into some kind of trap. But there would be no more barrels, no more crates. She threw them overboard. No provisions to keep them alive now. All the gnome had was her wits, and it was a paltry thing in comparison to an orc's strength.

She was done with the games now, and even the song of the butterflies was done. They wanted the gnome dead, and she would comply. With a savage roar she charged the front of the ship and the annoying gnome.

Her nose saved her once more, as she scented the anticipation rolling off the human. She dove into a roll, just as the jib boom swung where her head was. She came to her feet and lashed out with a right cross that sent the human to the deck so quickly it didn't even have a chance to scream in surprise.

Rusalka felt hot pain on her neck and realized with some annoyance that the gnome was on the jib boom, and jumped off onto her back. She was now stabbing with her little pricker in the back of Rusalka's neck. The rodent was squealing at her in its stupid little language, but she could hear her name interspersed within its laments. She could smell her own blood now, coming out the back of her neck, and it enraged her further.

Rusalka reached up, trying to grab at the creature on her back, but it squirmed away from each grasp, somehow managing to nimbly stay on her back and keep its little pricker buried in the back of her neck. She knew if she didn't do something soon, this prey's little bites might bleed her out.

She stumbled backward until her swinging arm struck the mainsail mast. A brutal thought came to mind through the rage and pain. With all of her might she slammed her back, and its occupant, into the mast.

Fire exploded in her neck, and she received a satisfying *oompf* from her assailant. The little thing fell slack against her and tumbled to the deck.

The butterflies danced with glee around her peripheral vision, and a single canticle echoed out to her... *consume.*

Rusalka felt for the limp thing on the deck and found it. She grabbed it by its face, feeling hot liquid splatter against her palm. She smothered its nose and mouth and hefted the tiny thing by its head.

Consume! The serenade continued again and again. *Consume!* Rusalka, wanting to please the butterflies, brought the still creature's neck to her mouth. She opened her tusks wide, and wrapped her jaw around the gnome's narrow, frail throat. Her tusks poked at its flesh, she could feel its pulse, quick against her tongue. She craved what was to come next. She reveled in the ecstasy of its final throes, as its life poured into her gullet.

Slowly, savoring each and every second, she began to bite down.

A CURIOUS THING HAPPENED TO RUSALKA AS HER JAW clamped down around the gnome's throat. She didn't get the rush of blood flowing into her mouth as the damn of flesh broke free from the artery in its neck. She didn't get the writhing rebuttal from the thing as the red liquid life left it, forcing it to shirk its mortal coil. This didn't happen.

Instead, her jaw... stopped working. It was the butterflies. The butterflies were distracted, and they no longer were telling her to consume. They were no longer playing to her. In fact, there was a voice now, over the violins, a lovely voice.

The voice of an angel.

"Well I've heard there was a hidden piece,

That Jasia sang and it pleased the priests,

But you don't really care for old stories, do ya?"

Her mind fog was as dense as the miasma in front of her, but she began to recognize the words of the song.

"Well it goes like this:

You set the scene, you add some action, you make them scream,

You tie it up, and you give them Hosanna."

It was a sorrowful song, but also a powerful one. It began to lift the cloud as the words poured forth into her ears, like crystal clear waters washing away the scree that blanketed her mind.

"Well her belief was strong but we needed reason,

We saw her chanting season after season,

Her resolve and her compassion it overthrew ya,

So you tied her to a wooden stake,

And you broke her heart, and she broke your faith,

And from your lips she drew forth the Hosanna."

The song did not abate but rose in strength. Rusalka found herself clinging to the words more fiercely than her mouth clung to the gnome's throat.

"Hosanna," the angel sang, "Hosanna."

She let the gnome fall from her mouth and she released her hand from the creature. She was completely taken by the words...

"But maybe we've been here before,

Upon this cold and empty shore,

You know, there were so many gods before I knew ya,

And I've seen your symbol on the colonnade,

And faith is not a hero's crusade,

It's a questing and it's a shattering Hosanna."

Tears began to tumble down Rusalka's face. Such a powerful melody, and the angel's voice was so pure. Purer to her than the chorus of butterflies, for now even their instruments were completely silent.

"I don't doubt in the Maker's wraith,

But all I've ever learned from faith,

Was how to crucify somebody who confused ya,

And it's not a hymn that you hear at dark,

It's not song to be sung on a lark,

It's a cold and it's a broken Hosanna."

The word *Hosanna* carried melodiously a dozen or so more times before all fell silent. There was no more song, and there was no more noise from the butterflies. Rusalka was dimly aware of a door creaking shut, and then a form cut a swath through the veil. She recognized the figure, and she recognized the voice.

It was a human that had transcended all barriers and become her friend. "Mari?" she whispered harshly.

The human nodded, and with more recognition, she glanced down at the gnome lying at her feet covered in blood. "Onna? Oh Maker, what have I done?" Rusalka cried.

As she reached for her gnome friend though, the pain proved too great, both in her heart, and throughout her body, and blackness finally took her.

It never felt more merciful.

CHAPTER TWENTY-EIGHT

Marissa de Cantor y Castile

Marissa opened her eyes. She could hear the surf crashing melodically against the shore and it reinvigorated her. The seaside scent tickled her nostrils, and the hot tropical sun kissed her eyelids. It wasn't an unpleasant burning sensation, but a restorative one. She couldn't remember the last time she ever felt so rested.

And her dream! She had the wildest dream of her life! Of returning home to Castile, of Augusto, and of a great chase out of Cuddle Cove and into the Pale! She'd never had a dream like that in all her life – she couldn't wait to share it, to figure out what it could mean.

She opened her eyes, expecting to see the small familiar confines of her captain's quarters. The plum drapes covering both windows. The dark oak frame, stained with sea spray. The chest of drawers that once held strange fineries from the previous captain. Either he liked to keep the garments of his conquests, or he secretly desired to dress as a woman when no one was looking.

She kept a few of the parcels when she took over, mostly the clean, relatively unused ones that seemed around her size. She particularly fancied the frilly crimson and black skirt, but it seemed ridiculously short for a Maker-fearing woman such as herself, though she secretly desired the thrill of wearing something so... robust.

He had also a tricorn cap with the same red frill that she had found comically endearing on the skirt. She placed it upon the dress, as a what-if scenario, of one day wearing. Though she knew the likelihood of such a thing, it was an outfit not conducive to working with rigging and booms, and more in line with pulling at men's heartstrings, or... other things.

All these things she expected to see, but a palm thatch roof was not one of them. Sunlight bit through the toothy holes between the fronds, leaving her swathed in serrated beams of light; one ironically cutting a long line across her face.

She blinked away the bright light and sheltered her hand over her dark eyes to take in the foreign surroundings. She was in some kind of single-room hut, and she was lying upon a thatched cot made of the same palm fronds as the ceiling. Around her in the circular hut were wicker furniture and baskets, all crafted from fronds.

Slowly, she sat up. An involuntary groan peeled from her lips as a throbbing ache wrenched at her abdomen. It took several breaths to even out the pain of her fatigued muscles, but after a few moments the sharp sting dulled into a muted pulsing. She pushed herself to her feet and noted with some surprise she was wearing a tattered blue dress... the same blue dress from her dream.

"What in the hells?" she muttered aloud. It was a dream, wasn't it? More confused than ever, she shambled her sore body to the door, which appeared to be made out of the flotsam of a wrecked ship, and she pulled it open.

The sun cast its rays upon a whole new world.

"Maker be praised..." she mumbled, "it's paradise."

Marissa surveyed the immediate landscape. Before her, as far as she could see, were rolling emerald valleys. Slowly she began to turn, and a wedge of sharp, copper mountain spires replaced the drapery of viridian plains. A further rotation still changed the landscape once more to bronzed, jagged cliffs, aged by time and the elements. All around, centuries of growth formed tropical rain-forests, forking rivers, and cascading waterfalls, all untouched by the races of man.

With one more turn, she opened herself up to a wide bay, the very ground laced with banks of auburn. At those banks were a handful of dinghies – all made from various pieces of flotsam. And berthed in the center of the bay was the *Bella Dahlia*. The sight of her ship added to the majesty that surrounded her, even though the poor vessel went through the hells and back again. It was true, she realized. It was no dream, everything was true... including her crew, and Rue.

Mari turned, urgently looking for the rest of her crew – surely she wasn't the only survivor? Facing the green valleys once more, she saw almost a dozen more huts like the one she emerged from. People with all manner of clothing ranging from simple loincloths to the ostentatious garb of the most prolific sailing merchants, were milling about, going about day to day activities like this was any other port harbor. There were men and women of all ages and races, though they seemed to be predominantly human. In fact, much to her surprise, she saw a scales talking with Anne and Badger. She scanned the people, looking for her other crew members. Where was Jocquotte, or Emmell, or Rue?

She spotted Onna talking to a striking woman dressed in Castile finery, though the clothes looked to be worn nearly thread-bare. As she looked at the clothes, Mari thought they looked very much like Cantor colors... Marissa felt her breath catch in her throat. No... no, this isn't possible, she thought. This can't be.

Onna saw Marissa and nodded to the woman she was speaking to. The human woman, who Marissa knew to be in her fifties, didn't look a day over forty winters, and as she turned her long, dark curly hair billowed backwards into the wind like a black flag. A smile came to her full lips, a smile that Marissa recognized all too well, for she saw it every time she looked into a mirror.

Marissa could hardly find her voice, "Mamá?"

The true Doña Cantor looked at Mari with a sparkle in her dark eyes. "Hello, my daughter."

"I'M EITHER DEAD, OR I'M DREAMING."

Doña Miranda Cantor smiled once more. "Neither, Mari," she looked around at the vista that surrounded them, "though I thought much the same myself when I made it to these shores."

Mari's voice cracked. "Mamá, is it really you?"

Doña Cantor's eyes began to water. "There's so much I want to tell you, but now I don't seem to have words."

Marissa felt her lips quivering. It was her! It was really her! "Mamá!" she cried. She ran towards her mother, kicking up long drags of sand as she barreled towards the awaiting Castellan woman.

Marissa lunged into her mother in a hug, and she found the woman much smaller than she remembered her. Her mother felt frail in her arms, but she was still whole. She was real! Marissa buried her face in her mother's hair and wept. And to her surprise she found the woman who she always thought so regal and pious doing the same. "I don't understand, help me to understand," Marissa sobbed into Doña Cantor's raven locks.

"I wish I could. Truth is, very few survive the Pale, and none escape." She pushed Marissa back, and waved at the people around them. "They, like I, were all members of a ship that was swallowed by the Pale. We were the stragglers that made it to this island, either by dinghy, or on a piece of floating hull that was once their ship." Doña Cantor pointed out towards the cliffs. "On the other side is a ship graveyard of the likes that you have never seen, Mari. There are reefs and rocks, and hundreds of other perils within the Stonewall Pale that mark the doom of any who sail within."

Mari scrunched her brow as she looked from her mother to the direction she was pointing. The cliffs blocked the sights she described, and Doña Cantor took a hesitant step away from her. Marissa immediately looked back at the woman.

"Your boatswain, Onna, has been telling me a remarkable tale, Mari. About where you've been, and what you've experienced since you made it back to Castile."

"I... left out the juicier bits fer ye to explain, Brains," Onna added. She had been atypically silent during Marissa's reunion with her mother. "I felt it'd be best comin' from family's mouth."

Marissa nodded dumbly. "Thank you, Onna."

The gnome looked suddenly uncomfortable. "Sure, sure. I'm just gonna check on the other ladies... we'll talk in a bit. We need ta have a discussion about Rue."

Mari grew suddenly alarmed. "Is she all right? Did she make it?"

Onna held up her hands. "Calm down, Brains. Rue's fine. An orc's skull is a lot thicker than we thought! Bolt barely even knicked her brain. There was a good deal of swelling though, from all we've been through. Emmell and I have already done worked on her, it's... other things that happened on the Dahlia that might be affecting more than the bolt ta her head ever did."

Marissa stared at her friend. She could hardly remember anything on the Dahlia after they sailed into the Pale. The harder she tried, the more it seemed as if that block of time was just... missing.

Doña Cantor placed her hands on Mari's shoulders. Mari looked to Onna, who gave her a nod, and then walked away. Mari focused on the woman before her. The winters of her absence had aged her mother. She was thicker now about the hips, and crow's feet were forming at the corners of her eyes. Though, truth be told, she'd held up remarkably well in comparison to someone like Adjutant Love. Her hands looked rougher now, too. Mari guessed that the title of Doña meant little when shipwrecked and stranded on an island paradise. "I want to hear it all, Mari. About where you've been? What the Enclave did to you? Onna tells me they abandoned you."

Marissa nodded.

Doña Cantor took an incensed breath. "We will talk about this, but first..." Marissa saw her mother pause, and she could read it in her body language. She was trying to summon the courage to say the next words. Finally, after several pregnant seconds, they came forward. "My husband is dead... isn't he?"

Marissa felt her eyes begin to water anew, as a rush of emotions that she'd been forced to bury down over and over again rose to the surface once more. She didn't even need to answer her mother – Doña Cantor could read it all over her face.

Doña Cantor's face twisted in pain, and she cursed vehemently as crystal rivers rolled down her copper flesh. "I knew," she said in the sob. "The moment I found my brooch missing, and the captain sabotaged the ship, sending it and his crew right into the Pale, I knew it was an attack on our family, and that my husband was going to die. Maker damn him!" she cried. "Maker damn that son of a whore, Cruz."

Marissa blinked back in sudden surprise. "You know it was him?"

Doña Cantor wiped away the tracks on her cheeks, and sniffed once, regally composing herself once more. "It could be none other. I'm sorry Mari, but Augusto is not the man you remember. His ambition has consumed the young boy you once knew. He was absorbing fiefs over the last few winters at an alarming rate. An unnatural rate. I knew he set his eyes on Cantor, even back when he was courting you. I think it was his plan originally to just marry into the titles, but your running off to join the Enclave put a massive damper on that."

Mari nodded. "I am only too well aware."

"Yes," Doña Cantor agreed, looking behind Marissa at the berthed *Bella Dahlia*, "I am sure you are." Her watery eyes focused back on Marissa once more. "How did he die, I must know?"

Marissa closed her eyes, the pain of Vicente's words coming back to her mind unbidden. How could she tell her mother how Papa died, how he was cut down with no more concern for his life than a farmer scything a sheaf of wheat? "Mamá... there are many awful rumors right now, no one can give me a clear answer on how he died. The predominant one is that he and Ser Corredor and a young woman all died in the woods at the hands of brigands."

Doña Cantor covered her hand over her mouth, trying to contain the expression of horror on her face. "Not Javier too?"

"Vicente is caretaker of Loja de Cantor right now."

"Oh, that poor, poor boy. He must hate us for this."

"He's angry, that's for sure, but he loves Cantor, Mamá. It's the reason he's still holding the castle from Augusto, even though Augusto controls everything else in Cantor." Telling her mother that sparked another thought as well. "In fact, Augusto would be fully in control of Cantor right now, and Vicente would likely be arrested – or worse – by the Castile Royal Guard and the Jasian Enclave, except..."

Doña Cantor looked at her expectantly. "Except?"

Marissa smiled and nodded in the direction Onna walked off

toward. "Except my boatswain may have swiped Papa's will and the fiefdom titles while we were in the Rhombus. Without those titles, Augusto will have to wait until new ones are drawn up at the Citadel. That should buy us something, I hope."

Her mother's mouth hung open in shock. "You stole the titles and will from Adjutant Love, in the Rhombus itself?"

Marissa shrugged sheepishly. "Yes...?"

A huge smile broke over the sadness. "Tell me. Tell me everything."

And so she did. She told her mother everything.

Hours later, her mother, Onna, Emmell, and the "not a faery," were all sitting together in a large community hut. Rusalka lay on a cot made of thatched palm fronds. Her head was shaved completely on one side and there was a long L-shaped incision that was stitched where the bolt had once been.

It wasn't pretty work, but it was efficient. A green paste that Emmell concocted out of local flora was smeared against the side of her head, outlining the wound. One of the women on the island, Delilah, was, at one time, a priestess for the Jasian Enclave and a Curate-in-training. She was the sole survivor of the lost Jasian Cog, The Reconniter. She did what she could to accelerate Rue's healing, and already, after only hours, the wound looked as if it was already a week old and healing nicely.

Rusalka herself was still unconscious since the event in the Pale.

Emmell and Onna explained what happened to everyone in the Pale, and the horrific results of Rusalka while under the nøkken's spell. Marissa could barely wrap her mind around it. Yes, Rusalka was an orc, and everyone knew what she was capable of, but to one of their own... it seemed impossible. There was a reason that only the three of them were in the room with her mother and the kållråden at the moment. Tensions in her crew were running high.

"So, let me get this straight," Marissa said to everyone in the room, "when the nøkken controlled Rue, she went... feral."

They all nodded.

"And she attacked us."

Again, silent nodding.

"And she bit off the first three fingers on Jocquotte's left hand."

No one answered her. It was a redundant question. Onna for her part scratched at one of the scabs where Rusalka's tusks pierced her neck. "It coulda been far worse, Brains."

"For who?" Marissa asked. "Jocquotte? Someone she trusted with her life just bit her fingers off!" She pointed at Rusalka. "And Rue..." Her voice caught in her throat. It took her a moment to find it again as she looked down at her friend in sorrow. "She's been working so hard to keep this part of herself down, and now this."

"It's not her fault," Onna tried to amend. "None of us here blame her."

Marissa pointed outside the hut. "But Badger, Anne, and Jocquotte do! They don't trust her."

"Only because that's the last thing they remember," Emmell pointed out. "You had your faculties when Rusalka fell to the song of the nøkken. It wasn't but a few moments after that you truly began to wane. Marissa, you admit yourself you couldn't remember one bit singing the song that saved us."

Marissa shook her head – it was true, she had no recollection of singing the song, or why she'd even chose that one. She'd sworn off singing Enclave hymns after the church left her to die a slave. To sing one that was so personal to her at one point... she couldn't fathom it.

"Quite the voice, too, for a mere mortal," a small voice added to the growing silence. They all turned to regard the kållråden, who up until this point had stayed quietly away from everyone but Emmell.

"My daughter has an exceptional singing voice," Doña Cantor agreed.

"Mother, stop, you know that's not true," Marissa protested.

Doña Cantor raised an eyebrow at her. "And yet, because of it, you have successfully done what no one has ever done before. You have navigated the Pale."

"Veil actually," Emmell interjected. "You've called it by the wrong name now for centuries, maybe even millennia."

"Excuse me?" Doña Cantor asked.

"The crimble is correct, mortal woman," the kållråden answered.

"Don't call me that," Emmell interjected.

The kållråden ignored her and continued. "The phenomena you call Stonewall Pale is actually the Stonewaël Veil – every self-respecting sidhe knows this."

"And yet, until you, young lady, I've never seen a sidhe in my life," Doña Cantor replied.

"That's because we are hidden to the eye, mostly. We are good at not being seen by mortals, and for the most part stay out of your affairs," the kållråden answered.

"Yes, why did ye help us? Not that I'm not fer bein' ungrateful and all," Onna added.

The kållråden looked between all of them with not an ounce of shame for what she said next. "I was promised Grains of Paradise. A great deal of them, in fact."

Everyone looked down to Emmell, and the small spriggan shrugged. "What? It was an easy barter – I mean come on, it's just a spice."

"It is not just spice!" the kållråden said, suddenly irate. She calmed nearly as quickly. "It's not."

Marissa looked at the sidhe in concern, before looking back to Emmell. "I take it she was paid at least with what she desired?"

Emmell fidgeted. "For giving me the information on how to save you she was... as for being the navigator to get you to this island, well..."

The kållråden shot up like a lightning bolt into Marissa's face, causing her to dart her head backward in surprise. "I was promised a barrel! An entire barrel of the Grains of Paradise!"

Onna whistled. "Em, have ye any idea how much that'd cost us?"

"I wasn't in a position to negotiate, was I?" Emmell replied defensively. "Every human was rolling around on deck sucking their thumbs and wetting their britches, and you and Rue were unconscious, soiling yourselves the other way. The whole incident reeked."

"Poop deck indeed," Marissa replied.

Onna's ears burned. "Not me fault, I was out cold, and it's not like we had a chance to take any potty breaks in the last twenty-four hours."

Marissa took a deep breath. "Either way, a deal was made, and we will now have to honor it. Plus, Em, you invoked the *Creideamh Sí* and we will keep it in good faith."

The kållråden nodded. "I normally avoid mortals, on account of your stupidity, but you, angel-tongue, you I could like."

"Uhm, thanks? I guess," Marissa replied.

"Do ye have a name little lassie, or are we gonna have to keep callin' ye a faery?" Onna asked.

Marissa watched as rage immediately took to the small thing's face. "Not a faery!" it howled. "And I do have a name." She almost looked abashed when she said it. "It's Nery."

"Nery, not-a-faery?" Marissa replied with a smile. Onna snorted.

Nery turned on Marissa, rage in her eyes, and Marissa thought perhaps it might have been a mistake to taunt the sidhe, when suddenly a large grin broke out on her bright, childlike face. "Oh... I see what you did there. You're a clever mortal, much higher on the primate's intelligence scale, more like a chimpanzee, and not like that little marmoset over there."

Marissa smiled wider, not sure how she should quite proceed. Was that a compliment? An insult? She didn't even know what a chimpanzee was.

"Is a marmoset bad?" Onna asked. "Is it a sidhe thing?"

"It's a tiny monkey," Doña Cantor told them all.

"Oh, okay, I'm good with that," Onna agreed merrily.

Marissa shook her head.

Emmell, however, changed the topic. "Now that we're all friends – for the most part – we need to get back to the topic at hand," she cringed at her own reference, "and discuss what we're gonna do with Rue when she gets up, and how we're gonna handle Jocquotte as well."

"What's wrong with telling them the truth? That you mortals get even stupider when you breathe in petrichor, and that the nøkken simply take advantage of it," Nery asked.

"I hope it's that easy," Marissa agreed, "though I fear it won't be."

"She lost three fingers, Mari – good ones too," Onna remarked.

"Are there bad fingers that are okay to lose?" Emmell queried. "I was unaware that we bore sacrificial digits on our persons."

"Well ye don't. A single finger lost and ye's down to only two. But humans have five on each hand. I mean, what are the last two even good fer?"

"All the same, I think Jocquotte would have preferred to keep them," Marissa replied. When nothing more was forthcoming, she sighed again. "You're going to make me talk to them, aren't you?"

"Yer the Cap'n. Comes with the title, Brains," Onna replied.

"I agree," Emmell added.

Marissa shook her head. "I knew you were going to say that."

Onna smiled wide, but just as quickly, Marissa saw another thought take its place. "Blimey, in all the chaos I was totally forgettin' ta show ya what I stole from the Adjutant and Cruz, Mari. It was important."

Onna turned and rifled through her pack, pulling out all the rolled-up documents. She placed them on the wicker table for all to see, and Marissa reached down to unroll them.

At the top of the stack was her father's last will and testament. She felt a knot catch in her throat as she looked at the beautiful calligraphy of Don Fernando Cantor. Doña Cantor reached down and tentatively picked up the document. This was one of the only things left, the last evidence of his life, and Marissa could see small diamonds blooming at the corners of her mother's eyes.

"When I snuck out from under ye dress, and ye left me in the room with the two men, I overheard them talking about a map and something about a 'pact.'" Onna reached up to the pile on the human-sized table and moved things around until she found that very thing. She grabbed the pact and handed them to Marissa.

Marissa began to read them over, her eyes widening as she soaked it all in. "A free and independent Castile?" she asked, handing the document over to her mother.

Onna nodded. "That's what they said. They want to make Castile its own nation."

"But how?"

"They're going to buy it," her mother said as she reviewed the pact further.

"With what money?" Marissa asked, confused. "I mean, I know Castile is a popular port, but our economy isn't great enough to possibly purchase the land as a nation. And all the capital of the Dons combined would only be a drop in the bucket for what the Enclave would charge."

Onna shrugged, but it was her mother who answered. "They

are purchasing it with lumber. Enough lumber to build a fleet five times over."

"Lumber? The average ship of the line would require 2000 oak trees for its construction. That's anywhere from 20-70 acres per ship. That's not accounting for all the waste wood. There are 430 ships to a fleet. Such an amount would de-forest all the woods we have on the peninsula, and that wouldn't be nearly enough to even build a quarter of the ships in a fleet, let alone five times that. Where do they think they're getting the lumber?"

Before she even finished, she thought she understood. Her mother finished her thought, showing her the paper. "They're using Elder wood, from the Shemma."

"Elder wood?" Onna asked curious, "I thought the wood elves said the Elder trees are sacred to them? Why would they let humans into the Shemma to cut down trees that are so important to them?"

"It says they have an agreement," Doña Cantor replied as she continued to scan the pact. "That as long as Augusto Cruz, or his descendants, maintains the peace of the Elder Accords then the Lefhym will let them cut down exactly 75000 acres of Elder trees."

"That's insane. That's how many square kilometers of land?" Marissa asked.

"303," Emmell replied instantly.

"That's a third the size of Halsbren," Marissa's mother said, to give them some context of sheer scale.

"That's why he needs Cantor," Marissa realized. "He needs to be in charge of the Elder Accords in order for this to work."

"That wouldn't be enough," her mother told her. "In all the time your father dealt with the chieftains of the Shemma and even the High Chieftain himself, it was constantly reinforced that we do not touch the Elder trees. They believe their spirits go into the trees after they die. Cutting down an Elder tree, to a wood elf, would be like someone denying our loved ones access to the Maker's heaven when they die by blocking the gate."

Marissa thought about it, "So it's a con. He's betting on a scam. But he's covering his bets by showing he's still representing the Jasian Enclave with the accords. He's lying to the Enclave more than the elves."

"Okay," Onna said, "so he's covering his arse with the Enclave, by controlling Cantor and absorbing the Accords. I can get behind that part, but how is he conning the elves? There's no way he could even cut one Elder down without them knowing, let alone..." she looked to Emmell for help.

"303 square kilometers," she answered.

"Right," Marissa said, "so what's his angle there?"

Doña Cantor shook her head, "I don't know, it doesn't say. This pact is only an agreement with the Supreme Pontiff of the Jasian Enclave, and Castile. In exchange for all that wood, Castile would be named a sovereign nation."

"And with Cruz as viscount..." Onna added.

"He would become its first king," Marissa finished. "That ambitious bastard." Marissa moved her family's titles out of the way so she could get a look at the map. "Where are you getting all the timber from, Augusto?" she mouthed. "Where?"

The map was hand-drawn and not overly precise. However, it did have coordinates and landmarks for her to follow. She traced her finger along an invisible path as she thought of the Sowle Sea and everything she ever knew about Castile, Cuddle Cove, and the cape of Cabo Hoorn. A lot of it didn't make sense until she saw a single recognizable landmark.

"Is that Beauty Rock?" Doña Cantor asked, looking down over her shoulder.

"That son of a bitch," Marissa muttered.

She knew. She knew without a doubt where Augusto was getting his Elders. In fact, she should have known all along. She discovered the damn place with him. It was theirs! "He needs Cantor lands because the Elders are in it."

"There are no Elders on Cantor lands," Doña Cantor said, quite positive. "I've covered every stretch of our land, child, and I assure you we have no Elders on the landscape whatsoever."

Marissa smiled at her mother. She knew something that Doña Cantor did not, that no one in all of Cantor knew – at least no one but she and Augusto. "That's because they're not on Cantor lands, mother, they are 'in' Cantor lands."

"Come again?" Doña Cantor said.

"It's a cave, beneath Cantor, accessible only by sea on a small dinghy."

"A cave to where?" Emmell asked.

"It leads to paradise," Marissa answered.

CHAPTER TWENTY-NINE

Marissa de Cantor y Castile

"Hold up, there's a place we could've hid in besides Cuddle Cove?" Onna asked.

"Obviously not," Emmell replied. "She just said it can only be traversed to by a dinghy."

Marissa nodded at Emmell. "I was looking to stow the *Bella Dahlia*, not abandon it."

Onna turned away. "Aye, sorry lass, that makes sense."

"So, let me get this straight," Doña Cantor interrupted, "there's a cave beneath Cantor that only you and Augusto know about, and it has Elders?"

"Yes."

Doña Cantor was astonished. "Just how big is this cave?"

"It's the largest cave I've ever seen," Marissa admitted. "I haven't exactly measured it, but the Elders don't touch the top."

"Oi!" Onna squeaked. "That's over six hundred feet tall!"

"At least," Marissa agreed. "It also takes almost six days to go from one side to the other."

"That'd put you well into the Shemma itself," Doña Cantor remarked.

"I thought so too," Marissa agreed.

"But how do they grow?" Emmell asked. "Trees like that need light and water."

"There's an underground river that runs through it, feeding nutrients to the trees. As for light, well, Augusto and I found dolines all across the cliff face that let in plenty of light," Marissa answered.

Doña Cantor shook her head. "In all my winters, I never knew..."

"No one does – that was kind of the point. And it appears not even the Lefhym know."

"Even if they did, what does it matter?" Onna asked. "If they just stick to the ones on Cantor land, they don't belong to the wood elves right? There's little they can do about it."

Doña Cantor was shaking her head. "It was all part of the accords. The Shemma peninsula was – is, technically – part of the wood elves' domain. When the Jasian Enclave set up the port of Castile on the cliffside, and began to build farms on the fields, the wood elves allowed it under the strict understanding that no Elders would ever be harvested for use in the construction of our town. Only the oaks and conifers in the smaller forests could be used. Should we break the accords and cut down the trees, the wood elves would eject us from this peninsula in a most violent fashion. The Cantor family was awarded the responsibility of maintaining the accords and policing the outskirts of the Shemma that fell within our purview. That is why Cantor has always hired the most people in all of Castile, to watch for any poaching lumberers."

Marissa nodded. "And now Cruz has performed that job for the last six months. Since ownership of Cantor was contested, as provisional viscount the job fell to him, just like he wanted."

"So no one would question his people milling about," Emmell remarked.

"Precisely."

"Didn't Vicente say there were brigands?" Onna added.

Doña Cantor looked down towards the gnome. "As a port, freebooters are a common problem. Occasionally they dip onto land to see what they can get away with, but only the most foolish would ever try and cut down an Elder. It'd take too long and they'd surely get noticed, if not by us, then the wood elves."

"Unless they worked for Cruz to begin with," Emmell pointed out.

"Perhaps," Doña Cantor agreed. "Such a thing cannot be ruled out."

"So, we know where he's getting his lumber, and we know why no one has seen it, but one would think that such an influx of laborers would be noticed," Marissa remarked. Then a more startling revelation struck. "Oh Maker help us, he didn't..."

"Didn't what?" Onna asked.

Marissa glanced to the curious gnome. "When I went to Corey Johns about the metal plate for Rusalka, he adamantly called Augusto evil. When I pressed him why he hated the man so, Johns answered the question with a question of his own. Where are all the regular people? You know, farmhands, field laborers, and such? Cantor was barren."

"I assume they found employment elsewhere," Doña Cantor answered.

"Which is what I thought, too," Marissa agreed. "I asked Adjutant Love to look into it, but things happened so fast that I found myself fleeing before I could get answers. But... what if they didn't leave voluntarily? What if they were taken?"

Doña Cantor seemed legitimately surprised. "Taken? That's preposterous – the dons and doñas would notice, not to mention people who had other family within Castile that wasn't part of Cantor."

"Maybe..." Marissa said, but she was sure she was on the right track. "Johns seemed to think there was more to it than that, and Cruz is taking up a lot of land, but what has he done with the displaced people? Castile didn't appear overpopulated."

"Wasn't that a concern of Cassandra's as well? The people were afraid of something?" Onna added.

"That's right!" Marissa replied energetically. "I think... I think he's using the people as a type of slave labor to cut down all those Elders."

Doña Cantor's eyes went wide.

"Think about it, Mother. Think about what kind of immense undertaking that would involve. The trees are hundreds of feet tall, dozens of feet wide. He has to convert it all into lumber, but do so in utter secret. Where could he do that and keep away from prying eyes? The cave – it all has to be done in the cave and then ferried out to ships. I know I'm right in this, I know it."

"If you are, then what does that mean now?" Doña Cantor asked.

"What do you mean?" Marissa asked.

Doña Cantor pointed to the map with the pact she still held in her hand. "Think Mari, we have his map, and his trade agreement with the Jasian Enclave. We could lead the Enclave to the cave, or worse the Lefhym. Do you have any idea of the repercussions that he would face at the hands of either?"

"Oi, but he thinks we be dead!" Onna pointed out. "No one survives the Pale."

"Point taken, gnome," Doña Cantor agreed. The room fell silent.

"The wreckage does," Nery said, speaking up for the first time in a while. Everyone looked to the sidhe. "The nøkken always send the wreckage out to the shores to teach you foolish mortals not to venture to close to the Veil. Not like you dumb apes ever listen, though."

"Augusto's too smart – he'd know that, and he wouldn't chance it. Adjutant Love couldn't chance it, for whatever his part in this might be." Marissa cursed quietly to herself. Vicente was right about the man after all. She should have listened to him from the start. Who knew how much of this could've been avoided...?

"Those people, those slaves, they are a liability to him now," Emmell voiced out loud what everyone was thinking.

"The whole cave is a liability," Onna added, "He'd need to eradicate it all."

Marissa found herself shaking her head. "That's too massive an undertaking, not to mention what it might do to Cantor. The cave is massive, and if he collapsed it all..."

"It would cause a sinkhole in all of Cantor," Emmell finished for her.

"Shemma too," Onna said.

"Hundreds of people would be killed. Perhaps thousands if it affected Castile at all," Doña Cantor added.

Marissa's mind reeled at the implications. "He wouldn't... would he?"

"He killed your father, Mari. He tried to kill me and the entire crew of the ship just because I was on it, all to get control of Cantor." Doña Cantor looked very old in that moment. "There have been a lot of deaths in the last five winters, the Marin's, the last viscount. The list goes on and on."

"So he's capable of it," Emmell stated the obvious.

"He's going to do it. He's going to kill all those people to cover up what he's done, and then he's going to buy Castile from the Jasian Enclave with the very thing we've been tasked to protect," Marissa could hardly believe it as she said it, but she knew it was true.

"So what ye thinkin' Brains? What kind of timeline do we have? Couple weeks? Couple days?"

"I'm not sure," she answered honestly. "Cantor was supposed to fall under Augusto's control tomorrow morning correct?" she asked.

Onna nodded. "That's what Vicente said, and that's what I heard from Love and Cruz, yeah."

"The trade happens tomorrow as well," Doña Cantor added.

Marissa looked at her mother, who was staring diligently at the pact. Doña Cantor looked up at her and pointed on the page with a bunch of signatures and dates. "It happens at sunset."

"He'll kill them tomorrow, then," Emmell said without a hint of emotion. Everyone turned to her. "It's the only way to be sure. If I were him, I'd be gone, on the ship delivering the timber to the Jasian Enclave when it happens. That way he will be able to deny the whole thing and have an alibi. And then in light of the tragedy, he'll rebuild, and after wounds begin to heal, he'll be able to announce that Castile is a free and independent nation. He'll be a hero to the people, and they'll accept his sovereignty eagerly."

Onna was nodding. "Spriggan's right, Brains, tis a savvy plan if e'er there was one."

Marissa shook her head. "One day? We have one day?"

Onna raised an eyebrow. "What do you mean, 'we'?"

Marissa looked at her like she'd just been smacked in the face. "What are you saying, Onna?"

Onna shook her head, "Don't mistake me, Brains, I go where ye go, but we're stuck here now, right? Stuck in the Pale? I mean, no one's e'er escaped."

"Your boatswain is right, my child," Doña Cantor told her. "No one has ever escaped the Pale."

Marissa shook her head, unable to accept that, "Yes, well no one has ever made it to the Sirens with their ship intact either, have they?"

Onna pointed at Nery. "We had a guide. She can see in the Pale. I'm all fer tryin' an all, but Brains, we get dumb when we breathe in the Pale. Passin' ta here was a one in a million chance – I'm not fer thinkin' it'll happen again."

"We need a way not to get dumb then," Marissa argued.

"Not going to happen," Nery interjected. "It's not some magic, or the like. It's the very air. Sure, you can sing the nøkken into not having you kill each other, but you can't control how stupid you get. Well, stupider."

"So how do we prevent that? We need to breathe?" Marissa asked.

Nery's little shoulders shrugged. "You can't."

"How long would it take to sail from this island and out of the Pale?" Marissa asked the kållråden.

The tiny creature gave it some thought, before looking down at Emmell. "An hour to the closest edge maybe?"

Emmell nodded. "I think that's a good assumption. Once we got the crew to stop fighting each other, it didn't seem to take long until we hit safe harbor again."

Nery nodded. "Yes, mortals only suffer the effects when they are fully in the Pale. But even then, it doesn't take long – it's more than enough."

"They went down in twenty minutes, Onna in twenty-five," Emmell remarked off-handedly.

"Twenty-five minutes?" Marissa said, thinking.

"Brains... I know that look."

"What if we had crews?" Marissa asked. "Emmell doesn't suffer the effects of the Pale and neither do you, Nery. What if three of us controlled the rigging until we became inert, and then another three took over for us right afterwards – that'd be fifty minutes right? You'd only have to navigate for ten alone?"

"Twenty," Emmell said. "Only Onna can last twenty-five minutes."

"Yeah, that's still too long," Nery returned, "the marmoset is right, you made it through only with my expert navigation skills, and far too much luck. It couldn't happen a second time."

"Dammit, we don't have enough people!" She looked to Emmell. "Get Badger, Anne, and Jocquotte in here. In fact, get any and everyone you can."

"What are ye plannin,' Brains?" Onna asked.

Marissa shook her head. "Everyone in here first, I want all of them to have a say."

Emmell nodded.

"I'll help!" Nery added, fluttering after Emmell.

Marissa looked down to Rusalka. She desperately wanted her friend to sleep and to heal, but she had a right to know everything, too. "Can we safely awaken Rue?"

Onna shrugged. "She's been out for a long time now, I don't see why not. Suren she's gonna have one hells of a headache though."

"Wake her up," Marissa ordered.

"You sure that's such a good idea?" Onna asked. "I mean after what we just talked about with Jocquotte and the ladies, I'm fer thinkin' a roused Rue might only be temptin' the beast and I ain't fer talkin' about Rue either."

"I understand," Marissa said. "I still want her up."

"Okay, Brains, yer the Cap'n."

It took about twenty minutes for Emmell to convince the three humans to join everyone in the hut. It appeared that Anne, Badger, and Jocquotte didn't arrive alone either, as it seemed almost every stranded person on the island tried to stuff themselves in the hut.

It was hot, crowded, and claustrophobic.

Rusalka sat in a corner, purposely not making eye contact with anyone. Marissa felt horrible for her, but there just wasn't time to console her friend and try to explain to her that it wasn't her fault.

Marissa glanced at Jocquotte, who stared at Rusalka with utter contempt in her eyes. Her left hand was heavily swathed in cloth freshly stained pink at the ends. Only the tips of her thumb and little finger were visible. Marissa shuddered at the thought of having her fingers chewed off. She didn't blame Jocquotte for being angry – enraged even – but the woman needed to understand that Rusalka was being manipulated. Marissa knew that was easier said than done, since no one actually saw the nøkken, and they were taking Nery on her word alone. Marissa would need to address it at some point, likely very soon, but right now she had other life-threatening matters to discuss.

"You all know who I am by now I'm sure, and for those that do not, I am Captain Marissa de Cantor y Castile. We are the first, ever, to successfully navigate the Stonewall Pale. This is not gloating, but simple fact. Now I wish I had time to get to know every single one of you personally, but I do not. I wish I had time to traverse this beautiful island, and explore its mysteries, but I do not. So, I am left instead with only the ability to offer you a choice."

The people looked at each other in confusion. She was actually happy that none of them tried to steal the *Bella Dahlia* while it was berthed. She supposed their prison walls of white murk dissuaded such ideas, though.

"A man by the name of Augusto Cruz is about to commit a crime that will endanger every living person in Castile, and could very possibly thrust the Jasian Enclave and the Lefhym peoples into a brutal and bloody conflict." The motley crew mumbled to each other. It seemed that more than a few in the crowd recognized the name. "I intend to stop him, but to do so, I have to go back through the Pale."

"That's impossible," a man in threadbare merchant's finery spoke up. "You'll never make it back through the Pale – you'll die for sure." There were more than a few murmurs of agreement.

"Maybe," she admitted. "But I have to try."

"Why, what's Castile to you? You've been gone. You ran away like a spoiled child!" another person exclaimed. Marissa looked to see who spoke and was surprised to see him wearing Cantor colors.

Marissa moved towards him, and the crowd parted eagerly, not wanting to get between the two. When she closed the distance, she saw he was small; smaller than her, his skin weathered from islander life. "You're right," she agreed. "When I left, I was a spoiled child." Marissa looked up to the crowd around her. "I was the daughter of a don; I was nobility in Castile and I could have anything I wanted. I was a dreamer, too! I dreamt of being the first woman purist! I wanted the juglares to sing epic canticles of my heroism! But do you know what happened?" People around her shook their heads. "I failed. My status afforded me nothing. The Jasian Enclave doesn't allow women to become purists." She felt the venom slip into her words. "So I became an exactor."

"Exactors are a myth," the merchant spoke up again.

She looked at him and smiled, "I assure you, they are no myth. On my first mission I was to cease hostilities during the Fermania Civil War. I was given a very specific parameter of missions. And can you guess what happened?" Again, people shook their heads. "I failed that too. I was captured, sold, and made into a slave. For five winters, I've been beat down, debased, and brought so low that I thought there would be no escape from that life. I was defeated. Nobility meant nothing – less than nothing in fact."

Marissa turned and looked at Rusalka, who slowly glanced up at her. Marissa smiled and continued. "I had given up everything but my life. All I knew was failure, fear, and regret. Then, someone came along and gave me courage." She pointed to

Rusalka. "This woman gave me the need to go on. She helped me understand my fear, acknowledge it, and put it aside." Rusalka's eyes widened at the comment, Marissa nodded to her in respect and then looked at the rest of her crew. "With the help of these brave women you see around me, we rose up against our oppressors and we took back our lives.

"Now I come home, and I see the same thing I rallied against: slavery. Worse, this man might cast my home into war. I've seen war, and I do not wish those horrors inflicted upon anyone. So I am going to fight! I am going to fight Cruz, I am going to fight his group of jacknapes and freebooters, and I am going to save Cantor and all of Castile."

"That's all well and good, lass, but you still have to go through the Pale," the merchant pointed out.

"I have a plan for that, and I will happily share it with all of you, for like I said, I have an offer for you."

"And what is that?" another woman in the crowd asked.

"Simple – to get through the Pale, I need no less than three crews. I need volunteers willing to sail through the Pale. It is imperative that I have three crews to make this work. Once through the Pale, you help me secure the people who have been made slaves, and then you are free to go about your lives. You are free of the Pale."

"But the Pale makes us dumb. We'll kill each other the moment we enter!" the merchant objected.

"The air you breathe makes you dumb. The nøkken make you kill each other," Emmell said to the crowd. "Marissa can subdue the nøkken, so no one will kill each other."

"But we'll still be made dumb, and if we're dumb, we can't man the ship!" the Cantor man said. There were rumbles of agreement.

"Yeah, Brains, how ye plan to get around that wee problem?" Onna asked.

Marissa looked at them all, "I can't stop that part. Two of the three crews will get dumb – this is unavoidable."

"But ye have a plan?" Onna pressed. Marissa nodded.

"Remember our escape from the Rhombus?"

Onna's eyes lit up. "That may just work!"

"What are ye talking about?" the Cantor man asked.

Marissa turned to Nery. "The problem is that we can't breathe the air in the Pale, correct?" Nery nodded, then Marissa pointed at her and then Emmell in turn. "But you two can."

"Yes," Nery agreed.

"What we need is to bring our own air with us into the Pale," Marissa explained.

"What? That makes no sense?" the merchant objected. "We can't transport air."

"Oh, but we can," Onna said to the group.

"The problem is that the air is finite, and once it's gone you will have to breathe the air in the Pale," Marissa told everyone.

"The petrichor," Nery corrected.

"What she said."

"And just how are we supposed to transport this air? I suppose you have some sort of magic for that?" merchant asked.

Marissa looked once more at all of them, and then at her mother who was smiling at her proudly. She smiled back, and turned to ask them, "How many dinghies do you have?"

CHAPTER THIRTY

Rusalka

Rusalka sat on the edge of a bronze cliff face, her legs dangled out into the open with a drop of over two hundred feet beneath her. The fall would be quite fatal.

She looked out at all of the people hard at work repairing the *Bella Dahlia*. It looked like the whole village was out there. Apparently the Jasian's little speech worked.

Rusalka watched as some of the men rigged a winch system. Slowly, but surely, they began raising a new anchor onto the ship. Others were attempting to patch the holes punched into Dahlia during their escape from Osprey. They would never be able to fix the ship to the level that would be required to take on Cruz's fleet. Time was against them, even if they had the materials on hand. But they tried anyway – the Jasian saw to it.

She smiled at the thought of Marissa, and of her words. When Rusalka met her, the Jasian was a terrified little shell of a woman. She was fearful and weak. Somewhere, though, she found strength and resolve to keep going. Now she was getting ready to charge headfirst into a conflict against the viscount and all the might he could throw at her. Where was that terrified little girl now? Rusalka couldn't see it anymore.

Rusalka took a deep breath and looked around at the island paradise. It was absolutely beautiful here, and with the minor exception of the small hut village down by the bay, it was completely untouched by man. It was a place someone like her could hide forever. Rusalka felt slightly guilty about slipping away from her crew while they and the castaways worked hard on repairing everything they could on the *Bella Dahlia*, but she knew it was better this way.

"Why ye be hidin' from everyone, Tusker?" a voice came from behind her.

Though startled, Rusalka did not bother to spin around. She was getting used to how deathly quiet Onna could be. Putting her thoughts to words, she said, "It's best for everyone if I am not around."

"Aye, that so?" The small gnome came and sat next to her, sharing in the picturesque landscape. "Oi, quite the view!"

Rusalka nodded. "This place calms me."

She felt Onna's eyes on her and glanced over at her diminutive friend. Rusalka flinched at the angry red marks on Onna's throat. They were just beginning to scab.

"So, what do ye think about Cap'n's plan?"

Rusalka shrugged. "I hope it works."

Onna snorted. "I think we all hope it works, Tusker. It's unconventional ta be sure, but what choice do we have? We're fer needin' ta get out of the Pale."

"And I hope you succeed."

The two were silent for a long moment before Onna spoke up once more. "I'm fer thinkin' that ye don't plan on comin' with us."

Rusalka remained passive. "I only endanger you."

Onna grunted. "Have ye actually seen Mari shoot? If anyone's a danger ta the crew, she is. Woman couldn't hit the broadside of a sea cow at five paces in completely still waters."

"Marissa is a fine shot with her pistols – you don't give her enough credit," Rusalka rebuked.

"Reason she has those flintlocks is cuz the lassie ain't no good in a scrap. Where we're going, we could really use someone that is."

Rusalka closed her eyes and shook her head. "I... can't, Onna. I just can't."

"Why not?"

She looked down at the gnome in shock. "I crippled Jocquotte! I almost ripped out your throat with my teeth! I'm a monster!"

Onna shook her head. "No Rue, yer an orc."

"Same difference."

Onna looked out at the dinghies ferrying people back and forth to the *Bella Dahlia*. "Ta some perhaps, but not ta us. Not this crew. Yer our sister."

"Jocquotte hates me, and she has every right to."

"Jocquotte's confused and hurtin' right now. She doesn't understand that it was not ye, but a product of where we was. Ye just happened ta be the first ta fall prey ta the nøkken, that's all. It could've been any one o' us that snapped."

"Even if that were true, that still makes me a liability. I'm weak-willed. If I lose it again, Onna... if I go berserk, I will kill you all."

Onna shrugged. "Maybe. Maybe not. Tusker, ye weren't in control, the nøkken were. They won't be a problem this time."

"Because the Jasian's going to sing to them?"

"Precisely."

Now it was Rusalka's turn to shake her head. "Do you know how ridiculous that sounds?"

"Not really... We've got a junky faery who's addicted to spicy pepper as our navigator, and a spriggan with no sense of humor as our sea artist. We have a war criminal as our Cap'n, an orc who mans the jib, and a gnome as a boatswain. We're about to travel through a poisonous cloud that makes us real stupid – a second time mind ye –that no one has ever survived, ta stop our Cap'n's delusional, sociopathic, definitely power hungry, ex-boytoy from collapsing half o' a city in on itself so he can sell some wood. On top of all that, if he actually does it, he'll be launching two nations into a brutal war, just so he can be king of whatever's left. Oh, and we've got to square away with the ex-boyfriend's supergirlfriend. All while bein' hunted by the people we're trying ta save. And ye think I've got a problem with Mari singin ta some faeries? Am I missin' anything?"

Rusalka shook her head. "You don't understand, Onna. Ever since we've freed ourselves from the Ayjub, I vowed to do right by you all. I've strived to put the beast within me at bay, because... because I wanted to be one of you."

Onna laughed. "And do ye think that's what we were wantin' of ye, Tusker? Ta be more like the Cap'n? Or ta be more like Anne, er Badger, er Jocquotte?" Onna shook her head at Rusalka, and the gesture made her more than a little irate.

"What's so wrong with that?"

"Rue, we like ye fer who ye are. We don't care that ye's an orc, and we don't want ye ta be anything less than ye are. We want ta educate ye, sure, it helps give ye greater perspective that way. But change who ye is, change where ye came from, what makes, ye... ye, no. We respect who ye are."

Rusalka didn't have an answer for that.

"Let me tell ye something Rue, that I'm not fer thinkin' ye be truly knowin'. If not fer ye, none of us would've survived the mutiny six months ago."

"That's not true..."

Onna held up her hand. "Let me finish," she demanded.

"Everyone played a part, this be true. But what the Cap'n be sayin' just a short while ago be the truth o' the matter. Ye gave her the strength necessary to take charge and lead us in taking the ship." Onna pointed at Rue's chest. "That was all ye."

Rusalka shook her head again. "She did it for Isa. We were trying to save her friend."

"And where did Mari find that courage? Huh? Ye not fer thinkin' I didn't know a coward when I saw one? Mari's not a fighter, ne'er was. But look at her now, Rue. How ye think she got that way? I'll tell ye how she did – it was ye."

"Me?" Rusalka couldn't even fathom such a thing.

Onna nodded and kept going, "All this time ye'r trying to be what? More human? She's over there trying ta do right by us by exemplifying yer courage. Ye're fearless in combat, Rue. Ye're fearless in the face of battle, and storms, and the open sea."

"It's only because..."

"Ye're an orc. I know," Onna agreed with her. "And yet, Mari, for better or worse, has found strength in ye, being ye. And that's just between the two of ye. We all bring something to the crew Rue, even Emmell. Ye want to continue to fight to better yerself and not lose yer cool, that's fine. That be a very noble pursuit, but don't let it take away from who ye are. I can tell ye, because Mari knows ye, she's the better for it, and in turn so are ye. Don't lose sight of that." Onna stood up and patted Rusalka on the shoulder. "The same goes for me, Tusker. Jocquotte will come around. It may not be today. It might not be tomorrow, but she will eventually. Yer a valued member of our crew, and Mari don't want to lose ye over something that ye had no control over... and neither do I."

Onna started to walk back down the winding trail before she stopped and called back to Rusalka, "Oh, and Tusker?" Rusalka turned and looked back at Onna. "Don't let Mari know we had this little talk. She bein' the Cap'n an all, we told her it was her job to talk to ye. Don't want it ta be seemin' I was takin' the wheel from her." She winked.

Onna saluted Rusalka once more, turned and walked down the path. Rusalka watched her friend disappear around the bend, though she didn't see a small-statured gnome walking out of sight, but someone who might very well have been a giant.

CHAPTER THIRTY-ONE

Marissa de Cantor y Castile

Marissa watched as the last of the dinghies were put in position, each one pulled firmly down with the heaviest shot they could spare and fashioned with chains against the hull. It would make the *Bella Dahlia* an ungainly sea beast for a while, but they only needed to hold the tempo for an hour.

Six dinghies were affixed to the hull, three on port, three on starboard. Ropes were slung over the rails on both sides, resting on the capsized minicraft. Everything was as good as it was going to be with the small time allotted them.

Marissa really wanted to sail to the other side of the island and look at the ship graveyard the castaways were talking about. She was sure there was plenty there that she could use, but Augusto already had a day's headstart on her. She could only imagine what he was doing with that lead. Would he execute all his indentured lumberers at crossbow point? Would he just trap them in the cave and collapse it on them? Or would he destroy the entrance and leave them trapped in the cave to their fate? The latter seemed the weakest option, since they could always attempt to scale the cliff face and climb out of the dolines.

No, it would be an execution, or full collapse – her gut told her collapse. It would be the only way to ensure that the elves never found out what he did. *Why Augusto? Why do something so terrible and reckless, for what? Power? You already made it to viscount – is king really worth it?*

She knew the answer already. While she spent her youth aspiring to be a purist, Augusto spent his aspiring to be a king. It was funny how little she had known of the person she once loved.

Marissa stood on the poop deck, watching the approaching dinghies now carrying all the fresh food and supplies they could muster from the island paradise. She watched her mother climb the stairs to stand beside her. Doña Cantor took in a deep breath and looked out at her home of the last six months.

"I wish I could've seen more," Marissa said.

"It truly is beautiful, Li Galli. But like all sirens, it is a dangerous creature." Marissa watched her mother look around at the large wan barriers that surrounded them. "This idyllic paradise is nothing more than a gilded cage."

Marissa took in the landscape again. It was easy to see how such a thing was possible.

"It's best that you not get attached to this place, captain," Doña Cantor told her.

Marissa looked at her mother wryly. "Really, Mother? Mari is fine."

Doña Cantor surprised her by shaking her head. "You are about to embark on a dangerous journey through the Pale, with a crew you do not know. Favoritism or division cannot happen – if it does, it will be fatal to us. In this I am no different than any other member of your crew. The last six months has taught me that my pampered life will not help me here. Being a Doña has little meaning in my survival outside of the domain of Castile." She chuckled darkly at her own comment. "It had little meaning on my survival, it turns out, within the walls of Cantor, too, thanks to Cruz. No, I will work as I must. I am not skilled in sailing these large ships as many who are joining you, but I'll help where I am able, even if that means I have to operate the bilge pumps."

"Mother!" Marissa said in alarm. "I would never!"

Doña Cantor held up her hand, "I will do what has to be done, as will you. You'll have a hard enough time as Captain, and singing to keep the nøkken at bay. I wish I had the voice you had, my dear. At least then I know I could effectively help. How long do you think you can keep it up?"

Marissa shrugged. "Emmell says when I began singing the first time, I had the mind of a child of maybe seven, and I sang for about ten minutes. The canticle Resolution has many stanzas."

Doña Cantor nodded. "Eighty-seven."

"At least now going in, I'll have all my faculties and wit about me. If I can give them all twenty minutes or more, that should help greatly."

"And what makes you think that these nøkken that bring violence upon us with their own music won't do so the moment you can no longer carry a coherent tune?"

"Nery," Marissa answered. "The sidhe have a code by which they abide. They're like toll collectors, and the toll is a song. I provide them with what they ask, and they in turn offer us the use of their bridge, so to speak. They honor this. Whether we die because we cannot breathe the air on their bridge is not their concern. Also, as long as we don't try and enter their home, they aren't bothered by what we do, either."

"As long as we don't venture too close to where this veil actually is?"

Marissa nodded. "Nery assures us, as a sidhe herself, she is going to be keeping us as far away from it as she can."

371

"And you trust this faery?"

Marissa quickly looked about for Nery's retaliation on her mother's choice of words, but didn't see the little kållråden anywhere. "Right now, Nery is under oath of the *Creideamh Sí,* invoked by Emmell, she won't betray that."

"I hope you're right."

Me too, Marissa thought. She recognized a drug addict when she saw one, and she only hoped that Nery wouldn't bail on them should another offer of the Grains of Paradise make itself available.

Doña Cantor changed the subject. "What are you going to do with Augusto Cruz if we stop him in time?"

Marissa was caught off-guard by this statement. She hadn't really thought that far ahead. "What do you mean?"

"I mean, are you going to kill him? It's the piratical way after all."

Marissa stared at her mother wide-eyed. "We're not pirates."

"No?" Doña Cantor asked.

"No! At most, we're mariners, since this has been our life for the last six months," Marissa defended.

Doña held out her arms and looked about the vessel. "And yet you sail upon a heavily armed scalesmade galleon, a rare ship on these waters. I've seen the holds, Mari – they are ample."

"And they held slaves," Marissa stated with ire.

"I do not mean to rile you, Daughter. You need to know what to expect the moment we come out of the Pale. You evaded the Castile Royal Navy and the Jasian Enclave. You will be labelled a pirate."

"What was I supposed to do, surrender?" she asked. "They would've killed Rusalka, and Emmell too, before even trying to understand them. Hells, might as well throw in Onna for good measure since gnomes were the enemy during the Fermania Civil War."

"The Enclave would've protected you..."

At that Marissa laughed. "I'm an ex-exactor. I can't get much more war-criminal than that, Mother. I was disavowed the moment Isa and I failed."

"Then what can you possibly hope to achieve by stopping Cruz?" Doña Cantor was clearly confused as to why Marissa was going to the effort. "If the Jasian Enclave won't help you, and they won't exonerate you, what can you possibly hope to accomplish?"

Marissa's countenance grew stern. "I was a slave for three winters. I know what it means to have no hope other than to live to see the next day. Right now, our people, our children, are suffering that same fate, and come tomorrow they will not have that hope to see another day beyond sunset. If I do nothing, they will die. If I don't try, then who will?"

Doña Cantor was quiet for several minutes, and Marissa wondered if she'd overstepped her bounds. She'd never spoken so sternly to her mother before, not even the night she left to become an exactor. Quite to Marissa's surprise a large smile took to her mother's face. "You have become so much like your father."

Marissa turned away, embarrassed. "Mama, please."

Marissa felt her mother's touch on her shoulder and when she turned to look at her, the smile was still there, but so were tears. "He would be proud of who you have become, Captain."

Marissa's ears burned. Growing up in Cantor, she rarely received praise from her mother. It was almost unsettling. Not that her parents were stern and unloving, which she had thought at the time. They'd been strict, but it was to teach her about life, not to take her away from it. Hindsight often taught one so much about their parents. Had Marissa's absence made the heart grow fonder? Did the loss of her father, give her a sense of perspective on the fragility of life that was otherwise absent living such a life of pomp as they did on Cantor? Had it done the same for her mother?

Her mother never praised her singing once growing up. Not

that Doña Cantor said that Marissa sounded like a mewling animal or anything harsh, but she never openly praised it. Yet, Doña Cantor had demanded a rigorous training regimen of singing that Marissa endured as a child.

It now appeared that this was their sole hope for survival against an adversary they could not see. The irony was not lost on Marissa. All her life, she wanted to learn to be this warrior who was such an amazing fighter that ballads would be sung in her name. Her reality was that she lacked the coordination and fine motor skills to be the fighter her father was.

But now...

She looked at her crew of women as they loaded barrels of fresh water onto the ship and she smiled. Ballads may never be sung of her heroism, plays never re-enacted of her valiant swords-manship – she wasn't that person, and she was okay with that. She was proud to call herself Marissa de Cantor y Castile again, she was proud to call herself Captain because of those women. So, if singing was to be her talent, then by the Maker, so be it.

She looked at her mother. "I'm sorry for how I was before I left, Mother."

Doña Cantor looked at her curiously. "You were a young woman, Mari, and you were in love with a dream. You have nothing to be ashamed of. We are all like that when we are young."

"Even Papa?" Marissa asked jokingly.

"Especially your papa," Doña Cantor answered seriously. "Your father, too, wished that he could be a purist."

"Really?"

Doña Cantor nodded. "Just so. I remember when he was courting me, he used to say, 'Miri, someday I am going to be a hero of the land like the great purists of old, and you... you will be my princess!'"

Marissa smiled. Had she not had the same dream? "What happened?"

Doña Cantor's eyes twinkled. "You happened, Mari. We were pregnant shortly before we eloped, and no one ever did the math, or if they did, they remained quiet about it."

"Mother!" Marissa said in astonishment. "But you're so devout to the Maker!"

Doña Cantor smiled mischievously. "I'm also human, Mari, and I was a very young woman, just like you were, with hormones the same as any girl in her late teens. And the way Fernando used to look at me... it sometimes stole my breath and lit a fire in my loins."

Marissa waved her away. "Okay, I really don't need to know any more about you and dad."

"I dunno, I could stand to ere' a bit more actually," a voice said from above them.

Marissa looked above to see Onna looking down on them, hanging from the mizzen top yard.

"Onna!" Marissa yelled.

Onna smirked at them. "Was just checking the lanteen rig Cap'n, ta make suren it was secure. Didn't mean ta drop no eves on ye'r conversation with ye mum. Carry on!"

Marissa watched the gnome quickly check on a few square knots, and then saddle down the rigging to check the top gallant mast sails.

Doña Cantor smiled as the gnome went off to work and looked back to Marissa. "Shortly after your grandfather passed away, Fernando was forced to become Don. He no longer had the luxury of choice. He had to be responsible. So the point, my child, is that we understood what you were going through when you left. And though Fernando would have never admitted it to you, I know he secretly hoped that one day you might succeed at becoming the first woman purist. Maker knows we're overdue for such a thing."

"'Really? You think he would've liked that?" Marissa asked feeling her heart swell at her mother's words.

Doña Cantor tilted her head to Marissa with a sad smile on her face, then reached up and cupped Marissa's cheek with her hand. Her touch was so warm, but not nearly as soft as Marissa remembered it to be. Her mother's voice was soft, and full of passion. "Your father loved you. You were his ondine – he would tell everyone when you were but a little waif of a girl. The little child with the beautiful voice that captured his soul. Your father would have given everything we had, titles, lands, all the wealth in all of Castile, just to see you again. You have to know that."

Marissa felt tears beginning to brim in her eyes as she cupped her mother's hand with her own, relishing the contact. "I said such awful things to him before I left. I just wish I could've said I was sorry."

"He knew," Doña Cantor told her comfortingly. "He knew the words, his words and yours, were spoken not in malice, but in the heat of the moment. A fleeting instant of passion. He always wanted you to be who you desired to be, nothing more, nothing less."

Marissa let the tears run down her cheeks, and she made no effort to wipe them away. They mingled with the heat of Doña Cantor's touch, leaving a growing warmth on the side of her face. Marissa let out a sorrowful little snort. "Youth truly is wasted on the young, isn't it? If I knew then what I know now, Papa may still be alive."

Doña Cantor lowered her hand and looked back to the people loading the ship, and Marissa followed her gaze. "People often say that, but I don't agree with that assessment," Doña Cantor told her. "I believe instead that wisdom is wasted on the wizened. All one can do is part with it, but very few will actually take it, least of all those that are the closest to you. If you're sharing it, they want no part of it. It seems that the lessons of life are not something we can teach, but that which must be learned on their own, by doing.

So, no, Mari, Fernando wouldn't still be alive, and you must never blame yourself for his death. That was all Cruz."

"One cannot have the wisdom of experience without first having had the experience."

Again, her mother wore a surprised expression. "Why Mari, what an intelligent thing to come up with."

Marissa smirked. "I didn't come up with it – Papa did."

"He could be a wise man sometimes."

"Yes, I guess he really was."

"So, you never answered what you were going to do when you get Cruz," Doña Cantor said.

"I am going to have justice," Marissa answered. "Not just for Papa, not just for you, but for all those in Castile that he's hurt in his ascension."

"But how? By killing him?"

"Killing would feel good, I won't deny it. Augusto may deserve death, but no, that shouldn't happen by my hand. True justice must be to first stop him from hurting anymore people, and then exposing everything he has done. Exposing the lies, and the evil he has inflicted upon Castile. I want to be there when he has lost everything he holds dear... when he recognizes in that moment that he has nothing... that he *is* nothing."

"And then?" Doña Cantor asked.

Marissa shrugged. "I have nothing past that."

"Good," her mother told her, "because after all that, I am going to kill him."

Marissa looked at her mother in shock. She didn't look back at her, but only stared out at the people hard at work. She shrugged. "What can I say, Captain, I'm fickle."

CHAPTER THIRTY-TWO

Don Augusto Cruz

Don Augusto Cruz watched as the string of longships flowed out of the cave with their loads of Elder timber. It was an ungainly and exceptionally slow process to transport the timber this way to his awaiting ships, but what choice did he have? If he blew the opening wider, others – freebooters perhaps – were likely to find the hidden cavern entrance, or worse, any Jasian Enclave ships on patrol down the coast might spot it. Then what would he tell the Enclave, or for that matter, the Lefhym? No, slow and steady was how he was going to win.

Osprey came up beside him and observed the lethargic string of long boats. He could feel her fervor radiating off her like waves crashing against him. The excitement was building in her. Augusto wasn't sure if her release was going to come in the form of violence or passion – probably a mixture of both.

"Are the explosives planted?" he asked her.

She nodded. "Just as you requested. Everything is in place."

"Do the people suspect anything?"

"Not a thing," she replied. "They believe you are going to use the explosives to go deeper into the cavern, clearing away stalagmites."

He nodded as he watched the line of oarsmen moving the boats along. Hired Ayjub corsairs "guarded" them with their heavy crossbows and strange pick-like axes. The Ayjub... his lip curled in disgust at them.

For this job, he couldn't afford to have anyone in Castile know what he was truly up to. He didn't trust Adjutant Love, or the purists he had in his pocket, for this particular assignment. No, it needed to be all mercenaries, and the Ayjub, being slave traders, were among the most discrete.

It helped that they already knew how to handle slaves as it was. It made this process more... efficient. Of course, the only way he could guarantee their silence was for them to keep twenty percent of the most able slaves for themselves to sell as they saw fit. His Castellan people sold like livestock.

He chuckled darkly to himself. Though he agreed to those terms, he would never allow it to happen. Castellans were his people, and no one else's. Little did the Ayjub know that they too were going to have several thousand tons of rock dropped on their heads as soon as everything was loaded on his cogs and they set sail to his rendezvous point with the Jasian Enclave.

As per the pact, the Enclave would take over all of his cogs loaded with timber, temporarily, to take back to wherever they planned on building their fleet in secret. This would leave his fleet woefully depleted for a few weeks, but it would be worth it.

As far as he was concerned, if the Jasian Enclave wanted to build the largest military fleet in all of Kuldarr, let them. He didn't care. He had an alliance with the Supreme Pontiff himself, signed, and in triplicate. Castile was going to be free. They were going to be an untouchable nation not dependent upon the whims of their neighbors. They were going to be just like Halsbren was. And he was going to be Castile's first king!

He felt his own anxiety rise at the thought. Finally, he was going to be a true king, not some empty title like "provisional viscount." Augusto always knew he was destined for this. He knew it since being born a noble. It wasn't some luck of the draw to be birthed into nobility, no genetic lottery that he won. No, this was destiny. He was meant for this.

He stared at the narrow cleft in the cliff face, so hard to see with the naked eye. It was funny really – while he always knew he would achieve greatness, this endeavor began because he stumbled into the cavern of Elders with Marissa when he was first trying to take her virtue. He wanted someplace where they wouldn't be seen, and while sailing, only glimpsed it because his other head was doing all the thinking.

Yet the moment they slid the ship into the tiny crag of rock, everything changed. He knew in that moment that he would need to have Cantor. His debaucheries with Fernando's only child weren't going to be the fleeting romp like he thought. No, he would need more from her than her body if he was to even hope to pull off his scheme. He would need to take Cantor.

So, he adjusted his sails, and began to court her. He made it appear to be "secret" while at the same time making sure Fernando knew Augusto was seeing his daughter. It was important. He wanted Fernando to accept the inevitable, since he knew the man would never warm to him.

Then the setback. Out of the blue, Marissa joined the Jasian Enclave and ended their relationship. Sure, she caught him with other women, but who cared? He was a nobleman – how could she expect anything less, really? Besides, in the end, it didn't matter. Papers or no papers, by morning he would be don over Cantor. Anyone of the Cantor line that could contest it was dead. It was funny, really, that daughter got to join mother in the Pale's embrace.

He turned and looked southward to the roiling mass of white, slowly turning pink in the light of the dying day. Like great undulating intestines the murk quivered before him. A beast that digested his ex-girlfriend only an evening before.

"What if she survived?" Osprey asked, speaking his very thoughts.

"No one survives," he answered.

"Pity," Osprey answered. "I wanted to kill the orc myself. It seemed almost worthy of being my prey."

Augusto nodded his head as he thought of Marissa. Yes, for the briefest of moments she seemed to be a worthy adversary, too.

He looked away from the swollen clot of ivory and focused once more on his cogs and the legacy they would bring him. Everything was so close now – he could almost taste it in the air. There was an electricity about it. Tomorrow, Castile would be free of the Jasian Enclave's influence, and then after that... he would become its king.

"All of this excites you," Osprey told him.

"What?" he asked surprised.

She nodded down to his torso. Augusto followed her gaze and saw that she was correct. If she expected him to be shy about it, he was about to disappoint her. He wasn't embarrassed about it. She had already seen plenty of him the night before, and he had seen all of her. "Yes, well, what can I say, I relish in victory."

"As do I," Osprey replied. "Tomorrow will be a glorious offering to the Warlord. This excites me, too."

And there it was, Augusto understood. The offer, from the night before, still stood. Even the muscle-laden warrior woman craved him, like so many others. And why wouldn't she? She was a woman, and he was power. All women lusted power.

He licked his lips at the thought of her hard body, her well-developed derriere. There was an exoticness in that form, something unusual, something new. While he preferred his women demure, so he could control them better, he would entertain her, at least for one night.

When he was king, he would have as many women as he wanted, as often as he wanted. He wouldn't be beholden to any of them, not that he really ever had been in the first place. Osprey though, didn't seem to care what he did with other women. She was a woman who lived for her passions. Sex and violence were one in the same to her. He could offer her both. That gave him power even over the indomitable Osprey. Yes, tomorrow he could reward her for a job well done. It was the least he could do for her, and it would sate his curiosity in what it would be like to bed a wilder.

He pushed the thoughts away, lest he give her the impression that she held influence over him. He watched as one of the crews in a cog almost lost an entire shipment of timber to the depths. While he expected to lose a little in this transaction, to watch it get so close to happening filled him with anger. How could these people be so stupid, so incompetent?

And that is why they are lessers, he understood. Because they lack the foresight that nobility is born with, that people with true greatness are born to inherit.

They caught it, barely, and transported it up to their main deck. "Should I kill them for you?" Osprey asked.

Cruz thought about it briefly, and then shook his head. "I don't want to slow production down any more than necessary. Just make sure that crew is closest to the explosives tomorrow. I'd like them to be at the focal point when it blows."

Osprey nodded, seemingly satisfied with the answer.

Cruz looked once more at the slow trail of dinghies. "This will finish in time, correct?"

"I will make sure of it," she reassured him.

"See that you do, Osprey. I want this place destroyed before any of the wreckage of Marissa's ship makes its way to our shores. I don't think you of all people need to be reminded of the price of failure."

Augusto watched Osprey's set jaw flex under his reproach. "That will not happen," she guaranteed.

"See that it does not," he added with a finality he knew he didn't need. He turned to one of his men standing by. A teniente. What was his name? Brian? Bran? Ben?

"Bevan," he said as he remembered.

The teniente snapped to attention, "Ser?"

"Round up a longship and an oarsmen or two. I am done here for the night."

Bevan saluted. "Aye ser, as you command."

Augusto smirked, and turned to face Osprey once more. "I think you are taken with that one – you seem to like keeping him around."

Osprey barely even glanced in the direction the slim guard departed. "For a Halsbrenian, he has proven himself... somewhat capable." As she said it, she turned and looked down at Augusto. "Do you want me to kill him for knowing too much?"

Augusto gave it a moment's thought. "I'll leave that to your judgment. He seems trustworthy. If you do decide to end him, I only ask that you don't do it in front of the others in the Navy. It'll squelch their morale unnecessarily."

"As you wish, milord."

"Yes," he answered, delighting in the sound. "As I wish indeed."

CHAPTER THIRTY-THREE

Marissa de Cantor y Castile

The morning rays crept over the surrounding vapor wall, casting the world around them in burnished gold. Marissa watched the azure waters, stained orange, crest on a beach that never seemed more beautiful.

Slowly men and women, young and old, began to shuffle out of their makeshift homes and make their way to the dinghies on the beach front. She could see those that were choosing to stay on this island paradise embrace the many who were risking the Pale once more after so long a stay.

Among them were her crew, going over everything in last-minute preparation. Nowhere amongst them, however, was Rusalka. A slight frown touched the corners of her mouth. Rusalka disappeared shortly after their meeting and no one remarked seeing her. Not that any of them minded not having an orc present among them, none but Onna, Emmell, and, of course, herself. She worried desperately for her friend's well-being. Rue barely survived being shot in the head, and she was still recovering from surgery. She should not be alone on the island. What if she passed out? What if she fell where no one could find her? What if something attacked her while she slept? All of these thoughts raced through her mind, but there was one that stood high up above all the rest. What if she simply doesn't *want* to come back?

That singular thought trumped all the others. What if Rusalka was intentionally staying away so Marissa would have to leave without her, leave her behind? Marissa knew, as much as she wanted otherwise, that she could not stay and waste any more valuable time. Hundreds, if not thousands, of lives were at stake.

And yet, she knew, deep down, that she would choose Rue over all of them in a heartbeat. She would make the selfish choice over the logical one if she could. Onna would expect it of her, and Emmell would keep her in line, like they had the last six months. So even though Marissa would throw it all away to find Rue, she knew, ultimately, she could not.

Rusalka would come to them, or she wouldn't... and the very thought of her not coming back ate at her soul.

"Ship's as ready as she's gonna be, Cap'n," Onna said from behind her. "Now all that's left is fer the Cap'n ta get ready to be er' Cap'n."

Marissa turned around to observe her friend. "What do you mean? I've been captain for the last six months – what do I have to do differently now?"

Emmell, Anne, Badger, and Jocquotte were breaking off from the castaways as the last of them got to their boats and began to sail to where the Dahlia was berthed. They were already informed of the positions they would be taking, so there was no need to mother-hen over them.

"Well ye see, ye been wearin' that tattered ole dress now fer going on three days. And not that it wasn't a fine dress, originally, when ye went to see Cassandra, but let's face it, it's been through a ringer and there ain't nothin' ta salvage from the thing."

Marissa looked down at the dress that she had indeed wore for the last three days. It was absolutely shredded at the hem, and a large portion of it was torn all the way up the seam revealing a bit more leg than most modest women would care to show. It hadn't been relevant at the time because she was surrounded by other castaways just as bedraggled as she.

"Well, I see little I can do about it," Marissa confessed. "Almost everyone here only has the clothes on their backs, it's not like I can ask them to part with their only garments. And if you'll remember, my chest with all my clothes was blown out into Cuddle Cove."

"Not all of it," Onna remarked.

"Yeah Cap'n, ye still got some left," Anne added.

The women filed a semi-circle around her, and it looked more than a little suspicious. "What are you girls going on about? You know I don't have anything left..."

Onna held up the frilly black and crimson skirt.

Marissa shook her head and felt her ears go red. "Oh Maker, hells no!"

"It's all ye got left Mari," Onna told her, and it was unfortunately true. It was, ironically the only clothing she had left.

"I'll look like a lady of the night in that thing," Marissa replied tartly.

"Or ye'll look like a confident woman who's not afraid of who or what she is. Just like a true Captain ought to," Jocquotte pointed out, waving black hosiery her way with elegant red stitching along the top.

"Joc is right, Cap," Badger added. "We're about to face off against a Navy and the Enclave. It's okay for ye crew to look a little bedraggled, but if ye wants ta be taken seriously by them, ye has to look the part." She held up a dark red bodice.

"You can't really believe that? You think they'll take me more seriously if I'm dressed like a prostitute?" Marissa retorted, but already she could feel her barriers beginning to wane.

"It looks nothing of the sort, Captain," Anne added to the conversation. "It makes you look proud to be exactly who and what you are. What we are, independent women." Anne held up a beautiful, white silk, short bell sleeve chemise. It was the kind of blouse her mother used to wear.

Her crew was determined, she would give them that. Still though, Marissa remained resolute, for propriety's sake. She saw her mother getting ready to board one of the last dinghies. "Mother!" she called, getting the Doña's attention. Doña Cantor looked up at her, and Marissa could see she was holding something wrapped in oilcloth.

"Yes, my captain?"

Marissa straightened at the address from her mother and returned with a regal appellative of her own. "Doña Cantor, do you see what these fustilugs are trying to make me wear?"

Doña Cantor broke off from the dinghy and walked the short distance their way. The crew let her in to the half-circle and Marissa watched as she observed all the articles of clothing with obvious concern. "Oh dear, my child, I can see why you're distressed, this... this won't work at all."

Marissa nodded, confident now that she had someone on her side. "See, ladies, I told you. This is coming from a lady of Castile herself, and she knows what..."

"Yes, yes," Doña Cantor interrupted, "to properly look the part, none of this ensemble will do..." Again, Marissa nodded, happy to have someone in her defense. Doña Cantor opened the oilcloth she was holding as she spoke, and all at once Marissa's face went stone cold sober. "Unless you have the right boots."

Marissa stared down at black leather buccaneer's boots. They looked easily knee high in length, with wide cuffs at the top and crossover straps with gold buckles. "Where... how...?" Marissa stammered.

Doña Cantor smiled mischievously. "Not everything washes up on Castile's shores. I told you, there is a whole graveyard out there."

"But..." Marissa stared at her mother in confusion, "you were in on this?"

"In on it?" Onna guffawed. "She set the whole thing up!"

Doña Cantor's face morphed from joviality to someone bound and determined. "When we clear the Pale, you are going to be facing off against Augusto Cruz. The man is a womanizer and a misogynist. It's time we used our own weapons against him. Nothing distracts that man more than a beautiful woman. It's time you remind him who we Cantors are!"

She raised hoots and cheers from all the women around her. And finally, Emmell spoke up through the din. "I'm afraid you're missing one last thing, Captain." Marissa looked down at her sea artist as she held up a black leather tricorn with red frill. "Every captain needs a good hat."

Marissa stepped out of her mother's hut twenty minutes later only to receive a bevy of whistles and catcalls from her crew. Slightly embarrassed, she reached up and straightened the tricorn on her head. "Well?" she asked.

Doña Cantor's eyes sparkled. "Cruz is never going to know what hit him."

"I agree," Onna added, handing Marissa her gun belt with her flintlocks. "Ye look striking fer the part, Mari."

"Oi! What was it we called her when we first took the ship from the Ayjub?" Anne asked.

"Brains?" Onna returned.

Anne shook her head, "No it was something else..."

Badger grinned, "Aye it was! Gory Mari or something, wasn't it?"

"Bloody Mari," A husky voice said from behind them all. Everyone turned to look. Marissa froze in the middle of putting on her belt and looked up. Rusalka stood alone, looking at them all, a little apprehensive. Her bandages were gone, revealing the shaved side of her head and a long angry scar. Somehow it looked very fitting on the large orc woman.

Marissa finished with the buckle quickly and walked between them towards the orc.

Rusalka looked down at them all. "I know I don't have any right to ask for forgiveness from any of you for what I did," Rusalka looked over to Jocquotte, "especially you, Joc. But, I know this is important to you all, and important to Mari, so... I'd like to help."

Marissa closed the distance and looked directly up at Rusalka. It was the most vulnerable she'd ever seen the orc in her life. For the first time since Marissa met her, she thought she saw fear in the woman's eyes. Marissa didn't let that fear linger, though, as she wrapped her friend in a tight embrace. "I thought I lost you."

Marissa felt the stilted shock on the orc momentarily before she was enveloped by large muscle-laden arms. "I will always serve you, Jasian, if you'll have me."

Marissa pulled back and put the orc at arm's length. "Of course we will."

There was an uncomfortable cough behind them, and Marissa turned around to see scornful expressions on Anne, Badger, and most of all, on Jocquotte. "Have we no say at all in this?" Jocquotte hissed.

"Of course," Marissa replied, "but I will remind you that Rue has been with us since the very beginning, so I see no reason for any objection."

"No reason?" Jocquotte replied, incensed. "How about three

of them?" She held up her bandaged hand that only revealed a thumb and pinky remaining. "Do you see this reason for objection?"

"Rue wasn't in control..." Marissa began.

"She's never in control!" Jocquotte barked. "It's just never been directed at us until now! She's always needed an outlet!"

"That's not true!" She was about to continue when she felt Rusalka's heavy hand on her shoulder. Marissa turned to look at the orc.

"It is true," Rusalka replied, surprising them all, most of all Jocquotte. "I have always had to find an outlet for this beast inside of me. I thought you all were a way to keep it down. I always felt different around you, as if it was you that tempered my rage. But, I've realized that is not the case."

"Rue, it was the nøkken, not you," Marissa told her, and everyone around her. "You have to understand."

"I must still take responsibility," Rusalka returned. "I have crippled Jocquotte, and I must make amends. I do not expect forgiveness. I only ask that you let me help you stop Cruz. After that, you can bring me back to this island, where I will remain."

"No..."

"She can come," Jocquotte interrupted. Marissa looked at the wounded woman now more confused than ever. Jocquotte shook her head in frustration, "We need her, we do. We need her strength. But know this! When we enter the Pale, she's not on my crew!"

The angry human turned and walked towards the dinghy. Anne and Badger followed to take their ship out to the Dahlia.

"Great, this is what we don't need," Marissa grumped. "Divided we will fall."

Onna, Emmell, and Doña Cantor closed around Marissa and Rue. "Don't sweat it, ye two," Onna piped up. "Jocquotte is just really hurt right now, and she needs a vent. Moment the shite gets lively, and it will, she'll be damn glad to have ye on our side." She finished by patting the orc on her knee.

Rusalka nodded in appreciation.

Marissa, however, took a deep breath, thinking. "Still, Jocquotte is right. You two should not be together right now. Not in the Pale."

"But ye can stop the nøkken!" Onna protested.

Marissa held up her hand. "She's a second stringer." Marissa looked to Rusalka. "You'll be third and final string. That way, if you do fade, it'll be right before we leave the Pale." The others were about to object when Marissa cut them off. "She'll also be the quickest to coherency and able to react more effectively the moment we leave." Marissa then looked to Onna. "I'm changing you from first string to third with Rue. This way, when we exit you should never degenerate at all. Onna, you'll be the captain until I regain my wits."

Onna opened her mouth to object, but then closed it and muttered, "Aye, aye Cap'n. Tis a savvy idea, e'er I heard one."

"How will I know when it's time for me to come out?" Rusalka asked.

Emmell spoke up. "Since Nery is not blinded by the Veil, she will fly to your dinghy and knock hard on it three times. We've affixed ropes down the hull to each dinghy. Take it before you go under so you won't have to search for it."

Rusalka nodded. "Got it. And if this doesn't work?"

"When ye get dumb, you'll let go of the dinghy and float away until ye drown!" Onna answered jovially. "Don't fret, Tusker, it'll work."

Marissa closed her eyes in acquiescence. She knew what had to be done next. She turned to her mother. "Doña Cantor, I'm afraid you now will take the place of Onna on first string. You'll be among the first to fall to the effects of the Pale."

Doña Cantor nodded. "It is a decision that has to be made."

"I'm sorry," Marissa apologized. "If it's any consolation, I'm going to be in the first string, and I too will fall to the debilitations of the Pale."

"It's okay, Captain, you do not need to explain yourself with me. Your decisions are sound."

"She's right, Mari," Emmell added, "your decisions are completely logical. Surprising for how emotional you normally tend to be."

Marissa raised an eyebrow. "Thank you... I think?"

"You're quite welcome," Emmell said with a nod.

Marissa shook her head at the spriggan and then looked at Anne and Badger nimbly scaling the hull to the top, helping Jocquotte all the way.

"All right, let's get this over with," Marissa said. "I don't know how much air everyone is going to have once we get moving, but I don't want it wasted."

MARISSA STARED AT THE SEA OF UNFAMILIAR FACES STARING up at her expectantly. Her crew was lost amongst them all, nearly impossible to find. Most of them were going to go down below on the gun deck and ready the culverins, something that she never thought she would use again. She separated the others with the most sailing experience into two other teams. They would climb back down to the capsized dinghies as soon as they set off. There they would wait like she and Onna had under the cog, waiting for Nery's signal to climb up and take over when Marissa's team was lost to the Pale. The rest, mostly unproven, were going to man the lines of the sails under Anne and Marissa's direction to start. It worried her to see so many strangers that would be depending on her direction; and she on them following orders.

Everything was riding on this initial start. If she didn't lull the nøkken into non-aggression, or if these castaways couldn't follow her directions, then when the second stringers climbed up the hull, they'd either be attacked or stuck on a boat that was hopelessly lost in the Pale.

"What am I doing?" Marissa muttered to herself. It should be Onna, not Anne, up here with me. Onna was a better sailor than any of us, and yet she told Onna to wait until the end. How had she thought that was a good idea?

"I think they want words of encouragement, Captain," Emmell whispered up to her, her blonde quills fluttering in nervousness.

"I just gave them a speech yesterday," she whispered back harshly.

Emmell shrugged.

"You mortals like your speeches," Nery added from Emmell's shoulder. "Make it sound encouraging, like 'we sail to certain doom' or something like that to start."

Marissa looked down at the kållråden in disbelief. "Remind me not to let you ever give us a speech." She looked back to the crowd before her and took a deep breath. She really hoped she didn't look like some kind of sex strumpet to these men right now, otherwise it would diminish the whole thing. She thought of her father, and what he used to say to his men. He would always make himself one of them.

One of them.

Marissa climbed off the poop deck and stood with them all on the main deck. "I know you all are expecting a rousing speech from your captain," she began, "something to alleviate the tension you all are feeling about traveling back into the Pale that has stranded each of you here for so long." A few shuffled nervously on the deck, looking towards her. "I know you're as anxious as I am to get this over with. The Pale is terrifying to you, as it is me, but it is what is on the other side that terrifies me more than this mind fog."

The crew began to murmur to one another as they looked upon her. Marissa took a deep breath and continued. "All my life I wanted to be someone who made a difference. I wanted to be... a hero. But the simple truth is that not all of us get to become the type of person we hope to be. And some of us fall very, very short.

"Augusto Cruz has become an immoral man. Greed has poisoned his soul and the souls of his men. And for that he needs to be stopped."

"Revenge ain't gonna bring your father back, Captain," the Cantor man said from the crowd. "All it will do is get us killed, and I ain't for dying for that."

Marissa stopped in front of him. Her speech faltered for a moment as doubt ebbed through her, as it always had. She searched about the crowd to see if all felt as this man before her and saw more than a few nodding in agreement. Was she really doing this for herself? For her father? Was she about be a selfish little girl once more? Her eyes roamed to the front of the boat, and there, by the jib, she spotted Rusalka. She stood as solid and implacable as the anchor she was next to. The sight of the orc stopped Marissa from her indecisions and her fears, and instead bolstered her courage, something she lacked until that woman came into her life.

She looked directly at the Cantor man, unabashed. "I agree. So what should we die for then? Cruz's fleet is going to be a tough nut to crack. All their cogs combined will have twice our guns and many times our numbers, and they will sell their lives dearly for the payload they carry. Though it may not seem it, Castile right this moment is under attack. Not by sword and cannon, but by treachery and lies from its very government. For a good many of you, this is your home. A home that still holds loved ones, and children. You want your children to one day inherit this home, do you not?"

There were nods of approval.

She lowered the timbre of her voice, but she remained loud enough so that everyone could still hear her. "We all do. Deep down I believe that's what all people want. To help one another as we look forward to a better tomorrow for our children. As beings, I believe we want to live by one another's happiness, not by their misery." The nods were intensifying now, and her voice was growing stronger, louder. "So, don't give your souls and the souls of your children to brutes, to those who despise you, enslave you, and control your lives."

"Yeah!" the crowd answered to her.

"When we come through the Pale, they expect us to be disorganized and afraid. They expect for us to run when our hull is splintered, and the cloth of our sails is rent. I say right now... that will not happen!" She was speaking passionately now, talking from her heart, and letting it guide her words, "No, by the sweat of our brow, and the strength in our backs, and the courage of our hearts, we will show them that it is they that should be afraid! They will hear the thunder of our culverins, see the glimmer of our steel, and feel our mettle, and of this they will know what it is we can do!"

The agreements echoed into cheers of approval across the deck.

"I make a solemn promise to each of you here and now. When this is through, and Castile is freed from the oppression that blankets it, imagine where you want to be and I swear I will take you there, together!"

The deck roared with life, and Marissa felt her heart swell. On impulse she yelled, "Hoist the colours!"

Swept up in the moment, and without a second thought, she watched Anne, Badger, and Onna pull the colours from where they'd been stored for the last six months. They tethered them expertly and pulled swiftly to the top of the main mast where the newly placed black flag billowed hard in the wind. The cheers echoed once more across the bay at the sight of the skull and crossbones.

"Positions!" Marissa yelled and her crew scattered across the decks to take their designated positions.

"Cruz wants to call us pirates? I'll show him just how piratical we can be." She glanced down at Emmell. "Take us into the Pale, Em. It's time to pick us a fight."

The spriggan's eyes glittered. "Aye, aye, my Captain."

CHAPTER THIRTY-FOUR

Don Augusto Cruz

Augusto watched as the last of timber was loaded onto the ship, *Pandion*. Osprey stood sentry at the loading plank while the captain, still heavily bruised from the beating she'd given him two evenings before, guided the workers on where to put the rest of it.

The hold was at maximum capacity, as were the stores, and almost all of the deck had timber loaded upon it. Though Augusto was no expert on matters of sailing anything larger than a sloop, he knew all of the Elder timber would slow the ship tremendously. For all intents and purposes, he was officially riding on a sea cow. Luckily, he wouldn't need to ride on it very long. He stared at the other fifteen cogs of his merchant fleet all loaded and just as heavy as the *Pandion*. It was a herd of sea cows all together, ripe for the picking.

Surrounding them all was Adjutant Love's escort, four heavily-armed war cogs ready to deter any potential freebooters of this massive payday. All of the purists and bellators were Love's people. He would not fear any retribution from them, unless they knew what he planned on doing within the caverns. Luckily, they would all be deep at sea when those caverns collapsed, securing his alibi.

After all, how could he possibly be to blame for such a thing, when he was surrounded by the purists themselves? Each and everyone faithful, devout, men of the Maker. Cruz smiled at the thought. It was foolproof. The only wrinkle that bothered him at this point was that Love didn't even have the decency to be part of the escort. It was no matter, though – by sundown the cave would be collapsed, all traces and witnesses of what he'd done gone, and the declaration of a free and independent Castile secure in his hands. Though he'd hoped to harvest more timber from the cavern of Elders, he knew when not to take unnecessary chances. Marissa's wreckage would be washing up any day now, and he couldn't risk anyone getting hold of the map. It was bad enough someone might land their filthy hands on the deeds of Cantor, but that was easily disputable through the Citadel, with which he'd have immense favor once this little transaction was finished.

Besides, in a couple months' time, he'd be king, and able to decide who gets what lands, and who owes *him*. The very thought of it brought a smile to his face. Soon all that he worked so hard for would finally be paying in dividends. All he needed was to be patient just a bit longer... that was something he could do.

"Don Cruz!" Osprey called excitedly.

Augusto looked back to the aftcastle deck. She never displayed excitement, not like he was hearing now. Osprey waved a large muscular arm, directing him to her. Such a rude gesture immediately wiped the smirk off his face. How dare she... and in front of his men! She may be a wilder, and brazen at times, but never was he summoned in such a fashion by anyone in a lesser station, save Adjutant Love, and that was under very special circumstances.

He debated briefly about refusing such a summons, but ultimately, he knew it would only be a petty gesture. While he cared little for what the plebeians of this vessel thought of him, he needed to maintain a modicum of control. So instead, he would answer her summons, but follow it with a fierce rebuttal, and punishment – possibly a flogging. It might interrupt the plans he had for her body that night, but there were other women he could celebrate with. There were always other women.

Mind made up, he climbed down from the forecastle and gingerly made his way past all of the lumber towards the aftcastle. Above him, in the crow's nest he heard the lookout begin crying out excitedly, "Pale! The Pale!"

Augusto tensed upon hearing those words. The cavern of the Elders was the one point that was furthest away from the Pale in all of the Shemma peninsula. That was, of course, unless it was shifting. Occasionally he witnessed the undulating mass of white mist shift and slither towards the shore for short amounts of time. It was never longer than a few hours, and it was never a sudden thing, but a slow and plodding motion that always allowed ships in its path a chance to escape from the vaporous tentacles. But if it were to shift now and block his way, as burdened as his cogs were, for even a few hours...

Thoughts of the punishment he was going to administer to Osprey vanished in the need to see what she saw. Clearly, she felt it urgent enough to breach the protocol. He made his way more matter-of-factly to the aftcastle, snagging his fine crème doublet on the corner of the timber once. He looked at the minute tear on his left shoulder in annoyance, but the lookout's continued cries about the Pale quickly doused any agitation over his finery being torn. He scaled up to the aftcastle deck and ran to the rear rail, where Osprey and the captain were staring at the rippling effluvium on the horizon.

The captain held a looking glass, and as he felt Cruz's approach lowered it. "Viscount Cruz, you need to see this."

He handed Augusto the looking glass and pointed in the direction of the Pale where he and Osprey were looking. Cruz put the glass to his eye and looked at the writhing wan mass. "What am I looking for?"

"Something was seen inside the Pale," Osprey told him, her voice anxious.

He lowered the glass momentarily and looked at the wilder. "Seen?"

She nodded tightly. "It was dark and large, like a moving shadow."

Cruz looked back into the glass. "Nothing is ever seen in the Pale except the Li Galli. Is that what your man saw?"

"With all due respect, Viscount Cruz, my men know what the islands o' the sirens look like. We've seen them many times."

"Then what else could it be?" Cruz asked, but as he said the words he wondered, could it be the wreckage, finally making its way out? Almost always it happened at night, but if it were true, how fortuitous it would be that the flotsam was ejected from the Pale right at the place he was located! No fear of reprisal from the Jasian Enclave or the Lefhym. He might not even have to collapse the caverns if he could get his hands back on the map! Truly then the Maker was on his side!

He looked back into the looking glass more diligently, trying to see what it was that the lookout saw. Above him, the lookout crowed again.

"There!" Osprey yelled. He was pretty sure she was pointing, but Augusto couldn't see it while looking through the glass. He searched over the massive alien fog but still couldn't see what it was that either the lookout or the wilder saw.

"I don't see anything!" he growled.

Without warning he felt a massive hand wrap around his head as easily as fingers squeezing a grapefruit. "Osprey what the hells..." With surprising gentleness, she turned his head in the direction everyone was talking about.

And there it was. A swollen black mass seemingly just on the other side of the alabaster curtain. "That's larger than some wreckage," he found himself muttering.

"Verily," Osprey agreed.

"Why can we see this?" he asked. "We never can see anything within the Pale except the Li Galli on occasion."

"Perhaps the sirens are coming to us?" the captain mused.

"Sirens," Augusto scoffed. "There are no such thing."

"I would ask that you do not discount myth, ser," the captain told Augusto politely. "It has kept many a wary sailor alive throughout the winters." Augusto lowered the glass and looked hard at the captain. Even with a heavily bruised face, he did not wither under Augusto's scrutiny. "Might I suggest, ser, that we get this convoy moving? Whatever is in the Pale, siren or no, it cannot bode well if it gets in our path."

Augusto started to hand back the looking glass, his attitude still soured from everything that was happening. "Signal the Enclave war cogs and get this floating payday moving."

"You do not desire to be back aboard your own ship, milord?" the captain questioned.

Augusto glared at the audacious man. "We will all transfer to *Reina del Mar* when I hold all the necessary documentation in my hands, and not a moment before." He withdrew the offer of the looking glass, keeping it for himself and causing the captain to grasp at the empty air.

"As you will have it, Viscount," the captain said with a brisk salute.

"Osprey, follow me to the forecastle," he told his wilder.

As they were just stepping away from the railing, Augusto heard the lookout call from above, "I see it! I see it! It's a ship!"

Augusto whirled around and brought up the looking glass once more. It couldn't be! He searched over the morass and watched in absolute disbelief as the prow of a scalesmade galleon cut a swath through the gale. Next to him he could audibly hear Osprey growling. "It's impossible," he told her, "no one survives the Pale."

But as he said the words, he already knew that he was wrong – the rest of the ship emerged from the murk and billowing strong on the mainmast was the unmistakable symbol of the skull and bones.

"Pirates!" one of the sailors on deck cried.

"It's not pirates – it's the sirens come from the islands for us all!" yelled another.

There were cries of confusion resonating not just from the *Pandion* now, but throughout the convoy. The name "sirens" could be heard on the tongues of dozens of men.

Augusto looked back down the prow and saw her clearly now. She seemed disoriented, led up the stairs by the orc, who pointed his way. There was a moment of stilled silence as her brown eyes bore down on him. He could only stare at her, barely able to comprehend what he was seeing. Then she mouthed the words, "I'm coming for you."

Jilted out of his bewilderment, he lowered the looking glass. "So be it, Mari. So be it."

CHAPTER THIRTY-FIVE

Marissa de Cantor y Castile

"We're too late! The convoy is already moving!" Onna called to Marissa. Marissa looked up, still trying to shake her grogginess. It was surprisingly not as severe as the first time they passed through the Pale. Of course, she was well rested and fed this time through, and they were better prepared about what to expect. Still, it was a little jarring. It was also jarring seeing Augusto and his convoy already. Of all the places to exit the Pale, Nery put them right on course with the cavern. Marissa was going to have to commend her on her navigational abilities. The little kållråden was turning out to be quite the boon.

"How are we gonna stop the convoy and save the people at the same time?" Onna asked.

Marissa stared at the slow-moving procession of ships that were already gaining a good distance away from them. She would have to save the people first, and then go for Cruz second. Her mother approached her on the bow. "I know that look Mari."

Marissa shook her head. "The people are the priority, not Cruz."

"True," Doña Cantor said. "And normally I would agree with you completely. However, if he makes it to the safety of the Jasian Enclave fleet, you will have no chance to stop him and he will win."

"This ship is faster than all of his ships," Marissa countered. "We can do both."

Onna came forward as well. "No, we can't," she said, siding with Marissa's mother. "It ain't gonna be like makin' a pit stop at the quartermaster's for some flour. We gotta get in there, scope out the dangers, possibly get in a tumble, and then try and get a whole bundle o' lads and lassies outta there. Ye gonna have to decide what's more important ta ye, Brains. Stop Cruz's deal, or save the people."

Marissa bit her lip in frustration as she looked from the cavern to the ever-widening gap that was growing between them and Cruz's convoy. She turned to her mother. "You're more knowledgeable on the politics of Castile than I am. If we let Cruz go now, but save the slaves, can those slaves testify against him? Can we call him out for what he's done?"

"To who?" Doña Cantor asked. "As soon has he has his ratified copy of the freedom pact in his hand, he'll be king. The voice of a few peasants, a Doña who's been declared dead, and a war criminal won't mean anything. Sure, there will be dissension amongst the peoples at his actions, but he'll still be the king, and he'll have the backing of the Supreme Pontiff, with all the might that the Jasian Enclave brings. Plus, many more may turn a blind eye to his actions if it profits them."

"You mean the other dons."

Doña Cantor nodded. "All those who would've voiced concern on Augusto's actions are all conveniently dead. This is no coincidence."

"But, what if we went to the Enclave instead? Petitioned against the illegality of what he did?" Marissa asked.

"And risk war?" Doña Cantor shook her head. "The Jasian Enclave will already be in possession of the timber. Possession is just as complicit as the act it took to get them the product. At this point they will be just as guilty as Cruz. In an ideal world, they would try and repeal the pact and declaration, and sentence Cruz for crimes against the Maker. But they couldn't risk going to the Lefhym with all the timber from the Elders and try to apologize for it. The breach of ethics is too great. Besides, that's fleets of ships they'd be throwing away. It's easier to let Cruz get away with it, and perhaps one day send an exactor to him with a polite reminder that you don't play games with the Enclave."

Marissa glowered; her mother was right. If anyone knew how the Enclave positioned the exactors, it was her. If she let Augusto go and saved the people, then he would win. It wouldn't be a clean win for him, but that really wouldn't matter in the end. He'd be king, and she'd still be a criminal. But could she do it? Could she leave those innocent people – her people – to die, just to stop a man from seceding their nation from the Jasian Enclave?

She looked down at the deck. "I can't do it. I can't leave those people to die, even if it's for the greater good."

"There's no good choices here, Brains," Onna told her. "None of us fault ye fer yer decision. It's not like there are two of ye, or two *Bella Dahlias*. Then maybe it'd be easier."

Marissa looked at Onna curiously, as an idea abruptly exploded like grapeshot in her mind. "But there could be!"

She swiftly moved to the side and looked over to the sea below. The capsized dinghies still clung to the ship like frightened ducklings.

"Ye gonna share what's goin' on in that melon of yers with the rest o' the class?" Onna asked.

Marissa looked back, and Anne and Jocquotte joined them on

405

the forecastle deck. Jocquotte maintained her wide berth from Rusalka. "Quickly, back to the quarterdeck. I need to share this with Emmell and Nery as well."

The women swiftly moved to the quarterdeck and encircled Emmell. The kållråden was sitting on the spriggan's shoulder. "Told you I'd get you through with no problems," the sidhe said proudly to Marissa.

"You did good, Nery," Marissa returned. "Now we need to modify the plan, and I need a sounding board. We don't have a lot of time to level this out, so I'm going to be shooting from the hip here."

"It's not like ye hit anything when ye aim anyway," Anne quipped.

"Where's Badger?" Marissa asked.

Anne stuck a thumb behind them. "Crow's nest."

Marissa nodded – it'd have to do. "We have to go after Cruz," she said to them. They all nodded grimly, knowing that it meant leaving behind innocent people to die. "But we will still save the people in the caverns, too."

"How ye figure?" Onna asked.

Marissa pointed at her. "Your idea."

Onna touched her chest in surprise. "Mine?"

Marissa nodded. "There's going to be two Marissas – at least that's what Cruz is going to believe."

"And how do ye plan on making two o' ye?" Anne asked.

"I don't, but that's what he's going to see," Marissa said, gaining wind with her plans. "Rusalka, Anne, and I are going to lead a team of volunteers to the caverns on the dinghies attached to the hull. I am going to stand in front of the lead dinghy where I will be easily seen by Cruz's convoy. Cruz will see me heading to free the people, and unless he has some means of signaling, he'll be forced to send one of the war cogs to stop us."

"That doesn't explain how there'll be two of ye?" Onna added.

"I'm getting there. In the meantime, Mother, you'll put on the last set of these clothes I'm wearing."

Doña Cantor raised an eyebrow. "That's a young woman's garb, dear, I wouldn't do it justice."

"Nonsense," Marissa countered, "you're every bit as fit as I am."

Doña Cantor snorted. "Have you seen your shoulders lately, Mari? They put most men to shame."

"Mother, we don't have time for this, will you please listen?"

"Sorry, go on, Captain."

"You will wear similar clothes – they're not identical, but they're close enough that I don't think Cruz will notice. You'll stand on the forecastle deck where we just were so everyone can see you. Onna will be captain of the *Bella Dahlia* while you go to stop Cruz."

Onna smiled in understanding. "Ye gonna use yer mum as a decoy!"

Marissa nodded. "Corey Johns made a comment that we look nearly identical. I'm hoping to use that to confuse Augusto. He thinks you're dead after all."

Doña Cantor was nodding. "This plan could work."

"Good, then I need you..."

Doña Cantor interrupted her before she could finish. "But it should be me that goes into the caverns, not you."

Marissa stopped and blinked several times in confusion. Finally, she shook her head, "No Mother, it's too dangerous. Too much could go wrong. Augusto could have a way to signal the cavern that we're unaware of and blow it to the hells just when we arrive. We don't know what kind of opposition is in there already. The war cog could open fire on you, or the purists could assault you in the caves."

Doña Cantor folded her arms over her chest. "All the more reason it should be me and not you, Mari. "

"No, Mama, I just got you back... I won't risk you so recklessly. You could die in there!"

"So could you! Besides, no one has seen you in many winters, I'm Doña Cantor, they know me. I would be better served rescuing our people than be a puppet dressed up for show. This way, we both will have a role to play, and you will still be the captain of your ship."

"But..."

"I hate ta argue with ye, Brains, but ye mum is right on this one," Onna told her.

"It's a logical choice," Emmell added. "The risk is great for the away team no matter who leads to the cavern. But the risk is exponentially greater to this ship if you are not its captain."

Marissa put her hands over her eyes, sighing into her palms. "Dammit Em, I don't need logic right now!"

"It's a good plan, Jasian, but I agree with your mother – she should go with Anne and me into the cavern," Rusalka added.

Marissa dropped her hands from her face, closing her eyes and taking a deep breath. If even Rusalka was agreeing with Doña Cantor over her, then it truly was a better suggestion. She could overrule it as captain, but now was not the time to create any more schisms. "Fine," she breathed.

Doña Cantor nodded. "Thank you, but you should keep your crew with you. Like you, no one knows this ship like they do."

Marissa opened her mouth to object, when Emmell interrupted. "It's another good point, Mari. We need everyone who knows how the Dahlia handles to be manning it."

Marissa closed her mouth and looked down at Emmell frustrated. "One day, your logic will fail."

"Doubtful," the spriggan replied.

Marissa looked to the Doña of Cantor. "Suit up, Mother. And please be careful."

Doña Cantor smiled at Marissa, and then swiftly wrapped her

in a hug. "Get him for me," she whispered into Marissa's ear. "Get him for your father, and all the people he's hurt."

Marissa's throat was tight. "I will," she croaked out.

Doña Cantor released the hug but held onto Marissa's arms. "Whatever happens, I want you to know that I am so very proud of the woman you've become." Her smile was radiant. "So very proud."

Marissa felt tears beginning to well in the corners of her eyes. "Just go, Mama, before I change my mind."

Doña Cantor released her and stepped back. She looked up to the clear sky and, closing her eyes, she took a deep breath. "Can you feel it, Mari? Your father is watching over us." With that she went into the Captain's Cabin. A dozen minutes later she came out straightening a tricorn on her head.

Onna let out a little whistle. "Ye two look like a matched set!"

Nery fluttered down to appraise the two and shrugged. "Hard to say, all humans look the same to me."

Marissa looked at her mother. "Last chance..." she said, hoping.

Doña Cantor shook her head. "I have to do this, Mari, for us, for your father, and for Castile. You have to lead your crew to stop Augusto."

Marissa nodded, "I understand." And really, she did. Marissa may call Castile home, but she wasn't close to the Cantor people as her mother and father were. They would respond better at the sight of Doña Cantor then they ever would Marissa.

Anne came back on deck. "I've rounded up about sixteen people that want to liberate the caverns. They're going to be making their way to the dinghies now."

"Thanks, Anne," Marissa said.

Anne saluted. "Aye, aye, Captain."

Doña Cantor touched Marissa's shoulder then. "Do you see why it needs to be me? These women will fight and die for you."

Marissa exhaled. She did see, and she knew her mother was correct. "Be careful."

Doña Cantor smiled. "You do the same."

Marissa watched as her mother calmly walked to the rail, grabbed a rope, and hopped over to the other side, climbing down swiftly. Marissa wished she could say more, but already Augusto was almost a league ahead of them – any more and it would be too late, and they wouldn't see the ruse at all.

She walked back to the helm. "Let's give them some wiggle room, Em." Obedient, Emmell nodded and spun the wheel, taking them out of the wind.

It was in her mother's hands now.

CHAPTER THIRTY-SIX

Don Augusto Cruz

Augusto looked back to see Marissa's galleon flagging behind. He was surprised, to be honest. With all the extra weight there was no reason that they should be outrunning them. Unless the ship was damaged from the Pale? When he last saw it, the galleon took a lot of cannon shot from Osprey's attacks. Perhaps something in the Pale crippled it even more?

Then he noticed movement at the bottom of the ship. To his surprise, small dinghies that were hidden against the hull began to roll over and pop out of the water like a dog giving birth to a litter of pups. Augusto put the looking glass up to his eye. A great many people were climbing into those ships and rowing towards the cavern. At the lead, standing tall and proud, he could see Marissa. She was going to save the people.

She knew. She knew that he would eliminate them to cover up what he planned. She'd figured it all out from the accords and the map. Of course, she would run off and help the poor people –

Marissa always wanted to play the hero. Saving lives would be more important to her than even stopping him. "Foolish girl."

As the sixth and final dinghy peeled away from the galleon, he watched the women aboard expertly redirect their sails to catch the same wind his convoy was riding on. Wait a minute... they were still coming for him after all, but without Marissa. Pity. At least Osprey would have her orc.

Still, he would be remiss if he didn't give Marissa something of a challenge. Sure, she would be surprised to see the Ayjub in the caverns, and they *might* stop her, but he wasn't one to take chances, not after she eluded his Osprey twice, and escaped the clutches of the Jasian Enclave to boot.

It was a risk to send purists into the cave where they might recognize the plot he had in store for the people within, but if he did nothing, Marissa might actually succeed in freeing them. Now, if any of them talked to the Lefhym...

No, this was an acceptable risk. He lowered the glass and proceeded to the captain. "Signal the war cogs covering our northern flank and the one on point. Divert them back to the caverns to intercept those ships."

The captain looked back to see the handful of ships leaving the galleon. "You want to sacrifice two war cogs on that, while we have a pirate galleon coming straight for us?" he said, nonplussed.

"Are you questioning my orders?" Augusto demanded. "We have two other war cogs to protect us against a handful of inexperienced women on an already damaged boat."

"Yes... Ser," the captain mumbled. "It just seems like a foolish bit of overkill, to waste half our defense on a handful of dinghies."

It was at that moment that Augusto knew a statement had to be made – a true declaration of exactly who the men of this crew were dealing with. Augusto turned around, "Osprey?"

Osprey looked back from where she was avidly watching the approaching galleon.

"This captain is proving to be vastly incompetent. Kill him."

"Now wait a…" the captain began, but Osprey was on him, just like two evenings before. Alone, she had him subdued in seconds, and with a massive arm around his head, she snapped his neck in a single brutal motion. His body was sent flying into the sea before any of his crew could react.

"Where's the boatswain?" Augusto asked calmly.

A mousey man with salt and pepper hair shambled forward. "Yes, milord?" he asked, voice shaking with fear.

"Did you hear my orders to the late captain?" The man nodded feverishly. "As new captain, what are you going to do, then?"

The mousey man studied Augusto for a second in confusion, but a single glance at Osprey forced him to straighten. "Signal the northern war cog and western cog, and send them after the dinghies."

Augusto smiled wickedly. "Good man." He then retreated back to the stern and watched as the signal was sent. Ever efficient, the war cogs furled their sails and dropped out of the convoy in pursuit of the dinghies.

Studying the pattern of the ships and of the inbound galleon, he knew both vessels would pass wide of one another. Still, in an effort to deter the galleon, the purists would try and take a few pot shots at the approaching pirates.

He wasn't disappointed.

Like a thunderstorm, half a dozen claps pealed across the sky in quick succession. Augusto watched with great humor as the cannons discharged in a shock of fire and plumes of dense smoke. Across the gap of open sea, a barrage of shot hammered into the water, crashing so violently into the deep blue that blasts of white froth blanketed the crew of the approaching galleon. In the span of only two heartbeats the second war cog erupted in a similar fashion, their aim only moderately better, but still short of the mark.

Then came the galleon's echoing reply.

Augusto saw twice the number of detonations of the previous two ships erupt from the gun deck of the galleon. The immense noise, even at their vast distance, thrummed in his ears. The rumble continued as the galleon's shot hammered against the choppy waters, cutting great swaths into the ocean, and launching geysers upon the war cogs in retribution.

One single shot of the dozen proved true as Augusto watched the aft portside hull of the trailing war cog explode into a mushroom of oaken confetti. The wooden debris cascaded into the angry, churning waters, a visible reminder of the wound the war cog suffered. Still, Augusto could see that the hole that remained was well above the waterboard and was no threat to the war cog, or the safety of the crew.

And then the ships were past each other. The galleon continued its pursuit of his convoy, while his war cogs bore down on Marissa's dinghy flotilla.

"She has spirit," Osprey commented next to him.

"That she does," Augusto replied, slightly bemused. The woman he knew as Marissa was a fearful bird, but this woman now...

He lifted up his looking glass to catch a final glance at the small ship parade as they neared the entrance of the cavern of Elders. He spotted her once more, and she turned to face him, only she seemed different... older, and thicker. That didn't give him too much pause though – it was hard to really see her at this distance. One thing did stand out though...

"Where are her hand cannons?" He asked.

He looked at Osprey, and then back into the looking glass. When he first spotted Marissa aboard her ship, she had them affixed to a belt on her waist. He'd admitted to himself that the picture of her that he saw, with the short skirt, exotic weapons, and tricorn was quite striking. Now though, she didn't have them – instead she had... was that a sabre?

A great swell of apprehension began to grow in his gut. He directed his looking glass at the approaching galleon, and the apprehension turned to distress. There at the bow, saluting him with the middle finger of her right hand, was the real Marissa de Cantor y Castile, the twin hand cannons still on her shapely hips.

She duped him! She outsmarted him! Such a thing might excite him if not for that fact that he just sacrificed two war cogs that he had no hopes of getting back in time.

It had been a long time since Augusto felt what he was feeling now, but he knew what it was – uncertainty.

CHAPTER THIRTY-SEVEN

Marissa de Cantor y Castile

"Those stupid jacknapes fell fer it!" Onna yelled in glee.

Around her, Marissa's crew cheered at the success of the plan, yet she herself only felt a growing disquiet. Her mother was going to square off against not one crew of purists, but two. Those odds... they weren't long – they were grim.

She sensed Rusalka looking at her from the jib and glanced her way. "Your mother understood the sacrifice. She was very brave. Let it not be in vain."

Hadn't Marissa heard the same thing when Isa sacrificed herself? The words nearly identical. Marissa failed to save her best friend then, a woman trained and honed in the crucible of war. Her mother... she was just an aristocrat. She couldn't fight a purist, let alone a crew of them.

"We should go back."

Rusalka let go of the jib and came her way. "There's nothing to be done for them now. You need to trust your mother. She survived the Pale and proved her resourcefulness, has she not? Besides you had to get your intelligence from someone?"

Marissa snickered at that. "My papa was pretty smart too."

Rusalka snorted. "The males of my people lack almost all sense. They desire only to breed and make war."

"It's a wonder how your kind continue to survive," Marissa said in jest.

"Wonder indeed," Rusalka returned. "But know this, Jasian, if your mother has even half of your intelligence, she will succeed."

The sentiment warmed Marissa more than she could say. The only response she could give was to place a hand on Rusalka's powerful shoulder. The orc nodded.

"Brains!" Onna yelled as Rusalka returned to the jib. "We're coming up on the convoy fast, and it's looking like the war cogs are getting ready ta greet us!"

Marissa turned from her friend and ran to the quarterdeck to stand by Emmell. "How's the wind?"

"Wind's on our side, Captain, even if we have to turn to give them a broadside, we'll regain far more quickly than they will."

"Nery, how close are we to the meet point with the Enclave?" Marissa asked.

The sidhe alighted from Emmell's shoulder and zipped into the captain's quarters to look at the map. She was back in less than a minute. "Just over a league, Captain!"

"At their speed of four knots, that's less than an hour away," Emmell replied.

"When will they be able to see us?"

Marissa watched the spriggan study the horizon. "If we don't stop them in about half a league, we'll be seen. Especially if they've got a spotter in a crow's nest. If they do, they might already have seen us. The difference really is how quickly can they respond versus how fast we can get away."

Marissa nodded and then yelled, "Badger can you see the Jasian Fleet?"

"Nay," came the reply.

Well, at least there's that, Marissa thought before turning and looking down at the main deck where her boatswain was. "Onna, how quick before the war cogs are on us?"

"Minutes Cap'n. Five maybe," the gnome yelled back.

Marissa's face grew determined. "This is going to be close."

"Aye," Emmell agreed. "We need to cut through them, and not have a prolonged engagement with the war cogs. Some of those cargo cogs also have cannons, so we might experience light resistance, but if the war cogs keep us bogged down..."

"Cruz will fall into the safety net of Enclave waters," Marissa finished for her.

"Precisely."

Marissa stared forward at the two war cogs which were forming themselves into a makeshift wall, facing opposite directions. No matter which direction the *Bella Dahlia* attempted to turn, one of the purist war cogs would be able to get several good broadsides on her before they could get a steady one of their own... unless they turned out of the wind now, but that would only increase the distance the convoy had on them, putting it even closer to the rendezvous point.

Marissa needed to cripple them both as quickly as possible, and yet also take her ship away from repeated broadsides. She wished that she concerned herself more with the culverins on her ship. All she had left were short cast-iron carronades. The bronze demi culverins they'd had were lost when they'd taken the ship from the Ayjub slaver. The carronades lacked the range of the long guns that the Jasian Enclave purists used. They were lighter, more versatile, and she had a lot more of them. A whole lot more. The only downside was she didn't have enough people to use them all. She lost so many with her mother on their rescue attempt. It didn't mean she was anywhere near defenseless, though – she just needed to be more cunning. She needed to be close to them, risking the long cannons once, maybe twice, and she needed to take them out right away. But war cogs were sturdy beasts of the sea. Slower, smaller, and less armed, but able to take punishment again and again.

"We can't hope to stop them in a single pass, their hulls can take too much abuse..." she mumbled absently.

"Agreed," the spriggan replied, thinking the comment was for her.

Marissa stared at the ships in their wall-like formation. Their sails unfurled but slackened due to lack of wind. Even without her sightglass she could see the riggers ready to redirect the sails back into the wind. Must be nice to only have to worry about a single mast, she thought.

...a single mast.

Her mind went back to the sloop they crippled when they first took the ship from the slavers. She rushed down to the main deck, where Onna was directing their own deckhands. "Onna, the war cogs are single masters."

"Aye, I know," she agreed.

"Like sloops!"

Onna nodded. "I get it, Brains. What ye on about?"

"Do we still have that bar-shot left?" Marissa asked hopeful.

A huge smile took to the gnome's face. "I savvy a plan ye got goin' on in ye skull, Brains!"

"That I do. When we took the sloop out with the bar-shot... can we do that again to the war cogs?"

Onna looked on; they were approaching the vessels swiftly. "Aye, but there's no avoiding a volley from each, and to be deadly accurate we'd need to be pretty damn close, I'm a'fearin'."

"But can we do it?"

Once again, the gnome nodded in approval. "Even the gree-nies down there won't be missin' if ye get us close enough!"

Rusalka turned and looked back at the comment.

"Not you, Tusker!" Onna barked to the orc.

Marissa snapped her fingers at the gnome. "Onna, pay atten-tion – how long will it take to switch ordnance?"

Onna's face scrunched up. "Too long, most of the cannons are already packed."

Marissa nodded. "Find our master gunner – I don't know who has that job – and tell them we're going to purge the starboard line into the sea."

Onna nodded, went to move, then halted, "Ye gonna turn us toward the Pale instead of inland?"

Now it was Marissa's turn to nod in agreement "It'll make the Enclave wary to pursue if we fail and will give us a moment to catch our breath."

Onna flashed a crazy smile. "That's why yer the Cap'n, Brains!"

Marissa climbed to the quarterdeck, just as the starboard of the *Bella Dahlia* began to bark its cannon fire into the sea.

"What's going on Captain?" Nery asked. "Why are we shooting at nothing?

"Quick change of ordnance, Nery," she said quickly, before looking at Emmell. "Em, how close can you get us to the ship's star-board side, while trying to minimize the long cannon fire?"

The spriggan looked at the ships and then the gap between the inland and the war cog. "Two hundred yards, but the *Bella Dahlia* will take fire – it's unavoidable."

"Make it so."

Marissa watched Emmell's face scrunch in concentration as she turned the wheel towards the shore. Marissa looked away from the spriggan and saw the horizon line turn. In seconds, Marissa saw the plumes of smoke from the first volley of long guns. They were already about fifteen hundred yards out, easily within range. Then they heard the thunder as the sound caught up with what they were seeing. "Brace yourselves!" Marissa yelled.

A shrill whistle was their only warning as the first cannon shot crashed into the forecastle. Oak blossomed outwards like a flower in full bloom. The second shot destroyed the starboard side railing on the main deck, and Marissa watched in horror as one of the castaways was hurled violently through the air into the churning sea.

A third shot drilled a furrow across the poop deck behind them. The next three shots were behind them, lost in the sea. "That southern war cog has a damn fine master gunner," Emmell commented, tight-lipped. "All three hits came from that ship."

Marissa stared at it grimly for only a second before turning to the kållråden, "Nery, get down to sea level and see if our deckhand survived. If he did, let's try to cast him a rope."

"We're moving too fast for that, Mari," Emmell commented.

"I want to at least know if they lived," Marissa returned.

"Okay, Captain, I can do that for you," Nery answered, and zipped away.

The sidhe rushed up to Marissa's side only seconds later. "One mortal quite deceased in the water, Captain. Would you like to know the nature of the wounds?"

Marissa closed her eyes. "No thank you, Nery."

"As you wish, Captain!"

Marissa stared at where she had last seen the man. She barely knew him at all – hells she didn't even know his name, and now he was gone.

"You can't save everyone, Mari, no matter how hard you may try," the spriggan told her calmly. "They all knew what they were agreeing to when they decided to leave the islands."

Marissa nodded to Emmell's cold logic once more. She hated to hear it, but she knew it was true. Meanwhile the *Bella Dahlia* clipped across the water at impressive speed, and Emmell closed the distance from fifteen hundred yards, to a thousand, then five hundred, and then closer.

"We're coming up for our starboard pass, Mari. The war cogs have prepared demi-culverins. We're going to get hit hard on this pass, so we need to make it count."

"Aye," Marissa agreed, "did you hear that, Onna?"

The gnome nodded. "We be given them a mighty punch in a moment, one they not be fergettin' any time soon, but we about ta get a bloody lip fer our troubles! Let's be given em' a tune for them ta carry ta Davy Jones' locker!"

The gnome broke off before Marissa could comment any further. Start singing? That actually wasn't a bad idea. Nery already commented that the nøkken were drawn to conflict, and if the last broadsides didn't gather their interest, the next wave would. If she could subdue them from her ship now...

She thought of one of her father's favorite pirate shanties, one that Cruz would know as well. A smile came to her lips – it would be most fitting to sing *Sea of Sirens*, wouldn't it? So, she opened her mouth and let the words flow.

The war cogs loomed close, and Marissa sang. She poured her heart into very vowel, every consonant, every verse, and every chorus.

"Avast ye scallywags!" she dimly heard Onna yell to the swiftly closing war cogs! "Ye hear the sound o' our siren! We's coming fer ye!"

Marissa sang. She sang with everything she had, as the world erupted around her in splintered wood, water, fear, and chaos.

CHAPTER THIRTY-EIGHT

Don Augusto Cruz

Augusto could only watch in disbelief at the maelstrom of smoke and violence that erupted between the three ships at close proximity to one another. Just before the battle was pitched, he'd heard her. He'd heard Marissa singing, of all things. "She's insane," he whispered to Osprey.

The wilder gave no answer to him, only watched as pieces of all three ships exploded skyward, mingling with the thick smoke and steaming water vapors all around them.

Marissa's ship was hammered mercilessly by the two war cogs. He saw wood flying in every direction and holes littering the hull. Still, he could see her through the haze and violence, standing on the quarterdeck, singing as her ship disintegrated around her. The galleon, though larger and swifter than a war cog, was not built for punishment.

It took the broadsides stoically, and it dealt its own damage in return. Round after round belched from the starboard of the galleon, thundering viciously into the war cogs' rigging, sails, and main mast. He saw rope and chains swing wild, he saw men scrambling to hold on to the rigging only to be flung wildly away, and he watched it all in detached horror as the main masts of both cogs splintered, ruptured, and collapsed into the deep blue. Then the cannon fire ceased, and all three ships disappeared in a thick fog of their own cannon smoke.

"Do you think they sunk her?" Augusto asked Osprey, hopeful that the war cogs were victorious.

"Hard to say," the muscular woman answered. "That ship was just brutalized."

As the roars of the cannons finally died away, silence reigned. Then Augusto heard something. Osprey cocked her head, and he knew she heard it, too. "No..." He couldn't believe it. It just wasn't possible.

The fog lifted, revealing the aftermath of the onslaught. Both war cogs' masts were gone, floating off to the sides in the water. Men were also in the water, swimming amongst the wreckage, scrambling to make their way to something secure. Both war cogs listed heavily, with nothing to give them direction. Through it all, the galleon was heading right for them. And there Marissa stood at the forecastle, singing loud and pure.

"It's... it's the siren!" he heard the recently promoted captain say in fear.

"It just wrecked the war cogs and we're next!" someone else agreed, adding to a growing panic on the *Pandion*.

"It's midday!" the captain cried once more. "It's true!"

Irritated, Augusto looked back at the former boatswain. "What are you rambling on about, you fool?"

The captain looked at him in wide-eyed fear. "The saying goes that her song takes effect at midday, in a calm. The end of that song is... death."

Augusto blew him off. "A sailor's superstitions, little more."

"And yet we have little wind, where the galleon seems not to have a problem," came the captain's terror-laced reply.

Augusto looked at the sails in growing concern. The captain was right about that much. There was almost no wind to be had for them. And when he turned to look back at Marissa and her incoming galleon, their sails were full.

Then that initial trepidation that was growing in the pit of his belly turned to dread. One by one, he watched as the cargo cogs all around him began to hoist white flags.

"No!" he screamed. He grabbed the rails so hard it hurt his hands. "No! What are you doing, fools!"

"What does it look like, Don," Osprey said with condescension dripping from her lips. "Your gutless navy is surrendering. You've lost."

Augusto spun around on Osprey. "By the Maker, I haven't lost yet!" he hissed.

He saw that teniente that Osprey liked so much preparing to raise a white flag as well. She still hadn't done anything with the immigrant. He was going to stop the teniente for his cowardice and kill him just for spite when an idea sprung to mind. *Two can play this game, Mari!*

"Teniente Bevan?" The young Halsbrenian looked up at Augusto's summons. "I need a word."

CHAPTER THIRTY-NINE

Marissa de Cantor y Castile

"I think I like this ship!" Nery cried in excitement. "You mortals are fun!"

Marissa's heart soared as she watched one white flag rise after another. "They've surrendered!" she said in glee.

A chorus of cheers resounded across the battered deck of the *Bella Dahlia.* All around, castaways and crew were congratulating one another. As she took in the sight of her ship, though, much of that cheer began to wash away like tears in the rain. Her people were ragged and bloodied. All were injured in some capacity, but several were severe. She saw Anne lying on the deck, while Onna hovered over her, her small three-fingered hands hard at work closing up a deep gash on Anne's abdomen, Onna's hands stained a rich scarlet.

The deck was cratered with holes, too. It looked like moles had burrowed into the belly of the Dahlia and were leaving broken oaken mounds all across the planking. The refabricated bowsprit once again hung limp, and the sprit sail was lapping at the water.

This was what it took to stop Augusto, and they weren't even done yet. So much pain, so much suffering. She didn't even know who was injured below decks. She didn't know the extent of the damage on the ship, other than it wasn't sinking. Was all of this... was all of the blood and agony really worth stopping a man whose goal was to free Castile from the chains of the Jasian Enclave?

And were they really even chains? Augusto might think they were, gilded ones to look pretty, but chains nonetheless. And yet, they were not. Marissa knew what shackles looked like, what they felt like. She knew what it was to be oppressed. Men like Augusto did not know. In fact, in his ignorance and arrogance, he had placed the people of Castile in heavier chains of oppression, just so he could sever the rope that bound them to the safe harbor of a gentle neighbor.

"Well, do we still sink them?" Emmell asked after seeing over a dozen white flags rise to replace Cruz's colours.

It was a simple, and yet troubling, question. There were thirteen ships out there with illegal goods that would inevitably lead two nations to war when discovered, and Marissa held no doubt that they would indeed be discovered. Maybe not today, or tomorrow, but it would happen, and then all the peace Castile ever knew with the wood elves would be replaced with horror. All for one man's greed.

But by the same token, the *Bella Dahlia* couldn't hold thirteen vessels worth of crews. There just wasn't enough space for them. These were men who were working for Cruz, many only to feed their families; not solely for greed but for survival. They were just as much victims of Augusto's desires as she and her family were. To kill the innocent in the hopes of preventing further violence later was a bitter apple to bite into.

Perhaps it would be different if she had time to spare. To send them to the shores and then scuttle the ships when they were safely away, or to try and unload everything back into the caves, but she didn't. There was no way the Enclave missed the rout between her and the two war cogs. Everyone around must've heard the thunder of her cannons. So no, she had minutes, only minutes before the proverbial sea cavalry arrived. She needed to do something, and fast.

Out of the corner of her eye Marissa noticed a shift on the horizon. She turned to face it, almost as if it understood her inner turmoil and was answering her call for help.

The Stonewall Pale was transforming.

It always fluctuated, of course. It happened often enough that ships would deviate course to avoid the alterations in the shape of the oscillating coagulation on the sea. But now, its morphing gave her pause, and with it an idea.

"Bring us within parley range of the cargo cogs," she instructed Emmell and then looked at Nery. "Nery, Onna is busy tending the wounded. Speak with the Master Gunner and have them load whatever standard shot we have in case the cargo cogs get bold enough to fire. White may mean surrender, but I will not be lured into a trap."

"Aye, Captain!" Nery said cheerfully before zipping below deck.

Emmell wasted no time in bringing their starboard side in line with the rear line of cogs, three in tandem. Marissa looked ahead and saw three more identical columns like the one she was aligned with now, and then at the very lead a sole ship as vanguard. She knew that would be where she found Augusto. She would deal with him in due time.

Instead she focused on the cog that her galleon was closest to. The *Bella Dahlia* dwarfed the cargo vessel, her three masts casting the ship in her eclipse. The lumbering crew all gathered upon the decks of the ship. They were looking at her... and her ship, with a sense of dread and awe.

"For those of you that don't know who I am, I am Marissa de Cantor y Castile!" she yelled down to them.

"Bloody Mari!" she heard Badger yell from the crow's nest above. A chorus of "Bloody Mari's" followed suit from the rest of the crew.

Marissa glowered down at the cog beneath her. "I do not desire to end any of your lives, but that doesn't mean we won't strike you down where you stand if you do anything brash."

"If ye ain't here to lure us to our death, siren, then what do ye need us for?" the lead man, a burly figure of hair and muscles that she assumed was the captain, asked her.

She paused only for a moment in shock at being called a siren. "I am here to stop Augusto Cruz from delivering these illegal goods, and to stop him from thrusting Castile into an inadvertent war."

"So ye seek to seize our stock like a common pirate!" she heard someone from the group yell.

Marissa tried to face the direction of that voice. "If that is how you choose to view it, I won't stop your opinion of it. But know this – I indeed have a plan for the lumber you carry aboard your ship, and it's not to pilfer it."

"Then what do ye plan to do with it?" the burly captain asked.

She turned and nodded her tricorn towards the undulating mass that was slowly rolling their way. "I want you to direct the ships towards the Pale."

He looked at her aghast, "Ye want us to sail into the Pale? Nay, siren that is not a melody we will follow. We'd rather be killed where we stand."

Marissa was afraid of this possibility, so she hoped to call his bluff with one of her own. She drew her flintlock and pointed it at the captain.

He stumbled at the sight of it, and she knew he, like she when she'd first come across it, had no idea what kind of weapon he was looking at. "We can do such a thing, but I do not desire your lives in the Pale, only your ships. Get the cog underway heading towards the Pale and then abandon ship. You should have ample time to find wind in your sails and then to escape on your longships."

He stared between her flintlock and her eyes, studying her intent. "And you'll let us go? You won't open fire upon defenseless prey in longships?"

She raised her pistol away from his face, "I swear to you as the daughter of Don Fernando Cantor that we will not open fire upon you or any of your people." She held up a finger, though, as she spoke. "But you must first direct the ship into the Pale."

The captain looked between his men on the ship, they were all nodding slowly in agreement to his unanswered question. Finally, he looked back to Marissa. "Ye spin an enchanting song siren, and ye have a fierce bite as we can see by the state of our guardians back there. Very well, we will do as ye say, under oath that ye not harm a one of us."

"We have an accord, captain. Put your vessel on the path to the Pale, then abandon ship, and none shall be harmed, – of this I do swear."

And so it went, more or less, for eleven more ships, until she found herself face to face with Augusto Cruz. The cogs behind her were already shifting and heading towards the Pale, the wind not exactly favorable for most and the going was painfully slow, but they were moving. On the western horizon she could make out the flotilla of the Jasian Enclave. A dozen war cogs at least, making all haste towards them. She was losing time fast.

Augusto looked up to her, his usual panache and charm still adorning his smug face. He didn't look like a man defeated, not yet. Behind him, Osprey stood, her massive crossbow loaded and aimed at Marissa. She saw the woman in action with that crossbow too many times to count, and she knew at their range, she would not miss a kill shot on Marissa. She tried to ignore the deadly weapon, and the intent written on the wilder's face.

"Augusto," she said peaceably.

"Mari," he intoned with a nod of his head, "fancy meeting you here."

She smiled mirthlessly. "I expect you've heard my demands to the other ships by now?"

He nodded slowly. "I have."

"And what is your answer?"

Augusto smiled a crooked smile up at her. "I am not some petty lowborn captain that will bow and grovel before a Doña. We are equals, you and I, Cantor and Cruz. Both our fathers' stations and standings were the same. So, do not speak down to me Mari – come aboard the *Pandion* and let us speak as equals to discuss the terms of my 'surrender'."

"Mari..." Onna murmured worriedly. During the course of talking to most of the convoy, the gnome patched up the more life-threatening wounds on the crew, and once again stood at her left side. As much as Marissa wanted Rusalka to stand with her as well, she knew for safety's sake, while dealing with the wilder, that Rue needed to stay out of sight. Still, Rue was listening to every word.

"He be stalling fer time, and baiting ye for a trap," Onna whispered.

"I concur. It is not a wise move," Emmell agreed.

"Noted," Marissa told them both before directing her attention to Augusto. "So then, you wish to parley?"

"Parley?"

He looked at her curiously, and she answered his confusion. "A conference, under truce, to discuss terms. There is absolutely no aggression what-so-ever." She nodded once to Osprey. "This is sacrosanct."

"I will accept those terms on two little conditions," he told her.

"While I'd say you are not in much of a position to be giving conditions, if you are willing to parley, I will hear you out."

"Most excellent, my dear, as my first condition is simple – I want my map back. No matter how this pans out, I want that map."

She nodded – simple enough. It wasn't like she didn't know where the cavern was anyhow. She looked over to Jocquotte and nodded, and the woman went to retrieve it.

"And the second?"

"This is a conversation between nobility only. You leave your... crew upon that vessel, and we discuss alone in the safety of the *Pandion's* captain's quarters."

"Mari..." Onna growled.

Marissa bit her lip, knowing this was a terrible idea. Every-thing about it screamed trap, but it was too obvious a ploy from Augusto, too blatant. That wasn't his style. But it might be... perhaps she made him desperate. She looked up to the horizon to see the war cogs bearing down on them with all haste. She knew the Jasian Enclave was likely growing frantic now.

A glance to her crew showed them all shaking their heads at her.

"Just sink 'is ship already," Onna told her. "It's the easiest thing to do."

"This be a bad idea," Anne added.

But still, if she could get Augusto to yield, if she could capture him alive... Would that not be a better victory than killing him? He would confess his crimes in front of the Dons and Doñas of Castile, before the Jasian Enclave, and even the Lefhym if need be. Would this not be the better solution? She would be cleared of her crimes on Castile. She would be granted her lands back. Her friends would be granted amnesty, and they could all live the lives they should have, not ones regaled to piracy.

Rusalka could live truly free for once in her life.

"Nery."

The kållråden flew up behind her head, "Captain?"

Marissa glanced back, just for a moment. "Climb in my hat. I'm not for going alone."

"Aye, aye, mortal!"

Marissa gazed once more upon her peers shaking heads, but her mind was made up. Though she knew she controlled the high ground, and though she knew how much of a snake Augusto was, if ever she was going to be able to negotiate the freedom of her crew, the safety of Rue, it would be now. She had to do this for them. Jocquotte handed her the map. "We have an accord," Marissa said firmly.

Augusto's predatory grin widened. "Wise choice, darlin'. If you would but kindly extend a gangplank, we can get this 'parley' underway."

The plank was lowered and Marissa crossed quickly onto the cog. She walked right up to Augusto and scowled. "Don't ever call me darling."

His grin had grown absolutely feral as he mocked a slight bow. "Whatever you desire, Bloody Mari."

Marissa followed Augusto as he led her to the Captain's Quarters on at the stern of the ship. She could feel the eyes of his crew upon her. The tension on the ship was so heavy she could almost taste it. Behind her, Osprey followed, like an ever-present shadow. When he reached the door, he opened it for her, all pomp and gentlemanly accord. Hesitantly, she entered.

Augusto closed the door behind them, and Marissa eyed him

speculatively. When she heard the bolt latch shut, she knew in an instant the betrayal was in full.

She reached for her flintlock, but Augusto was on her. He grabbed her arm, keeping the pistol jammed in its holster, and slammed her against the table. She gasped as pain rocketed up her spine. "You... son... of... a... bitch..." she groaned out. "You never violate a parley!"

Augusto backhanded her, sending her tricorn spinning on her head. "Dumb bitch, I'm no sailor, or soldier, or pirate, I'm a lord! Your trivialities mean nothing to someone of my station!"

Marissa's jaw throbbed and she felt copper flush her mouth. She must've bitten her tongue. She thought his hand was coming up to strike her in the face once more and she raised her other arm to defend herself, but instead his fist went hard into her stomach. She doubled over in pain, her hand coming from her flintlock. His, however did not, and as she fell over onto the floor, she felt the weapon pull free from her belt.

Groaning and spitting gobs of red onto the wooden planks, the world around her spun. She knew this was a bad idea, and she did it anyway! All in the hopes that somewhere in Augusto was the decent young man she remembered. The room fell deathly quiet as everything around Marissa faded away. The only thing she heard was the single click of Augusto locking the hammer back.

Marissa stared up at him, looking up the barrel of her own weapon. He glared down at her in menace. That cruel, all-white smile took to his face once more. "Map," he said.

Marissa reached behind her back and pulled out the map, throwing it to his feet. Slowly he squatted down and picked it up, glanced at it with a grin, and tucked it away behind his back.

"You kill me, and the *Bella Dahlia* will open fire and demolish this ship," she croaked out.

Augusto shrugged nonchalantly. "Doubtful," he answered.

"You're the one with the hand cannon, Mari – when it goes off, they'll think you killed me," he said with a nod over to the right.

Marissa, puzzled, turned away from him for a moment to glance where he nudged his head. Laying behind the desk, where she hadn't been able to see from her vantage before, was Bevan Ó Cuana. His eyes were wide open and staring emptily up to the ceiling. A ring of bruises danced across his throat where he'd been strangled.

Marissa closed her eyes, "Oh, Bevan." When she looked at him again, she noticed he was wearing the same finery as Augusto. She turned and looked back at the viscount, aghast.

"You think you've ruined me, Mari? You've barely even set me back. Thanks to your miraculous return, I no longer have to destroy the cavern. You've given me the map, and you were the only one to truly know its location. I'm sure your crew could find it again, but since you've done the luxury of flying the colours of a pirate for me, the Jasian Enclave will now crush your ship on sight. All I have to do is pull this trigger, dump that body out the back window, and wait. Osprey will see it and lose her mind. She'll fire upon your crew. Disorganized and without their leader, your crew will scramble before they think to open fire. And even if they do attack out of vengeance, this is a cog. It can take more abuse than you can mete out before reinforcements arrive to drive your crew to the inky depths." He laughed mirthlessly to himself. "Hells, if I'm lucky, we might even be able to stop those other ships before they enter the Pale. Probably won't get all of them, but a few will be enough to secure goodwill for the Supreme Pontiff. He'll understand after being told of the pirate attack upon the convoy."

He was right. Marissa knew he was right. It wasn't a perfect plan, but it was a damn clever one for how little time he had to put in place. He was willing to sacrifice everyone for it. Even Osprey. It showed her in that moment just how low the man had become.

"Truly a remarkable piece," he commented, bringing her back

to look at him. He pointed the weapon in her face. "I was talking about your ass by the way, not this cannon," he added with a twisted smile. "You know it's funny, your father died in very a similar way, at my feet. Give him my regards, won't you?"

"Nery!" Marissa screamed.

Augusto pulled the trigger.

CHAPTER FORTY

Rusalka

Rusalka heard all the protestations from her companions through the cracked door of the Captain's Quarters. She was ready, harpoon in hand, just in case the wilder attacked. Rusalka didn't agree with the reasons they asked her to wait in this chamber, but she accepted them. The humans felt that the wilder would do anything she could to try and kill Rusalka, and it would jeopardize any chance for peaceful surrender. As much as it chafed the proud orc, she acquiesced, her own failures of control still on her mind.

But now the ever-emotional Jasian wasn't listening to any of her crew, not even Emmell. Rusalka knew that when Mari was set, it would do little good to talk her out of something, no matter how logical. So, the Jasian was going to cross over onto the enemy's ship alone to parley.

It felt like forever that she was squatting in the Captain's Quarters, waiting for the all clear, or the cry for help, or something. Then the worst thing possible happened – she heard the thunderous crack of the Jasian's pistol.

There was a moment of stunned silence, and then a splash. Only a breath later, she heard a scream of primal rage. Rusalka recognized the fury in that scream, and its owner, the wilder. Commotion erupted on her own deck as shrill whistles ripped through the air. She recognized the thuds on the hard, salt-stained boards. The wilder was shooting her people! Unable to remain hidden any longer, Rusalka barreled out of the door, her harpoon in hand.

She stared at the carnage before her, so many of her companions lying on the deck, blood coursing out like rivers from thumb-sized holes punched through their bodies. She saw Onna, lying face down, a growing puddle of crimson blossoming from her throat. Anne and Jocquotte were hunkered behind the main mast while a constant stream of bolts shattered and splintered the thick cylinder of wood. Near them, almost every castaway from the island lay dead or wounded.

Her eyes hastily searched for Emmell and found her taking cover on the stairs leading to the poopdeck. The intelligent little sea artist was cognizant enough to seek shelter from the incessant barrage of iron death that the wilder was unleashing.

It seemed inhuman how many bolts the woman was firing, and how swiftly. Rusalka found her, this Osprey, standing on top of a load of Elder timber so that her tall mass was level with that of the galleon's main deck. Her skull-like helmet contorted the proportions of her face in rage. Her eyes bore the single-minded intensity of murder within them. The wilder bellowed a war cry as bolt after deadly bolt left the massive crossbow.

Finally, Rusalka saw the hammer fall forward and the cable set to neutral for the last time. Rusalka watched the wilder remove a case from the device and deftly begin to load more bolts into it. Recognition then dawned on the orc – this weapon could fire multiple bolts in rapid succession! The damage aboard the ship already demonstrated the weapon's danger, and the throb in her head was a none-too-gentle reminder of how devastating a device it was.

Her eyes fell to the fallen Onna once more, and her blood boiled. The orc roared, drawing the Osprey's face to look into her own. There was a new need in those eyes now. A need to hunt her prey. Rusalka would give this wilder that which she sought.

Rusalka charged the railing just as the Osprey slapped the cartridge back into the crossbow. With proficient hands, and immense strength, she cranked the firing cable back into position as Rusalka reached the railing. Rusalka lunged one foot up on the railing and, using all of the strength of her dense thigh muscles, catapulted herself into the air.

Osprey raised the crossbow and methodically took aim at the soaring orc as she leapt between ships. Rusalka saw Osprey draw a confident bead on her and lock in her trajectory, but this time Rusalka was prepared. History wouldn't repeat itself today.

Osprey might be a master crossbowman, but she was reliant on being motionless. Rusalka however, was adept at fighting while moving. She hoisted her harpoon and locked onto the motionless statue of muscle and sinew. She let the harpoon fly.

The blade buried itself through the Osprey's forearm, driving the crossbow down just as she fired. Rusalka felt the bolt clip and deflect off her ribs as it whistled past. There was no chance for another shot as the savage orc in full bloodlust fell upon the wilder, knocking them off the timber and to the deck below.

Both women scrambled to their feet at the same time and collided forward in fury, an unstoppable force slamming into an immovable object. It was a battle of titans, and Rusalka, unfazed by the scorching shot across her right flank crashed into the towering wall of muscle that was Osprey. Osprey seemed equally unperturbed by the blade of the harpoon that was driven completely through her forearm. She dropped the crossbow and met the might of the orc head on.

Rusalka clawed with her fingers and snapped at the wilder with her tusks, while the massive woman began to drive her down with sheer tenacity. Rusalka was surprised to see her own muscles, rippling and taut with exertion, begin to flag under the brute force of Osprey. She had encountered wilders before, but never one whose strength surpassed an orc enraged!

Rusalka growled and adjusted her footing, trying to vie for better stability. The adjustment turned out to be a mistake. The moment she shifted her momentum, Osprey capitalized on it, and the powerhouse kicked out a leg, sweeping wide and destroying Rusalka's balance. She then hammered the elbow of her good arm into Rusalka's sternum. The air left Rusalka's lungs in a great "oompf!" as she fell backwards.

Not finished, the dexterous wilder grabbed Rusalka's face as she was falling backwards, and violently drove her skull into the hard oaken deck. Rusalka felt the boards snap and crack against her thick skull, and pain exploded like cannon fire. A cloud of fire-flies danced before her eyes.

With no air in her lungs, and mini-torches swaying across her vision, unconsciousness threatened to take her. She knew if she let it, though, her friends would all be dead. Not just Onna, but Emmell, Anne, Badger, Jocquotte, and Mari.

Mari!

The thought of the Jasian who believed in her, when she didn't even believe in herself, fueled the rage within her. If Mari died, she didn't know what she would do, how she could go on. Rusalka let forth a battle cry of her own, one that went deep to her very bones, to the culture of her people. She slammed the palms of her hands to the wood – boom, boom, boom.

Massive hands grasped her throat. The dancing lights before her eyes wouldn't abate, and she realized with some shock that she couldn't really see anymore. The world seemed bathed in orange. Everything was blurry and indistinct, like she was looking through the flickering flames of a fire. She could only see shapes, little else.

Her fists struck the deck again: BOOM, BOOM, BOOM. She found the tempo of her people. She was orc! Rusalka didn't need to see to fight, for she could smell. And right now, what she smelled was a wounded animal. Blood was easy to track, and nothing excited an orc more than the scent of blood. Except for the taste of it, perhaps.

Rusalka reached out and clamped onto the shaft of the harpoon and twisted. Osprey's tolerance to pain was impressive, but the serrated blade of the harpoon tearing tendon and sinew, grating on bone, caused the wilder to cry out. The vice grip on her throat became pliable. Even steel weakens under heat. With her other hand, Rusalka batted away the wilder's meaty hand, and drawn to the blood, the lust of need coursing through her, she drove her tusks down onto Osprey's exposed flesh.

Rich, scarlet life poured over her tongue, coating her throat, re-invigorating her. She could hear the bellow of the wilder in surprise. Her actions did not disarm Osprey though – far from it. Wilders, like orcs, were most deadly when wounded.

Osprey slammed her head down upon Rusalka's, and another round of agony detonated in her skull. She felt the stitches on her scalp split, and her own liquid essence begin to pour hot down the side of her face. She released her grip on the harpoon and pulled her face away from the wilder's fierce head-butts. The two pulled away from each other just as quickly, rolling in opposite directions and coming to their feet.

Rusalka spit out the mouthful of blood, some hers, though most of it belonged to Osprey. She smiled, and though she couldn't see, she could smell the blood pouring from Osprey's wounds. More than that, she could smell doubt. It wasn't as pungent as fear, but the scent was there, floating between them. It was a bouquet of lilies to Rusalka, enticing and invigorating.

Her nose crinkled, and there was something else on the air, a tang she recognized – burning pitch, and… black powder.

She heard the hiss of a slow match, the odor of burning twine became suddenly apparent. But who was going to fire, the *Pandion*, or the *Bella Dahlia*? Rusalka knew it didn't matter. They were too close, side-by-side, an explosion at this proximity…

Rusalka never had a chance to complete the thought as half a dozen demi-culverins fired near-simultaneously at point blank range.

CHAPTER FORTY-ONE

Marissa de Cantor y Castile

Her temple burned like white hot fire. Her brain felt like it was being branded with the Cruz heraldry – one round bullet.

"Don't move," a voice whispered in her head. *"He thinks you're dead."*

I'm not? Marissa wanted to reply. It certainly felt like she should be. The last thing she saw was the hammer of her own flint-lock drop and the flint strike the frizzen pan. A wash of sparks, thunder's roar. There was molten fire in her temple, and she felt herself fall. But now she realized she wasn't dead; something else... held her body immobile.

Through the burning, it dawned on her – Nery stopped the bullet! She didn't know why she didn't realize it sooner. Nery could use magic! Of course, she could! She was sidhe. She already admitted to being able to remove herself from mortal views. The nøkken were invisible as well, and they manipulated the minds of

443

mortals with their arcane songs. Why wouldn't a kållråden be able to manipulate the strings of the supernatural as well?

Marissa heard Augusto grunt as he lifted the corpse of Bevan and hoisted it out the rear window. It took only a second before Osprey's cry cut through the silence. Augusto chuckled darkly above. "So predictable women are."

His words cut at her. Outside, she could hear bedlam. Men scrambling on the deck to ready the ship to break away from the *Bella Dahlia*. Osprey's guttural war cry as Marissa heard shot after shot pounded against her ship at her beloved crew. All of this was caused by the snarky, arrogant bastard above her, hiding out while Osprey thought him dead!

Though Marissa held no love for the wilder after what they'd been through over the last few days, she felt a pang of sorrow for the woman. She could hear the suffering in Osprey's cry, the anger, the torture, and it broke Marissa's heart. Meanwhile, Augusto merely hummed to himself as he waited.

"Let me up!" Marissa hissed.

"*Not yet... wait for it,*" the sidhe replied in her head.

Wait for what? She wanted to ask, but a second later she heard it. A roar.

Rusalka...

The whole deck quivered as they felt the orc vault aboard. The roar mixed with a guttural yell from Osprey, and Marissa could only imagine what was happening out there.

"*Now!*" Nery whispered excitedly.

Marissa saw a shimmer of cerulean light before her eyes, and then a small ball rolled off her temple and struck the treadworn planks before her. A sudden surge of mobility filled her, and she felt her arms again. Slowly, she reached up and touched her temple. She felt a divot in her skin, and it was tender to the touch, but her fingers didn't come back slick with blood as she expected.

Nery snickered in her ear. "Silly mortal. Don't think too hard about it. Now get up and stop this bad guy! I'm having a blast!"

Outside, the commotion was growing even more frantic as the duel between wilder and orc continued. The men were all yelling, and she could hear something heavy being dragged across the deck. Still, she tried to push it to the back of her mind while she focused only on what was in this room. Where was Cruz? She knew he was above her, but behind? In front? Nery "faked" Marissa's death convincingly enough, but that now left her face down, and she didn't think she could move her head very far before he noticed. Unless he was paying more attention to the pandemonium going on the other side of the door... Marissa remembered she had eyes on her shoulder.

"Where is he now?" she whispered as quietly as she could. Luckily the turbulence on deck masked her own susurrations.

"Behind the captain's table, studying your boomstick," Nery murmured. "He kind of looks bored, actually."

Figures, Marissa mused. He killed a hapless guard, shot his ex-girlfriend in the head, and riled up a huge maelstrom outside, all while organizing one of the biggest betrayals in Castile history... and he's bored.

Well, time to liven up his day. Marissa shimmied her hand slowly down to her other flintlock, and as deftly as she could she drew the weapon and hopped to her feet, all in one motion.

She expected to see a surprised look on his face, something along the lines of a startled deer. Instead he was staring at her in a calculating way, her stolen pistol pointing right where she alighted to her feet.

"Took you long enough," he said dryly.

"How...?" Marissa stammered.

Augusto rolled his eyes. "You sound like a swine in labor, you breathe so heavy."

Breathing... right... dammit!

"Didn't think about the breathing bit – you mortals can be vexing things sometimes," Nery confessed. "Sorry, Captain."

"Don't worry about it," Marissa said with a nod.

Now Augusto did look surprised as his eyes drifted away from hers and to the side of her tricorn. "So that's how you did it?"

She cocked the weapon and pointed it at him. "Did what?"

"Survived the shot." He stared at the side of her head bewildered. "I must say, Marissa... my dear, you continue to astonish. Not only do you have the most sophisticated ship on the Sowle Sea, and these fascinating hand cannons, but you also have a faery!"

Marissa felt static build up on the side of her head, and her hair begin to rise. "Now you did it."

He looked at her in curious amusement for a moment, before regarding the rising current of electricity that was dancing through her hair.

"I...AM...NOT...A...FAERY!" Nery bellowed at Cruz.

Marissa couldn't even track the lightning bolt that was Nery as she zipped to Augusto. His keen mind didn't even have time to react as the small kållråden was suddenly on him, her insect-like wings shimmering rainbow hues, they moved so swiftly. More entrancing was the fact that something seemed to be sifting off her wings and drifting lazily all over Augusto.

His concern though, was not the dust that was covering him, but the mercurial miniature person that was darting all about his face screaming at him with the most crude, and simultaneously most creative, inflective uses for profanity that Marissa ever heard. She didn't even realize that so many words like that could be strung together to form complete logical sentences, and yet she was listening to it now as Nery spewed them forth with gusto while raking his face with her tiny claws.

Finally, Augusto broke from his trance, swatting at the kållråden, and hollered, "Enough!"

Seemingly satisfied, the sidhe flew back to Marissa's side. "Give him a minute," she said.

Marissa arched an eyebrow. "What'd you do?"

"Dusted him."

Marissa wanted to know more, but the click of the pistol brought her back to Augusto. She raised her flintlock back at him as well. "Mari, you enthrall me, I confess," he told her, while starting to scratch at his neck. "I haven't had sport like this since... well ever, really."

"Glad I could challenge you," she said dryly.

He laughed a genuine laugh. "I wouldn't call it a challenge." His eyes gleamed. "I've still won, you must see that. I set out to delay your ship until the Enclave arrives, and..." he nodded out the window, "I've succeeded."

Marissa looked out the window and saw Augusto was right – the fleet was visible and closing fast. They would never be able to outrun them at this distance. She focused back on Augusto, and his copper skin was beginning to welt. "You've still lost most of the Elder wood to the Pale," she pointed out.

He shrugged, sweat dampening his brow. "That hardly matters now. With the map in hand, I don't have to destroy the cavern. I must admit, this is the most fun I've had in a long time."

This was fun to him? Marissa couldn't believe what she was hearing. People were dying just on the other side of the door, and he was having fun? Her friends were in danger, hurt, or dying, and this was all a joke to him?

She knit her brow and leveled the weapon at his face. "It's over now, Augusto. Fleet or not, I will have your surrender or your death."

Augusto stopped laughing and looked at her darkly. His free hand reached up and scratched his cheek as large pink splotches formed all over his tan skin. "You're beautiful, and intelligent, and have a cunning that I just didn't know was there," he told her. "But what you lack is moxie and courage. For all your bluster and veneer," he waved at her outfit, "you even dress the part like a confident woman, but I know the girl. I know your roots. Within that disguise of a cocksure piratess lies the truth. You are a coward. Without your friends here, you don't have what it takes to pull that trigger and kill me where I stand. I, however, have already demonstrated that I do." With that, he leveled the weapon directly at her eyes, yet his breathing was becoming raspy. "Tell me, Mari, can your faery catch cannon fire twice?"

"Not a vulnerable place like the eyes, no," Nery whispered to her.

Marissa though, did not waver. The old Marissa might have. The unsure one that needed Rusalka's encouragement six months ago to fight for her own life would have. But Augusto was wrong. While her friends indeed bolstered her, they had also done something else. Something remarkable. They'd taught her confidence. They gave her self-assuredness. They gave her hope. And that was something she could now call hers.

She may never be brave, but she could be bold. Besides, she knew something Augusto did not. "Last chance, Augusto."

He smiled. "Even now you pontificate when you should pull the trigger. I've got a read on you, Mari. You're weak, just like all women. Soft. You should've stuck to what you did best – singing. Goodbye, love."

He pulled the trigger. Once more Marissa watched the hammer drop. The flint struck the frizzen pan and a swath of sparks scintillated in the noon light, before disappearing into a flash of white, acrid smoke.

Marissa smiled sensually at Augusto. "Should've studied the weapon a little more... love. It's exactly like a cannon – you only get one shot."

Augusto, at a loss for words, stared now at the single weapon between them, in her hands. He swallowed hard. The swelling on his face was getting comical now.

"Seems the cat's got your tongue."

"Pull the trigger, Captain," Nery told her. "End this paltry mortal so we can go and shoot the big chick next!"

Marissa cocked her head. "What say you, Augusto? Still want to see if I lack... what was the word you used? Moxie?"

"Perhaps we..." Augusto wheezed as the ship lurched violently starboard. A great detonation of raw, primal sound reverberated in her ears, and a fusillade of shot pounded into the tethered *Bella Dahlia*.

The concussive force of the blast between the near proximity of ships slammed into her like a battering ram. Unprepared, it threw both her and Augusto from their feet, but not before she pulled the trigger. Her aim, now awry, was angled away from Augusto's face, but still drove the bullet home, right into the meaty part of his shoulder. He screamed as they flew. Marissa slammed into the nearby armoire, while Cruz tumbled into what looked like barrels of some vintage liquor, probably rum.

Her world spun, as a dull throbbing pain wracked her body. It felt like her bones were struck by a hundred fists all at once. She tried to right herself, tried to see where Augusto was, where Nery flew off to, but her head spun from where she struck it against the armoire.

Then she saw him. He was up, stumbling, limping on his right leg. He was going to the door. If he opened it... she couldn't hope to stop the wilder.

Marissa tried to scramble to her feet, but she felt a shooting pain lance up her own leg. She screamed and fell over. Her ankle twisted.

Unable to stop him, Marissa could only watch as Augusto disappeared outside. She gritted her teeth and forced herself to bear the pain. Using the armoire, she stood and hobbled out after him. The deck was a mass of writhing bodies, all driven to the oaken floor by the back blast. Marissa could see both Rusalka and Osprey lying stunned on the deck. Neither were in good condition – they did quite a number on one another.

Both ships were listing heavy to starboard, and she could see a half dozen gaping craters in the side of the *Bella Dahlia,* thick smoke roiling from the puckering wounds.

"My ship!" she cried, before focusing on Augusto making his way for a longship. He was trying to run? Why was he trying to run now?

"Cruz, it's over!" she yelled.

He looked back at her and she could see for the first time true, absolute fear in his dark eyes.

"We need to move right now!" Nery said, suddenly materializing right next to Marissa.

"What? Why?" Marissa asked.

Nery looked back in the same direction as Augusto. "Too late," she whispered.

And the waxen brume of the Stonewall Pale engulfed them all.

CHAPTER FORTY-TWO

Rusalka

R usalka pushed herself to her feet as a wash of song enveloped her. She could barely see, but she recognized the lilting melody from before.

"No," she hissed. "No!"

Yes, the song encouraged. *Yes, do what you do best, orc. Finish what you have started.*

Rusalka shook her head, trying to fight the beautiful music filled with suggestion. The bloodlust was still running fresh through her veins, the adrenaline fueling her desire. "Stay away from me!"

But the anthem wouldn't abate. It only poured into her more fervently. Harder, and harder. It wanted her to do what she did best. It wanted the violence to sift from her, just like the tune so effortlessly sang from their instruments.

She felt herself succumbing to the madness. It encircled her, embraced her, and told her to accept herself as she was, as she was meant to be. As a killer.

A bug-shaped silhouette flew into her periphery. "I found her!" it said. She swatted at it. Then there was a hand on her. She growled, the music compelling her easily to the violence within her.

"Hey, hey it's me! It's me, Rue," the disembodied voice said.

Rusalka recognized the familiar voice, and the scent, but the lullaby wreathed her with dark promises, with a release she so desperately sought.

Then she felt the soft touch of a hand on her face. Delicate, peaceful, steady. She knew that touch...

"Jasian," she whispered. The song of the nøkken faded.

"It's me, Rue," Marissa's voice, it held so much emotion, so much promise, of friendship, of love, of family. Rusalka gripped at the hand, "I can't see..."

"That's because of the Pale," Marissa told her.

"No," Rusalka commented back. "I'm blind."

There was a brief silence, and Rusalka held her breath. Her people would leave her behind. She was useless to them. But Mari, she was different, she was compassionate.

"Come on, I'll hold your hand," Marissa told her encouragingly.

"I'll guide you," Nery chirped through the darkness. "Just follow my voice."

Together they crossed the ship as people moaned, some cried in fear, and others cackled in madness. Rusalka knew they didn't have long. Minutes maybe, they were all so hurt, and the nøkken were quite adept at what they did.

They found their way to the gangplank and crossed it with little trouble. Already, her brain was becoming muddled by the petrichor, and the deadly suggestions were growing more insistent in her head. She was fighting them, though, and Mari's touch gave her strength.

After they crossed the gangplank, Rusalka heard Marissa cast it off. "Do not move, and do not succumb," Nery ordered. "I will cut the lines tethering us to the neighboring ship."

Marissa continued to hold her hand, feeding her with strength.

"Help!" Rusalka heard a weak voice say somewhere by her feet. "The song, it is so beautiful."

It was Jocquotte. Rusalka squatted down feeling around for the woman. Her hand grazed over a wounded limb and Jocquotte cried out in pain. "I've got you," Rusalka encouraged.

"Rue?" Jocquotte said in panic. "Please, please don't kill me!"

"It's okay," Rusalka said. "I'm in control..."

She helped Jocquotte to her feet in the mists. "What's happening?" the human asked.

"Nery is cutting the tethers," Mari answered.

"Done!" Nery chirped as she zipped by. "Directing the crimble to get you all out of here!" the voice said, fading back to the quarterdeck. Within another minute the ship began to lurch forward.

Rusalka felt her mind drifting, and Marissa began to sing.

CHAPTER FORTY-THREE

Don Augusto Cruz

Augusto Cruz finally understood what it was like to be defenseless and afraid. As the Pale consumed them all, he couldn't seem to find the longship. And his brain, normally so brilliant and so quick, felt sluggish and choked. Everything around him just seemed so baffling. Thoughts, even simple ones, were encumbering.

All he knew was that he needed to get to a longship. To escape. In the distance he heard a beautiful song, and a magical voice.

"Mari..." the thought of her, and her singing brought a smile to his face. Such an adversary. So surprisingly brilliant.

A heavy hand struck his shoulder, turning him around. Though he couldn't see her, he could feel the heat radiating off her.

"Osprey," he said with relief. "Oh thank the Maker – quick love, help me find a longship."

Osprey didn't answer him, though. Instead her wet hands

crept up from his shoulder to the side of his face, to the top of his head.

"Yes, it's me. I'm alive," he said irritated. "Come on wilder, we have to get out of here."

Osprey continued her silence, her grip turning vicelike on his skull. Pain exploded through his head. "Let... go! You're hurting... me!"

"Butterflies," Osprey whispered. Those were the last words Don Augusto Cruz, provisional viscount of Castile, ever heard spoken to him again.

CHAPTER FORTY-FOUR

Rusalka

The screams... they were awful. The sound of fighting and dying happening only a hundred yards away was sickening. The ripping sounds were wet, the screams burbled. This was the horror that the nøkken were capable of... she had no idea.

Marissa continued to sing beautifully, and the nøkken's melody vanished from her mind. Instead, Rusalka was aware of something else, another presence.

Jocquotte reached out and took Rusalka's other hand. "I'm sorry," she whispered. "I... didn't believe it, but now I understand. It wasn't you."

It wasn't you. Words she needed to hear, and now with the massacre occurring so close, she knew that they were true. It *wasn't* her.

"Those things I said," Jocquotte continued, "I was wrong to say them. You're not a monster."

Rusalka closed her eyes and drank in the words. Words she

desperately longed to hear. She turned to look where Jocquotte stood. "No, you're correct. I am a monster," she told her friend, "but I am *your* monster." Jocquotte's fingers squeezed hers.

For the first time in Rusalka's life she did not feel alone. A curious sensation tickled her face, and to her astonishment, she realized she was crying. Rusalka smiled to herself and began to laugh.

CHAPTER FORTY-FIVE

Marissa de Cantor y Castile

When they broke through the haze of the Pale, Marissa was alarmed to see that the Enclave was in full retreat. She thought for sure they'd be surrounded by an armada. Instead it seemed as if the ships wanted nothing to do with the arcing spiral of the Stonewall Pale. Now they were just visible on the horizon. If they actually saw the *Bella Dahlia,* they wanted no part of her.

Marissa felt a deep worry in her gut as they bore down on the cavern of Elders. Was her mother all right? Did they collapse it on everyone? Was half of Castile gone? Was Cantor gone?

It turned out, she needn't have worried. When she arrived, there were dozens of dinghies and longships bringing out everyone trapped within. Nearby on the beach, three dozen Ayjub slavers were in manacles.

The two purist war cogs were still there, and there was some initial concern, along with primed cannons, at their arrival, but it was quickly snuffed out; for on the quarterdeck of the lead ship talking to the captain was her mother!

They sidled up alongside and tethered to the war cog, and Marissa raced over to her mother. She embraced the woman in a fierce grip. "Mama," she cried, "I thought I'd never see you again!"

Doña Cantor laughed and nodded to the captain. "It turns out we needn't have worried, my love! When the captain saw the Ayjub slavers, and what was happening inside, the purists quickly came to our side! It seems the Jasian Enclave wasn't as deep in his pocket as Augusto thought."

The purist captain saluted her. "Indeed not, milady. We were simply under orders from Adjutant Love. We had no idea what horrors Viscount Cruz planned for his people. It was unspeakable! We could not follow such a heinous plan any longer."

Marissa smiled – this was almost better than she hoped possible. Augusto finally made a mistake, and now the Jasian Enclave knew about it.

"YE MEAN I MISSED THE WHOLE FIGHT?" ONNA EXCLAIMED in fury. Behind her, the sun was beginning to settle into the mountains.

Marissa was happy that her boatswain was not as injured as first perceived. She had indeed been shot by Osprey during the initial volley, but it was only a glancing blow across her neck. The near miss made the normally elusive gnome stumble and strike her head against the rail, rendering her unconscious. The action probably saved her life. Emmell warned her about how incredibly lucky she was. "It missed your jugular by about three centimeters," Marissa's sea artist exclaimed while tending to the bandages on her neck.

The gnome batted her away. "Quit swaddlin' me, ye blasted spriggan, I ain't yer baby."

Emmell harrumphed. "Don't come crying to me when it gets infected. You know we amputate on this ship, right?"

"Yeah, yeah," Onna grumbled. "Ye'll cut off me head, I get it. Who's the sawbones ere,' anyhow?"

Emmell dismissed her with a petulant wave, "I'm going to check on Jocquotte's bandages. Nery will be with me, Captain." Marissa nodded as the spriggan loped across the deck with a zipping firefly in tow.

She turned back just in time to see the gnome look over to Rusalka in obvious awe. "Can't believe I missed ye square up against Osprey, Tusker! That musta been a sight ta behold!"

"Oi! Crazy orc leapt between the two ships and crashed down on the wilder! Looniest thing I ever saw!" Badger exclaimed merrily.

In a rare moment of affection, Rusalka grinned. "It wasn't that dramatic," she insisted. "I just needed to stop her from shooting at my friends."

Badger walked up and swatted Rusalka on the shoulder, while looking at both Marissa and Onna. "The Tusker's bein' modest! She soared through the air and skewered the wilder like a fish with her harpoon!"

"Fleet inbound!" Anne called from the crow's nest, interrupting the revelry.

Everyone quieted as they turned southeast to face Castile. There, right at the edge of the waterline, they could see the masts of a dozen ships.

Doña Cantor, who was busy dealing with their liberated people, came over to Marissa. "It will be okay," she said quietly.

But Marissa said nothing.

The purist captain also came by to stand with her. "Rest assured, Captain de Cantor, Adjutant Love will be made well aware of all of your heroism, and that of the bravery of your crew. This... this should've never happened."

"I am grateful none of your men were seriously hurt in our little scuffle," she replied.

"I'd rather have broken ships then dead men. I thank you for such discretion. It truly is the better part of valor."

Marissa looked to the purist, and he really did seem a kind man. She hoped that he was telling her the truth, that they were ignorant in all of this, as so many seemed to be. Still though, a hollow lingered in her stomach. She knew Adjutant Love was on one of those ships. She knew he was affiliated with Cruz's actions. He knew of the pact. Hells, he was probably the inter-mediary. It would make sense. He knew of the map, which meant he knew of the people being held here. But did he know they were held against their will? Did he know they were enslaved? Or was he kept just as oblivious of Cruz's real game plan?

She glanced at Onna. "What do you think?" She wanted to add, 'You heard the conversations that no one else did,' but that part was left unspoken.

Onna shrugged, "I say we hear it out, Brains. Then decide, savvy me?"

"Spoken like a true pirate, I'd wager," Marissa added with a smirk.

"I am what I am," Onna agreed with a mock bow, and then groaned, grabbing at the bandage around her neck. "Blast it all to hells. Stupid wilder an' her good arse shootin'."

Marissa surveyed the forecastle deck and all the mounds of cloth that lay there in three very long rows. So many dead. She promised them an escape from the island, and instead delivered upon them their end of days.

She felt her mother's hand wrap around her shoulder, and she placed her head against Marissa's. Her thick raven locks tickled

Marissa's cheek, smelling of the sea. "That is not your doing, child."

"I promised them freedom," Marissa said.

"Freedom always has a price," Doña Cantor answered. "They died knowing that what they were doing would help those they loved. Their husbands, wives, and children. That there was a chance that they might see those loved ones again as well, was merely icing on an already too tempting cake. Remember, the Pale could have consumed us just as easily, but it did not. You gave them a chance to see their home one last time, if only briefly. And you gave them a chance to fight for it."

Marissa clasped her mother's hand and smiled. "Thank you."

Doña Cantor shook her head. "No, my child, it is I that should thank you. Before you came through the Pale, I thought I had lost everything. My people, my husband, you... " She paused as if uncertain on how to continue. "Though I will mourn Fernando for the rest of my days, and though I shall miss him terribly, I can rest easy now knowing that the best of him lives on – in you."

Marissa's eyes welled up. It was probably the best praise she could ever hope for. How she wished her papa was still alive. The things she would say to him! But most importantly, she would tell him how much she loved him.

"Peace lanterns are lit!" Anne called down.

"Well, at least they're not fer shootin' this time," Onna mused. "Just please don't agree to any more parleys."

Marissa chuckled and wiped her eyes. "No promises."

Rusalka groaned.

"MARI!" A FAMILIAR VOICE CALLED AS SOON AS THE gangplanks were dropped on Adjutant Love's two-masted, heavily modified war cog, *the Avondster*. Marissa looked to the voice and could see the robes of the Jasian priestess.

"Cassandra!" Marissa called back excitedly. "How?"

Cassandra scurried across the gangplank and wrapped Marissa in a tight hug. Marissa smiled, though she felt a little awkward. Their initial reunion was so short, and their bond was never as strong as Marissa's had been with Isa. Still, she had to admit there was a connection there. Perhaps it was through their shared love of Isa that they were stronger for it.

Cassandra pulled back, "When I heard you went into the Pale, I feared I'd lost you again forever." She wrapped Marissa in another tight hug. "You are my only connection left to my sister. I can't lose that, not again."

As if realizing that they were surrounded by people, Cassandra pulled back, her face beet red. "I mean... it is good to see you, Doña Cantor."

"Oh, I am not Doña Cantor!" Marissa said with mirth. She gestured over her shoulder. "She is."

Cassandra looked over her shoulder, and her expression became one of mystification. Marissa laughed at her befuddlement as her mother said, "Hi Cassie, you look well."

"Do... Doña Cantor... you're alive," the priestess stammered.

Marissa dislodged herself from the lithe young woman, so she and her mother could face each other. As she did, she saw Cassandra's bodyguard hovering menacingly nearby. "Maria," she said by way of greeting.

"Marissa," the hulking exactor replied.

Doña Cantor began to explain to Cassandra how she survived the Pale when the purist captain called all on deck to attention. Winters of habit actually forced Marissa to attention for a handful of seconds, as Adjutant Love came aboard their ship.

Though heavy, he seemed at home on the open sea. She could see a liveliness in him now that wasn't there in his quarters.

"Adjutant Love."

Love snickered at the formal address. "Captain de Cantor."

He continued to walk aboard the ship to survey the galleon, its damage, and most importantly its crew. His eyes fell upon the orc. "So, you survived."

Rusalka, knowing nothing of the Jasian Enclave's etiquette simply nodded.

He looked over to Marissa and then back to Rusalka. "She cares a great deal for you. Remember that."

"I... will," Rusalka answered flummoxed.

Adjutant Love made his way over to Marissa, Cassandra, and Doña Cantor. He did not seem as surprised as Cassandra was. He must've been notified of her "resurrection" before boarding. Adjutant Love formally greeted the Doña with kisses on the tops of both her hands. "It does this old man's heart good to see you alive, Doña Cantor."

"You are too kind, Beneford," Doña Cantor said to him, rather informally.

Adjutant Love straightened and faced Marissa. Around them, purists and bellators began to board the ship to remove the casualties and help aid both the castaways, and the recently liberated. Most of her crew watched in mild amusement, dotted with slight apprehension.

"So Mari, I didn't think we'd be talking again so soon," Love said.

Marissa looked at him keenly. "Nor did I, to be honest."

He looked over to the cavern that was darkening with each passing minute of the setting sun. "Yes well, you uncovered a great many disturbing developments that happened right under my nose."

Off to the side, Onna scoffed.

Love looked over to the gnome and raised an eyebrow, "Is there something you would like to add, miss?"

Onna shared a look with Marissa, and she shook her head minutely. "Tis' Onna. And nay, pray continue." Marissa let out a small sigh of relief.

"Yes, well," he turned back to Marissa, "as I was saying, you brought an abhorrent crime to light, committed at the hands of the provisional viscount Augusto Cruz. For that, I am indebted to you."

"But you were aware of the pact?" Marissa asked. This wasn't so much about calling him out, more a gentle reminder that his hands weren't completely clean.

Adjutant Love didn't bat an eye. "I did, in fact. I ratified them. Though I am Enclave through and through, young captain, I have called Castile home since before you were born. I thought this a very good step in Castile's future."

"On the backs of its people?" This came surprisingly from Marissa's mother.

"I assure you, Doña Cantor, I had no idea that the people were being enslaved in such a manner," he stated adroitly. Marissa could tell he was lying through his teeth. "I have also been recently informed that Cruz planned on destroying this cavern with the people in it. I find such actions outrageous and revolting! I assure you I had no knowledge of anything so atrocious!" That statement, Marissa was not so sure, though it made little difference. He knew of the slavery, and he knew of the cave and the violation to the peaceful accords that they had with the Lefhym. Though she could condemn him outright, she had no proof – yet.

"So what happens now?" Doña Cantor asked.

"Now?" Adjutant Love asked as he looked across the deck. "Now we see to our wounded. We reunite loved ones with their families. We celebrate the victory of life and we mourn those who died so that others may live. You, Doña, will return to Cantor, with full restoration of title, lands, and all rights therein." He looked about at the other castaways milling about the deck. "These fine men and women will return to a home that has desperately missed them."

Many of the castaways thanked Adjutant Love profusely, and Marissa saw what was happening. He conquered the moment, and just like that he pulled the sway of the people away from her, and to himself. She hated politics.

As the people shuffled off the ship, Marissa became all too suddenly aware that there weren't enough people left to man the *Bella Dahlia,* save those fully within the Jasian Enclave. Her gut began to tighten.

Adjutant Love turned to regard her. "As for you, Marissa de Cantor y Castile. I'm afraid I must place you and your entire crew under arrest."

"What?" Cassandra squawked.

Marissa watched it all unfold against her masterfully. Once again, she put too much faith in the system, and it failed her.

Four fully-armored purists had swords drawn and leveled at the seated orc in the blink of an eye. The injured and blood-deprived gnome was manhandled like a child and forced down against a barrel, her signature knives stripped from her. Suddenly Anne, Badger, and Jocquotte all appeared, being led at crossbow point. Emmell was screaming and writhing from an oilcloth sack, and Nery's foul vociferations could be heard pouring out of the bag as well. Marissa slowly stood up. She was unarmed, having lost both her pistols on the *Pandion* in the Pale.

"This is really how it's going to be, Love?" she asked bitingly. "You think we don't know?"

"I really could care less what you think you know, Mari," he told her. "I do what is necessary for both the Jasian Enclave and Castile. You've saved lives that will not be forgotten, but you are also a war criminal of the worst kind. An ex-exactor. There's no absolution for that crime. You've turned your back on your god and your people. No dismissal or exoneration can I provide. Furthermore, you and your crew have been charged with theft, larceny, public destruction, resisting arrest, impersonating a Doña..."

"Hold up – I *was* a Doña!" Marissa argued.

Love ignored her and continued. "Piracy, assault, and murder in the first degree, multiple counts."

Onna snorted. "Is that all? No public offenses to bein' an orc in the streets mayhaps? Releasing monsters on the general populace? That'd be a great addition. Really rolls from the tongue, when listing the accolades afore ye make her dance a hempin' jig."

"I'm sure we can find something equally impressive for you," he assured her.

Onna flashed him a bitter smile.

"You... you can't be serious about this, Beneford!" Cassandra said, flabbergasted. "After... after everything she has done here? She's saved hundreds, perhaps thousands of lives! She's brought our missing loved ones back from the Pale! If that's not grounds for absolution, I do not know what is!"

Love shot her a patronizing look. "Priestess Marin, know your place! This is not a religious matter, it is a military one. Though I serve the Maker with body and soul, I also serve law. There is a distinction. Mari has violated law, a great deal of them in fact. She must be held accountable. Perhaps the Maker will seek to forgive her when she ascends, but that is not for *us* to decide."

Marissa saw Cassandra's cheeks and ears flush crimson. She recognized the family trait from her sister Isa. This wasn't embarrassment, it was rage. "This is barbaric!"

Before anyone could react, Cassandra vaulted herself at Love, barreling into his broad chest. She reached up and slapped the surprised Adjutant once, twice across the face. He reached out and grabbed her before she could do it a third time.

"Cassandra! Get ahold of yourself! Or I'll have Maria detain you for your own good."

Marissa looked over to Maria, who seemed to not be enjoying

this moment in the least. Marissa empathized. Maria was an exactor, and this very well could be a reality for her in the future.

Marissa turned back to Cassandra right as she ripped away from Adjutant Love. She swiped her hand over her mouth in disgust. Without another word she turned and strode up to Marissa. Marissa watched the priestess curiously.

"Cassandra, what are you doing?" Adjutant Love demanded.

Cassandra didn't answer him, and Marissa was surprised to see she only had eyes for her. It was a curious thing, this moment between them. Then, like with Love, Cassandra lunged at Marissa, except she didn't strike her face with a slap. No, she was kissing her.

Marissa's eyes widened in surprise. The kiss was long, and full of passion. Not knowing how to react at the moment, Marissa went with the amorous gesture. This seemed to invoke more hunger from the younger woman who was leaning fiercely against her.

"What in the Maker are you doing?" Love roared.

Marissa felt Cassandra open her mouth, wanting – probing. She replied in kind, and felt Cassandra's hot tongue pierce into her mouth, seeking, needing... sharing. Marissa's already wide eyes bulged as she felt the sultry reward, and then all too quickly it was over as purists pulled Cassandra away.

Marissa stared at the beautiful woman in a new light. She never would've imagined Cassandra as that type of person.

"I will fight for you," Cassandra whispered ardently.

The purists pulled the priestess away, while others detained Marissa and locked shackles upon her arms and legs. Marissa watched in silence as the rest of her crew was also similarly humiliated.

"What in the hells do you think you're doing?" Love demanded of Cassandra. "You're a priestess of the Maker! That's blasphemous!"

Marissa watched with humor as Cassandra stared up at the Adjutant hotly. "Priestess yes, and I'm not allowed to marry or have intercourse with a man, ever. The rules never say anything about another woman."

Adjutant Love stood dumbfounded as Cassandra began to march proudly back to the other ship. "Maria come – I've things to prepare for." The exactor looked over at Marissa, with a small smile creasing the corner of that stern visage. She nodded once, and then followed Cassandra onto the boat.

Doña Cantor was pulled away from Marissa, pain in her eyes. "It won't end like this, child! I promise you dear, we will fight!" Two more purists then escorted her off the *Bella Dahlia*.

Marissa's eyes burned with fury as she redirected them back to Love. "Any more witty retorts?" he taunted.

Marissa could say nothing more; she had to look towards her crew now.

He laughed at her. "Very well... Bloody Mari." The Adjutant looked to the group of men surrounding her "Take them to the brig below deck. Let them ride in the cell of their own ship as we bring it back to Castile."

"Very good, ser," a purist answered him. "I'll assemble a skeleton crew for the task."

Love glared back at Marissa. "You can rot in your own cell for a while so you can really think on what you've done. Then... we'll see what kind of discipline will be best for a deserter." And Love spit on her. Marissa didn't flinch as the hot liquid spattered on her face, dribbling slowly down her cheek. Love flicked his wrist in the air. "Take this traitor away."

Marissa watched him turn and leave with his retinue, heading back to his own ship. The women were herded to the cells below. Each one fought, kicking and screaming the whole way. All but Marissa.

—————

"Well, ain't this some shite," Badger told them after their jailors left them alone in their cells. "We done saved the day and rescued all kinds of people, and we're branded criminals fer it!"

"Well, technically when we first fled the authorities, we were criminals," Emmell commented, now free from her oilcloth prison, only to be placed in a cell. "And Mari was a criminal from the start."

"Tit fer tat, lass," Onna objected. "Point is, we saved the whole town and now that crepuscular arse-breathed Adjutant going to be taking credit fer it! Mark me words."

"He's got to try and recover from this somehow," Rusalka added. "Otherwise he just looks bad."

"Oi, orc, don't be throwing logic into this, that's Emmell's job," Onna shrilled.

"Yeah!" Emmell agreed.

"Fine!" Rusalka grumbled, "Where's Nery anyway?"

"I'm here," the small kållråden squeaked.

"Well?" Rusalka pressed.

"Well what, ogre?" Nery fired back. "I already told you the moment we came down here, I'm spent for the day. Magic has limits, and I hit mine the moment I stopped the Captain from being shot in the head."

"Then how about we figure out how we're going to get out of this mess?" the orc groused.

"Pssh!" Onna snarked, "Like that's the most pressing thing ye all need ta be talkin' about right now!"

"Then what is?" Anne asked, curious.

Onna nodded to Marissa. "The fact that no one's talking about that kiss! Didn't ye see that priestess get all hot and spicy on the Cap'n there?"

"We all saw it," Anne replied.

"Yeah, Cap'n, what's up with that? We didn't know ye liked girls," Jocquotte asked.

"Not that we cares if ye do, yer still our Cap'n," Badger quickly added.

Marissa smiled at them all, and before she could give them the big reveal, Onna leaned forward and asked. "So how was it? Was it everything ye thought it could be? Was it better than a man be doing?"

"Well..." Marissa mumbled. She rolled her tongue around and slid the reward she'd received from Cassandra out between her teeth.

Onna's smile went wide. Everyone else saw what she had, and they too, one by one, began to smile broadly, with the exception of Rusalka. Marissa countered those smiles with one of her own as the manacle key that Cassandra stole from Love sat poised between her teeth. "I must admit, I found the whole sensation to be very... liberating."

EPILOGUE
CASSANDRA MARIN

T hree weeks later...

"LADY CASSANDRA?" MARIA'S HUSKY VOICE CALLED FROM the doorway.

"Hmm?" Cassandra answered, her eyes sliding across the parchment, devouring the words written on the page.

Maria stepped into the room, forcing Cassandra to put the paper down and give the exactor her full attention. The heading, *The Sirens of Sowle strike again!* still managed to catch her eye one last time before Maria made her way to the desk.

Maria glanced down at the paper and snickered, "Sirens of Sowle?"

Cassandra pushed Castile's local paper, the Oyez Castile Post, underneath a stack of other documents. "That is what the royal navy and the mariners have taken to calling them, yes." The Oyez Castile Post wasn't read by Dons and Doñas; it was considered too lowbrow, only meant for the middling classes that weren't quite nobility but were still literate. Dons and Doñas were supposed to have subjects that brought them such intelligence and did not have to hear about it days later in a town crier's written work. Cassandra, however, had taken to the paper. It had a certain charm to it. It told a story, instead of merely reporting information.

"Why Sirens?" Maria asked.

"Well, mainly because Mari and her crew are the only ones that can come and go from the Pale."

"Ah, yes, and since the islands are called the Sirens..."

"Easy fit," Cassandra agreed. "Also, the purist crews swear that they hear someone singing right before they are attacked."

"Bloody Mari and her Sirens of Sowle – it has a nice ring to it," Maria said, shaking her head. "I can't believe they stole their ship back right underneath Love's nose."

Cassandra allowed herself a small smile. "Yes, funny how things work out. Now, was there something you wished to discuss?"

"Actually, there is. A man is here to see you," Maria told her. "I wanted to know if you still desired me to play the role of Lady Cassandra while you dressed as a guard?"

Cassandra stood, her curiosity peaked. "Oh, so I assume we don't know this person?"

Maria shook her head. "He is claiming to come from Doña Cantor herself. Says he has a delivery only for Lady Cassandra Marin and no other."

"Did he offer a name?"

Maria nodded. "Vicente something... I'm sorry I seem to have forgotten his surname. I make a terrible aide."

Cassandra laughed. "Well, it's a good thing you're not really an aide then, isn't it?"

Maria nodded. "So, am I to be Lady Cassandra, then?"

Cassandra thought about it briefly, and then shook her head. "Not today, Maria – go ahead and show him in."

Maria looked at her in surprise. "In here? Not in the Maker's Eye antechamber?"

"It's fine, Maria," she told her bodyguard. "I trust the Lady Cantor."

Maria raised an eyebrow. "Which one?"

Cassandra rolled her eyes and deflected the question. "Just show the man in, please."

Maria saluted Cassandra, an odd habit she had taken to doing ever since Cassandra stood up to Adjutant Love. "As you will have it, my lady."

Maria stepped out, and Cassandra seated herself back behind her father's old cherry desk. She discreetly placed the Oyez Castile Post firmly underneath a large stack of letters she prepared to send to the Citadel and elsewhere in an attempt to have Marissa's exactor status annulled. She'd tried reaching out to everyone in the last few weeks, but so far, her luck was few and far between. Adjutant Love's reach extended much further than hers.

There was another knock, and Maria's announcement, "Ser Vicente Corredor, here on behalf of Doña Cantor, mi'lady."

"Do show him in," Cassandra added with the usual pomp that accompanied her station as Doña of Marin.

A tall, thin man only slightly older than she entered. He stood proudly, wearing the Cantor livery. He was gaunt, with rich, black curly hair and swarthy skin. He bore a beaklike nose, and his dark gaze was intense. When he reached her desk, he saluted her, and then bowed.

"Well, Vicente it appears that you've grown since we last met," Cassandra admitted.

"As have you my lady, though I must confess I am rather at a loss at the moment. Do I address you as priestess or Doña?"

Cassandra smiled and stood up. "Either is fine, ser Vicente.

I've only recently submitted a formal reinstatement of the Marin's holdings to the new provisional viscount. It's not official yet, but I am acting in the capacity of Doña now."

Vicente nodded. "As you will then, milady."

They stood awkwardly for a few moments before Cassandra asked, "I was told that Doña Cantor sent you?"

Vicente blinked for a moment in surprise. "Yes..." he stammered, "how unprofessional of me." He stood a bit straighter and reached into a hip pouch at his side. He pulled out a short, cylindrical scroll case.

"My lady wishes you to have this. She is an acting proxy in this case." He held out the scroll for her.

"Proxy?"

Ever inquisitive, her thin fingers plucked the scroll case from his dark hands. A dense red wax covered one end of it to show that it was sealed. If it was tampered with in any way, the wax would be cracked. Pushed into it was a symbol, but it wasn't the horses of Cantor like she'd expect, but...

The blood drained from her face.

Vicente smiled at her. "I think at this time I will leave you to it, mi'lady." He bowed once. "Have a good day, Doña Marin."

Cassandra nodded her agreement, her eyes studying the symbol in the wax. "Thank you, Vicente." She mumbled. "I hope to see more of you in the future."

Vicente stopped for a moment and dipped his head again. "As you wish, mi'lady. And might I only add one thing?"

Cassandra looked up from the case.

"Thank you for believing in her when no one else did... even me." Vicente dipped his head one last time and exited out the door.

Cassandra fell back into the plush chair looking at the figure pressed into the wax, a bird with the head of a woman. A siren.

She cracked the seal and felt the wax crumble in her sweaty

palms. Carefully she slid the rolled sheaf of paper out, and she could immediately smell the salt from the sea. Her eyes drank in the written words:

My dearest Cassandra,

I'm glad you are back at Tossa de Marin – I was afraid after you stood up to Adjutant Love that he'd force you to remain in the Rhombus for a time. I don't like the idea of you rattling around a military compound surrounded by those that might wish to do you harm.

We all need family, and those at Tossa de Marin are yours, the Castellan people are yours, much more so than mine. The last several winters away has changed me in ways I did not expect. Though Castile is, and will always be, where I am from, it's not home anymore, that's clear to me now. Perhaps that's why I felt I had to leave in the first place. But now, aboard this ship, with these women, I finally can say I've never belonged anywhere more.

I hope after all you've witnessed that you haven't lost your faith. I heard that you filed to become Doña and that once that happens, Tossa de Marin won't be classified as consecrated ground, not protected by the Jasian Enclave. I hope that doesn't mean you've forsaken the Maker. I would hate to think that I've influenced that in some way. I've always loved the Maker, but I think my faith is not so much in a god, but in people. I'm happy to say that for the most part, with few exceptions to the rule, that people have never let me down. Isa never let me down.

So this is why I hope you understand that I cannot let them down either. These women, they need me just as much as I need them. Ships can always be replaced, buildings repaired, walls rebuilt, and viscounts newly elected. But... maybe they shouldn't be.

I made a promise to your sister to watch over you, to protect you as your guardian, and now I feel like I've made you more of a target than ever. For that, I am deeply sorry.

I hope you do not look bitterly upon me because of this. I wish that things were different. I wish I came home, and both our families were safe, and we could have the same kind of friendship that I had with your sister. But as long as Adjutant Love is in power, I can't risk you like that.

You're smart, Cass, and you do what you believe is right. I like that about you. Keep doing that, and so will I. Have faith in me, like I do in you. And no matter what you hear about me, no matter what evil is spread about my name, and the names of my crew, I promise you, when you need us...

When you need me...

I'll be there.

- M

~Fin~

www.ingramcontent.com/pod-product-compliance
Lightning Source LLC
Chambersburg PA
CBHW070827260626
47170CB00007B/2292